FELIX FRANCIS
Guilty Not Guilty

**SIMON &
SCHUSTER**

London · New York · Sydney · Toronto · New Delhi

A CBS COMPANY

First published in Great Britain by Simon & Schuster UK Ltd, 2019
A CBS COMPANY

Copyright © Felix Francis, 2019

The right of Felix Francis to be identified as author of this work has been
asserted in accordance with the Copyright, Designs and Patents Act, 1988.

1 3 5 7 9 10 8 6 4 2

Simon & Schuster UK Ltd
1st Floor
222 Gray's Inn Road
London WC1X 8HB

Simon & Schuster Australia, Sydney
Simon & Schuster India, New Delhi

www.simonandschuster.co.uk
www.simonandschuster.com.au
www.simonandschuster.co.in

A CIP catalogue record for this book
is available from the British Library

Hardback ISBN: 978-1-4711-7316-5
Trade Paperback ISBN: 978-1-4711-7317-2
eBook ISBN: 978-1-4711-7318-9

Typeset in Sabon M Rules
Printed and bound by CPI Group (UK) Ltd, Croydon, CR0 4YY

Guilty
Not Guilty

With my thanks to

Miles Bennett, barrister
Julia Needham, barrister
William Barlow, BH Steward
Jo Dickinson, my editor

and, as always, to Debbie

Foreword

In England and Wales, lawyers fall into two categories, barristers and solicitors, dependent on their course of qualification. Barristers are regulated by the Bar Council and solicitors by the Law Society. Scotland and Northern Ireland have their own separate judicial systems.

A barrister specializing in criminal law acts as an advocate in court, arguing cases in front of juries in the Crown Court or in front of senior judges in the Court of Appeal, the High Court of Justice, and the Supreme Court of the United Kingdom, whereas a solicitor does everything else that requires compliance with the law, such as wills, contracts, divorce petitions, transfers of property etc. In addition, in criminal cases, solicitors generally prepare the 'brief', the documentation in the case. A barrister may act as either the prosecution or defence counsel, but not as both in the same trial!

In the English criminal justice system, the accused will generally appoint a solicitor to advise them (or have one appointed for them). If the case goes to trial in the Crown Court, the solicitor will instruct a barrister to act as the advocate in the proceedings. Throughout the case, the solicitor and the barrister work closely together to plan strategy. There is no distinction in seniority due to their separate roles.

A Queen's Counsel, QC, is a senior member of the legal profession, usually, but not always, a barrister, and the term is an honorary title that conveys esteem, experience and recognition within the ranks of lawyers. Persons appointed QC will have made a substantial contribution to the administration and delivery of the law.

Unlike in the United States, where it effectively means 'lawyer', the term 'attorney' in the UK is reserved for someone who is appointed to act specifically on someone else's behalf, often through a power of attorney document. Such an attorney may be a lawyer but is often a non-legally-qualified family member.

Judges in England and Wales are selected by the politically-independent Judicial Appointments Commission. They are chosen solely on merit from the ranks of senior lawyers, mostly barristers. Judges are never elected, nor appointed by the holder of a political office.

In this book, lawyers, both barristers and solicitors are referred to using these terms, and the court proceedings are described in accordance with generally accepted practice in England and Wales.

PART ONE

October

1

It is said that everyone over a certain age can remember what they were doing when they heard that President Kennedy had been assassinated, or that Princess Diana had been killed in a Paris car crash, but I, for one, could recall all too clearly where I was standing when a policeman told me that my wife had been murdered.

'Detective Sergeant Dowdeswell, Thames Valley Police,' announced the plain-clothed officer, holding out his police warrant card. I glanced down at it. 'This is PC Roberts, Warwickshire Constabulary.' He indicated towards a uniformed officer by his side. 'Are you The Honourable William Gordon-Russell?'

I was, although I never used that name.

'Bill Russell,' I said, nodding. 'That's me.'

The detective seemed slightly confused but quickly recovered.

'From Banbury in Oxfordshire?'

'Yes,' I said. 'Well, I live just outside Banbury.'

'The Old Forge in Hanwell?'

'Yes,' I said again, nervously. 'That's right. Now what's this all about?'

'Bit of bad news, sir, I'm afraid,' he said.

Not more. I'd had nothing but bad news for weeks.

'What is it now?' I asked with a sigh, fearing the worst.

That's when he told me. Brusquely and without any compassion.

'Murdered?' I said, my voice somewhat squeaky from the sudden constriction I could feel in my throat. I also felt weak at the knees.

'I'm afraid so, sir,' the policeman said.

'How?' I asked. 'And where?'

'All in good time,' the policeman said. 'Now, sir, we would like you to come with us.'

It all sounded rather official.

'Where to?' I asked.

'The station,' he replied, and I didn't think he meant the railway station.

'I'd rather go and see my wife,' I said.

'I'm afraid that won't be possible at this time. You need to come with us.'

There was something about the policeman's tone I didn't like.

'Am I being arrested?' I asked.

'No, sir. We just need to ask you some questions.' He said it in a manner that made me think that I might very well be arrested if I didn't play ball.

'But I have duties to fulfil here,' I said. 'I can't just leave.'

That seemed to flummox him somewhat.

'What duties?'

'I'm a steward.'

'A steward?'

'Yes,' I said. 'I am one of the four stewards at the race meeting this afternoon. We are responsible for ensuring the Rules of Racing are observed.'

'Oh,' he said, suddenly nodding in understanding. Perhaps he'd thought I would be serving drinks or keeping the crowd in order.

The three of us were standing alone in the Stewards' Room, which was attached to the weighing room at Warwick Racecourse. It was just after one-thirty in the afternoon. The first race was due off at two.

'Someone else will have to take over,' stated the detective unequivocally.

Indeed they would. Even if I hadn't had to go with the policemen, I was no longer in a fit state to adjudicate on a children's game of tiddlywinks, let alone six competitive horse races.

I suddenly felt very unwell.

I sat down heavily on one of the chairs and leaned my head down on the table.

'Are you all right, sir?' asked the detective.

'No,' I said, without looking up.

Murdered!

'Here,' said the policeman, holding out a glass of water. 'Drink this. My colleague has gone to fetch medical assistance.'

I drank the water.

'I don't need medical assistance,' I said. 'It's just the shock, that's all.'

How could Amelia be murdered? Suicide I could have understood. We had lived on that knife-edge for the past three years. But murder? Surely not. Who would have wanted to murder the kindest and gentlest person on this earth?

'Her brother,' I said, glancing up at the detective. 'Now that's who you ought to question.'

'That's funny,' he replied without smiling. 'That's exactly what he said about you.'

'So you've spoken to him?'

He didn't answer and I sensed he was berating himself for revealing anything at all.

One of the racecourse doctors arrived carrying his regulation bright-red medical kit slung over his shoulder. Dr Jack Westcott. I knew him well. He was a long-time friend. His regular job was as my GP but his role at the races was to be on hand to tend to any fallen jockeys. An unwell steward was clearly also within his remit, especially one who was his regular patient.

'Hi, Bill,' he said, crouching down to my level. 'What's the problem?'

'I feel a little faint, Jack, that's all. I've just had some bad news.'

'Not Amelia, I hope,' he said.

He was only too well aware of how badly our lives had been in turmoil. Over the previous three years, Jack had acted not only as our family doctor, but also as our confidant and unofficial therapist.

I nodded. 'She's been found . . .'

I stopped. I couldn't bring myself to say it.

'Dead,' said the detective, over my head.

'My God, Bill. That's awful.'

Jack laid a comforting arm across my shoulder.

'Doctor, can you just hurry up and check him over?' the detective said impatiently. 'Mr Gordon-Russell needs to come with me.'

'For God's sake, man,' the doctor replied, looking up at him. 'Have some sympathy. The man's just heard his wife has killed herself.'

'She didn't kill *herself*,' Detective Sergeant Dowdeswell said bluntly. 'She was strangled.'

If Jack was shocked, he didn't show it.

'There must be some mistake.'

'There's no mistake,' replied the detective. 'Mrs Gordon-Russell was found on her kitchen floor with a ligature still round her neck.'

I wondered if the policeman had again said more than he should. It was certainly more than I wanted to hear. I felt ill again.

'But you surely can't suspect Mr Russell,' said the doctor.

'Mr *Gordon*-Russell,' – the detective placed the emphasis on the Gordon – 'needs to come with me in order to assist us with our inquiries.'

'And if he won't?'

'Then he will be arrested for obstructing a constable in the execution of his duty.'

At least it wasn't for murder.

I looked forlornly at the doctor and he stared back at me.

'I didn't kill her,' I mouthed at him.

He wrinkled his forehead with incredulity and shook his head as if the thought had never crossed his mind.

It had mine.

I had often wondered if I could have done more to alleviate Amelia's mental anguish. Had I done enough? Was her death now a further manifestation of her psychiatric problems? Or was it something entirely different and infinitely more sinister? *Murder?*

I still couldn't quite believe it.

'I'm not at all sure that Mr Russell is well enough to go with you,' Jack declared, standing up. 'I consider that he needs to go to hospital for a full medical check-up.'

To say that DS Dowdeswell was unhappy with this announcement was an understatement – he was apoplectic.

'He will be seen by a doctor at the police station,' he said decisively.

'No!' Jack replied loudly with even greater determination. 'Mr Russell should go to hospital now. And I trust you won't be arresting me for obstructing a constable in the execution of his duty.'

I knew what he was doing. He was trying to protect his friend. But it was like attempting to hold back the tide – hopeless and impossible.

'It's all right, Jack,' I said to him. 'I'm feeling a bit better now. I'll go with the police. I have nothing to hide.'

'Are you sure?' he asked, looking straight at me. 'I can still insist that you go to hospital.'

'No, Jack. I'm fine. It's best if I go with them now. They won't give up.'

He smiled. 'I'll send you a cake with a file in it.'

I glared at him. 'I didn't do it.'

'No, of course not.'

But I could see a touch of doubt creeping into his eyes.

'Please tell George Longcross that I can't act as a steward today after all.'

'He won't like it.'

'Tough,' I said. 'It's not as if I have any choice.'

George Longcross was the designated chairman of the stewards for this day's racing, and he was a stickler for everything to be done exactly by the book. He abhorred absence or lateness and was determined that nothing should go amiss on his watch.

As if on cue, George Longcross walked into the Stewards' Room, no doubt having enjoyed a lavish luncheon courtesy of the directors of the racecourse. Not that I hadn't been invited. But I had learned from experience that a plate of roast beef and Yorkshire pudding in the middle of the day, together with all the trimmings and a dessert, was no good for my waistline, and also had a tendency to send me to sleep at the very time when I needed to be alert and on my mettle.

George took a quick look around the room, and then settled his stare on the uniformed policeman.

'What is going on here?' he asked in his usual booming authoritarian voice.

There was a brief pause before the detective sergeant answered.

'Mr Gordon-Russell has had some bad news,' he said.

9

The chairman of the stewards transferred his gaze to the detective in his open-fronted leather bomber jacket over a black T-shirt, blue jeans and trainers. George Longcross, meanwhile, was, as always, attired in a dark pin-stripe suit, highly polished brogues, white shirt and silk tie, with a matching handkerchief in his breast pocket. I couldn't imagine that he even possessed a black T-shirt or a pair of jeans, and certainly not a leather bomber jacket.

'And who are you?' he asked in an accusing tone.

'DS Dowdeswell, Thames Valley Police.' The detective again flashed his warrant card. 'Mr Gordon-Russell needs to leave.'

'But I require him here,' George said. 'He's a steward.'

'Find somebody else,' said the detective decisively. 'He's coming with us, and right now.'

It seemed to take the wind out of George's sails.

'Oh,' he said. He looked at me. 'It's all very inconvenient. Very inconvenient indeed.'

I felt like telling him that it was not as inconvenient as one's wife having been found murdered, but I said nothing. I just turned away and accompanied the policemen out of the door.

I may not have been arrested but it certainly felt as if I had, especially if the reaction to my departure was anything to go by.

The weighing room was filling up as the time for the first race approached, with trainers and officials milling around completing their duties, and jockeys weighing out.

However, as I was being escorted through the throng by the police, the general hubbub died away to silence and I could almost feel the stares of those watching.

2

'You are being interviewed under caution,' said the detective sergeant formally. 'You do not have to say anything. But it may harm your defence if you do not mention when questioned something which you later rely on in court. Anything you do say may be given in evidence.'

We were sitting in a stark windowless interview room at Banbury Police Station. Alongside the sergeant was another plain-clothed policeman who was introduced as Detective Constable Parkinson.

'So I am under arrest?'

'Not at all,' said the DS with a forced smile. 'This is simply an opportunity for us to ask you some questions concerning the death of your wife. I have cautioned you solely to ensure that whatever you say can be used in future court proceedings if there are any. Hence, we are recording this interview, but you are free to leave whenever you like.'

'Should I have a solicitor here?' I asked.

'Is there any reason why you need one?'

'No,' I said. But I wasn't sure if it might not be a good idea anyway.

The detective nodded as if pleased. 'For the recording, state your full name.'

'Bill Russell.'

'Your full name, please.'

'The Honourable William Herbert Millgate Gordon-Russell,' I said. 'The last two are hyphenated.'

'Quite a mouthful.'

I ignored him but he was right. That's partly why I called myself just plain Bill Russell.

'How do you get to be an Honourable?' the DS asked.

'My father is an earl.'

The ninth Earl of Wrexham, to be precise.

'So you'll be an earl when he dies?'

'No chance,' I said. 'I have two older brothers. And they both have two sons apiece. Far too many members of the family would have to die first for me to inherit the title.'

'But it *could* happen.'

'Only in the movies,' I replied.

Specifically in *Kind Hearts and Coronets*.

When I'd been aged about twelve I'd obsessed over that film, watching Alec Guinness in black-and-white on an old video recorder, daydreaming for hours about cunning ways I could emulate him and elevate myself up the family pecking order. Third-son syndrome, I called it. Neither the heir, nor the spare. Hence the chances of inheriting anything were slim, let alone the title and the family seat – not that I'd ever been very keen on the draughty thirteenth-century castle in the Welsh Borders where I'd been raised.

Fortunately, my childhood obsession with bumping off my brothers in order to become the tenth earl hadn't progressed beyond fantasy, not least because I had adored my siblings. I still did, albeit from a safe distance.

The detective sergeant changed tactic. 'You don't seem very distressed by the news of your wife's death.'

'I am devastated,' I said. 'My wife and I were very close.'

'That isn't how it appears to me.'

'But you can't see how I'm feeling on the inside,' I replied.

I had been taught as a child not to display my emotions. 'Big boys don't cry' had been a mantra for my grandfather, the eighth earl, with whom I had spent much of my early years.

I *was* devastated. I hurt, badly, and part of me wanted to scream and shout, but the 'Captain Sensible' within simply asked what good it would do, so I didn't.

And it was not as if I hadn't prepared myself for this moment.

For the previous three years, I had half-expected on a daily basis to hear that Amelia was dead. She had seriously tried to kill herself twice and openly discussed the likelihood of taking her own life almost every week.

Over time, I had discovered that there was a limit on how much I could accompany and chaperone her. If someone was determined to kill themselves, then it was nearly impossible to stop them. To keep Amelia safe for every single moment of every day was unachievable short of locking her up in a mental hospital – something that had happened more than once in the recent past.

'When did you last see your wife?'

'Yesterday afternoon about five,' I said.

'Can you account for your movements over the past twenty-four hours?'

'I was at work in my study yesterday until about four,' I said.

'Where is your study?'

'At my house. I'm a self-employed business consultant. I work mainly from home unless I have meetings, and they are usually in London. Mostly with insurance companies.'

The look on his face indicated clearly that he didn't think much of insurance companies. Not a lot of people do.

'Doing what, exactly?' he asked.

'I'm an actuary.'

I could see a quizzical look spread into his eyes.

'I deal in all sorts of insurance but mostly life cover and annuities.'

I don't think it helped him much.

'Basically, I calculate risk against reward,' I said. 'I calculate mortality rates and investment risk and then I turn those into insurance premiums.'

'Clever, then, are you?' he asked with irony.

I shook my head. 'Just good at maths.'

'So what did you do after you left your study?'

'I changed into a suit and then drove myself to Birmingham. To Edgbaston. I attended a charity event in the banqueting suite at the cricket ground. It started at seven and finished about eleven. Then I stayed the night in a hotel.'

'Which hotel?'

'The Edgbaston Manor Hotel. It's near the cricket ground. Walking distance. I checked in around six and walked to the ground.'

'It's not far from your house to Birmingham. Why didn't you simply drive home afterwards?'

'Because the event was a dinner and I knew I'd be drinking.'

'Drink often, do you, Mr Gordon-Russell?'

Was he trying to rile me?

'No,' I said calmly. 'I had maybe three or four glasses of wine throughout the whole evening. Too much to drive but I certainly wasn't drunk, if that's what you're implying.'

'Why didn't your wife go with you?'

'Charity dinners are not really her thing.'

Were not.

'Is there anyone who can vouch that you were at this dinner?' he asked.

'Lots of people,' I said. 'I sat at a table with friends.'

'And were they staying at the same hotel?'

'Not that I'm aware of. I walked to the hotel alone.'

'For a nightcap?'

'No,' I said patiently. 'I went straight to bed. I needed to be well rested for my role as a steward at Warwick Races today.'

'Did you call your wife?'

'I spoke to her at about six, before I went to the dinner, to tell her I'd arrived safely at the hotel. She told me she was just

15

going out for an hour to meet a friend at the village pub for a drink.'

'What is the name of this friend?'

'Nancy Fadeley,' I said. 'She lives right across the road from us in the same village.'

The detective sergeant nodded as if he already knew.

'She was spoken to this morning as part of our house-to-house inquiries.'

'What did she say?' I asked.

He ignored me.

'Did you call your wife again later?'

'No. It was after eleven when I got back to the hotel and I didn't want to disturb her. She might have gone to bed early. She often does when I'm away.'

Did.

'And she knew she could call me if she needed something. I always have my phone on. I leave it by the bed all night when I'm away, just in case.'

'But she didn't call?'

'No.'

'How about this morning?'

'I tried the house number about nine but there was no answer so I thought she must have gone out. She often goes food shopping in Waitrose on Wednesday mornings.'

Went.

'How about her mobile phone?'

'I tried that too but there was no answer. It went to voicemail so I left a message saying I'd be home around six-thirty. The last race at Warwick today is at five but we have to complete our report before we can leave.'

'So you also work for Warwick Racecourse.'

'It's not exactly work,' I said. 'Not paid work anyway. I'm what is called an honorary steward. For the BHA – the racing authority. It's a volunteer role. I suppose you could call it my hobby. I act for about thirty-five days a year at the local race-courses – Warwick and Stratford mostly. It is something I choose to do in addition to my usual day job.'

The detective made some notes before again looking at me.

'Did anyone see you at the hotel last night?'

'Not that I specially remember. The restaurant staff would have seen me at breakfast. Plus the receptionist when I checked out.' I dug into my pocket and produced the credit card receipt from my wallet and put it on the table. 'There. I checked out at . . .' I glanced at the slip. 'Nine fifty-two this morning.'

'But no one saw you from the time you left the dinner until breakfast. So there would have been plenty of time for you to drive home, kill your wife, and get back to Birmingham.'

'That's nonsense,' I said, standing up. 'I didn't kill her. In fact, I've had enough of this. You said I was free to go at any time, so I'm going. Which way is it to the exit?'

It was obviously not what he'd been expecting.

'But we need to ask you some more questions.'

'Then you will have to make an appointment. I will attend only with my solicitor. I want to see my wife.'

'As I told you before, that's not possible.'

'Why not?' I asked belligerently.

17

He said nothing but his sidekick finally broke his silence. 'Post-mortem.'

Oh, shit.

Too much information. I'd have been better off not knowing.

'Don't you need official identification first?' I asked. 'It may not be Amelia at all.'

'We already have a positive identification,' said the DS. 'Joseph Bradbury, your wife's brother, confirmed it was her.'

'How come?' I asked angrily. 'What's he got to do with it? He's not her next of kin. I am.'

'Formal identification of a body doesn't have to be done by the next of kin. A close relative is good enough, and Mr Bradbury was there. He was the one who called the police. He says he went to visit his sister and found her lying dead on your kitchen floor.'

'How did he get in?' I asked with rising rage.

'He said he looked through the kitchen window and saw her.'

'And you believed him, I suppose?' I shook my head in frustration. 'He's the man you should be questioning, not me. If I were you, I wouldn't have confidence in a single word my brother-in-law says.'

'Why is that?' the DS asked with all seriousness.

'Because the man's a pathological liar. He wouldn't know the truth if it punched him in the face.'

'He told us where to find you.'

'And I suppose he told you that I'd killed my wife.'

He nodded. 'And he also said you'd deny it.'

'Of course I deny it. Because I didn't do it.'

He looked up at me. 'Then answer my questions.'

'Not without my solicitor being present.'

'But you said there was no reason for you to need a solicitor. Changed your mind about that, have you, Mr Gordon-Russell? Why don't you just tell us what really happened between you and your wife?'

The detective clearly believed I had murdered Amelia. It was plain to see in his manner.

'I am leaving now,' I said.

'I could arrest you.'

'What for?' I asked. 'Murder? You don't have any evidence. If you did, you'd have done it by now.'

3

I stood outside Banbury Police Station in a bit of a daze.

I'd half-expected to be prevented from leaving but here I was alone on the side of the road, not quite knowing what to do next.

The detective sergeant had unhelpfully told me that I wouldn't be able to go home as my house was sealed off and it would remain so for some time, maybe for days, or even weeks. And my car was still in the officials' car park at Warwick Racecourse where I'd parked it that morning, with my overnight bag in the boot.

But at least I had kept hold of my mobile phone, in spite of the detective wanting to take it from me.

'Have you got a warrant?' I'd asked as he'd held out his hand for it.

The police may have been allowed to forensically search my house as a crime scene, but I was damned if they were going to do the same to my phone. Not yet anyway. Not without arresting me first.

I looked at its screen: 15.58.

Racing at Warwick would still be going on but there was no point in going back. My car would be quite safe in their car park. I would collect it when I felt a little better.

I called my brother. Not the to-be-earl. The other one.

'Douglas,' I said when he answered, 'I'm in a bit of trouble. Can I come and see you?'

'Sure,' he said. 'When?'

'Right now.'

There was a slight pause from the other end.

'Is it a big bit of trouble?' he asked.

'Huge.'

Another pause.

'I won't be home for another forty minutes.'

'I'm still in Banbury,' I said. 'The train takes an hour to London. I should be with you about six.'

'Come,' he replied. 'I'll be waiting.'

I hung up.

Good old Douglas.

No ifs, no buts, no questions – just *come*.

Ever since I could first walk and talk, Douglas had been the port I had run to in a storm. Eight years my senior, he had always seemed to me to be so calm and wise, traits he now employed daily in the courts as a QC, a Queen's Counsel.

I made my way through Banbury town centre to the railway station without really feeling my feet on the ground.

Amelia murdered.

It had to be a mistake or some sort of cruel joke.

The detective sergeant had said during the interview that I didn't seem very distressed by her death and I had replied that I was devastated, but, in fact, I was totally numb. I didn't feel anything.

It was as if this was happening to somebody else, like a drama unfolding on the television. It wasn't like reality.

Except that it was.

I bought a train ticket from the machine using my credit card.

My cognitive brain was working fine – I could remember my PIN without a moment's hesitation. But my emotional brain was in disarray, with synapses failing to fire as if anaesthetised.

I knew I ought to be sad, miserable even, or inconsolable and grief-stricken. I should be wretched and in despair, unable to bear the torment of my loss.

But I was none of those things.

If anything, I was angry.

I was angry with Amelia for getting herself killed but angrier with her brother, whom I was absolutely certain was responsible.

I stared out as the rolling green hills of Oxfordshire and Buckinghamshire gave way to the great metropolis of London, and the daylight began to dwindle towards darkness.

The second half of October.

It had never been a favourite time of the year for me. The clocks would go back in a few days and then we would be into winter, with many seemingly endless months to come before the re-emergence of spring. That in itself was depressing enough without the knowledge that I would now be spending them alone, cruelly deprived of my soulmate.

And, as if to add to my woes, it started to rain, beating loudly against the carriage windows. Hence I took a taxi from Marylebone to Chester Square in Belgravia where Douglas lived in a four-storey town house.

The rain was still hosing down as I climbed out of the taxi and I was pretty well drenched even by the time I'd walked across the pavement and pushed the doorbell.

Douglas opened the door almost immediately.

'My God, William, you look terrible. Come in, dear boy. Come in.'

He led me through to his kitchen. 'What's the problem?'

'Can I have a drink? G and T. And make it a strong one.'

And to hell with DS Dowdeswell.

Douglas clinked ice into two tumblers, added generous portions of gin plus a splash of tonic water and some slices of lemon from the fridge.

'There,' he said, handing me one of the glasses. 'Get that down your neck.'

I drank deeply, enjoying the effect of the spirit in my throat.

Douglas looked at me expectantly.

'Amelia's dead,' I said.

His shoulders slumped but there was no look of great surprise on his face – more one of resignation. My brother was fully up to speed on my family situation. He had been quietly advising Amelia and me for months.

'She was murdered,' I said.

Now there was shock in his eyes. 'Are you sure?'

'The police told me she was strangled. And they think I did it.'

He looked straight at me. 'And did you?'

I told myself it was the lawyer in him.

'What would you suggest if I had?'

'I'd call the best criminal solicitor I know and arrange to meet him, with you, at Charing Cross Police Station in half an hour.'

'Well,' I said, 'I didn't, so there's no need.'

'Good. I didn't think so.'

I told him everything that had happened to me on that day and what I could remember from my interview with the detective sergeant.

'You should have never allowed yourself to be interviewed without a solicitor being present, especially after the police cautioned you.'

I knew he'd say that. And he was right.

'So what should I do now?' I asked.

'There's not a lot you can do. The police will conduct their investigation and, undoubtedly, they'll want to speak to you again. But make sure you have a solicitor present next time.' He wagged his finger at me as if to emphasise the point. 'So why do they think you did it?'

'Because . . .' I couldn't even bring myself to say his name. 'Amelia's damn brother told them I'd done it. More likely it was him. What was he doing there otherwise? He hasn't been to our house for well over two years. And neither Amelia nor I have been in contact with him for months, so why did he turn up out of the blue? And on the day Amelia died? That's bloody fishy if you ask me.'

'I'm sure the police will have worked that out.'

'But shouldn't I tell them what's been going on? Especially before he puts his oar in with all his nonsense.'

'He's probably already done it,' Douglas remarked.

'Isn't that all the more reason to show them the sort of man he is?'

Douglas stroked his chin as if thinking. He was always keen for me to take a 'stand back and watch' position rather than jumping in with both feet. But I found it was hard sometimes not to respond to my brother-in-law's lies.

'How about Amelia's mother?' Douglas said, changing the subject and not answering my question. 'Does she know her daughter is dead?'

'I've no idea. And, what's more, I don't really care.'

'But I thought you had a good relationship with your mother-in-law – what's her name?'

'Mary Bradbury. And you're right in so far that I *had* a good relationship with her, but not any more. Her damn son has turned her against us with his lies. She, of course, accepts as true every word he says. I gave the old bat more credit but Joe keeps whispering in her ear about how wonderful he is and how awful Amelia was, and eventually she believed it. God knows why after all Amelia and I have done for her, taking her on holiday with us and so on. We even took her with us on a Mediterranean cruise.'

'How old is she now?'

'Seventy-five. But she's a very old seventy-five. Nothing like our dad. I'm certain she's losing her marbles, but her doctor keeps telling her she's fine and has still got full mental capacity.

And Joe Bradbury exploits that fact to get her to sign all sorts of papers. He now controls her completely. I think he must have been jealous of how close Amelia was to her mother so he set out to drive a wedge between them, and he managed it.'

'I suspect it wasn't only that that made him jealous,' Douglas said.

'What do you mean?'

'What does he do for a living?'

'He's a High Court enforcement officer,' I said.

Douglas looked at me. 'So he's a glorified debt collector. I bet that doesn't make him much. Does he own his own house?'

'No. He lives with his wife and three girls in a rented flat in Uxbridge.'

'There you are then. He is obviously jealous of your lifestyle – successful in the City, making lots of money, living in the country in your own home, two-car family, cruises to the Mediterranean. I bet jealousy has been eating away at him for years.'

'You might be right,' I said. 'Last year, Joe returned the Christmas presents we sent for his girls with a curt note stating that they didn't need our charity.'

'There you are then – he's clearly insanely jealous.'

Funny that, I thought, *when Amelia had been so incredibly jealous of him for having children while we did not.*

'He also tells everyone that, because Amelia has been a patient in a psychiatric hospital, she is totally unhinged and not to be trusted.'

Was.

'But that's rubbish,' Douglas said. 'Winston Churchill had

psychiatric problems and where would we be now without his astute wartime leadership. Everyone trusted him.'

'Exactly. But that hasn't stopped that damn Joe Bradbury from saying it.'

I was getting quite agitated.

'Here,' my brother said, 'let me refill your glass.'

Douglas had a masterly way of taking the heat out of any situation. He always had. 'Justice is determined by the facts,' he would often say, 'not by how we feel about the facts. Sentiment should have no place in court.'

He handed me another strong gin and tonic.

'Have you eaten?'

'No,' I said. 'I've not had anything since breakfast. But I'm not hungry.'

'You need to eat, dear boy,' he said. 'It's important to keep up your strength.' He clapped his hands together. 'Now, do you fancy taking a chance on my signature spaghetti Bolognese or shall we nip out for a Chinese?'

Difficult choice.

I didn't really feel up to going out but the opportunity to sample Douglas's culinary masterpiece didn't particularly thrill me either. Whereas his former wife had been Cordon Bleu trained, Douglas had always boasted that he couldn't even boil an egg.

'How's the cooking going?' I asked.

He pulled a face. 'I miss Charlotte in many ways, but mostly for her food.'

Charlotte had walked out on him four years previously, claiming that she could no longer live with a man who never stopped work-ing, one who regularly left home at six in the morning and often didn't return until nearly midnight, even at weekends. She wanted more romance in her life and had left him to find it.

In truth, they had simply drifted apart after twelve years of marriage and, with their two sons away at prep school, Charlotte had become bored with preparing gourmet meals for a husband who never came home to eat them.

In the end Douglas and I went to the Chinese, not least because, on close inspection, the minced beef in the fridge that he had planned to use in his Bolognese sauce was well past its use-by date and was looking a touch green.

We didn't have a reservation but that didn't seem to worry Douglas.

'The best Chinese restaurant in London,' he informed me as we walked round the corner into Ebury Street and to Ken Lo's Memories of China, where he was greeted like a long-lost family member.

'So what do I do?' I asked over crispy duck pancakes.

'Nothing,' Charles replied. 'Other than grieve.'

'What about funeral arrangements?'

'There's no hurry,' he said. 'I'm sorry to tell you this but, in murder cases, it is usually some considerable time before the victim's body is released by the coroner. It can take several weeks or even longer.'

'Oh.'

The prospect of Amelia's funeral was bad enough without having the agony prolonged.

'As the next of kin, do I have to register the death?'

'That will be a job for the coroner once the inquest has concluded. That too could be some time off as it would likely be after any criminal proceedings. There really isn't anything you have to do. Just wait and see how the police investigation unfolds.'

'It seems all wrong,' I said. 'I feel I ought to be doing something.'

A waiter placed an iron plate of sizzling chicken in black-bean sauce down on the table between us. The smell was magnificent and I found that I was more hungry than I'd realised.

'Can I stay tonight?' I asked between mouthfuls. 'I've got nowhere else to go.'

'Of course you can,' Douglas replied. 'But you'll have to go in one of the boys' rooms. The spare is being redecorated. I had a leak from a pipe. Damn nuisance.'

'I'll find somewhere else tomorrow,' I said.

'No need. Stay as long as you like. I'd enjoy the company. I keep the boys' beds made up ready, just in case, although they won't be back until Christmas at the earliest, that's if their mother lets them come at all.' He smiled lopsidedly at me.

In a strange way, I felt sorry for Douglas. Amelia and I had never enjoyed the delight of having children, not that we hadn't tried. Five rounds of fertility treatment had ultimately proved fruitless and, by the time we reached our mid-thirties, we had reconciled ourselves to spending our lives childless. But Douglas had become accustomed to a house full of young voices only for them to be snatched away when custody of the boys had been awarded to their mother.

'How frequently do you see your kids?' I asked.

'Not as often as I would like. They're so far away.'

Charlotte had not only left him but London too, choosing to spend a large portion of her divorce settlement purchasing a property in the Yorkshire Dales. She had also cancelled the boys' registrations for Eton and had sent them instead to Sedbergh School, nearly three hundred miles north of Belgravia.

'I do try to get up there to see them occasionally, especially if they are in a play or something, but I'm so busy. I have to work so hard down here just to pay the school fees.'

I thought it was a poor excuse, but probably a true one with independent schools now charging a king's ransom every term.

We walked back to Chester Square for coffee, arriving in time to watch the BBC ten o'clock news on the television in Douglas's sitting room.

Amelia was the third item.

'Mrs Gordon-Russell, the daughter-in-law of the Earl of Wrexham, has been found dead at her Oxfordshire home,' voiced the newsreader over a photograph of Amelia taken by the paparazzi outside Royal Ascot the previous year – all smiles with a large hat. 'Police inquiries are continuing at the house near Banbury after Mrs Gordon-Russell's body was found at about ten o'clock this morning by her brother, Mr Joseph Bradbury.' There was footage of some men in white overalls and masks going into the house while a uniformed policeman stood guard outside. 'Sources have told the BBC that the death is being considered as suspicious and Thames Valley Police have confirmed this evening that they are conducting a murder investigation. Mr Bradbury made the following statement to journalists.'

The shot showed Joe Bradbury standing on the road with my house clearly visible in the background.

'The family are understandably devastated by the death of my darling sister,' he said, self-assured and looking straight into the camera, his horn-rimmed spectacles reflecting the multiple flashes from the assembled press photographers. 'We are helping the police in every way to bring the perpetrator of this horrendous crime to justice. I would ask that anyone who knows anything about my sister's death to come forward and speak to the police.'

It almost made me vomit just to watch it.

Seeing the news report, with its happy-looking image of Amelia and the police activity at my house, seemed to bring home to me the appalling reality of the situation.

My gorgeous loving wife was dead and I would never again see her smiling and laughing as she had done at Ascot in the summer, as in the photo.

My eyes began to well up and my stiff upper lip started to tremble.

'I'm sorry,' I said to Douglas, trying hard to fight back the tears. 'I need to go up.'

I stumbled through the sitting-room door and almost ran up the stairs.

'Second floor, on the right,' Douglas shouted up after me.

I didn't quite make it.

I lay down on the stairs and sobbed, my whole body

convulsing as I gasped for air. I cried and cried for what seemed like an age, until I simply ran out of the energy to cry any more.

When I had finished, Douglas came up, his eyes also showing red from weeping.

'Come on, my dear chap,' he said, putting a kindly hand on my shoulder. 'Let's get you to bed.'

He almost lifted me to a standing position and guided me up the last few steps to the second floor and then into his elder son's bedroom, the one with 'Philip's Room' painted on a small oval ceramic plate screwed to the door.

Philip may have now grown into a burly fifteen-year-old rugby-playing teenager but his room had changed little since he'd left it as an eleven-year-old child. Dozens of miniature *Star Wars* characters stood to attention, staring out from a shelf, while the bed was covered in soft toys, which Douglas now threw onto the carpet as I removed my shirt, trousers, shoes and socks.

I climbed in between the sheets, exhausted.

'Thanks,' I said.

'No problem,' Douglas replied. 'Sleep as late as you like. I'm currently prosecuting a murder case at the Old Bailey and I have several meetings to attend before the court sits so I need to be gone from here by seven. I'll see you tomorrow evening.'

'Okay. Thanks again.'

He started to go but turned back to me.

'Be assured,' he said, in a rare expression of raw emotion, 'we'll get even with the bastard who did this.'

4

In spite of my tiredness, sleep would not come and I lay awake in the darkness for hours longing so much for things to be different, to be as they had been just a couple of days ago.

Why had I gone to the dinner? Why hadn't I made her come with me? Why hadn't I gone home afterwards? Why? Why? Why?

Why was she dead?

Was I somehow to blame?

Before I eventually drifted off into restless and sporadic sleep, I experienced two more overwhelming bouts of sobbing.

It felt like it was all too much to bear but I had no choice in the matter.

Misery, it seemed, was not an option and I discovered that my former attempts at advance mental preparation were, in the end, of no benefit whatsoever in relieving the devastating heartbreak of the actual loss.

Grief was the price we paid for love – the greater the love, the worse the grief.

My love for Amelia had been absolute and, consequently, my grief was desperate.

By the time the morning light began to show through the curtains, I was a wreck.

I turned on the bedside light and looked at my watch. Seven-thirty. I may have been in bed for more than eight hours but I'd been asleep for less than half of that time. I did not feel rested.

I dragged myself out of bed and walked across the landing to the bathroom.

I had a vague recollection of having earlier heard Douglas leaving the house but he had not forgotten me. He had left a pile of clothes outside my door with a note on top – 'hope these fit'. Pants, socks, blue corduroy trousers and a new checked shirt still wrapped in the maker's plastic.

I showered and put on the clothes. All was well except for the cords, which were far too long, so I replaced them with the trousers from my suit. It was not a surprise really. Douglas was a good five inches taller than I, although our upper bodies must have been similar as the shirt fitted fairly well.

I went down to the kitchen where, once again, Douglas had come to my aid, leaving out the essentials for making breakfast. There was even a spare front-door key on the kitchen counter with another note saying that I could come and go as I pleased. He would be back later.

I was so lucky to have such a brother. We had always been close, even though Douglas had been much nearer in age to Edward, the eldest son. Indeed, the two of us had often ganged up together against our elder brother on the grounds that, as the heir, he would have his day later. And he never let us forget it, reminding us constantly that, in time, it would be he who would become the earl and own the castle, and not us.

Nevertheless, I smiled at the happy memories of our childhood spent largely in make-believe adventures within our grandfather's medieval castle, with Edward always as the baddie – often the wicked Sheriff of Nottingham up against our Robin Hood and Little John, although, in our case, Little John really had been little, i.e. me.

Somehow, I had not inherited from our father the 'tall' gene like my older six-foot-plus siblings but, overall, this omission to my genetic code had served me well. Not only had it helped make me the undisputed castle hide-and-seek champion but, in my twenties, it had enabled me to fulfil my ambition of becoming an amateur jockey.

There had been a period of about eight years when my whole life had been determined by the date and venue of the amateur steeplechase races around the country. Saturdays and Sundays were fine but taking my annual leave as midweek days off work to ride half a ton of racehorse at thirty miles an hour over huge jumps without a seatbelt was not my boss's idea of a sensible way to behave, especially since, as he often pointed out, my day job was to calculate the risks to other people's lives, not to totally disregard those to my own.

Nevertheless, he regularly released me to go to the big events like the Foxhunter Steeplechases at Aintree and Cheltenham, and he even seemed pleased one year when I won one of them. And he didn't seem to mind too much when I had turned up on

Monday mornings with a bruised and battered body after things had not gone quite as planned on the track.

And it had been an injury rather than the pressure of work that had caused me to hang up my riding boots permanently. A horse I'd been on fell at the open ditch on the far side of Sandown Park in the early December of my thirtieth year. The fall itself had been easy enough but another horse behind had kicked me as he landed and had fractured two of the cervical vertebrae at the base of my neck.

The surgeon who had operated informed me in no uncertain terms that a severe weakness now existed and another similar incident would probably result in me being paralysed from the shoulders down, that was if I lived at all.

I had quickly done the maths and concluded that the gain-to-loss ratio was insufficient. Indeed, it was a no-brainer.

I'd had a good run and had been contemplating my retirement from the saddle anyway, so it simply accelerated my decision, something that Amelia had been absolutely delighted about. As she had often said, she was fed up of picking up the pieces from whichever hospital I ended up in.

And as one racing door closed, another magically opened when I was invited to attend an honorary stewards' training day.

I'd been on the stewards list now for five years and I greatly valued my continuing involvement in the sport.

But neither the race riding nor the stewarding paid the bills. That was the role of my job as an actuary.

I had joined Forehanded Life Ltd, one of the large London insurance companies, direct from Cambridge after their chairman had come to the university to give a careers talk to the third-year mathematics students. The firm had then sponsored me through a postgraduate master's degree in Business Analytics at Imperial College, after which I entered their actuarial department as an eager young buck aged just twenty-two.

Four more years of study on the job had led to a fully fledged qualification from the Institute and Faculty of Actuaries and a promotion into a new team within the same firm.

'Your job is simply to predict the future,' my new boss told me in all seriousness.

'If I could do that,' I said, smiling, 'I'd have won the lottery by now.'

He laughed. 'You just have, by passing your exams.'

And, in a way, he was right.

On days when I wasn't race riding, I had looked forward to going to work and being thrust into a world of probability and statistical analysis, financial planning and risk management – crunching numbers on a computer and then explaining my conclusions in simple terms to those who needed to know.

I absolutely loved it.

Insurance is all about spreading risk and we all use it on a daily basis, whether to insure our houses, our cars or our lives, to say nothing of our pensions and investments.

My job was to study data from the past and the present for such things as the economy, interest rates and inflation, and to combine that with my judgement and experience to foresee what was likely to happen ahead, and hence to determine the premiums for life policies, or the contributions needed for a certain level of retirement income.

If I got it right, everyone was happy and the company was profitable. But if I got it wrong then we might not have enough reserves to pay out our claims, or provide the level of pensions that we'd promised.

And then I would get fired.

Fortunately, that hadn't occurred and I had steadily climbed up the greasy pole of the corporate structure.

That was until Amelia had become unwell.

She and I had first met at one of the regular dinners held in London for Cambridge alumni. The seating plan had us placed next to each other and we'd hit it off immediately.

She was an art historian and was working as a curator in the historic royal palaces, maintaining the fabric not so much of the buildings themselves but of their contents – paintings, furniture and tapestries mostly, with the occasional sculpture or antique timepiece thrown in for good measure.

At the end of the evening, we had swapped numbers and within a week we were an 'item', spending as much time together as our busy schedules would allow. Six months later she moved in to my flat in Harlesden and we started looking for a house to buy together in Wimbledon.

We were married on her twenty-seventh birthday in the private chapel of my father's castle and I'd never been so happy, before or since.

The first years of our married life were blissful other than the fact that Amelia was failing to become pregnant as we had hoped and tried for. While most of her girlfriends seemed to be dropping babies left, right and centre, my wife was becoming more and more stressed by her own inability to conceive, all the more so when the doctors couldn't identify the reason. 'Maybe it's an abnormality with your ovaries,' they said, shaking their heads. So we had tried using donated eggs. They had fertilised happily in a petri dish but had failed to convert to a full-blown pregnancy.

The situation was not aided by her mother, who kept going on at her about wanting grandchildren, while totally failing to grasp the fact that we were trying our best to do just that.

Amelia became obsessed that I would leave her for someone more fertile, someone who could bear me children. I tried to reassure her that I wouldn't but she didn't really believe me.

The issue affected her work, which began to suffer from inattention and carelessness, neither particularly helpful attributes when you were dealing with the nation's priceless treasures, and she started coming home every night in tears. In the end she had no option but to resign from her job before she was dismissed.

That made her deeply unhappy, so I decided we needed a complete change of scenery, a change of life.

We went house-hunting and fell in love with a Grade II listed converted blacksmith's workshop in the tiny village of Hanwell, a few miles north of Banbury in Oxfordshire. It meant my journey to my London office was much longer but it was all worth it as Amelia threw herself into village life and seemed so much happier.

We were welcomed by the locals, not least because Amelia was immediately drafted in to help with the cleaning and flower arranging in the parish church, parts of which dated back to the twelfth century, as well as arranging coffee mornings in the village hall and becoming a major help at HanFEST, the annual food and farming festival.

Life for us returned pretty much to normal and the lack-of-baby thing faded into the background as we were accepted for who we were, not for whom we might become.

But then her stupid brother waded in with his size-twelve boots and abusive emails, upsetting her again badly and pushing her into full-blown clinical depression.

Just the thought of him raised my blood pressure.

It had all started with a quite innocuous-looking email from him to Amelia concerning the sale of the family home.

Their father had died of bladder cancer not long after our move and Amelia had convinced her mother that it was sensible for her to sell their big house in commuter-belt Surrey and move into something smaller up in Oxfordshire, to be closer to us. It would also release the funds she needed to support herself.

As my work with pensions showed, widows were often left asset-rich but cash-poor, with so much of their wealth tied up in their home. This had certainly been true of my mother-in-law, so much so that Amelia and I had had to help with her day-to-day expenses in spite of her living in a multimillion-pound seven-bedroomed mansion. As one of my financial advisors regularly pointed out to those who ignored his recommendation to buy shares as an investment rather than property, one can't sell just a single window when a little money is needed.

That first email from Joe had asked for the name of the estate agents Amelia had appointed on her mother's behalf to sell the property.

A simple enough request that Amelia had happily answered, naming the local Weybridge office of a big national firm, one that she had been assured would market the property extensively.

The abusive email she received back from Joe by return had taken our breath away.

'How dare you appoint that firm,' he wrote. 'Are you stupid or something? They are the worst estate agents in the world and very expensive. I have been in touch with them and cancelled the arrangement forthwith. I have far more experience than either of you in selling houses and I will appoint a different agent who will sell the house more cheaply.'

There had been neither salutation nor valediction on the email.

Almost as soon as it had landed in Amelia's inbox, she had received an irate phone call from the manager of the Weybridge office who was, understandably, confused and not a little upset. Joe, it seemed, had been rude to several members of the agency staff, calling them lazy and arrogant, and he had demanded the cancellation of the contract. Hence the manager had removed the property from his company database. But, as he pointed out to Amelia, a colour brochure had already been prepared and a full-page advert placed in the upcoming *Country Life* magazine as well as on various websites, so her mother would remain liable for those costs in spite of the fact that any responders to the adverts would now be advised that the property had been withdrawn from sale.

Amelia had immediately called her brother to tell him that it was *he* who was the stupid one but she had received a tirade of abuse in return, to the point where she'd had to hang up the call and burst into tears.

And that had been just the start.

Since that point, for the past three years, Joe had waged a spiteful campaign of calls and emails, all seemingly designed to undermine Amelia's confidence and self-worth. And he'd also been incredibly rude both to me and about me to anyone who would listen; and there were, sadly, far too many of those.

I wasn't sure of his motive other than, it seemed, to place a firecracker in the centre of his and Amelia's family and blow the whole lot of them to smithereens.

Amelia and Joe had been the only two children of Reginald and Mary Bradbury, but their parents had each come from large families. Hence Amelia had a multitude of uncles and aunts, plus several dozen cousins, many of whom were now not talking to me, or to each other, due to Joe's efforts to divide us with his lies.

It was not something that especially bothered me, but Amelia had been much saddened and troubled by her loss of contact with some of those with whom she had spent many happy school holidays as a child.

Reginald Bradbury had been a successful stockbroker in the City of London and he had been almost fifty before he had finally married for the first time, to Mary, his personal assistant, who'd been some fifteen years his junior. Amelia had arrived two years later, followed by Joe, four years after that.

Not that the Bradburys had enjoyed a particularly happy marriage.

Amelia often described to me how her parents had fought all the time. Memories of her childhood home, rather than being full of fun and happiness as mine had been, were of a battleground of shouting, recriminations and tears. From an early age, Amelia had had to protect her mother from a domineering husband. It was one of the reasons mother and daughter were so close . . . at least they had been until Joe had started his antics.

My phone rang and brought me back to the here and now.

'Hello,' I said, answering.

'Hi, Bill,' said a female voice. 'Virginia Lutton here, racecourse manager at Warwick.'

'Yes, Virginia. How can I help?'

'Is that your silver Jaguar sports car in the officials' car park? George Longcross said you left early yesterday with the police.'

Was it me or did she make it sound like an accusation?

'Yes, that's right,' I said. 'I did leave early and left my car behind. I had some bad news.'

'I'm very sorry to hear that.' She paused for a sympathetic moment before continuing. 'But, the thing is, we need it moved as we're having that part of the car park resurfaced and it's sitting right in the middle of where the workmen want to start.'

'Okay,' I said. 'I'd better come and get it, but I'm afraid I won't be there for a couple of hours or so. I'm in London.'

I could hear her suck the air in through her teeth in annoyance. 'We need it shifted before then. Is there anyone else who could move it?'

The only spare key was in a drawer of the kitchen dresser at the Old Forge in Hanwell, and I wasn't about to call DS Dowdeswell to ask him to get it to move the car, even if he would have done. He'd have probably impounded the vehicle and carried out a fingertip forensic search looking for evidence. And my laptop was in the boot along with my overnight bag; I didn't want him getting his hands on that, not because I had anything to hide but because I needed it for my work.

My work.

I'd better do something about that too. I was due to attend a meeting later in the day with some pension-fund managers in Henley-on-Thames. I would have to cancel. I didn't feel up to meeting with anyone.

'I'm sorry, Virginia,' I said. 'I'll be there as quickly as I can. There's no one else I can ask.'

She wasn't happy but, short of organising a crane, there was nothing she could do. 'Right,' she said with resignation. 'Please get here as soon as possible. I'll go and tell the men to start somewhere else.'

She hung up.

There's no one else I can ask.

Oh, God!

How could I survive without Amelia?

5

It was just after midday when I arrived by train and taxi at Warwick Racecourse.

Virginia Lutton's workmen were clearly a bunch of jokers.

They had dug up the tarmac all round my Jaguar, leaving it as if on an island. It was surrounded by red and white plastic barriers, clipped together in a tight rectangle almost touching the car's paintwork.

I looked about me. Plenty of their big bright yellow machinery stood silently doing nothing but there was not a workman in sight. It must be lunchtime, an early lunchtime.

I unclipped the plastic barriers, climbed in and drove carefully off the island and across the site to the exit.

Where to?

I had called the fund managers in Henley to tell them I wasn't able to meet with them but they were well ahead of me, having themselves already cancelled on the assumption I wouldn't be coming.

'I saw it on the TV news,' said the young man I spoke to. 'Dreadful.'

Amelia's murder was not just on the television. Every daily newspaper on the newsstand at Marylebone Station had the story on its front page, all of them carrying that same smiling picture taken at Ascot.

The man who'd been sitting opposite to me on the train had been reading the *Daily Telegraph* and I'd craned my neck to peruse the article beneath the picture.

While the journalist hadn't openly accused me of being responsible, he all but had, reporting the fact that I had been escorted by the police from Warwick Racecourse to Banbury Police Station for questioning under caution, but had not yet been arrested.

How did he know all that? I wondered.

There had even been a small head-and-shoulders photo of me at the bottom, lifted from my website, no doubt, and without my copyright permission.

I'd kept my eyes down and hoped that neither my train neighbour, nor anyone else, would recognise me.

It was an action I'd sadly have to become familiar with.

I turned right out of the racecourse car park and drove the twenty miles home to Hanwell village.

There was a single marked police car and a small white van stopped on the road outside my house blocking the drive. Not that I wanted to park there anyway. I went past them and round the corner to the village pub, where I left my car in their car park. The publican was a good friend and I was sure he wouldn't mind.

I walked back to my house.

There were lines of yellow tape everywhere around the property with CRIME SCENE – DO NOT ENTER printed in bold black capital letters continuously along its length. It was stretched across the driveway and also across the path from the road to the front door, which itself was wide open. There was no sign of the police guard I had seen on the TV news the previous evening.

I stood by the tape barrier. 'Hello,' I shouted. 'Anybody there?'

There was no answer.

I almost ducked under the tape and went in but there was a little voice in my head telling me not to upset the police more than I had to.

It would be out of my control if they chose to arrest me for something I hadn't done, but giving them a good reason to arrest me for something that I had would be just plain stupid.

I stayed where I was and called out again, louder this time, but with the same lack of result.

So I waited.

Eventually a figure appeared through the front door. It was wearing a full head-to-toe white forensic coverall, complete with hood, facemask, gloves and overshoes. Such was the formless nature of the baggy suit that I was unable to tell if it was a man or a woman.

'Excuse me,' I shouted. 'Who's in charge?'

The person in the suit ignored me completely as he or she

walked across the drive towards the van, bending down slightly and lifting the yellow tape overhead.

I walked along the road.

'Excuse me,' I said again. 'I live here and I need to collect a few things.'

The figure turned towards me and a blue-gloved hand pulled down the facemask. It was a man. He had stubble on his chin.

'Don't know about that,' he said unhelpfully. 'I was told not to allow anyone in.'

'So who can let me in?'

'The senior SOCO. Scene of Crime Officer.'

'And where is he?' I asked, trying my best to keep my cool.

'Oxford.'

Oxford was almost an hour's drive away.

'Can you please call him?' I asked.

The man peeled off his gloves and unzipped the front of his plastic suit to extract a mobile phone from a pocket within. He dialled his boss and handed the phone to me.

'What sort of things?' asked the senior SOCO when he came on the line.

'Clothes,' I said. 'And some papers from my desk.'

'I'll have to check with the officer in the case. I'll call you back.'

The senior hung up.

His subordinate and I waited.

'Found anything?' I asked.

'Like what?' he replied.

'Evidence.'

'I never know what's evidence and what isn't. I'm just the

dabs man. I go through the place recording all the fingerprints I can find.'

'Not the DNA?' I asked.

'I can if necessary but that's mostly the job of the blood team. They were here yesterday.'

'Where are they, then?' I asked, nodding at the marked police car.

'Round the back in the garden, digging. They're waiting for a JCB excavator to arrive.'

'Digging?' I repeated. 'What for?'

He never had a chance to reply as his phone rang. He answered.

'It's for you,' he said, holding it out.

It wasn't the senior SOCO but DS Dowdeswell.

'Sorry, Mr Gordon-Russell,' he said. 'I can't let you into the property until we have finished our investigation and search of the crime scene.'

'But I need some more clothes. I only have what I'm standing up in.'

'Sorry,' he said again, not sounding it.

'Can I at least go into my study?' I said. 'It's next to the conservatory. I can get in there without going through the rest of the house. There are some papers on my desk that I require urgently for my work.'

There was a slight pause while he thought it over – very slight.

'No,' he said. 'That won't be possible.'

'Why on earth not?' I demanded. 'Are you being deliberately obstructive?'

He didn't deny it.

'Mr Gordon-Russell,' he said, 'you have to appreciate that we have a murder to investigate. Do you not want us to determine who is to blame for your wife's death?'

'Of course I do,' I replied. 'And please call me Mr Russell.'

'I will call you only by your proper name.'

Now I was certain he was trying to rile me.

I remained un-riled – at least on the outside.

'Why are your officers digging in my garden?'

There was a slight snort from the other end as if he was annoyed that I knew. 'We are carrying out our investigation in accordance with accepted practice. It is normal to thoroughly search the area surrounding where a body has been discovered in questionable circumstances.'

'Are you anticipating more?' I asked sarcastically.

'A geophysical survey of the garden indicated two areas of interest and a dog specially trained to find dead bodies gave a positive response at one of them. We need to investigate.'

'A geophysical survey *and* a cadaver dog,' I said. 'My, you have been a busy boy.'

He refused to rise to my goading. Two could play at that little game.

'So when can I gain access to my home?' I asked.

'Not until after we have completed our search. It's difficult at the moment to say when that will be.'

'Have a guess,' I said, consciously suppressing the anger that was rising in my throat.

'I would hope we'll be finished over the weekend. Monday, maybe. It depends on what we find.'

'Do I get a hotel allowance?' I asked.

He laughed. 'No.'

It was Thursday today. Could I stay with Douglas for four more nights or was that pushing the boundaries of brotherly love too far?

I sighed.

My life seemed to be unravelling around my ears. Amelia's murder was back in the I-don't-believe-this-is-happening category. And I wasn't even sure that I ever wanted to go into the house again anyway.

How could I carry on living there without Amelia? How could I go into the kitchen without looking down at the floor and thinking . . . ?

Oh, God.

I could feel the grief rising in me once more and I fought it for control.

'And I also need to ask you some more questions,' the DS went on. 'We didn't finish yesterday.'

'Then you will have to make an appointment with my solicitor,' I said.

'It's not for the police to arrange meetings with your solicitor. That's your job. Who is it, anyway?'

'Simon Bassett,' I said.

'I don't know him. Is he local?'

'No. He's a partner at Underwood, Duffin and Wimbourne. It's a London firm. Chancery Lane.'

'Humph!' said the DS. He clearly didn't like London firms.

Tough.

Simon and I had been undergraduates together at Cambridge, and firm friends ever since. He was also up to speed with what had been going on vis-à-vis Joe Bradbury, and had provided Amelia and me with advice on how to proceed – mostly by not replying to or even acknowledging any of Joe's plethora of emails – which had annoyed him even more.

'I would like you to attend at Banbury Police Station tomorrow,' said the detective. 'Shall we say at ten o'clock in the morning?'

'Make it eleven,' I said. 'My solicitor will have to come from London. And I'll need to confirm to you that he's available.'

'Eleven it is, then,' he said, ignoring my last comment.

The DS hung up and I handed back the phone to the man in the white suit.

'Thanks,' I said to him. 'But no thanks.'

A bright yellow JCB digger came along the road and stopped. One of the policemen from the back garden came out to guide it down the side of the house, its great rear wheels chewing up Amelia's lovingly tended flower beds.

'Is that really necessary?' I asked of no one in particular as the digger disappeared from sight behind the house.

How ridiculous. There was nothing to find and they would just make a dreadful mess everywhere. But did I care?

I walked down the road to the pub to my car.

Where to now?

My life was routinely what one might call incredibly busy. As a rule, my diary was full to bursting and hardly a moment existed when I didn't have some work to complete, usually something that had to be finished by yesterday.

Yet, here and now, I had nothing to do.

My mobile phone, customarily ringing five or six times an hour, had been silent all morning, and my inbox lay strangely quiet, with the arrival of just a couple of spam emails.

I sat in the driver's seat of the Jaguar and banged my hands on the steering wheel in frustration at not being able to turn back the clock.

After a while I called Simon Bassett.

'Bill, I'm so very sorry,' he said. 'Amelia was lovely. I can't think why anyone would want to harm her.'

Simon had known Amelia for as long as I had. Indeed, he had been seated on the other side of her at that alumni dinner and had often bemoaned the fact that he had let me speak to her first while he had turned the other way.

He'd even been my best man.

'How can I help?' he asked.

'I have an interview with the police tomorrow at eleven in Banbury. I'd like you to accompany me.'

There was a pause from the other end.

'At eleven, you say?'

'Yes.'

'What's the purpose of the interview?' he asked.

'The police think I killed Amelia.'

Another pause.

'I assume you didn't.'

I wasn't sure if he was making a statement or asking a question. At least he hadn't asked me straight out, as Douglas had.

'Can you come?' I asked. 'I really need you.'

'Why do the police think you are responsible?'

'Because that damn Joe Bradbury has been telling them so. He's been filling their heads with his lies.'

'But is there any physical evidence?'

'Of course not.' I was slightly exasperated. 'I didn't do it. Can you come or not?'

'Yes,' he said slowly. 'I could, but I'm not at all sure that I am the right person.'

'Why ever not?'

'I know you and I knew Amelia. Both very well. And I've met Joe Bradbury. He was at your wedding, remember. There's far too much scope here for a conflict of interest.'

Bloody lawyers. Why do they always make things so damn complicated?

'I could send one of my colleagues. Someone who specialises in criminal work more than I do.'

'I want *you*,' I said despairingly. 'I need my friend.' Try as I might, I couldn't keep an emotional quiver out of my voice.

Yet another pause, longer this time.

'Okay, Bill,' he said. 'I'll come. Of course I'll come. I'll rearrange things. But you will have to appoint someone else if you are charged.'

'Charged! But I didn't do it. Don't you believe me?'

'Listen,' he said slowly but forcefully, 'it's not what *I* believe that's important. Charges are laid by the CPS, that's the Crown Prosecution Service. It is solely what *they* think that matters.'

If only that were true.

6

Simon Bassett and I walked through the front door of Banbury Police Station on Friday morning at eleven o'clock precisely.

We had caught the train together from Marylebone after I had spent a second restless night in my nephew's bed in Chester Square.

I had nowhere else to go.

The Welsh castle hardly seemed an option in spite of its abundance of spare bedrooms. It was so far away from London, from where I needed to be for my work. Not that I had much work to do.

A big London insurance company, with whom I'd been in final contract negotiations to produce a detailed analysis of their full-life business, had emailed me late on Thursday to say that, in the light of the previous day's events, they had decided to appoint a different actuarial firm to do the work.

Bad news clearly travelled fast, and I regretted all the time and effort I had already put in on research for which I would now not get paid.

At least it meant I didn't need the papers on my desk at home any more.

On Thursday afternoon I'd spent time buying some new outfits, enabling me to give my suit a rest and wear some casual trousers of the right length.

I had wandered around the shops at an out-of-town retail park on the outskirts of Banbury more in a trance than in a determined effort to provide myself with a coordinating new wardrobe. Hence, when I'd boarded the train to London, I carried a motley collection of bags from Marks and Spencer, Next, River Island and Primark containing four shirts (all blue), two pairs of chinos (also blue), a blue sweater and two packs each of blue underwear and blue socks.

My mood must have subconsciously dictated my choices.

Only when I'd unpacked it all at Douglas's house did I realise the uniformly monochrome nature of my purchases.

At least it had made me smile, if only fleetingly.

So, when I walked into the police station, I was *The Blue Boy* both in dress and demeanour, although I felt more like the boy in the painting *And When Did You Last See Your Father?* than in the Thomas Gainsborough version.

Simon had impressed on me to be extremely careful when answering the police questions.

'They are very adept at getting their interviewees to give away more information than they mean to,' he'd said to me on the train.

'But I have nothing to hide,' I'd retorted. 'The more information that I can give them will surely help them catch the person who is really responsible – Joe Bradbury.'

'I know you believe that your brother-in-law is guilty but it would be far better if you let the police work that out for themselves rather than stating it straight off.'

I looked at him, wondering if he really did think I'd killed Amelia.

'You wanted me to come to advise you,' he'd said quite sternly. 'So take my advice.'

'Okay, okay,' I'd replied. 'I will.'

So here we were, sitting side by side, in the same interview room as I'd been on Wednesday afternoon, with Detective Sergeant Dowdeswell and another man who kicked things off.

'I'm Detective Chief Inspector Priestly,' he said, pushing a business card across the table towards me. 'I have been assigned to this case as the senior investigating officer.'

I picked up the card. A detective chief inspector, no less.

I knew the case had a high profile as some forty-eight hours after the event, and much to my angst, it still featured large on every newspaper front page and had been the second item on the morning's television news, complete with aerial footage from a drone of the digging activity in my back garden.

Clearly, it had been a slow news day. Where was a royal baby announcement or a tsunami when you needed one?

'My client wants it recorded that he is attending here today entirely voluntarily,' Simon said.

DCI Priestly looked at him and then at me. 'Yes, of course, thank you for coming in. But can I remind you, Mr Gordon-Russell, that you are still being interviewed under caution.'

'Yes,' I said.

'Good. Now will you please tell us everything you did between lunchtime on Tuesday until ...' He glanced down at the notes in front of him. ' ... DS Dowdeswell approached you at Warwick Racecourse at one twenty-six p.m. on Wednesday afternoon.'

'I've already told him,' I said, nodding at the sergeant.

'Yes, as may be,' said the DCI. 'But now tell me.'

I went through everything again exactly as before: worked at home, drove to Birmingham, checked in to the Edgbaston Manor Hotel, walked to the cricket ground, attended a charity dinner, walked back to the hotel, slept, breakfasted, drove to Warwick Races.

'We will need the names and addresses of those at the dinner with you,' said the DCI.

'All one hundred and fifty of them?' I replied. 'It was a big affair.'

'Those that were on your table, then.'

'Why?' I asked with irritation. 'Don't you believe I was there?'

Simon glanced at me with a minimal shake of his head as if to say, 'Don't go there.'

'We need to verify your story,' explained the DCI.

'It's not a story,' I said flatly. 'It's the truth. Check the hotel CCTV. It will show that I was there all night.'

He changed tack. 'How would you describe your relationship with your wife?'

I stared at him. What was he trying to do now?

'Very loving,' I said.

'Did you have any problems?'

'No,' I said.

'No problems at all?' he asked again.

Only her brother, I thought, but Simon had said not to talk about him.

'None.'

The detective looked down at one of the papers in front of him, and then up at me.

'But Mrs Gordon-Russell had been under the on-going care of a psychiatrist, indeed, she had been an in-patient in a psychiatric hospital on several occasions over the past three years. Wouldn't you call that a problem?'

'It was a medical problem, yes. But it was not a problem in our relationship. If anything, Amelia's medical condition brought us closer together.'

'So you hadn't been close before?'

I now understood why Simon had been so insistent that I be careful with my answers.

'I didn't say that,' I said. 'We were always close, but her troubles made our relationship even stronger than it had been.'

'Hmm,' the DCI uttered, as if he didn't believe it. 'But is it not the case that you and Mrs Gordon-Russell regularly attended marriage-guidance counselling?'

'No,' I said with surprise. 'That is not correct.'

'No? Not every third Monday in the month with a certain Doctor Andrews in Oxford, a specialist in matrimonial problems?'

The DCI slid a piece of paper across the desk towards me. I glanced down. It was a printout of the front page of Dr

Andrews's website with the headline LET ME SAVE YOUR MAR-RIAGE written large across it.

'Well, yes,' I said. 'We have been to see Dr Andrews each month but it was not for marriage guidance in the way you are trying to imply. It was part of our family therapy to complement that which Amelia received each week from her own psychotherapist.'

'Family therapy?' the DCI repeated. 'That sounds very much like marriage guidance to me.'

'It was to help us cope with Amelia's illness,' I said, trying hard to keep calm. 'To teach us how to live a low-stress lifestyle. To help me to manage her mood swings and to recognise the symptoms and potential dangers. I loved my wife and she loved me.'

'I am sure that O. J. Simpson loved his wife too – at some point.'

'Come now, Chief Inspector,' Simon Bassett interjected. 'That cheap jibe is uncalled for. As I said at the start, my client is here voluntarily. If you want him to remain, I suggest you moderate your comments.'

The DCI looked at him in a manner that I took to be contempt. He clearly didn't like being told how to behave, especially by a solicitor.

The chief inspector looked back at me. 'Was your wife ever the victim of domestic violence?'

'No,' I said. 'Never.'

He again looked down at his papers.

'But wasn't your wife treated at Banbury Hospital emergency

department on three separate occasions in the past year for injuries sustained at home?'

'Yes,' I said. 'That's true, but they were not as a result of domestic violence, at least not violence perpetrated by me. One was accidental and the other two as a result of her self-harming. Sadly, my wife was very troubled and sometimes felt that she was a bad person and needed to be punished. When things were really bad, this misplaced need for punishment could lead her to cut herself. Twice it was severe enough for me to take her to A and E.'

'And the third occasion?'

I didn't particularly like where this was going.

'She needed treatment for a facial injury.'

'What sort of injury?' he asked, while clearly already knowing the answer from having read her medical notes.

'She had a cut over her left eye that required stitches.'

And a huge black eye, I remembered, but I decided not to mention that.

'And how did she come by this cut?'

I stared at him. 'She walked into a door,' I said. 'To be precise, she walked into the end of a kitchen cabinet door that she didn't realise was open. I wasn't even in the same room as her at the time of the incident.'

I could tell that he didn't believe me, and who could blame him, but instead of pursuing the point he reached down to the floor and lifted a large brown paper envelope, laying it on the table and removing a clear plastic bag from within.

'Do you recognise this?' he asked, holding up the bag with its contents.

'Yes,' I said. 'It's a leather dog lead.'

'Have you seen it before?'

'It looks like the one we had hanging on the back door in our kitchen.'

'But you don't have a dog,' said the DCI.

'We used to.'

I suddenly laughed out loud.

'What's so damn funny?' demanded the detective crossly.

I managed to stop laughing – but only just.

'When we first moved out of London we bought a Rhodesian Ridgeback puppy. Lovely little chap, he was, but he grew into a large dog, a very large dog. Sadly, last year, he died from an inherited heart condition. I buried him in the garden.'

I'd only just remembered. And the burial site had been exactly where I'd seen the big yellow digger working on the morning news.

'Found his bones yet, have you?' I said, trying hard not to chuckle.

The DCI wasn't pleased, or amused. And he soon put paid to my own amusement too, big time.

'This dog lead was the murder weapon,' he said. 'Mrs Gordon-Russell was found with it still tight round her neck.'

'Oh.'

Reality struck back. I felt embarrassed at having laughed.

The DCI put the lead back in the large brown envelope and returned it to the floor. I had the impression that he'd rather enjoyed showing me his prized exhibit.

'Can you tell us what your wife was wearing when you last saw her?'

I thought back to Tuesday afternoon. I was notoriously bad at remembering what Amelia wore, even on special occasions, and I had no reason to imagine that, when I left to go to Birmingham, it would be the last time I would see her.

'Blue denim jeans, I think,' I said, 'with a red sweater. I can't really recall. She was out in the front garden clearing leaves wearing a green Barbour jacket and gloves as I drove away. I do remember that. She waved at me.'

I could feel a surge of pain and anguish sweeping over me at the memory. I swallowed hard and tried desperately not to blink for fear that the tears collecting in my eyes would run down my cheeks and be visible to the policemen.

Why, I wondered, was I so fixated with not showing my emotions?

Amelia would often harangue me for not opening up to her with regard to how I really felt about her illness instead of being 'so bloody restrained' all the time.

It was my way of coping, I suppose. It was how I'd been brought up.

I did my ranting and crying in private.

'I would like a few moments alone with my client,' Simon said, perfectly aware of what was happening. He had known me for a long time.

'Interview suspended at eleven forty-eight,' said the DCI, stopping the recording machine.

He and his sergeant left the room and Simon passed me his handkerchief.

'It's all right,' he said. 'Show them you care.'

I wiped my eyes and shook my head, more in frustration than as a negative to his comment.

'I'm sorry,' I said.

'Don't be,' Simon replied. 'I feel the same way. I cried myself to sleep last night over Amelia.'

That made two of us.

After five minutes I had regained my composure and the two detectives returned. The recording was restarted.

'Now, Mr Gordon-Russell,' said the DCI, 'tell me about your financial circumstances.'

'What have they got to do with things?'

'Do you stand to gain financially from your wife's death?'

'What sort of question is that to ask?'

'Please answer it.'

'As her husband, I suppose I am her next of kin,' I said. 'Therefore, as we have no children, I will inherit everything she owns, including her half of the house, as she would have done if I had died first. But I also inherit her half of the mortgage liability.'

'Does she leave a will?'

'Somewhere,' I said. 'We both made one when we were first married, leaving everything to each other. They'll be in a filing cabinet in my study.'

'How about investments and savings?'

'Huh!' I uttered. 'We used to have those but there's not much left.'

'Why is that?'

'Mental illness is not cheap, you know.'

'But, surely, medical care in this country is provided free on the NHS.'

'It can be but that's not the only consideration. When I was with Forehanded Life I was part of their private health-insurance programme. It covered Amelia too, as my wife. When she first became ill, she was referred to the very best private psychiatrist I could find in Harley Street, and, when she needed it, she was an in-patient at a private psychiatric hospital in Marylebone.

'Then, two years ago it became obvious to me that being in London every day was not sensible. Twice, when I was at work, she overdosed on her medication in failed but serious attempts at suicide, so I decided that I needed to keep a closer eye on her, to keep her safe. Hence, I resigned from Forehanded Life and set myself up as a self-employed consultant working as much as possible from home.'

'Did you resent that?' asked the DCI.

'No, of course not. She was my wife and she needed me. However, as a result of me leaving the firm, their health-insurance scheme stopped paying for her treatment. By then, she was well used to her psychiatrist and psychotherapist and I was advised that continuity was vital. So I paid the huge private health-insurance premium myself and things went on as before, at least for a while.'

'What happened then?'

'The health-insurance company wrote to me and said that they had unilaterally determined that her condition was chronic rather than acute, and their policy didn't cover chronic conditions other than cancer. So they stopped paying. For the past year I have been funding her treatment out of our savings – monthly appointments with the psychiatrist and twice-weekly visits to the psychotherapist. Not to mention two further lengthy stints in hospital at five grand a week.'

'So you're broke?' asked the detective.

'No,' I said. 'I'm not broke, but let's say my retirement nest egg has taken rather a hit.'

'So it is very convenient for you financially that your wife is now dead.'

I stared at him. 'Don't be ridiculous.'

The chief inspector again shuffled the papers in front of him. He read from one of them and then looked up at me.

'And is it not also the case, Mr Gordon-Russell, that you now stand to benefit to the tune of a million pounds from your wife's life insurance policy. A policy you took out only eight months ago?'

7

'I have to say that I'm quite surprised they let you go.'

Simon Bassett had never been one to mince his words.

We were walking together out of Banbury Police Station.

'But they have no evidence. They can't have. I didn't do it.'

'But they think they have a motive,' Simon said. 'That's often enough on its own for them to arrest. They then search for evidence later.'

I had tried to explain to the detectives why I had taken out such a large insurance policy on Amelia's life but they hadn't really understood, even if they had wanted to. To them it was simply a further reason why I had murdered her.

'The policy had a no-pay-out-for-suicide clause,' I'd told them. 'So it wouldn't pay out if Amelia killed herself. She knew that. It was one of the ways I tried to stop her doing it. I told her that if she died of self-inflicted injury or an overdose, or by jumping in front of a train, then I would get nothing. Strange logic, maybe, but she referred to it often, claiming that the thought of me losing all the premiums for no return had prevented her from doing anything stupid on more than one occasion.'

'But the policy *does* pay out for murder.' The DCI had said it more as a statement than a question.

'I suppose so. Only death by suicide was specifically excluded.'

'In that case there was a huge incentive for you to kill her before she could kill herself, in order to collect the insurance?'

Clearly, my efforts at explanation had been falling on deaf ears.

'I didn't want her to die,' I'd pleaded to them. 'I was just trying to keep her alive. I loved my wife and I miss her desperately.'

What did they want me to do to prove it? Break down and cry?

But that was not in my make-up and forcing myself to weep would surely appear as contrived and false and, worse still, as proof in their eyes of my guilt.

I looked up at the dark threatening sky and sighed. 'I don't think they believed a single word I said. You could see it in their faces.'

'But it gave them something to consider,' Simon replied. 'Trust me, if they really thought you'd killed Amelia, you'd be in the cells now and not out here.'

We started off towards the station but there was a shout from behind.

'Mr Gordon-Russell.'

I half-expected it to be DCI Priestly or Sergeant Dowdeswell calling me back to arrest me but, when I spun round, I found myself confronted by two press photographers who busily snapped away with their cameras. I turned away from them in disgust.

'How the hell did *they* know I'd be here?' I asked.

'Tipped off by the police, I shouldn't wonder,' Simon replied as we hurried along. But the two weren't giving up that easily. They ran past us and continued to take more shots, their flashguns going off like strobes in a nightclub.

I started to cover my face with my arms.

'Don't do that!' Simon said sharply. 'It makes you look like you have something to hide.'

So I put my hands down and walked along with my head held up high, or at least as high as my five-foot-eight-inch frame would allow.

Eventually, after about five minutes, the two obviously decided they had enough pictures and they peeled away, eager, no doubt, to send the images off to their editors.

I sighed again.

'How long before they lose interest?' I asked of no one in particular.

'Not until the next juicy story breaks,' Simon replied.

We caught the train back to London. I wasn't sure where I was going but Simon needed to get back for some meetings and I just went with him.

At Marylebone we were met not by a couple of photographers but by a whole TV-news crew complete with cameraman, sound recordist and female reporter.

'Mr Gordon-Russell, have you any comment to make about your wife's death?' shouted the reporter as I passed through the ticket barrier.

I glanced at Simon and he shook his head. 'Whatever you say to them they will distort to fit their agenda. So don't say anything.'

I kept my mouth shut and walked straight past without giving them a second glance.

'This is ridiculous,' I said when we were safely on our way in a taxi. 'Surely they have more important stories to follow.'

'Spoilt rich aristocrat being quizzed as a suspect in the murder of his commoner wife? Just up their commie street.'

'I'm not spoilt or rich,' I objected.

Simon looked at me. 'But you were brought up in a castle, weren't you? There's nothing the press like more than having a bash at the upper classes. If they can't find Lord Lucan, then you will have to do.'

He obviously wasn't much of a fan of the news media, nor, it seemed, of the aristocracy, although it was hardly my fault that my father was an earl.

The taxi dropped me off as Simon had to rush back to his office for a meeting, so I wandered down Baker Street on foot, not really sure where I was going, or for what purpose.

One must have things to arrange after the death of one's spouse. How about deciding the order of service for a funeral or memorial service? Or completing necessary paperwork, such as registering the death, sorting out bank accounts, wills and probate?

Plus a myriad of other things to be done. Surely?

Why, then, did I have nothing to do?

It was not just that I had no practical arrangements to complete, but now there was no work for me to do either.

I had checked my emails on the train back to London and discovered that the two other insurance companies for whom I was engaged as a freelance consultant had both suspended the agreements.

I wondered if I should sue them for breach of contract, but that would hardly bode well for any future relationship either with them or any other firm. The world of insurance was quite cliquey, with everyone knowing each other's business. To upset one was likely to upset them all. I would just have to grin and bear it, and hope that the suspensions were short.

I drifted aimlessly along, staring into shop windows.

I was horrified to see that Selfridges already had their Christmas window displays up and running, more than two months before the day itself.

Christmas. Oh, God!

In spite of her saying that it was all too commercial and complaining about how much work was involved, Amelia had always adored Christmas, and she revelled in finding me a present that I would love, despite also declaring that I was 'impossible' to buy for.

I had already bought hers for this year.

Back in July she had tried on a gold necklace in a small jewellers in Brighton when we had been there for a day. She loved it but claimed it was far too expensive; but I had managed to sneak back and buy it without her knowledge. It was hiding at the back of one of my desk drawers.

Now what would I do with it?

Here, surrounded by a multitude of shoppers on Oxford Street but effectively alone, my eyes did fill with tears.

How could anyone possibly think that I'd killed her? I worshipped her and would do anything to have her back.

I stood on the kerb waiting for the traffic lights to change while several London buses swept past me at speed, and I seriously wondered about stepping out right in front of one of them.

Quick and easy, and it would put an end to this dreadful pain.

Perhaps the only reason that I didn't was because everyone would then conclude that I had indeed killed my wife, and the real culprit would get away scot-free. And I was still positive that that was Joe Bradbury.

Sandwiched between the emails from the two insurance companies, there had been yet another of his rants, as usual full of abuse and untruths.

'How could you do such a thing?' he had written. 'Amelia always said you were dangerous and now you've proved it. If it weren't for you, my sister would still be alive. Your marriage to Amelia was, without doubt, the worst thing that ever happened to our family. I have tolerated your behaviour up to now for the sake of my sister. But no longer. How could you? . . . how could you? . . . shame on you.'

I had hardly bothered to read it. I certainly wouldn't be replying.

As another twelve tons of bright-red double-decker thundered past inches from my nose, I resolved to stay alive long enough to expose my brother-in-law as the fraud and liar that he was, and to bring him to justice for the death of my wife.

It was easier said than done – the staying alive bit, that was.

8

On Saturday I went to the races at Ascot.

I'm not sure why, because I wasn't acting as a steward, but I'd had enough of kicking my heels aimlessly around Douglas's house. And I needed something else to occupy my mind rather than spending all the hours that God gave yearning that I could reverse the passage of time, like Superman.

However, I received some strange looks from my fellow race-goers even before I'd passed through the turnstiles.

The press had obviously received inside information from the police, and more than just telling them when I'd appear outside Banbury Police Station. Features of the crime were being widely reported by the media, including the gory details of how Amelia had died in spite of the fact that the post-mortem report had yet to be completed.

Friday had been another sparse news day and the police fail-ure to make an arrest in what was now being described as the 'dog-lead murder' was still prominent on both broadcast news bulletins and in the papers. All the front pages included the picture taken of me with the police station in the background, and the evening TV news had had the footage of me arriving at Marylebone.

All of their stories included the fact that I had recently taken out an insurance policy on Amelia's life and implied that I had killed her in order to collect, without actually stating it in so many words. Close to libel but not quite. The lawyers had been busy.

So much for the presumption of innocence. That was clearly a myth and the crowd at Ascot had obviously believed everything they had read and heard.

'Shame on you,' one man shouted at me, echoing the email from Joe Bradbury.

'Murderer,' yelled a young woman wearing a full-length black coat, who then encouraged those around her to join in the abuse.

I realised that it had been a huge mistake to come and I sought refuge from the mob in the Stewards' Room, using my authorised pass to gain entrance to the weighing room complex beneath the grandstand concourse.

Even though I wasn't down to act in an official capacity at the meeting, it was quite common for qualified stewards to report early to the day's chairman just in case there was an emergency and more stewards were needed than had been booked.

However, on this day, even the Stewards' Room was not a safe harbour in my storm.

'What the hell do you think you're doing here?' George Longcross demanded.

Oh, shit! I hadn't appreciated that he was acting as chairman.

'You are not welcome,' George said. 'You've brought the sport into disrepute.'

'How exactly?' I asked.

'Stands to reason,' he replied arrogantly. 'By being accused of murder.'

'I haven't been accused of murder,' I pointed out. 'And I have not been arrested. I have simply been questioned by the police about the murder of my wife, but not as a suspect.'

'Humph!' he uttered in disbelief. 'That's not what the papers are saying.'

And it was also not how I felt.

'Then the papers are wrong. Otherwise, how would I be able to be here?'

For a moment he seemed confused but he was not going to back down. George Longcross had probably never once backed down in his whole life. I had always considered him to be an overbearing pompous snob and nothing about this exchange had encouraged me to change my opinion.

'I order you to leave,' he said angrily. 'Right now.'

I wondered if he had the authority to make such an order but decided that putting it to the test was unlikely to make me any friends in the racing establishment.

So I left, and not only the Stewards' Room but also the whole racecourse – but not before half a dozen or so more members of the public had vented their rage at my presence. One of them was even acquainted with me slightly through our time riding together as amateur jockeys, and he was particularly vitriolic, accusing me of bringing disgrace on a noble family.

'Your father must be horrified,' he shouted at my face from about six inches away.

'I haven't done anything wrong,' I protested, but it fell on deaf ears. He'd read the newspapers – he knew.

But I was, indeed, very apprehensive of what my father might be thinking. And my mother too. For the most part, my parents lived in their own ivory tower in the Welsh Marches, where they were more concerned with how they could afford to keep the castle roof watertight than they were with the major news stories of the day.

I knew that they were aware of Amelia's death – Douglas had phoned them on the first evening I'd been in his house – but I had yet to be in contact with them myself.

I'd never been that close to my parents; indeed, as a young child I had been cherished far more by my grandparents. I believed that my mother had been more 'hands on' when my two elder brothers were born but, by the time I arrived eight years later, she was far too busy running the local church and history groups to worry about her new baby. In those days, before my grandfather's death duties had laid waste to the family fortune, there had been an army of domestic staff to cook my meals and wash my clothes, and, later, even a chauffeur to drive me to and from my boarding schools. Not that I'd felt particularly deprived of maternal affection at the time. It was just the way things were, and I knew nothing different. Only much later, as a teenager and after my grandmother's death, did I start wondering if my arrival into this world had been a huge blunder on my parents' part.

So I hadn't called them yet, not least because my father, in particular, would have been hugely embarrassed if I'd been in an emotional state with him on the telephone. But perhaps now was the time to remind them not to believe everything they read in the newspapers.

I caught the train back to London from Ascot station while many were still arriving for one of the great days of British racing – Champions Day, the last great hurrah before flat racing on turf went into hibernation for the four and a half long months of winter.

Why had I come in the first place?

I had been humiliated, especially by George Longcross.

He and I had never really seen eye to eye. He was a harsh judge and was always quick to blame the jockeys for the slightest interference, even when it had been completely accidental or due to one of the horses reacting without warning. I, on the other hand, tended to try and give the benefit of the doubt to the riders.

Professional jockeys are self-employed and hence don't get paid unless they are racing, so any decision to suspend them from riding affects their ability to earn a living. Nevertheless, and irrespective of their fame and fortune, George Longcross treated them like servants, referring to them always by their surnames alone. I had a more sanguine approach, while at all times upholding the strict Rules of Racing.

I felt there had to be a delicate balance between carrot and stick, considering most of the people the stewards deal with have hugely more experience of racing than we do, and far greater earnings. It's similar to football, where a Premier League star earning hundreds of thousands of pounds a week is under the control of a referee who is paid only a small fraction of that in a full year, and is most unlikely to have ever played the game professionally.

I believed that respect should be a two-way process but George Longcross demanded absolute subservience both from the sport's participants and from his fellow stewards, with no place for empathy, compromise or compassion. It didn't do much for his popularity rating at any time, and especially not with me at the moment.

I kept my eyes down on the train to Waterloo, thankfully arriving without any unpleasant confrontations with my fellow passengers.

'Chester Square, please,' I said to the driver of a black cab at the station taxi rank.

We set off and I wondered if it was my paranoia or was he really looking at me via his rear-view mirror more than at the road ahead?

But he must have been paying more attention to the traffic than I'd realised, as we made it safely to Chester Square without so much as the slightest bump or scrape.

I stood on the pavement and paid him through the open window, including a tip.

'Good luck, mate,' he said.

I looked at him enquiringly, but he wasn't finished, not by a long way.

'But you're going to need more than luck where you're going.'

'I didn't do it,' I said, but I could see from his expression that he didn't believe me.

I nearly asked him for my tip back.

Douglas wasn't at home. I knew he wouldn't be. He'd left on Friday afternoon for a rare day's partridge shooting in Somerset. He was staying down there with friends and not leaving until after lunch on Sunday.

He had offered not to go. He said he would remain in London and look after me, but I had insisted he went. I told him I'd be fine if I could stay in the house – 'As long as you like, dear boy' – and I knew how much he enjoyed his shooting.

It was partly why I'd gone to the races, as the hours until Douglas's return seemed to stretch interminably ahead with nothing for me to do. The choice was either to sit in front of the television all day and get drunk, or go to the races and stay sober.

Now I wished I'd chosen the former.

But it was not too late.

I fetched a bottle of Merlot from the wine rack in the kitchen – not one of Douglas's finest – and took it along to the sitting room.

I was still in time to watch the last three races from Ascot but I found myself mostly just staring at the screen without really taking in what was happening.

The short-priced favourite won the Queen Elizabeth II Stakes, but it had been boxed in on the rail and appeared to barge its way through to get home by a neck. It would be something for George Longcross to sort out and, sure enough, a stewards' enquiry was quickly announced.

I could imagine George and his fellow stewards studying the footage from the various cameras and interviewing the appropriate jockeys in the Stewards' Room.

From what I could see from the head-on shot on the TV, the fast-finishing winner had taken a bit of a liberty by forcing himself through a gap that was hardly big enough in the first place while, at the same time, the horse in front, which had subsequently finished second, had begun to hang towards the rail, making the gap even smaller. Contact between the two had been inevitable.

It was a difficult call but I would have argued that, on balance, the fault was six by one, half a dozen by the other, and I would leave the placings unaltered.

But I wasn't George Longcross.

To massive boos from the crowd, the horse that had been first past the post was demoted for causing interference and the race was awarded to the second. And then, to add insult to injury, it was announced that the jockey on the favourite had also been suspended for two days for careless riding.

A little while afterwards, the young man in question was interviewed by the TV presenter and he was not happy, and not particularly diplomatic either in his criticism of the stewards, something that might cause him more trouble later.

'They didn't consider the facts,' he protested loudly. 'It was as if they made up their minds without even bothering to look at the evidence. I've been unjustly accused of something I didn't do.'

I knew exactly how he felt.

9

At eleven o'clock on Sunday morning I received an extremely irate and rambling call on my mobile from Mary Bradbury, Amelia's mother.

'You're a horrid little man,' she shouted down the line. 'How could you have killed Amelia?'

'I didn't,' I replied.

'Ha!' she squawked. 'Joe told me that you'd deny it.'

'I deny it because it isn't true.'

'Joe says it is.'

'That's because Joe is lying to you, as he's lied to the police.' And to everyone else. Some of the so-called exclusive revelations in the Sunday newspapers concerning Amelia's history as a psychiatric in-patient had Joe Bradbury's fingerprints all over them.

'He says you killed her for her life insurance money.'

'Mary,' I said earnestly, 'I didn't kill her. I loved her, as you know all too well.'

'Joe says—'

I interrupted her. 'I don't care what Joe says. He's not telling you the truth.'

'Why would he lie?'

Why indeed.

'Why don't you ask him what he was doing at our house when he found Amelia. He hasn't been there for more than two years. He wasn't welcome. Yet he appears on the very day Amelia died. Don't you think that's rather suspicious?'

'You're not seriously suggesting that Joe had something to do with Amelia's death? Don't be ridiculous, he's her brother.'

'But you think it's not ridiculous that I did have something to do with it when I'm her husband?' I asked with strong irony. 'Come on, Mary, use some common sense.'

Common sense had always been something she was short of, and all the more so recently as her age-related confusion had grown.

'But Joe is adamant that you killed her. He told me that he has proof you did it.'

'Then he's lying to you again,' I said, but she wasn't listening.

'I just hope I live long enough to see you found guilty,' she said. 'It's a real shame you won't hang, if you ask me. Namby-pamby do-gooding abolitionists. Not like when I was a girl. Murderers got what was coming to them then – the long drop at the end of a rope. And good riddance. Prison's too good for the likes of you.'

She was getting quite agitated and breathless.

'I'm sure you'll live for a long time yet, Mary,' I said, ignoring her vitriol.

'I will if this cancer doesn't see me off.'

Cancer? What cancer? That was news to me.

'I'm sorry to hear that, Mary,' I said.

However hard I tried, I found I couldn't be angry with the old witch. I'd loved her dearly for such a long time, as Amelia had done. It was not her fault that her shit of a son had taken advantage of her increasing impairment to brainwash her so completely.

'In the pancreas, they say. Found out last week. Quite advanced, spread to my liver. Seems it could see me off at any time. They say I'm too ill for an operation – it would kill me. But the damn cancer will kill me too.'

'I'm so sorry,' I said.

In a strange way, I was pleased that Amelia had never known – at least I assumed she had never known because, if she had, she would have surely told me. She would have been devastated. In spite of everything that had gone on over the past three years between them, she had still loved her mother very deeply.

'Well, dear, I must go now,' Mary said, as if she had completely forgotten why she had phoned me in the first place. 'It will be time for my lunch soon.'

Away with the fairies, but not so much that she couldn't do me considerable harm if I wasn't careful.

We disconnected but my phone rang again straight away. I thought it must be Mary calling back with more insults but I was wrong.

'William!' stated a humourless male voice loudly. 'It's your father.'

Oh, hell!

'Hello, Pa,' I said in my best try-not-to-antagonise-him tone. 'How lovely to hear from you.'

'Don't give me that claptrap,' he said. 'Seems like you're in a bit of bother.' He coughed, as if there was more he wanted to say but didn't. Then he got it out. 'Not something you can handle on your own. Your mother wants you to come home here so we can help.'

I could have cried except that he wouldn't have wanted that, or liked it.

'Thank you, Pa,' I said. 'Maybe I'll come tomorrow.'

'Good,' he said. 'I'll get Mrs Jenkins to make up your room. Your mother and I would be pleased to see you.'

'Thank you,' I said, but he had already gone.

That was as near as he ever got to expressing his love for his sons.

I was my father's son and, throughout my life, it had only been with Amelia that I had been able to express my true feelings about anything.

And now, God help me, she was gone.

Another series of huge bouts of sobbing left me completely wrung out and by the time Douglas returned about eight in the evening, I was pretty much ready for bed.

'Good weekend?' I asked.

'Lovely,' he said. 'Although I felt guilty at having left you alone the whole time. Especially with all that nonsense printed in the newspapers.'

I waved a dismissive hand as if I could handle all of that, even though I couldn't.

'Fancy a drink?' he asked. 'I had to refrain at lunch because I was driving. Bloody shame. Tony had a really nice magnum of Châteauneuf-du-Pape 2007 that I could have got deeply stuck into.' He sighed.

'I'd love a drink,' I said, 'but make it just a small one. I don't feel much like celebrating.'

'No,' he agreed, and he poured two small glasses of a somewhat lesser-quality red wine than the Châteauneuf.

'Pa called me,' I said, taking a sip.

'Oh.' Douglas's hand stopped abruptly as he raised his glass towards his lips. 'How did that go?'

'Pretty well,' I said. 'In fact, much better than I expected. He asked me to go home so he could help.'

'Blimey!' Douglas exclaimed. 'But I bet he's more concerned about you tarnishing the family name than your personal welfare.'

'Maybe,' I said. 'But, strangely, he really did seem to care. I was quite moved. He mentioned Ma for a start. Said she'd be pleased to see me.'

'He must be getting soft in his old age.' Douglas laughed loudly.

'I think I'll go tomorrow, but just for a couple of nights. I need to be back by Wednesday as the police have informed me that Amelia's inquest will be opening in Oxford that afternoon.'

'But that will be just a formality at this stage,' Douglas said. 'The coroner will simply open the inquest, and then adjourn it.'

'Yeah, but I think I should be there as her next of kin. Don't you?'

'Maybe,' he said thoughtfully. 'I don't want you to get too upset by what you might hear.'

'Like what?' I said.

'Preliminary results of the cause of death. Method of identification. Stuff like that. I've acted in several Coroners' Courts. Usually after industrial accidents where a firm is worried about being tried for corporate manslaughter. It always seems to me that the deceased is rather dehumanised, just a "thing" rather than a person. It can be quite upsetting for the relatives.'

'Everything is quite upsetting at the moment,' I said, hanging my head. 'I don't really know where I am or what I should do. I'm only going home to see Ma and Pa because I can't think of anything else to do. I don't want to be in the house in Hanwell on my own, that's for sure, even if the police do let me back in. And I can't go on staying here for ever.'

'Why not?' Douglas said. 'You're welcome to stay as long as you like.'

'Thanks,' I said, meaning it. 'But I think I'll go to Wales. My life seems a bit lost at the moment, as if I were starring in a horror biopic without a screenplay, and no director. I feel I should be doing something but I have absolutely nothing to do. At least up there, I'll be put to work on some project or other and I'll feel useful.'

Our mother always had her pet projects on the go, to somehow improve the castle in her eyes. Such as tree planting or path laying, converting outhouses into craft workshops or organising local workers into chain gangs to confront the never-ending scourge of ivy before it could attack the ancient stonework.

I would simply get swept up by her enthusiasm and maybe, just maybe, the physical labour, even for a day or two, would enable me to forget briefly the agony that existed in my heart.

'As you like,' Douglas said. 'But if I were you, I'd skip the inquest and stay longer at home. It will do you good.'

'Won't it look bad if I'm not present?'

'I wouldn't worry about that,' Douglas said. 'The way the press have been hounding you, it's probably best to avoid them, and you can bet they'll be there in force.'

I still didn't like it. The media would accuse me of hiding, and not caring.

'I'd go on your behalf,' Douglas said, 'but I'm busy with this trial at the Bailey. The judge is currently doing his summing-up and the whole thing should be through by the middle of the week, but one never knows how much time the jury will take. In my experience, juries are always a bit of a lottery. But here's hoping this one makes the right decision.'

He lifted his glass.

'Guilty, you mean.'

'In this case, yes,' he said firmly. 'It's a gay lovers' tiff and the defendant is as guilty as hell.'

'How can you be so sure?' I asked.

'His DNA was all over the murder scene for a start.'

'So?' I asked. 'My DNA will be all over Amelia's murder scene too. I live there. It doesn't mean I killed her.'

'Hmm. Good point,' Douglas said. 'But the defendant in this case maintains that he had an argument with his neighbour and killed him by mistake while defending himself with a fish-filleting knife. What complete nonsense. No one carries a knife like that unless they have the intention of using it. And he also claims that he'd never been in the victim's flat before and that his DNA found all over the victim's bed was planted there by the police.'

'Are you sure it wasn't?'

He looked at me strangely. 'You don't seem to have a very high regard for the Old Bill.'

'Would you in my place?' I replied. 'They seem to take Joe Bradbury's word for it that I killed Amelia without investigating him at all.'

'You don't know that.'

'Don't I?' I said. 'I've just received another of his diatribes by email. In it he continually mocks me as being the only suspect. Then he accuses me of being abusive and aggressive towards his mother on the telephone in spite of the fact that I wasn't, and that it was she that called in the first place to abuse me. He also maintains that I'm a bully when it's really he who's done all the bullying. I'm totally fed up with him. Amelia and I were advised by Simon Bassett never to respond to Joe's lies, but he's sorely testing my patience at the moment. So it hasn't been a great day, to say nothing of those damn newspaper headlines. They really hurt.'

'Why did you look at them?' Douglas asked.

'It's a bit difficult not to when you have them delivered and they were lying open on the doormat.'

'Sorry about that,' he said. 'But they're only delivered on Sundays, mind. You'll be spared tomorrow.'

'Surely by tomorrow they will have found something else to write about.'

'I wouldn't bet on it,' Douglas said. 'Felicity and Tony hosted a big Sunday lunch today for ten of their friends. In spite of them knowing that you're my brother, it was all they talked about. I had to spend the whole time defending your character and reputation.'

'I'm sorry,' I said.

'Don't be.' He smiled. 'It was my pleasure. The damn media should be ashamed of the hatchet job they've done on you. I hope you sue.'

'Douglas, you know as well as I do, in fact better, that suing newspapers is a mug's game. They will have cleared everything through their lawyers before they printed it.'

'Yeah, you're right. The media are so careful these days. Especially after the BBC quite rightly got done for invading Cliff Richard's privacy. And then there was that dreadful case in Bristol when the landlord was accused by the papers of murdering one of his female tenants.'

I looked at him blankly.

'You must remember. They made a TV film about him and he was a star witness at the Leveson Inquiry into press ethics – not that that seems to have done any good, if this case is anything to go by. What the hell was his name?'

'I can't help you,' I said.

'Jefferies!' Douglas said, clapping his hands together in delight. 'That was it. Christopher Jefferies.'

'What about him?'

'Turned out he was completely blameless, so he sued for libel. And he won, too. Received substantial damages from eight national newspapers, no less, two of which were later also found in contempt of court and heavily fined on top. The combined press had tried and convicted him in the eyes of the public without any evidence whatsoever. Assassinated his character just because he had long white hair and looked a bit odd. It was disgraceful.'

No more disgraceful than what they were now doing to me.

10

On Monday morning I packed up my meagre possessions and set off from Chester Square to Wales. But first I would have to collect my Jag from the pub in Hanwell village where I'd left it while in London, having taken a taxi to the station. Hence, I caught the train from London to Banbury.

While on the train, I called the number on the business card that Detective Chief Inspector Priestly had given me at our interview. A voice answered but it wasn't the DCI.

'DS Dowdeswell.'

'Ah,' I said. 'You'll do. This is Bill Russell.'

There was a pause while he worked it out.

'Yes, Mr Gordon-Russell,' he said. 'What can I do for you?'

'I'd like access to my property. I need some clean clothes.'

There were some mumblings from the other end that I couldn't really hear, as if the sergeant was speaking to someone else with his hand over the microphone. Then he came back to me.

'That shouldn't be a problem. We have finished our forensic examination of the murder scene.'

'Great,' I said. 'I'm on my way there now.'

'Then you will need the locks removed.'

'What locks?'

'We applied hasps and padlocks to the external doors to prevent anyone gaining access before we had completed our investigation.'

'Me, you mean?' I said cynically.

'Well, yes,' he agreed. 'But there is also some damage to the external kitchen door, which needed securing.'

'Damage?'

'Yes,' said the detective sergeant. 'It was through the kitchen door that Mr Bradbury made his entrance when he saw Mrs Gordon-Russell lying on the floor. Basically, he kicked the door down.'

'And you're certain that that was done after she was dead?' I asked.

'What do you mean?'

'Why are you not considering the possibility that Joe Bradbury broke into my house to kill his sister?'

'Who says we're not?' he said. 'We consider all possible scenarios.'

At least that was a start.

'So why are the newspapers reporting that I'm the murderer?'

'I can't speak for them.'

'Why not? You're giving them the information.'

'I am not.'

'Well, someone in the police is. Otherwise, how would two press photographers have known that I was at Banbury Police Station on Friday? They must have been tipped off.'

'Perhaps it was a coincidence,' the DS said.

I snorted my disbelief but realised that continuing to argue the point would get me nowhere. 'So how do I get the padlocks removed?'

'I will get our works department to do it.'

'When?' I asked. 'I'm on my way there now.'

'It won't be done right away. Probably tomorrow or the next day.'

'Then can I come and collect the keys from you? I'm currently on a train to Banbury and I need access today.'

There were more mumbling discussions in the background.

'Yes, okay,' said the DS finally. 'The forensic team left the keys here. I'll leave them at the front desk for you to collect, but we'll need the locks and keys back after you've been to your house.'

'I'll be with you in half an hour,' I said, and hung up.

I stared out of the window as the world rushed by.

Did I really want to go into my house? Especially into the kitchen.

The very thought of it was making me shake but I needed some stuff apart from clothes, particularly the chargers for my phone and computer. I suppose I could have bought new ones but there were other things I needed too, not least the medication I took each night to keep my cholesterol in check, having now exhausted those that I'd had in my washbag.

A previous passenger had left a copy of a newspaper on the table to my left and I glanced at the bold headline on its front page: STILL NO ARREST IN DOG-LEAD MURDER.

For goodness' sake! Is there still nothing more important to report?

Even though I knew that I shouldn't, I could not help but read the start of the article beneath the headline.

'Thames Valley Police are coming under increasing pressure to make an arrest for the murder of Amelia Gordon-Russell, found strangled in her own home near Banbury last Wednesday. A police spokesman has told this newspaper that their investigation is proceeding and they expect to detain a suspect in the near future.'

And we all knew who that would be, didn't we?

I tossed the paper back onto the table. I didn't want to read any more. *Police spokesman, my arse!* Someone was making it up. But perhaps going to the police station was not such a good idea after all. The phrase 'putting my head into a lion's mouth' sprang to mind.

I might never get it out again.

I took one of the taxis waiting outside the railway station and asked the driver to wait outside while I went in to collect the padlock keys from the police. I didn't really expect to be detained, did I? But my anxiety heightened somewhat when I found that the keys were not at the front desk as promised.

'Are you sure?' I asked the woman sitting behind the glass screen.

'Quite sure,' she replied.

At that point DS Dowdeswell came into the foyer and my heartbeat ramped up a few notches.

'Ah, there you are,' he said.

He came towards me but there were no handcuffs at the ready in his outstretched mitts, just the bunch of keys for the padlocks.

'There are four of them,' he said. 'We put locks on all the doors including the conservatory, and the French windows in the dining room. I don't know which key works which lock. You'll have to try them.'

He hesitated as if there was something else he wanted to say, but I wasn't waiting around to give him time to change his mind. I took the keys from him and walked briskly out of the door, hardly daring to breathe, and quite expecting to be recalled. But I made it unchallenged to the taxi and we quickly set off with me sighing deeply on the back seat.

Calm down, I told myself, *you've done nothing wrong.* I was glad to be away from there, nevertheless.

'Hanwell village, please,' I said to the driver. 'Drop me outside the pub.'

Which he duly did.

I walked down the side of the building to my Jaguar, which was waiting in the corner of the car park where I'd left it.

I was just turning it round when Mark Thornton, the publican, came out to see me.

'I thought that must be yours,' he said gruffly. 'You're lucky I didn't call the police over the weekend to report an abandoned vehicle, but someone from the village recognised it.'

'I didn't think you'd mind,' I said.

He clearly did.

'Don't leave it here again, do you hear. Some of my regulars aren't happy about it and nor am I. Not with everything about you in the papers.'

I forced a laugh. 'But surely, Mark, you don't believe all that guff.'

'You're not welcome here and neither is your car,' he said in all seriousness. 'Amelia was very popular with people in the village and feelings are running high.' There was no flicker of warmth and no hint of compassion for my loss. 'Next time, I won't be able to stop them scratching the paintwork or slashing your tyres.'

'I didn't kill her,' I said for the umpteenth time, but I could see that I was wasting my breath. What chance did I have when even my closest friends thought I was guilty?

I drove the hundred and fifty yards up the road to the Old Forge.

The yellow crime-scene tape of last week had been removed so I pulled the Jag into the driveway.

Someone had sprayed the word KILLER in white paint in foot-high capital letters across the dark green of the garage door. Charming. Why was it that, with the emergence of social media, ordinary people, probably my kindly neighbours, who wouldn't have dreamed of doing such a thing in the past, now felt that it was acceptable to vent their anger in such a fashion?

Especially when it wasn't true.

But did they care?

Not one bit. They had probably filmed themselves doing it, and shared the footage with their supposed 'friends' and 'followers' on Facebook, Twitter, Instagram or Snapchat, possibly all four.

With mounting trepidation I walked over to the front door.

As DS Dowdeswell had indicated, a large padlock hung on a shiny metal hasp that had been firmly attached to the heavy oak door and surround without any thought for the damage caused to the listed woodwork. English Heritage would have had a fit if they'd known.

The third key I tried fitted and the shackle snapped up.

I pushed open the door and stepped into what felt like an alien world of no warmth, no joyous delight at my arrival, no exclamation of love – no life.

Amelia and I had adored this house. We had transformed the dark drab interior of our purchase into a bright vibrant living space where we loved to entertain or just have quiet dinners *à deux* on our laps, sitting side by side on the sofa facing a roaring log fire in the space that had once held the blacksmith's furnace.

But now it was cold and dark and silent – unwelcoming.

I switched on the lights in the hall but it made little difference.

It wasn't so much the house that was dead, more my aching heart.

I picked up the post that had accumulated on the mat, most of it online shopping brochures addressed to Amelia, many of them encouraging early purchases for Christmas. But among the other detritus were three white envelopes addressed to me. *Bills,*

I thought, and stuffed them into my trouser pocket, unopened.

Next I went upstairs to the master bedroom, collecting my black suitcase from a landing cupboard on the way.

So far, I had held things together pretty well, but the sight of our bed made me gasp out loud. My side was undisturbed while the other was turned back as if Amelia had just got out to go to the bathroom, her reading glasses still on the bedside table where she would have put them after checking her emails, something she had done every night before she went to sleep.

I lay down and wept, pushing my face deep into her pillow to try and detect her pheromones, to smell her scent one last time, but nothing remained. It was as if she had never been there.

After a while, the bout of sobbing subsided and I was able to get up and continue my packing, but I had no heart for it.

I wasn't even fully aware of what I was putting in the suitcase, although I was careful to include my black tie. My father had a penchant for demanding that we dress for dinner, especially if there were guests in the castle. It was like travelling back to the 1920s.

'One has to maintain standards,' he would claim, as if what one wore made a huge difference.

At least he didn't insist on white tie and tails, even if he did sometimes wear them himself.

I went into the bathroom.

Every surface was covered in a fine silvery dust and I remembered back to my conversation with the dabs man, the fingerprint finder. I wondered what prints he'd been looking for. No one had taken mine to eliminate them.

I collected my medication from the bathroom cabinet along with a fresh razor and a new tube of toothpaste, mundane necessities in extraordinary circumstances.

I took the suitcase back down to the hall and left it ready by the front door, along with my wellington boots, waxed Barbour jacket and tweed cap – essentials for a trip to Wales in October.

My computer charger was in the study so I went in there and collected it, along with some other bits and bobs from my desk. But I couldn't find my phone charger.

Where was it?

I needed it as my phone was already running on reserve.

Then I remembered that I had last used the charger in the kitchen on Tuesday afternoon before I'd left for Birmingham.

The kitchen.

I stood in the hall seriously considering leaving it where it was and buying a new one, but where would I find a charger shop on the rural roads between Hanwell and North Wales without going miles off my route, maybe into Telford or Shrewsbury?

Perhaps I could use the internet to order one to be delivered direct to the castle, or simply go without. There was hardly ever any phone signal up there anyway.

But I told myself I was just being silly.

'Stop being such a wuss,' I said out loud. 'Just go in and get it.'

So I went into the kitchen.

It looked just as it always had, apart from the slimy fingerprint dust on every surface and the splintered wood around the back-door lock.

I stared down at the floor but there was no sign of the horror that had occurred. No blood, no stains – nothing, just the washed flagstone floor, same as usual.

I didn't linger – I had done enough crying for one day – so I picked up the charger from the worktop and left, collecting my stuff from the hall on the way out.

I reapplied the padlock to the front door – I may as well use the extra security – and loaded everything into the boot of the Jaguar. Then I drove out of the village, paused briefly at the main road before turning north, away from Banbury and towards Wales, with the padlock keys in my pocket.

I couldn't be bothered to take them back to Banbury Police Station.

The police might arrest me for murder but they were unlikely to do so for stealing four keys.

11

Llanbron Castle sits in a commanding position on the top of a small hill overlooking a curve in the River Dee, just south of Wrexham in North Wales. It was constructed in the late thirteenth century as part of the ring of fortifications built by King Edward I of England to suppress and control the Welsh hordes.

Over time the castle had undergone many changes, not least in the mid-seventeenth century when, after surviving the English Civil War intact, it was besieged and then sacked by parliamentarian forces as a reprisal for supporting the Cheshire Rebellion of 1659, when a group of English and Welsh noblemen unsuccessfully attempted to revive the monarchy.

However, a year later, with Charles II now safely restored to the throne of England, Sir Thomas Humberly, owner of the castle at the time of the revolt, had his neck saved from the axe by the returning king, who then generously rewarded him for his loyalty. He was granted a sum sufficient to restore the structure to its former glory, with enough remaining to transform the former rather austere living quarters into something more luxurious for the period.

Over the next hundred years or so, the castle had again fallen into disrepair before being acquired by the Gordon-Russell family in a somewhat questionable manner.

My six-times-great-grandfather, Herbert Gordon-Russell, later created the first Earl of Wrexham in equally dubious circumstances, had reportedly accepted, unseen, the near-derelict castle as payment for a huge debt run up during a game of whist played in a London house of ill repute.

The afternoon light was beginning to fade as I drove up the long driveway, the sharply defined castle battlements silhouetted against the still-bright western sky.

I wondered what my ancestor Herbert must have thought of his gambling acquisition when he came here for the very first time, taking almost a week to travel from his London home by horse-drawn carriage. Did he consider it a millstone round his neck, as my father did, or as a safe haven from the stresses of an unfair world, as I hoped it might be for me now?

I pulled up in front of the imposing main entrance and my father came out to greet me, as if he'd been watching for my arrival.

'Hi, Pa,' I said, climbing out of the Jaguar.

'William,' he said, coming forward across the gravel to shake my hand. There were no hugs between male members of the Gordon-Russell family. Even as a small child, I'd only ever greeted my father by shaking his hand and it wasn't about to change just because my wife was dead. 'Good journey?'

'Fine,' I said. 'Just the usual heavy traffic around Birmingham.'

I lifted my suitcase out of the car boot.

'Here,' I said. 'I bought this for you.'

I handed him a bottle of his favourite Glenmorangie ten-year-old single malt.

'How lovely,' he said, and he smiled broadly, which was quite an unusual occurrence. The way to my father's heart was definitely through his whisky decanter.

'I also have some flowers for Ma,' I said, lifting them out of the boot and giving them to him. I'd picked them up from a petrol station on the way and had been careful to remove the price label.

'You shouldn't have.'

But I always did. This was like a game and he would have been disappointed if I'd arrived empty-handed.

'Let's get in,' my father said. 'It's getting cold out here.'

But it would be no less cold inside. 'Why spend money on heating the damn place,' my father would often say, 'when one can simply wear a sweater?'

I was thankful that I'd remembered to pack one, and some fleecy pyjamas.

We went in through the massive wooden door of the main castle entrance, my father slamming it shut and bolting it behind us as if still keeping out the barbarian mob beyond.

My mother was waiting in the small sitting room, as it was known, and there was indeed a welcoming log fire in the grate.

'Hello, my darling,' she said, offering her cheek for a kiss. 'I'm so glad you've come. I have some jobs for you to do.'

I smiled at her. It wouldn't have been the same if she hadn't.

'Be quiet, woman,' my father said with a mixture of authority and tenderness. 'Give the boy a chance to sit down. He's not here just to potter in your garden.'

But why was I here if not to busy myself and keep my mind off the void?

'I'll be happy to help tomorrow,' I said, and smiled at her again.

For twenty minutes or so, we sat and drank cups of tea, making small talk and avoiding the elephant in the room until my father finally cut to the chase. 'Now what's all this stuff about you in the papers and on the television?'

My mother gave him one of her how-dare-you-ask-that-question stares, but the subject had to be broached sooner or later. After all, that was the main reason I was here.

In the least distressing terms I could muster, I outlined how Amelia had been murdered while I was away from home for the night, how she had been discovered lying on the kitchen floor of our house with a dog lead still round her neck. And I described how I had been informed of her death while at Warwick Races, and I told them of my subsequent interviews at Banbury Police Station.

'The police are so certain that I'm guilty that they are telling it to the press, hence it's all in the papers. But it's all nonsense, of course.'

'Of course,' my mother echoed.

105

My dear mother would never have believed that any of her children could do anything illegal, and especially not murder.

'But *why* do the police think you did it?' my father asked.

'It's a long story.'

Up to that point I had kept my parents in the dark with respect to the trouble that Amelia and I had been having with her brother, and the effect it had had on her mental health. One's wife having psychiatric problems was not the sort of thing one shouted about from the rooftops, or even to one's parents. I was certain that my father would have considered it a weakness, so I hadn't told him. But maybe now was the time.

'It all started about three years ago,' I said. 'When Mary Bradbury moved out of their family home and into a quaint "chocolate-box" thatched cottage in West Oxfordshire to be closer to us. Joe didn't like it and he's been waging a war of abuse and vilification against me ever since, even though the move was not my idea or my doing. And every time he wrote his lies about me it was like a knife in the heart for Amelia. She became really upset that it was *her* brother who was attacking *her* husband.'

'Didn't you confront him about it?' my father asked.

'We tried. But he simply twisted everything we said and threw it back at us with interest. We were advised by a lawyer to stop responding to his emails or communicating with him in any way, but that appears to have made things worse. He now accuses us of trying to destroy him when we're not even in contact. It's bizarre.'

My parents sat quite still, staring at me and waiting for me to go on.

'However, bad as all that is, it pales into insignificance compared to what else he did. He turned his own mother against Amelia. He kept telling her that Amelia was mad and not to be trusted. In the end she believed it. It was as if Joe was jealous of their close relationship so he set out to destroy it. And he managed it. It was that which caused Amelia the most heartbreak and it was what finally tipped her over the edge.'

'What do you mean, it tipped her over the edge?' my mother asked.

So I told them everything – the psychiatrists, the therapists, the hospital stays, even the suicide attempts. I told them the whole shebang.

They were shocked. My mother was even in tears.

'My poor darling,' she said. 'How dreadful. Is there nothing you could have done to stop him?'

'Nothing, short of going to court and getting an injunction. And that would have cost a fortune. Thousands at least.'

'But exactly what has all that to do with the reports about you in the papers?' my father asked.

'Because Joe Bradbury has been telling the police, and the press and anyone else who'll listen, that I killed his sister and, for some reason, they all believe him.'

My father had always been one for keeping his emotions in check, as he had taught me to do, but now he let down his guard. I had rarely seen him so angry. He stood up and marched back and forth across the room, continuously bunching and relaxing his fists. 'There must be *something* we can do to shut this man up.'

'Douglas says it's best to do nothing,' I said. 'Not to give Joe any more ammunition that he can then fire back. Douglas is fully aware of what's been going on and he's been absolutely wonderful. In fact, I don't know what I'd have done without him. I've been staying at his place in London because the police wouldn't allow me back into my own house.'

'Why ever not?' my mother asked.

'Forensic examination,' I explained. 'They've been searching for evidence.'

My mother looked appalled at the thought.

'I could do with a drink,' my father announced. 'Want one?'

'Why not,' I said.

'Whisky?'

He didn't wait for an answer but went out the door, presumably to the drinks cabinet in the dining room.

'Why didn't you tell us before?' my mother said quietly, but she was already aware of the answer. 'I suppose your father would have told Amelia to get a grip and stop making a fuss.'

'It would have made things worse.'

She nodded. She knew him even better than I did. Much better in fact.

'Edward and Stella are joining us for dinner.'

'Great,' I said, not meaning it.

My eldest brother and his wife lived in another part of the castle, as my parents had done when my grandfather was still alive. It had become a tradition in the Gordon-Russell family for the heir apparent to the earldom to live on site but, unlike for former generations, the tax benefits were now being properly utilised. There clearly were some advantages to having a family member in the financial services industry.

In reality, my parents were now houseguests of Edward in his castle, the estate having been transferred to him several years ago. It was a transaction that I had initiated and managed in order to try to prevent another crippling round of inheritance taxes resulting in a total loss, a fate that had befallen so many British stately homes now owned by the National Trust on behalf of the nation after the taxman had come calling once too often.

When questioned by Her Majesty's Revenue & Customs as to whether my parents would henceforth pay Edward a commercial rent, I had asked whether it was now the taxman's practice to expect all parents who had given up their own home to pay their children commercial rents when they lived with them in their old age, and the matter had been dropped.

My father returned with a glass of white wine for my mother and two cut-glass tumblers with an ample measure of amber spirit in each for him and me.

'Bugger the lot of them,' he said, lifting his glass high in a toast, then he tossed a third of his whisky down his throat in one large gulp.

I smiled ruefully at him as I sipped at mine. It wasn't that easy just to dismiss them all with an expletive. Maybe I could try telling the police to bugger off, but they probably wouldn't have taken any notice.

And they didn't.

12

I had a disturbed night and it was not just because my bedroom was cold, although that hadn't helped.

Dinner was not easy.

My elder brother, Edward, was not particularly happy that I was there at all. It was clear from his body language.

'How are the boys?' I asked, trying to make things civil.

'Away at prep school,' Stella said. 'Near Chester.'

'You must miss them,' I said.

'I do,' she replied, smiling at me wanly before glancing rapidly at Edward to check his reaction. 'But they're home for the half-term break this Friday. I can't wait.' This time the smile was genuine.

Edward, meanwhile, was building up a head of steam and it finally blew loudly and tactlessly over the main course.

'You're blackening our family's good name,' he said directly to me across the table.

I looked down at my food and ignored him – it was less stressful than getting into a fight.

'Now, now, Edward, dear,' my mother said, stroking the back of his hand. 'William has enough trouble without you adding to it.'

It did not noticeably appease my brother, who pompously expressed his opinion that the common people looked to families such as ours to provide role models for their behaviour.

He had clearly forgotten that the first earl, our ancestor, had been a depraved and shameless womaniser who had acquired this castle as a result of a bet on cards in a brothel, and then had allegedly demanded a title in exchange for keeping quiet about an eighteenth-century royal scandal in the same establishment.

Nowadays that might have been called extortion.

'It's an outrage him being here,' Edward muttered to no one in particular.

I looked up at him. 'I've done nothing wrong,' I said quietly.

I could see from his face that he thought I was lying, and he was about to say something else when our father cut in sharply. 'That's enough, Edward. You heard your mother.'

We all sat there in awkward silence for a while, the only noise being the clinking of our cutlery on the plates. And any conversation during the remainder of the meal was somewhat uneasy and forced, such that I think we were all relieved when it was over and Edward and Stella could return to their own quarters at the far end of the castle.

'I'm tired,' my mother announced. 'I'm going up to bed.'

She offered her cheek for a goodnight kiss.

'I think I might do the same,' I said. 'It's been a long day.'

'How about a nightcap?' my father said, raising his bushy eyebrows at me in a manner that suggested that it wasn't really a request, more of an order.

'Fine,' I said.

'Don't stay up too late, you boys,' my mother said with a hollow laugh as she disappeared out through the door.

'Whisky?' my father asked. 'Some of that Glenmorangie you brought with you?'

'Just a very little,' I said.

I wasn't a habitual drinker of alcohol, let alone neat spirits, but on this occasion I welcomed the sharp warming sensation it made in me as it slipped down.

'Now then, William,' my father said, clearing his throat. 'I think it's time you fought back.'

'What do you mean?'

'You can't just stand by and let all this happen to you without responding. Look at this evening at dinner. You let Edward off without as much as a whimper, sitting there with your head down as if he were right and you are guilty. The same with this Bradbury man. It's time to fight back, boy.'

I stared at him. Part of me agreed with him, and strongly so.

'But I have been advised by my solicitors not to respond in any way.'

'I don't care what their advice is,' my father said, banging his hand on the table to emphasise the point. 'Your silence has got to stop or else everyone *will* believe you killed Amelia. And I'm assuming you didn't.'

'No, Pa, I didn't.'

'Then say so. Shout it from the ramparts and sue the damn papers for libel.'

'Suing newspapers is extremely expensive,' I said.

'Only if you lose.'

I shook my head. 'It would be expensive anyway. Even if you win, you never get all your costs back, and your lawyers expect you to pay them what they call a retainer before they will do anything. All of it, up front, just in case you lose. It would run into the hundreds of thousands. I haven't got that sort of cash lying around, and neither have you.'

'It's so bloody unfair,' my father said in frustration.

It certainly was.

We finished our drinks and then I made my way up the cold stone spiral staircase to my bedroom high in one of the towers that had made up the main defences of the castle.

The original thirteenth-century structure had been rectangular with a round tower at each corner and another midway down each side, the towers joined by curtain walls between them. It had not been built for comfort but simply to house a garrison of troops to defend itself and to dominate the surrounding countryside.

It had been Sir Thomas Humberly who had converted the interior of the towers from damp fetid dungeons into proper living accommodation, including the installation of square windows set high into the stonework, not an easy task considering the four-feet-thick fortified walls that sloped gradually inwards from ground level.

This bedroom was not where I'd spent my early childhood

nights, that had been in the part now occupied by Edward and Stella, but this had been my space since I'd been a teenager when my father had inherited. The only difference since that time being the swapping of the single bed for a double after my marriage – something that, in itself, had been quite a task as it had had to be dismantled, carried up the narrow stairway in pieces, and then reconstructed in situ.

I sat down on the side of that bed and felt very alone. Amelia had loved this place, although more so in the warmth of the summer rather than now, as winter approached, with the bitter cold already seeping into my every joint. Central heating remained one of the modern-day comforts that the castle was still lacking although, thankfully, electricity, running water and sanitation had been installed in the first quarter of the twentieth century.

I undressed quickly and put on my warm pyjamas together with some bedsocks and my sweater. While folding my trousers, I came across the three envelopes that I had stuffed into a pocket at the Old Forge.

As I'd assumed, one of them contained a bill that could wait, but the other two did not. They were both letters and I read each of them through several times, absorbing the bad news.

The first was from the chairman of the BHA telling me that my services as an honorary racecourse steward were no longer 'in the best interests of British racing' and therefore my name had been struck from their list; all my future appointments as a steward had been cancelled.

But it was the second letter that was the real worry.

It was from my bank, informing me that there had been an insufficient balance in my account to cover the recent direct-debit demand for my monthly mortgage payment. It further reminded me that, unless I placed more funds in the account as a matter of urgency to cover the debt, they could commence proceedings to recover the loan by foreclosing on the property.

That was all I needed.

Kick a man when he's down, why don't you?

I'd lost my wife, my job, my hobby and my reputation, and now I was in danger of losing my home as well.

No wonder I didn't sleep well.

I woke early from a combination of cold and anxiety and I lay for a long while as darkness gave way to daylight, wrapped tight in the duvet, wondering if my father was right.

Perhaps I should start fighting back.

Did people only believe Joe Bradbury because there was no one telling them that he was lying through his teeth? Maybe I should conduct my own interviews with the newspapers, accusing him of being the murderer.

But would they listen?

Simon Bassett had claimed they would only distort what I'd say to match their own agendas. But could that really make things worse for me than they already were?

I had to be joking. Of course it could.

Still wrapped in the duvet, I lay prone on the deep window seat with my phone pressed up close to the glass – it was the only spot in the room with any signal – and downloaded my emails.

There was wireless internet access in my father's study but, with such thick walls in the castle, the waves didn't make it into the next room let alone all the way up here.

There were only six emails in total, far fewer than I would have normally expected, and not one of them to do with any work, either past, present or future. It was as if I had fallen off the actuarial planet.

Indeed, five of the six were spam or unwanted advertising and the remaining one was from the local Hanwell village round-robin email service informing me of the dates and times of upcoming services in the parish church.

At least I hadn't been struck off that list, not yet anyway.

I sighed. At the very time I needed the support of a loving wife, she was not here to provide it.

Even in our darkest hours, when Amelia had been hospital-ised with mental health problems, she had still been there for me, understanding what I was going through as her husband, and helping me believe that she would soon be well and home again.

Now, there was no possibility of that.

I would simply have to cope on my own, one way or another.

My bedroom window faced slightly south of east and I looked out into England, across the flatness of the Cheshire and Shropshire plain, towards the Wrekin, the hill faintly visible in the far distance. Much closer, I could just make out Bangor-on-Dee Racecourse where I had once ridden two winners in a single afternoon and had been presented with a trophy for the second victory by my own father, with Amelia looking on in admiration.

Happy days.

As I watched, two cars made their way up the long driveway towards the castle and, to my dismay, one of them was a marked police car.

What the hell did they want?

My dismay deepened considerably when, having pulled up on the gravel outside the main entrance, I saw that DS Dowdeswell was one of the four men that climbed out of the vehicles. And I was sure he wasn't here for his health or the view.

The maxim is often quoted that an Englishman's home is his castle. Although technically a Welshman, my father's home was indeed a castle and, if it had been down to me, I would have raised the drawbridge – that's if we'd had one – and let the sergeant stew outside. I might even have been tempted, like that medieval garrison, to pour boiling liquids down on the invaders through the 'murder holes' constructed for the purpose above the entrance.

My father, however, must have let them bypass the castle fortifications and walk straight into the building as, presently, I heard him at the bottom of the stone staircase.

'William,' he shouted up. 'There are some men down here to see you. They're police.'

I felt cornered.

My heart was beating fast, with adrenalin coursing through my body. Part of me wanted to kick out the window and use knotted bedsheets as a rope to make my escape, like some swash-buckling hero of a 1950s B movie.

Instead, I dressed quickly and went down to face the music.

'William Gordon-Russell,' said the detective sergeant imme-diately I arrived at ground level, 'I arrest you on suspicion of the murder of Amelia Gordon-Russell.'

13

'You must be mistaken,' my father said loudly, just as soon as the DS had finished telling me that I had the right to remain silent but anything I did say might be used in evidence.

'No, sir,' the detective said firmly. 'I am not mistaken. I have driven here from Oxfordshire this morning to arrest your son. He will come with us. I also need his belongings, and his car.'

'But it's preposterous,' my father exclaimed, going a little puce in the face.

'It's all right, Pa,' I said. 'Please keep calm. And do something for me. Call Simon Bassett and ask him to meet me at Banbury Police Station.' I turned to DS Dowdeswell. 'I assume we are going there.'

He grunted, which I took to be confirmation.

My father, however, wasn't finished yet.

'I think it's monstrous that you come in here without any appointment, force your way into my property, and arrest my son without so much as a by-your-leave. I intend to complain to the Home Secretary.'

He was going even redder in the face and I was seriously worried that his blood pressure was going through the roof and that he might easily have a seizure.

'Pa,' I said loudly. 'It's fine. Calm down. They are only doing their jobs. I'll be back here before you know it.'

I went to make a movement towards my father and that was my error.

The two constables holding my arms must have sensed the tightening in my muscles and they clearly mistook it as an attempt to flee.

In a flash, a pair of handcuffs were out and being snapped tightly onto my wrists, which did nothing to help calm my father. Only the arrival of my mother on the scene did that. She had always been the pragmatic one in the relationship.

She took one look at the situation and went straight over to stroke my father's arm. 'Now, now, dear,' she said to him. 'We won't help William by getting all upset, now, will we?'

My father looked down at her and smiled, the tension instantly draining out of his features. Not that my mother couldn't also give her own acerbic opinions when she wanted to. She turned to the detective sergeant. 'You're going to look very foolish when you find there's no evidence.'

The policemen ignored her and went about their business, collecting my suitcase and possessions from my bedroom and taking them out to their cars.

'Mobile telephone?' the DS said to me.

'In my left trouser pocket,' I replied.

He removed it.

'Laptop?'

'In my Jag.'

'Where are the keys?'

'In the other trouser pocket.'

He took those too. Then it was my turn to be taken to the police car.

I turned my head. 'Pa,' I called over my shoulder as I was taken out. 'Don't forget to call Simon Bassett. Look up the number on the internet. His firm is Underwood, Duffin and Wimbourne in Chancery Lane, London.'

'I'll do it straight away,' my father replied, having finally regained his composure.

I took one last look at the castle as I was placed in the back seat of the marked police car and wondered, in spite of what I'd said to my father, how long it would really be until I was back here. They wouldn't have arrested me now, and not before, unless they had found something else, something new.

'How did you know where I was?' I asked as we drove away.

'Dead easy,' said one of the constables. 'We traced your phone.'

That was sneaky. Now I rather wished I *had* left the charger in the kitchen and let the battery run down. *But why?* I asked myself. *I have no reason to hide. I've done nothing wrong. Have I?*

It took nearly three and a half hours for us to get back to Banbury, which gave me plenty of time to think but still I couldn't come up with a single reason why the detective sergeant should consider it necessary to have gone all the way to North

Wales to arrest me today when I'd been voluntarily at his police station only yesterday.

He had simply to invite me back and I would have come, meek and mild, to his own front door without the need for histrionics, henchmen and handcuffs.

But we didn't go in through the police station front door this time. Instead, the cars pulled into the yard behind the building and I was ushered through a rear door into the lobby of the custody suite, where the cuffs were finally removed.

'Name?' asked the burly uniformed custody sergeant behind the high desk.

'Bill Russell,' I said, rubbing my wrists.

'William Gordon-Russell,' said DS Dowdeswell, and the uniformed sergeant typed the longer version into a computer on the desk.

'Date of birth?'

I told him.

'Address?'

I told him that too, and he entered it.

'Offence?'

I said nothing.

'Murder,' announced the DS with a bit of a flourish.

The custody sergeant glanced up at him and then back to his screen.

'Murder,' he repeated, typing it into the computer. 'Any medical concerns? Or medications?'

'No,' I replied. 'Other than I take a statin each night for high cholesterol.'

'Mental health problems?'

'No,' I said. There had been plenty of those in our family but they were not down to me.

He typed some more then looked up at the clock on the wall. 'Mr Gordon-Russell, I authorise your detention here at Banbury at twelve-thirty p.m., in line with the Police and Criminal Evidence Act 1984. Do you need to let anyone know you are here?'

'Has my solicitor arrived?' I asked.

'No one has asked for you. But I can arrange for you to see the duty solicitor if you want.'

'No thanks,' I said. 'I'll wait for my own.'

The DS next to me snorted slightly as if to imply that he wouldn't wait too long.

'Anyone else?' asked the custody sergeant.

'No,' I said. 'No one else. No one at all.'

The only person I really wanted couldn't be here; indeed, I was only in this situation *because* she couldn't be here.

Oh, Amelia! Help me.

'Empty your pockets,' instructed the sergeant.

I took out my wallet, a handkerchief, Douglas's key and a few coins and placed them in the grey plastic tray provided. Next came the keys to the four padlocks on my house, which caused DS Dowdeswell to raise his eyebrows. He picked them up from the tray.

'Belt?' said the custody sergeant.

I removed my leather belt and put that in the tray.

'Watch?'

123

It joined my belt.

'Anything else?'

'No.'

'Any drugs?

'No.'

'Phone?'

'I've already got that,' said DS Dowdeswell.

The custody sergeant nodded and made another note in his computer.

'Remove your shoes,' he said.

I nearly said *please* to him, like my grandmother would to say to me as a small child, but the sergeant wasn't asking, he was ordering.

I removed my shoes and put them in the tray with the other stuff.

I was then searched – thankfully more of a frisking than a full-body strip search. Nothing found.

Next I was photographed and fingerprinted, and then a DNA sample was taken by a none-too-gently swabbing of the inside of my cheek.

'Sign here,' said the custody sergeant, pushing a sheet of paper across the desk towards me.

'What is it?'

'Custody report. Confirms you have been told your rights.'

I signed even though I didn't know if I'd been told my rights or not.

'Cell number seven,' said the sergeant to another uniformed officer, and I was escorted by him past the line of other doors and into cell seven.

The door was slammed shut behind me, leaving me alone in a space about six feet by ten, painted throughout in calming cream.

A solid bed was built-in down one side of the cell, complete with a thin blue plastic-covered mattress. On the wall opposite the door, there was a small frosted-glass window and, in one corner, a stainless-steel lavatory with no movable seat, plus a tiny washbasin built totally into the wall with push-buttons for taps.

All of it had been constructed to avoid there being any fixture or fitting from which an inmate could hang themselves.

I kept telling myself that wasn't a consideration and I should not fret. The whole custody procedure had clearly been specifically designed to unnerve the prisoners – and it was working.

I sat down on the bed, took some deep breaths, and waited . . . and waited . . . and waited.

Without a watch, I found it impossible to know exactly how long it was before I heard a key in the door, but it felt like at least half a day, although it couldn't have in fact been that long – it was still light outside.

'Your solicitor is here,' said the policeman who opened the door. 'She wants to see you.'

She?

I was taken along the corridor to a legal consultation room where a woman in a smart dark-blue suit and white blouse was waiting.

'Where's Simon Bassett?' I asked.

'He's in court,' she said. 'He sent me instead. I'm Harriet

Clark.' She handed me one of her business cards. 'I'm a specialist criminal solicitor in the same firm.'

I wondered if Simon Bassett really was in court or whether it was his concerns over a potential conflict of interest that had made him step aside. Either way, Harriet Clark was all I had.

I glanced up at the clock on the wall of the room and was dismayed to find that it had been less than two hours since I'd arrived. Doesn't time fly when you're enjoying yourself – not!

'I assume you haven't been interviewed yet,' Harriet said.

'Not today.'

I explained that I'd been interviewed before, on Friday, but she knew all about that. Simon had given her some notes.

'I don't understand why I've been arrested,' I said. 'It doesn't make any sense.'

'No doubt we'll find out in due course,' she replied in a rather matter-of-fact tone.

'I didn't kill my wife,' I said earnestly.

'That's not what's important at the present time,' Harriet said.

'I assure you, it's pretty important as far as I'm concerned.'

'Yes, well, as maybe. But, right now, I'm more interested in deciding our tactics for this interview.'

'What do you mean by tactics?'

'Basically, are you going to answer their questions? Or should you reply "no comment" to everything?'

'I have nothing to hide.'

'That, again, is not what's important here. This interview is our opportunity to discover what they have. They might think they will get information from you, but we intend to turn things around and find out something from them, to determine the strength of their case.'

'They can't have a case,' I said. 'I didn't do it.'

'Then we should definitely give them nothing. I strongly recommend you answer "no comment" to anything and everything they ask.'

'But won't that make me sound guilty?'

'It's not what you sound like in the police interview that's important. It's what evidence they have. Remember, we don't have to prove your innocence – it's up to them to prove your guilt.'

'But they said that it could harm my defence if I didn't say something now that I later rely on in court.'

'Poppycock,' Harriet said with a laugh. 'That's just the standard caution. And you can always blame me. What really hurts your defence is to say something now that is completely different from what you say later in court. So it's better to say nothing now, and especially nothing you haven't already said in your previous interview. But I'd much rather you say nothing at all. Any slight change to your story, however small and insignificant, maybe due only to a minor lapse of memory, will be picked up and thrown right back at you – and at the jury – as proof that you are lying.'

Why was all legal advice seemingly always to say nothing? And do nothing?

Harriet banged on the door, which was opened from the outside.

'Tell them we're ready when they are.'

We were taken into the same interview room as before, again with Detective Chief Inspector Priestly and DS Dowdeswell. The only difference was that, this time, it was Harriet sitting next to me instead of Simon.

The recorders were started again with a long beep.

'I remind you, Mr Gordon-Russell,' the DCI said, 'that you are still under caution and anything you say may be used in evidence. Do you understand?'

'Yes,' I said.

'Good,' he said, shuffling the papers in front of him. 'Now, Mr Gordon-Russell, would you describe yourself as a violent man?'

'No,' I said. 'I would not.'

I received a nudge from Harriet under the table.

I looked at her. Surely there was no harm in answering that question.

'But is it not the case, Mr Gordon-Russell, that you have been violent in the past?'

'No,' I said and, after receiving another nudge, I added, 'comment.'

The DCI looked up at me from his notes.

'Was that no, or no comment?'

'No comment,' I said.

'So you have been violent in the past?'

He was twisting my answers, or rather my lack of them.

'No comment.'

'Do you know a young girl called Victoria Bradbury?'

Where was this going? Victoria was Joe and Rachael Bradbury's ten-year-old daughter.

'No comment.'

'We have received a complaint from her father that you have

been violent in the past towards Victoria Bradbury. That you picked her up by the arms, shook her violently and shouted at her. Is that true?'

I sat and stared at him. Of course it wasn't true.

'Well?' said the DCI. 'Is it true?'

I looked at Harriet and she shook her head very slightly.

'No comment,' I said.

'Did you shout at her because she wouldn't do what you wanted? And was that something of a sexual nature?'

What nonsense was this?

'Was that why you killed your wife? Because she found out about your sexual depravity with her niece?'

I didn't like this, not one bit. I could feel my palms beginning to sweat and my heart was racing.

'I wish to consult alone with my solicitor.'

'Interview suspended,' said the DCI, and he stopped the recorder.

Harriet and I were shown back into the legal consultation room.

'What is it?' Harriet asked, the irritation clear in her voice.

'I can't just sit there saying "no comment" to such an allegation.'

'Why ever not?'

'Because it's not true, dammit. I've never laid a finger on that girl, and Joe Bradbury knows it. Why would he say such a thing?'

'Because he's trying to wind you up,' Harriet said. 'And so are the police. Ignore it – unless there's some proof to back up the claim.'

'There isn't.'

'So let it all wash over you.'

Easier said than done.

Sexual interference with a young child was considered *the* most horrendous of crimes – far worse even than murder. And yet it was so easy to accuse someone of sexually abusing children and have the police and others believe it. Look at how some senior politicians, including a former prime minister and other men of rank and influence, had been lambasted on the TV and in the press, having had false accusations of rape and sexual abuse made against them by a liar and complete fantasist. The police may have grudgingly apologised to the accused eventually, but not before one of them had died and the others had had their reputations destroyed for ever.

And I had no doubt that this latest unjustified claim against me would also make it into the newspapers.

'I want to fight back,' I declared. 'If no one is telling them that Joe Bradbury is lying, then they will all believe him.'

'They'll all believe him anyway,' Harriet said depressingly. 'It's human nature. People want to believe everything bad about the perceived villain and, in this case, that's you. If Joe Bradbury told them that you had two heads and scales down your back, most of them would believe it absolutely. You simply claiming that he's lying will make no difference.'

'It's so unfair.'

'As maybe, but unfair false accusations are not evidence. It is still better for you to say nothing at this stage. Trust me.'

'Okay,' I said. 'I'll try.'

'At least we now know why they went all the way to Wales to arrest you.'

'Why?' I asked.

'So that they could search your phone and computer for sexual images of children before you heard about Joe Bradbury's allegations and destroyed them.'

'I assure you, they won't find any such images,' I said. 'Not unless Joe has managed to store them there remotely.' I was suddenly worried. 'He can't do that, can he?'

'I wouldn't think so, not without sending them as emails and showing his hand as being the one responsible.'

That reassured me, but only slightly. Joe was a bit of a wizard with computers and I wouldn't put anything beyond him at present.

'Are you ready to continue?' Harriet asked.

'I suppose so.'

But I wasn't looking forward to it. And with good reason.

14

'I ask you again, Mr Gordon-Russell,' DCI Priestly said when we were all again in the interview room with the recording restarted. 'Was the reason you killed your wife because she found out about your sexual depravity with her niece?'

I still felt uneasy. I wanted to shout, *No, of course not, you fool. Not only did I not kill my wife, but I have never had any sexual feelings towards any young children, let alone my wife's niece.*

But, instead, all I said was 'No comment.'

I could see that the DCI took my reply as a minor victory. In his eyes, it clearly implied my guilt.

I felt sweaty and unwell.

But the DCI wasn't finished. Not by a long way.

'Does the name Tracy Higgins mean anything to you?'

I blushed.

I know I blushed. I could feel the warmth of the blood in my neck and face.

'No comment,' I said.

But the policeman had seen. And both he and I knew he'd seen.

'Did you not admit to having sexual intercourse with Tracy Higgins when she was under the age of sixteen and was therefore still a child?'

'No comment.'

'And did that admission not result in your name being placed on the sex offenders register.'

I gritted my teeth. 'No comment.'

How mistakes in your past can come back to haunt you.

I'd been in my first week as an undergraduate at Cambridge when, at a freshers' party in my college, I'd been approached by a beautiful young woman with very long legs and a very short skirt. She told me that she'd also just started at the university, and wasn't it fun to be finally living away from home.

One thing had led to another and, at her express invitation, we had ended up indulging in the pleasures of the flesh in my room. Only at one o'clock in the morning had I discovered that things were not as they appeared, when the college security officer banged on my door.

The young woman's father had turned up at the porter's lodge enquiring after the whereabouts of his fifteen-year-old daughter, whom he had dropped off there earlier in the evening.

In spite of the fact that she had lied to me about being another student at the college, and that she had fully consented to our sexual activity, I had been arrested for having had intercourse with a minor, with her father demanding loudly that I be sent down for a long stretch in the slammer.

I should have contested the charge in court as the law at the time actually stated that a man under the age of twenty-four who had sex with a girl over thirteen but under sixteen was not guilty of an offence if it was consensual and he had reasonable grounds to believe that she was older. But I was a frightened naive nineteen-year-old and I was badly advised to accept an official police caution because, I was told, that that would be the end of the matter and my university career would not be affected.

What I hadn't realised at the time was that, by accepting the police caution, I was not only admitting guilt of an illegal act but also acquiring a permanent criminal record. As such, my name had been added to the then newly created sex offenders register for five years and, even though that period had long since passed, the police obviously still had a record of it.

And it didn't look good.

I so wanted to explain the circumstances, to make the chief inspector realise that it had been a huge misunderstanding and that I wasn't the one at fault, but I could see that what Harriet had said was right. He believed the worst of me and no amount of explanation would ever change that.

'Still fond of young girls, are you, Mr Gordon-Russell?'

'No comment.'

The grilling lasted another half-hour or so but, basically, the DCI asked the same few questions over and over again, and he received the same answer – 'No comment'. Eventually, he gave up and terminated the interview.

Harriet and I went back into the legal consultation room.

'I think that went pretty well,' she said when the door was closed.

'Pretty well?' I said with incredulity. 'I thought it was disastrous.'

'But it showed they have nothing on you other than Joe's tittle-tattle, innuendos and the dragging up of past events. Don't forget, they can't raise that previous conviction in court as evidence in this case.'

'It wasn't a conviction,' I corrected. 'It was a police caution.'

'Okay, I agree,' Harriet said. 'Technically a caution is not a conviction, but you know what I mean. And they concentrated all their efforts on the child-abuse thing instead of confronting the reason for your arrest. It shows that they have nothing new to connect you with the murder of your wife. Not enough, I would have thought, to charge you, anyway.'

'So what happens now?' I asked.

'We wait.'

'For how long?'

'Legally they can detain you for twenty-four hours, thirty-six with the agreement of a senior officer, a superintendent or above, and they're almost certain to get that in a murder case. After that they have to apply to a court to keep you longer, up to a maximum of ninety-six hours in total, but I don't think they have enough to convince a magistrate to extend that long. Then they have to either charge you or let you go. Of course, we're assuming they won't find anything incriminating on your phone or computer in the meantime.'

That was beginning to worry me more and more. One hears such dreadful stories of how hackers can remotely get into other people's computers to do all sorts of stuff such as turn on their webcams to spy on them. God knows what Joe Bradbury might have done to mine.

'I'll try and find out some information from them,' Harriet said. 'Like if they intend to interview you again today, which I think is most unlikely as they will need time to trawl through your hard drive. I have to get back to London now but I can come back again in the morning if necessary.'

'So what do I do?'

'You just have to sit and wait.'

'In a cell?'

'I'm afraid so.' She smiled a sort of lopsided apologetic smile. 'I could ask them if they have anything you can read but I wouldn't hold out much hope. They consider that sitting in a cell alone with nothing to do is part of the process of encouraging a prisoner to confess.'

'Well, I certainly won't be doing that,' I said. 'But something to read would be good.'

I was taken back to cell seven and, shortly afterwards, some reading material in the form of a thick booklet was brought in and handed to me.

They must be having a laugh.

The booklet was entitled *Police and Criminal Evidence Act 1984: Code of Practice for the Detention, Treatment and Questioning of Persons by Police Officers.*

I lay down on the thin blue mattress and stared at the ceiling.

What was happening to my life?

I watched as the daylight coming through the small frosted window diminished to darkness. It was exactly one week ago that I had left to go to Birmingham on that fateful day, with Amelia waving to me from the garden as I'd driven away.

Just a single week. It felt more like half a lifetime.

And the time went on dragging as I lay on the bed feeling sorry for myself. Eventually, in desperation, I sat up and read through the code of conduct booklet. At least then I really *did* know my rights, which I'd previously signed for, one of which was that I was entitled to have access to this very document.

So they had done me no special favour in supplying it. I was not surprised.

However, another thing of interest that I discovered was that I should be offered three meals within every twenty-four hour period, two light and one main. And, if I had special dietary requirements, I was even be permitted to have food brought in by my friends or family, at my own expense, as long as it didn't conceal drugs or weapons.

So far today, I'd had absolutely nothing to eat, not even break-fast, and I was hungry, very hungry. That was surely a special dietary requirement. Maybe I could order a super-size takeaway from the Thai Orchid restaurant in Banbury town centre – I was on particularly good terms with the head waiter and I'm sure he would deliver it as my 'friend'.

If only I could contact him.

I pushed the cell-call button set into the wall next to the door.

I waited for five minutes but nothing happened, so I pushed

the button again. This time an eye appeared at the peephole in the door and then the hatch beneath was slid open.

'What do you want?' said an unfriendly voice.

'I'm hungry,' I said. 'I've had nothing to eat all day.'

Before I had the chance to say I'd like a double portion of Thai green chicken curry with sticky rice, the hatch was slammed shut again.

Damn it. Are they trying to starve me into submission too?

But I hadn't been ignored.

After a while, the hatch reopened and a cheese sandwich in a cardboard container was held through it. I took it and the small plastic bottle of water that followed. It wasn't quite what I'd had in mind but it would do.

'Thanks,' I said through the hatch just before it was slammed shut again.

It must have taken me all of two minutes to eat the sandwich, although I managed to stretch out drinking the water for just a fraction longer.

Now what?

I lay down again on the bed and once more stared at the ceiling.

At least I knew I'd done nothing wrong and was totally blameless of the crime for which I had been arrested.

I tried to work out in my mind which was worse: to have done something really bad and be facing the prospect of a long stretch in prison, or to be totally innocent but hopeful that this was only a short-term incarceration until innocence was established.

There was a third scenario, of course, and one that was truly scary – that, in spite of being innocent, you were nevertheless convicted, and hence facing the same long sentence as the guilty.

I tried hard not to dwell on option three, but without much success.

The hours passed and I started to imagine the DCI finding all sorts of incriminating evidence on my computer hard drive.

After what seemed like an eternity, the cell door was opened by a young policeman who handed me a musty blanket and a far-from-fragrant lumpy pillow.

'What time is it?' I asked.

'Ten-thirty,' he replied.

Too late to place an order from the Thai Orchid.

'Is there any more food? I've only had a single cheese sandwich to eat all day. According to this . . .' I tapped the cover of the code-of-practice booklet, ' . . . I'm entitled to a main meal.'

'Main meals are served at lunchtime,' he said. 'Midday.'

When I'd still been on the road from Wales.

'Are there any more sandwiches?'

'I'll see what I can find,' he replied, and he slammed shut the door again.

But, true to his word, a few minutes later the hatch opened and another sandwich was passed through – egg this time – and another bottle of water.

'Eat it quick, though,' the policeman said through the gap. 'Lights out in five minutes.'

That was a great relief. The overhead strip lights, built flush into the ceiling, were particularly bright and I had wondered how I would ever get to sleep with them on.

However, when the main lights did go out, it was far from being completely dark in the cell as there were several night lights built into the same fitting. But it was a huge improvement and I snuggled down beneath the musty blanket for my seventh restless night in a row.

At least it was warmer here than in Llanbron Castle.

15

Wednesday morning started much the same way as Tuesday finished, with me lying awake on the cell bed staring at the ceiling wondering what the hell was going on, and why was I here?

The bright overhead strip lights were turned on without warning and, presently, the hatch in the door opened and my breakfast was passed in – an individual small packet of cornflakes, a small half-pint cardboard carton of milk, a plastic bowl and a flimsy plastic spoon. What did they think I'd do with a metal one? Dig a tunnel through the concrete floor?

'What time is it?' I asked through the open hatch.

'Eight,' came the reply just a fraction of a second before the hatch was slammed shut again.

Eight o'clock. I'd been arrested at the castle just before nine. So in an hour's time their twenty-four would be up and I should be released.

Either that or I would have to be brought before a senior police officer or a magistrate.

I ate the cornflakes, drank the rest of the milk, and wished I had a toothbrush.

The isolation was beginning to get to me and I'd been here less than a day. I couldn't imagine what it was like for those in long-term solitary confinement – no wonder it was considered to be torture by the United Nations.

It was not being aware of what was going on outside the cell door that was causing me the most distress. That and also not knowing the time.

My whole life was normally determined by the clock – meeting times, appointments, race-start times, train departures – everything. Yet here I was, trying to estimate the passing of a single hour without one, and getting it hopelessly wrong.

When I was certain it must be at least nine o'clock, I leaned on the cell-call button and kept on pressing.

I was fed up doing nothing. It was time to fight back.

First an eye appeared in the peephole and then the hatch was opened.

'What do you want?' shouted an irate voice through the slot.

I took my finger off the button.

'It's nine o'clock,' I said confidently. 'I've been in custody for twenty-four hours.'

'It's only eight-forty and you haven't. So shut up.'

Oh! Damn. But I wasn't giving up.

'I demand to be released.'

The hatch was slammed shut again.

Once more I leaned on the cell-call button, but no one came for a long time.

Finally, the hatch opened again.

'Be quiet,' came the order.

'I know my rights,' I said, holding up the code-of-conduct booklet. 'I demand to be released.'

The hatch shut again and no amount of call-button pushing made it open again. Perhaps they had a way of disconnecting the bell for 'difficult' prisoners. And I intended to be 'difficult'. My detention beyond twenty-four hours, for something I hadn't done, was an outrage and I was becoming incensed by it.

In frustration, I banged on the metal cell door with my fist, but that did nothing more than give me a sore hand.

In the end, I sat down on the bed and almost cried.

Amelia, my darling, where are you when I need you?

In a mortuary; cold and lifeless.

I rather wished I could join her there.

By the time the cell door was finally opened some considerable time later, I was totally depressed and suicidal. Perhaps it was a good thing there were no hanging points after all.

'Out,' said the policeman, jerking his thumb at me.

I was escorted back to the custody-suite lobby and told to stand in front of the high desk, across from the custody sergeant.

'Why have I been detained for more than twenty-four hours?' I asked before he had a chance to speak.

'You haven't,' the sergeant replied.

I looked up at the clock on the wall. It indicated half past eleven.

'I was arrested at nine yesterday morning. I make that

twenty-six and a half hours ago.' I stared at the sergeant with my angry face on.

He ignored it. 'The relevant time from which the twenty-four hours run is the time you were booked in at the police station, which was ...' He consulted his record. ' ... twelve-thirty yesterday. We are well within the time limit.'

'So being confined in a police car for three and a half hours wearing handcuffs doesn't count?' My voice was full of irony.

'No, it doesn't,' said the sergeant firmly. 'The twenty-four hours started when I authorised your detention here on your arrival.'

'But that's ridiculous,' I said.

'It's the law. Police and Criminal Evidence Act 1984, section forty-one, subsection two-point-A-one.'

He rattled off the provision without having to look it up and I was sure he must know. He would deal with this many times every day.

But I still wasn't happy.

'I wish to see my solicitor.'

The sergeant sighed.

'As you wish,' he said, 'although you have been brought out here now to be processed for release.'

'Release?'

'Yes,' said the sergeant. 'You are being released under investigation. Sign here.'

He pushed a piece of paper and a pen over the desk towards me.

'What does "released under investigation" mean?' I asked.

'It means exactly what it says. You are being released from custody but the investigation of your involvement in the murder of your wife continues and you may be required to return at some time in the future for further questioning, or to be charged.'

'So it's like being on police bail?' I said.

'Similar, but there is no fixed date to report to a police station, and no conditions.' He handed me an envelope. 'The details are in here.'

'But I'm free to go now?'

'As soon as you sign this paper.'

I signed quickly before he changed his mind.

'How about my stuff?' I asked.

He passed across the grey plastic tray from yesterday. I put on my watch, shoes and belt, and placed my wallet and handkerchief in my pocket along with the loose change and Douglas's front-door key.

'Where's my phone?'

The sergeant consulted his computer.

'Your phone is subject to a police evidence seizure notice, as is your car and your computer, so they will be held by us for the time being while forensic investigations continue.'

'How about my wife's car?'

'Where is it?' asked the sergeant.

'I assume it's in the garage at my home but I don't know. I didn't check. And where are my house keys, anyway?'

'You have it. I just gave it to you.'

'That was my brother's house key,' I said. 'Where are mine?'

'I've no idea,' said the sergeant. 'The only key in the inventory of your belongings is the one you've already got.'

That would be because the padlock keys hadn't in fact been *my* keys in the first place.

'But there's a black suitcase and a coat in the store under your name.'

'Good,' I said. 'I'll take those.'

One of his staff appeared with my things and, much to the custody sergeant's obvious irritation, I lifted my case up onto the top of his desk and opened it.

It had clearly been thoroughly searched, with the pockets of my dinner jacket and trousers pulled inside out to ensure they were empty, but, as far as I could tell, everything I had taken to Wales was still there – other than my dignity, and my welling-tons, which I assumed were still in the boot of the Jaguar.

'Can you ask DS Dowdeswell for the keys to my house?'

'Does he have them?'

'I presume so. They're the keys to the padlocks that you lot applied.'

A call was made but the outcome was unsatisfactory, at least as far as I was concerned.

'It seems your house remains a place of interest to the investi-gation. A second search of the premises is being conducted there even as we speak.'

'Looking for more dog bones, are you?' I asked sarcastically, but he didn't know to what I was referring and my joke fell completely flat. 'When can I go back there?'

'Not until the search is complete.'

'When will that be?'

'Depends on what they find,' the custody sergeant said unhelpfully. 'We'll let you know.'

'How?' I said. 'You have my phone and my computer.'

'You'll have to contact us, then. But I'd give it at least a day or two.'

'Can I get my wife's car from the garage in the meantime?'

I don't know why I bothered to ask. I knew the answer would be no.

'Not until the search is complete.'

I put on my coat, picked up my suitcase, and was escorted through to the public side and then to the front door. Here, I paused, checking for any sign of more press photographers, but all looked clear so I stepped out into the late-October sunshine.

I stood for a moment looking up at the blue sky and real-ised how we all took liberty for granted. Only when we were deprived of it, albeit even for a very short period, did our lack of a distant horizon become so significant.

Where to now?

I couldn't go home to the Old Forge in Hanwell and I had no available car to get to Wales, even though, I suppose, I could have taken a train from Banbury to Wrexham and then asked my father to pick me up from there. But I didn't have any appetite for going back to the castle, only to have another fight with my elder brother.

I decided that I'd return to Chester Square. Douglas had said I could stay as long as I wanted, so I was sure he wouldn't mind me sleeping in Philip's unused bed for another couple of nights.

I walked down through the town to the railway station, stopping off at a mobile-phone shop to buy a pay-as-you-go smartphone.

Instant communication was another thing we took for granted. There are now officially more mobile telephones in the world than there are people, and being disconnected from the network was tantamount to being a non-person, an outcast, a reject from society.

'Name?' asked the young man in the shop.

'Why do you need my name?' I asked.

'Regulations.'

'Jones,' I said. 'Henry Jones.'

'Any ID? Driving licence or a utility bill? Something with your address?'

'Not on me,' I said, patting my pockets.

'Doesn't matter,' he said, smiling. 'No one will ever know.'

He typed Henry Jones into a computer without question.

'Address?'

'It's 262 West Street, Coventry, CV1 7QT.'

He typed that in too without checking, which was just as well because I'd also made it up. I had no idea if there even was a West Street in Coventry and that wouldn't have been the post-code even if there were. It seemed easier than telling him that I was William Gordon-Russell, notorious accused husband of the woman recently murdered down the road in Hanwell village.

'How much data do you want?' the young man asked.

'How much do I need?'

'Depends what you intend doing. Downloading films and

videos takes the most. That and streaming live TV, or internet gaming.'

I shook my head. 'Just enough for my emails and some
Google searches.'

'Five gigs should be plenty for that,' he said. 'You can always
top up if you need more.'

He showed me how to add email accounts and I paid for the
phone with cash, to avoid giving him a bank card with a different name on it than Henry Jones.

Hence I became, once again, a fully fledged member of the
human race.

I walked on to the station but I didn't catch a train to London.

Instead, I took one to Oxford, and, contrary to Douglas's
advice, I went to the opening of Amelia's inquest.

16

My presence in the Coroner's Court caused quite a flurry of excitement and not just among the assembled media. Not that I had intended it to, but circumstances overcame me.

The hearing was scheduled for two o'clock and I had caught the train from Banbury at just after midday, arriving into Oxford station at half past. Hence, I had been early at the court and had slipped into the public area unseen, partly by wearing my tweed cap, and with my Barbour jacket collar turned up. I chose to sit on the back row of benches.

As the time drew near, the court began to fill up; due, no doubt, to the extensive media coverage and the public's love of anything morbid, and especially of violent death. I shuffled along the bench until I was tight against the wall in the far corner from the door, still with my cap pulled down to my eyebrows.

'All rise,' announced the court usher, and the coroner came in and took his place behind his bench. He sat down and we did too.

The court itself was a very fine affair, having been built in

1841 with magnificent tall arched windows and an extremely high ceiling. It had originally been the city's Assizes and Quarter Sessions court, and later served as the Crown Court before the construction of the new Oxford Combined Court building in St Aldates in the mid-1980s. It was now part of Oxfordshire County Council offices and access was gained, rather ignominiously for such a grand setting, through the staff canteen.

The interior had changed very little since its time as a Crown Court, with extensive grey-painted wooden divisions separating the different areas. In the centre of the court, with a high solid back to prevent access for the defendant to and from the public, was the old dock with its steep flight of wooden steps leading up from the holding cells beneath, still connected in turn via a subterranean passage to the nearby Oxford Prison, itself now converted into a luxury hotel.

The dock served no purpose in the current usage, other than to block the floor of the court from my view, but it was here in July 1976 that the infamous Donald Neilson, nicknamed the Black Panther, had stood trial for the kidnap, ransom and subsequent murder of seventeen-year-old heiress Lesley Whittle.

'Ladies and gentlemen,' the coroner began. 'We are here today to open and then adjourn the inquest into the death of Amelia Jane Gordon-Russell. As I am sure you are all aware, this death is subject to police inquiries and, as such, a date for the full hearing will not be set at this time.

'The purpose of an inquest is to establish the who, where, when and how of an individual's demise. *Who* was the deceased?

Where did they die? *When* did they die? And *how* did they die? It is *not* the purpose of a Coroner's Court to apportion blame to any specific individual or organisation. That is the role of the criminal courts.

'Today we will be mainly concerned with evidence of identification of the deceased, and the time and place of death, plus we will hear brief updates on the medical circumstances and the police investigation.'

He shuffled his papers.

'Do we have the investigating officer present?'

'Here, sir,' came a voice from behind the old dock, out of my sight.

A man I knew well appeared in view and went to stand in the witness box to the left of the coroner as we looked. He was sworn in by the usher.

'Detective Sergeant Dowdeswell,' said the man. 'Thames Valley Police, based at Banbury Police Station. I am one of the investigating officers in this case. The senior investigating officer, Detective Chief Inspector Priestly, sends his apologies. He is detained elsewhere.'

The coroner nodded in understanding as he wrote down the details on a pad in front of him. Clearly the presence of a DCI at an inquest opening was not expected or required.

'Thank you, Sergeant,' said the coroner. 'Can you please briefly outline the circumstances of the death?'

'Yes, sir.' The detective referred to his pocket notebook. 'The police emergency line received a call at ten-seventeen last Wednesday morning informing us that a woman's body had been found in the kitchen of a house in the village of Hanwell, near Banbury.'

'Do we know who made the call?' the coroner asked.

'Yes, sir,' said the DS. 'It was made from the premises by the deceased's brother, Mr Joseph Bradbury. It was he who had discovered the body and it was also he who provided the official identification of the remains as those of Mrs Amelia Gordon-Russell.'

The coroner looked up from his note-taking.

'Is Mr Bradbury in court?'

'Yes, sir,' said another voice from out of sight behind a wooden division.

'Good,' said the coroner. 'Sergeant, will you step down a moment but remain within the court as I will require you again shortly.'

DS Dowdeswell exited the witness box.

'Mr Bradbury, if you please.' The coroner waved a hand towards the now-empty space.

I watched with gritted teeth as Joe Bradbury made his way into the box. He was handed a Bible and he read from a card: 'I swear by Almighty God that the evidence I shall give shall be the truth, the whole truth and nothing but the truth.'

He handed the Bible and card back to the usher.

This will be interesting, I thought. I hadn't heard him say much that had been even the slightest bit true for a very long time.

'Please state your full name and occupation for the record.'

'Joseph Reginald Bradbury. I work as a High Court enforcement officer.'

So far, so good. I knew that bit was true even if, as Douglas had said, it was just a fancy way of saying he was a debt collector.

'Thank you, Mr Bradbury,' said the coroner. 'Can you please tell the court what happened on the morning of Wednesday last?'

'I arrived at my sister's house about ten o'clock. There was no answer at the front door so I walked round to the back. That was also locked so I looked through the kitchen window. My sister was lying face down on the floor. She didn't respond to me knocking on the glass so I kicked the lock off the door and forced my way in.'

Joe stopped, looked up to the high ceiling and took a deep breath.

'Take your time, Mr Bradbury,' said the coroner. 'I realise that this is very difficult for you but it would be most helpful to the court if you could continue.'

Joe took another deep breath.

'I reached down to Amelia to try and wake her but her skin was cold to the touch – very cold. She was clearly dead. Had been for hours, I reckon. Then I saw the strap around her throat. That was when I called the police.'

He paused again, swallowed hard, and tears appeared in his eyes.

Crocodile tears. The bastard.

He and Amelia had been at loggerheads for the past three years, with some of his texts and emails reducing her to real tears, and he was the main reason she had ended up in hospital with mental health problems.

I found it impossible to believe that he was really upset by her death. After all, it was he who'd been doing his utmost to drive her to suicide.

'What did you do while you waited for the police to arrive?' asked the coroner, still writing notes on his pad.

'I can't really remember,' Joe replied. 'I was in shock.'

The coroner looked up at him with misplaced sympathy. 'I won't keep you much longer, Mr Bradbury, but can you confirm that you formally identified the deceased to the police as your sister, Mrs Amelia Jane Gordon-Russell?'

'I can. There was no doubt about it.'

'Thank you,' said the coroner, making another note. 'Just one more thing. Can you tell us why you went to see your sister that particular morning, a weekday morning when you would normally have been at work?'

'Because she asked me to. She called me at home on Tuesday evening. Our mother has just been diagnosed with stage-four pancreatic cancer and Amelia wanted to discuss her treatment, and how we could make her remaining time a little easier for her.'

'Liar!' I shouted loudly.

I didn't mean to. I hadn't planned it. It just slipped out.

All eyes in the public gallery swung round in my direction, as they did in the courtroom below.

'Silence!' ordered the coroner. 'You,' he said, pointing up at me with his right forefinger extended. 'Who are you?'

I removed the tweed cap and stood up.

'I'm Bill Russell. Amelia Russell's husband. And her brother is lying.'

My outburst brought the inquest proceedings to a halt, at least for a while.

I was warned by the coroner that I could be held in contempt of court.

'I don't care,' I said. 'Joe Bradbury is lying to you when he's just sworn an oath to tell the truth. Surely that's more a contempt of the court than a bit of shouting.'

'That would be committing perjury not contempt,' the coroner corrected.

'Well, that's what he's doing. There is absolutely no way on earth that my wife would have invited her brother over to our house. She'd have rather cut off her own hand with an axe. She hated him with a passion for what he'd done to us over the past three years.'

'Mr Gordon-Russell,' said the coroner. 'In the light of the loss of your wife, I can understand your anger and frustration at a perceived wrong, but this is neither the time nor the place for this conversation. Please resume your seat.'

'It's not a *perceived* wrong,' I said. 'It's real. And this is the time. I'm fed up of not saying anything and letting him get away with it. Joe Bradbury is nothing more than a habitual liar and all his smarmy protestations otherwise are yet more lies.'

The coroner had run out of patience. 'Mr Gordon-Russell. If you don't retake your seat immediately and be quiet, I will have you forcibly removed from the court.'

All through this exchange, Joe Bradbury had been standing silently in the witness box, a supercilious smirk on his face.

'I object to being called a liar,' he said haughtily. Then he turned to the bench with his nose held high in an arrogant pose. 'Your honour,' he said, addressing the coroner incorrectly, 'I am an officer of the High Court and I take severe exception to having my name blackened in such a manner by that man.'

Sue me, then, I thought. *That will give me a chance to prove his lies.*

I sat back down and the coroner had the good sense to excuse Joe from the witness box and recall DS Dowdeswell.

But my troubles weren't over. Far from it.

'Now, Sergeant,' said the coroner, clearly relieved to be getting the inquest back on track. 'I am sure I don't have to remind you that you are still under oath.' The detective nodded at him. 'Good. Before I deal with the pathologist's interim report, could you please give us a brief update on the progress of the police investigation?'

'Yes, sir,' said the DS. 'The police are treating the death of Mrs Gordon-Russell as one of murder and, as such, a murder inquiry incident room has been set up at Banbury Police Station under the leadership of DCI Priestly.'

The coroner wrote it all down. 'Has it not been reported in the press that an arrest has been made?'

'Yes, sir,' replied the detective. 'A forty-year-old man was arrested yesterday morning on suspicion of murder. However, at this time, there is insufficient evidence to charge the individual so he has been released under investigation.'

As he spoke, the detective sergeant stared straight at me from the witness box and no one in the courtroom, nor anyone in the public gallery, was left in any doubt about who was the forty-year-old individual concerned. Those sitting near to me shifted away slightly, as if too close a proximity might cause them to be contaminated.

'But we continue to search for and examine the evidence and we are hopeful of tabling charges against the man in the near future.'

It wasn't a hope I shared.

'Thank you, Detective Sergeant,' said the coroner. 'Have you anything else to add at this time?'

He hesitated for a moment and I wondered if he was going to ask the coroner if he could arrest me for contempt of court but then he shook his head. 'No, sir.'

'Then you are excused.'

The DS left the witness box but continued to stare up at me as he walked back to his place in the body of the courtroom.

'Next I come to the post-mortem results,' said the coroner. 'Dr Nicholas Brewster, the Home Office pathologist who performed the examination, will attend the full hearing as and when that is convened. However, for the purposes of the official recording, I will read out loud his interim report.'

He lifted a single sheet of paper from his desk.

'*Having been informed by Thames Valley Police that a suspected murder victim had been found, I attended the scene at a house in the village of Hanwell, Oxfordshire, at eleven-thirty a.m. The body was that of a female aged approximately forty years of age. I confirmed that life was extinct and conducted an initial examination in situ, including recording the core temperature of the deceased.*

'This temperature, plus the fact that rigor mortis was already detectable in the eyelids, neck and jaw, indicated that death had probably occurred between two and eight hours previously. General lividity of the body, that is the pooling of the fluids after death due to gravity, indicated that the victim had likely died where she was found.

'I had the body removed to the mortuary at the John Radcliffe Hospital in Oxford where I conducted a full post-mortem examination.

'An external inspection of the corpse showed considerable pinpoint haemorrhaging, known as petechiae, in both the skin and in conjunctiva of the eyes, a clear indication that asphyxia was the likely cause of death.

'Dissection and removal of the larynx, with the tongue attached, showed that the hyoid bone was fractured and that there was evidence of contusion haemorrhage in both the superficial and deep musculature of the neck, all positive indications of strangulation, and something that was in keeping with the deceased having been found with a ligature still in place around the neck. In addition there were several abrasions on the neck consistent with damage due to finger and thumbnails and, from the angle of the wounds, they were most likely the nails of the victim fighting to remove the ligature. Skin found under the nails matched that of the deceased.'

The coroner paused and took a drink of water and I realised what Douglas had meant about the body being considered as an 'it' rather than a 'she'. The post-mortem examination of Amelia was not something that was easy for me to think about.

'I conclude that, subject to the results of various toxicology tests yet to be received, the deceased died from asphyxia as a consequence of being strangled by pressure to the neck. This pressure created an obstruction of the jugular veins, causing a backup of venous blood in the head that would, within a minute or two, have resulted in passive congestion within the vessels of the brain. This, in turn, would have cut off the supply of oxygen to the surrounding tissues, leading to unconsciousness, depressed respiration and, eventually, to death.'

The coroner laid the piece of paper down on his desk and looked out at the courtroom.

'There will be an opportunity to ask questions of Dr Brewster at the full hearing, but does anyone have any comments to make at this time?'

Nobody did.

I was trying to come to terms with the knowledge that it had taken 'a minute or two' for Amelia to become unconscious and how she had been so desperate that she had dug her own finger-nails into her neck while fighting for her life.

How awful that must have been for her.

'At this point,' said the coroner, 'I will adjourn these proceedings until the full inquest, to be heard at a date after the conclusion of any criminal proceedings.'

As he spoke the last part, he looked directly at me.

'All rise,' shouted the usher.

17

I tried to slip away from the inquest as quietly as I'd arrived by employing the pull-my-cap-down-over-my-eyes-and-keep-walking-regardless game, but it didn't work, and the assembled media weren't playing by the same rules.

'Did you kill your wife?' shouted one particularly belligerent journalist who stepped straight into my path.

It was a stupid question. I was hardly going to say 'yes' even if I had.

I ignored him, remembering what Simon Bassett had said about having one's words distorted by the press, but the man had caused me to stop and now all the others gathered around me like a cackle of hyenas at a zebra carcass.

They all shouted questions at the same time.

I didn't answer any of them but took tight hold of my suit-case and pushed my way through the rabble, only to come face to face with Joe Bradbury, which was certainly not on my planned agenda.

'You're a fucking disgrace,' he shouted at me from a distance of about twelve inches, ensuring that all the media could hear. 'You killed my sister and I can't believe it that you're not locked up.'

'You're the one they should lock up,' I replied rather more quietly. 'You killed her and you know it.'

'Look in the mirror, loser. It was you that was arrested.'

He looked around to ensure the waiting press were all listening before pressing on with his vitriol.

'You're a hateful, hateful man that's like a plague in our family. You made my sister mentally ill and now you're driving me crazy too.'

'What nonsense,' I said, although I was quite hoping that I was indeed driving him crazy. It was no more than he deserved after the horrendous way he had treated his sister.

'And now you've totally destroyed any chance of happiness for my mother during the last few precious months of her life.'

'What's that about your mother?' asked one of the journalists, his notebook at the ready.

'My elderly mother is dying of cancer and that beastly man . . .' he pointed at me, ' . . . has made her life hell for years and now he's robbed her of her daughter at the most vulnerable time of her life. Prison's too good for him. He should be strung up. Anyone got a rope?'

I wasn't about to wait and see if he could recruit a lynch mob. I pulled my suitcase through the throng and walked out of the building and off down New Road in the direction of the railway station. A couple of photographers chased me for a bit until they were happy they had enough snaps and then they, too, peeled away.

I was seething.

Once again I felt like it had been *me* on the defensive when I was the one who had done nothing wrong.

'That bloody man,' I said angrily out loud, and received a very strange look from someone walking the other way.

I'd calmed down a bit by the time I reached the station.

Now where to?

I still had the key to Douglas's Chester Square house in my pocket, so I bought a ticket to London and caught the next train to Paddington.

'You were right,' I said. 'I shouldn't have gone.'

'So when are you going to start taking some notice of your big brother?'

I sensed that Douglas was quite cross with me.

'Don't you start,' I said. 'I have enough trouble as it is.'

'Much of it of your own making.'

I was quite taken aback. 'What do you mean by that?'

We were in Douglas's kitchen watching the television evening news, which covered the gory details of the inquest opening at Oxford Coroner's Court together with some unfortunate footage of the fracas outside afterwards. There was also an interview with Joe Bradbury, clearly conducted after I'd left the scene. Needless to say, he was not very complimentary about me, and that was putting it very mildly.

'I just can't understand why the police allow this wicked man to roam the streets. None of us are safe with this killer on the loose. I have been accused of being involved but that's total nonsense. I loved my darling elder sister. I am just the unfortunate individual who found her dead after her husband had done his worst. And now I'm accused by him of lying. It's an outrage that he's not locked up.'

It was close to slanderous – maybe even over the line. Perhaps I should sue both him and the television company, but first I had to prove my innocence.

The TV picture dwelt on Joe's self-righteous face for a fraction too long before returning to the studio.

'Why on earth did you go?' Douglas said again with irritation, now for the third time.

'I don't know,' I said miserably. 'Perhaps I thought it would somehow make me feel closer to Amelia.'

'And did it?'

'No. And now I have images in my head of how she died that I would rather not have.'

'I told you so,' Douglas said, throwing his hands up in frustration.

'Okay, okay. I'm sorry,' I said. 'I should have listened. Can we now please drop the subject?'

We sat in awkward silence for a few minutes while Douglas emptied the dishwasher.

'I could do with a G and T,' he said. 'Want one?'

'Yes,' I replied. 'Make mine a double.'

He clinked ice into two freshly washed glasses and added generous portions of gin with a little tonic and slices of lime.

He pushed one of them across the counter to me and we both drank deeply.

'It could be worse,' he said finally. 'You could've been charged.'

'They have no grounds, other than what that damn man says.'

'In my experience, grounds are sometimes the least of their concerns. If the public demand that someone is put behind bars, they tend to comply and sort out inconveniences like lack of evidence later, at a trial.'

'Talking about trials, how's yours going?'

'Stupid jury,' he said.

'Wrong verdict?'

'No verdict. Not yet anyway. They've been out for ten hours now and the judge has sent them home for a second night. God knows what they're talking about. Open-and-shut case as far as I can see. Defendant is guilty as sin.'

'What do you do while you're waiting?' I asked.

'Sit in the robing room twiddling my thumbs, mostly. I try to read future case notes but I find it difficult to concentrate in such circumstances, especially when we keep having to go back into court so the jury can ask the judge a question, as they've done repeatedly in this case.'

'What sort of questions?'

'All kinds of things. Mostly about the evidence or the law, but they even had us all back in court today so they could ask if three of them could go outside for a smoke.'

He rolled his eyes.

'And did they?'

'Of course they did. But the judge had to tell the others not to deliberate without those three being present, so they all had to take a break. It just adds to the time. I got so bored this afternoon that I even spent some time on a casino app playing blackjack.'

'Did you win?' I asked.

'Did I hell! I reckon it's fixed.'

It had clearly not been his day either.

'What happens if the jury can't decide?'

'The judge has already said he'll take a majority verdict – that's when at least ten of them agree – but they haven't even got that far.'

'How long do they get?'

'How long's a piece of string?' He forced a laugh. 'The foreman said that he still thinks they might be able to reach a verdict tomorrow, so the judge has given them more time. If they can't, then there'll be a retrial with a new jury. I can't see the CPS giving up on this one. But it would be a complete waste of everyone's time, not to mention the money. And I've got a very full list for the next few months. Fitting it in will be an absolute nightmare.'

No wonder he'd been in an irritable mood.

He refilled our glasses.

'But enough of my problems,' he said. 'What are we going to do about you?'

'What do you suggest?'

'Well, first of all, keep out of the way of the press and especially of that brother-in-law of yours. All you do is pour fuel on his fire and give him more ammunition to shoot back at you.'

'But I surely have to do something,' I said.

'I agree,' Douglas said. 'And I think that rather than trying to prove who did kill Amelia, you should concentrate on proving who didn't.'

Now he was talking.

'It's quite clear to me,' Douglas went on, 'that the police are not going to investigate anyone else unless we can show them beyond any doubt that you couldn't have done it. That will force them to look elsewhere.'

'Where do we start?'

'We simply prove that you were in that hotel room in Edgbaston all night and that your car never moved from the car park. If that's the case, you couldn't have done it.'

'I assure you it was the case,' I said.

'So let's prove it?'

'The police are trying to prove the reverse.'

'And if they could, they'd have charged you by now. So we will start from the opposite premise and provide absolute proof that it was physically impossible for you to have been in Hanwell at any time between five o'clock on Tuesday afternoon until after Amelia's body had been discovered. We will provide you with an unbreakable alibi.'

He smiled at me.

'Do you know what *alibi* actually means?' he asked. 'It's Latin for "elsewhere". It is an absolute defence. If you can prove you were elsewhere when the crime was committed, then you have proved your innocence. Only then will we try to show who really did do it.'

I loved his enthusiasm. It was almost catching.

'So we start with the hotel,' he said. 'Get a copy of their CCTV film and other electronic data, such as from their door locks.'

'Door locks?'

'Yes, door locks. Did you use a metal key or a card?'

I thought back.

'It was a plastic card, like a credit card.'

'Then there will be an electronic record of when you used it to enter your room. I prosecuted a theft case last year in Luton where the defence was able to show conclusively that three different cards were used to enter a particular hotel room around the time the valuables went missing. It was enough to put sufficient doubt in the minds of the jury to acquit the accused.'

'But won't the police already have that information?'

'Maybe, or maybe not. I'd not heard of it before. But, either way, they're looking for proof of a different scenario. If they find something that doesn't match their theory, they disregard it. They'll go digging for something else instead. And they won't tell us something that will help us prove your innocence, certainly not at this early stage in the game. That's up to us.'

It was good to hear him being so positive, and inclusive.

'And if the hotel key system or CCTV doesn't prove it, we'll find other footage from shops, houses and even dashcams in other cars, anything that shows that your car was in the hotel car park all night. There must also be an ANPR camera somewhere between the hotel and your house.'

'ANPR?'

'Automatic Number Plate Recognition. There are thousands of cameras, on all the motorways and main roads, recording the number plate of every car that passes them. Thirty million or so hits every day. They will show if your car moved, unless you used only very minor roads. I assume the police have checked your mobile phone but just because your phone didn't move doesn't mean that you didn't. You could have left it in your hotel room for that very reason.'

He knew all the arguments.

'Tracking my phone was how they knew I was in Wales.'

Douglas nodded. 'People don't realise how easy that is. And mobile phones and computers are the very first things to be seized on arrest. Everyone thinks of their electronic devices as their faithful friends but they have no sense of loyalty. They will grass up their owner's secrets to anyone who has access to them.'

'How about passwords?'

'Forensic extraction technology has a way around those. I see it all the time in organised-crime cases, but it applies to everyone.'

'That's scary,' I said.

'It certainly is. And smartphones contain the record of our whole lives these days – photos, emails, calendar, contacts, texts, calls, social media, the lot. Nothing is safe from Big Brother if they have your phone.'

I could imagine DS Dowdeswell trawling through all the mundane things on my phone, such as texts from my dentist about an upcoming appointment or to my local dry cleaners about mending a coat. At least he would also see the lovey-dovey messages between Amelia and myself, and find no evidence that I had a bit-on-the-side. Indeed, I had nothing to hide on either my phone or my computer, just as long as Joe Bradbury hadn't hacked in and stored something I hadn't seen.

'I just hope the police read Joe's foul emails. It will show them what he's really like. Getting hold of *his* phone is what they ought to do. He claims that Amelia called and asked him to come over on that Wednesday morning, but he's lying, and the phone records will prove it. She'd have never done that. She wanted absolutely nothing to do with him.'

'Let's not jump the gun,' Douglas said. 'First, we prove it couldn't have been you that killed Amelia. Only then will we set about finding out who did.'

18

'I'd like to see the manager, please,' I said.

I was back at the Edgbaston Manor Hotel on Thursday morning, having caught a train from London to Birmingham.

'What about?' asked the female receptionist defensively.

'That's between him and me,' I replied. 'It's not a complaint.'

'It's a *her* actually,' she said. 'The manager is a woman.'

'Great,' I said, giving her a smile.

The receptionist disappeared into an office behind the desk but soon returned with another woman dressed in a three-piece pinstriped suit, white shirt and dark tie. The manager may have been a woman but she was dressed like a man.

'I'm Karen Wentworth, the manager,' she said. 'How can I help you?'

'I stayed here last week . . .'

'I know, Mr Gordon-Russell,' she interrupted icily. 'The police came here about you on Monday.'

'Oh,' I said, slightly taken aback that she recognised me so readily. 'What did they want?'

'To search the room you stayed in.'

'Did they find anything?'

She shook her head. 'I told them it was a waste of time. Two other guests had been in that room in the interim so it had been cleaned three times since you were there.' She smiled. 'Our cleaners are very good.'

'But the police searched it nevertheless.'

'They did,' she agreed. 'Took the drains apart beneath the shower and the wash basin too. They made quite a mess.'

DS Dowdeswell was nothing if not thorough.

'Did they want anything else?'

'Copies of all our CCTV recordings.'

'That's what I was hoping you might give *me*.'

'But why should I help you?' she asked. 'The papers claim you're a wife killer who should be in jail.'

She started to turn away.

'But the papers are wrong,' I said quickly. 'I haven't killed anyone. I was asleep in my room at this hotel for the whole night while someone else was murdering my wife and I need your CCTV footage to prove it.'

'So why were you arrested when the police already have a copy of our recordings?'

It was a very good question and one that I'd been asking myself as well.

Karen Wentworth turned away again.

'Please,' I cried in desperation, my voice cracking with emotion.

'It's bad enough that the woman I adored has been taken from me without also being accused of killing her. You are my only hope.'

She slowly turned back.

'Come with me.'

I followed her past the reception desk and into the office behind.

'I'm afraid our CCTV system is quite old,' she said over her shoulder. 'It is due to be upgraded next month.'

Old will do, I thought, *as long as it shows what I need.*

But it didn't.

The image of the car park only showed the exit and, at night with car headlights on, the image was so grainy it was impossible to tell even the make of the vehicles that went in and out, let alone their number plates.

'We've recently decided to install a barrier at the exit,' Karen said. 'To stop people parking in there who are not hotel guests. It gets particularly bad when there's a big match at the cricket ground.' She paused as if in apology for even mentioning it. 'But we haven't done it yet.'

Shame.

'What else have you got?'

She pulled up the images from the hotel lobby but they were equally useless. There was only one black-and-white camera in the reception area and that concentrated on the desk itself rather than the front door. It had clearly been designed to catch staff stealing from the till, rather than the hotel comings and goings.

'Is that all?' I asked in disappointment.

'I'm sorry,' Karen said. 'To be honest, I didn't realise just how poor it is. No wonder we're replacing it. The only decent camera is the one we recently installed in the indoor pool area, so we could see if someone is in trouble. We had a nasty incident last year when an unsupervised child nearly drowned.'

I looked at the image of the swimming pool on the screen and it was bright, sharp and in colour. I obviously should have gone swimming in the middle of the night.

I remembered what Douglas had said.

'How about the electronic door locks?' I asked. 'Does the system keep a record of when they were used?'

'I think so,' Karen said. 'It certainly records the last time someone unlocked the door, but I'm not quite sure how to access it. I'd have to ask our IT man.'

'I can wait,' I said encouragingly.

She pushed a button on the desk. 'I've paged him. He'll be here soon.'

'Didn't the police ask for that information?' I asked.

'Not that I'm aware of.'

We waited in silence and, presently, a twenty-something bespectacled young man wearing blue dungarees came into the office.

'Ah, there you are, Gary,' said Karen. 'Mr Gordon-Russell here wants to know if our room locks keep a record of when they were used.'

'Sure do,' Gary said. 'Last sixty times for each one.'

Things were looking up.

Gary sat down at one of the computer terminals and started tapping on the keyboard.

'Which room?' he asked.

'Three-ten,' Karen said.

I was glad she could remember the number. I only knew where it was.

Gary tapped some more.

'There you are,' he said triumphantly. 'Easy as pie.'

I looked at the list on the screen

The last sixty times, Gary had said, and it was none too many. It seemed that room 310 was regularly opened many times per day and the sixty activations of the lock only took us back to Tuesday morning of last week, the very day of my arrival. If I'd left it another day, the data would have disappeared for ever.

'Can you print this?' I asked.

Gary looked at Karen, who nodded.

'No problem,' he said and tapped yet more.

A printer on the side whirred and out popped a sheet of paper with the information neatly tabulated upon it.

Not only did the list give the time the lock was opened but it also recorded the reference number of the card that opened it.

'Those first two are Lindy, one of the chambermaids,' Gary said. 'I know her keycard number.' I had the impression it wasn't the only number of hers he knew. 'And the next one is Jess, the housekeeper.'

'She would have been checking that the room was ready,' Karen said.

'Then that must be me arriving,' I said, pointing to an activation at seven minutes past six with the code 4579053.

'Gordon-Russell, you say?'

'I checked in as Mr Russell.'

Gary tapped some more on the computer.

'It *was* you,' he said. 'I cross-referenced your name against the machine that programmes the cards. Keycard 4579053 was created at eighteen-oh-four in the name of Mr Bill Russell.'

The next activation was at 23.34.

'That's me returning from the dinner at the cricket ground.'

And the very next activation on the list was at 09.21 on Wednesday morning, with nothing in between.

'That's me coming back from breakfast,' I said with a degree of excitement. Was something finally going my way?

Maybe not.

'But the system doesn't record it when someone leaves the room, only when they arrive,' Karen Wentworth said.

'That's right,' Gary said. 'It only registers when the keycard is used and you don't need the card to leave the room – there's a handle on the inside that opens the door without it.'

So, even though the system clearly showed that I hadn't *entered* the room between 23.34 Tuesday and 09.21 Wednesday, it didn't prove that I was in there all night. I could have left at any time, not just for breakfast.

I sighed.

'Thanks, anyway,' I said. I folded up the piece of paper. 'Can I keep this?'

'I don't see why not,' Karen said. 'Do you also want a DVD of the CCTV tapes? Gary can burn you one easily. He made the copy for the police on Monday.'

'Gordon-Russell,' Gary said slowly, the cogs in his memory obviously now turning. 'Bloody hell . . .'

'I know what you're thinking,' I said. 'But I didn't kill my wife, and I'm trying to prove it.'

With the useless DVD and the inconclusive lock data in my pockets, I walked down the side of the building to the hotel car park, and specifically to the spot in the far corner next to the rear wire fence where I'd parked my car the previous week.

I stood and looked about me.

The car park backed on to the rear of a parade of local shops, with a service delivery road between them and the car-park fence. I went over to the fence for a closer look. I could see that one of the shops had a security camera pointing along the service road. Maybe the images would also show the hotel car park.

I walked back round the hotel to the shop. It was a local grocery store

Yes, the woman behind the counter told me, the camera made an on-going recording of the previous twenty-eight days, but why did I want to see it?

Rather than explain the real reason, I made up a story of having had my car vandalised while in the hotel car park and their camera might have caught who had done it.

'Don't know about that,' she said unhelpfully. 'It's only there to cover our back door.'

'Please could I see anyway?' I asked patiently.

She looked around as if wanting some customers to make her too busy, but the shop was deserted.

'I'll have to get my husband,' she said. 'He deals with the CCTV. We had it put in last year after someone tried to rob us.'

She looked at me suspiciously as if I might have the same mission.

'And where is your husband?' I asked.

'Having a rest. We open from seven in the morning until eleven at night, seven days a week. Every day but Christmas Day. It's a lot of hours for just the two of us.'

'It must be,' I said in my most sympathetic tone. 'But this is very important to me.'

She hesitated but then went over to the door to the rear, all the while keeping her eyes firmly on me – just in case I tried to pilfer something.

'Faisal,' she shouted through the door. 'There's a man here to see you.'

A bearded man appeared, rubbing his eyes as if he had been woken by the call.

'What do you want?' he asked gruffly.

I repeated my story about having had my car vandalised and asked if he could show me the recordings from the camera out the back. The man didn't seem to be at all happy at being roused from his slumbers for such a paltry reason and he gave his wife a severe stare. She, meanwhile, patently ignored him.

'This way,' the man said reluctantly, and I followed him into a room behind the shop that was crammed full to the ceiling with boxes of spare stock.

He moved a case of Heinz tomato soup tins from a chair and then sat down at a desk.

'What date did you say?' he asked.

'A week last Tuesday. Nine days ago.'

'Time?'

'About quarter to six in the afternoon.'

He entered some numbers into the CCTV recorder via a remote control and an image appeared on a screen above.

In the very top corner of the screen, I could see the car-park wire fence and a little way beyond it, but there was no car visible.

'Can you fast-forward?' I asked. 'I arrived a little after that.'

The image shimmered a little as he did so and then, as if by magic, we could see the back end of my silver Jaguar appear as I reversed into the empty space. The number plate was clearly visible,

'That's my car,' I said excitedly, placing my finger on the screen. 'Can you wind it on a bit more? Until after it got dark.'

He did so and the colour drained from the image as the system switched from visible to infrared but, crucially, the back of my car was still visible, in ghostly grey.

'Please wind it right on to the following morning,' I said.

'What time was it vandalised?' the man asked.

'I'm not sure. Sometime during the night.'

He pushed some more buttons on the remote and the image flickered as he fast-forwarded it, the time-recording in the top corner racing on from six in the evening to midnight and then beyond.

The colour returned to the image with the coming of daylight and still the car was unmoved. Only at 9.56 a.m. by the on-screen clock did the car finally disappear from the image, and that was when I drove it out of the car park to go to Warwick Racecourse.

'I didn't see any vandalism,' the man said.

'No,' I agreed. 'It must have been done further forward out of sight of the camera. But that is fabulous nevertheless. Can I please have a copy?'

'But it didn't show anything.'

'I know, but it does at least prove my car was in that car park all night and I'll need that for the insurance company.' *And for DS Dowdeswell*, I thought.

I felt elated. I finally had the proof I needed.

19

'You could have used some other form of transport,' said the detective sergeant.

'Don't be stupid,' I said. 'What other form of transport do you think I had access to, a racehorse?'

I had gone direct from Edgbaston to Banbury by train and had walked with a jaunty step through the town to the police station, where I was now talking to DS Dowdeswell in the entrance lobby.

'There's always public transport,' the DS said.

'Don't be ridiculous. Every bus and train has CCTV. If I'd come back from Birmingham by public transport I'd have been filmed. And how would I have then got from Banbury to Hanwell village? By taxi? Have you found the driver? And what did I do then? Ask him to wait outside on the road while I just nipped inside for five minutes to kill my wife?'

He said nothing.

I had laid the grocery-store CCTV evidence before him, together with the data from the hotel keycards.

'I demand that you stop this nonsense and release me from this laughable investigation. You have no forensic evidence against me, nothing on my phone or computer, and now I have proof that I couldn't have been in Hanwell when Amelia was murdered. I was "elsewhere". That's what alibi means in Latin. I am told by a QC that an alibi is an absolute defence. So it is high time you started looking for the real culprit. And that's Joe Bradbury.'

'You could have arranged for someone else to kill your wife when you knew that you could prove you weren't present.'

'Now you really are grasping at straws,' I said. 'And who is this mystery person? And how did I contact them, by telepathy?'

'What about your wife's life insurance policy? That's a powerful motive.'

'I explained all that,' I said. 'It's not relevant.'

'We'll see,' he replied patronisingly. 'And there is also the abuse complaint we have received.'

'That's malicious nonsense and you know it.' I was quite cross. 'I not only demand that you release me from this investigation but also that you inform the press and media that I am no longer a suspect in the murder of my wife.'

'Well, that's not going to happen.'

'Why not?'

'Because you do remain a suspect.'

It was like talking to a brick wall.

'I want my car back,' I said. 'And my house, plus my computer and my phone.'

I wanted my life back too, my lovely life with my gorgeous Amelia, but that wasn't going to happen either.

'I will need to speak to DCI Priestly,' the DS said.

'Fine,' I replied. 'You do that. I'll wait.'

I sat down on one of the seats in the police station lobby, crossed my legs and folded my arms. I could also be bloody-minded.

I waited a long time and I began to worry that they must have more evidence against me than I thought.

It had always been a bit of a risk coming back to the police station and part of me had argued strongly against it – the memory of being in that cell, even for only one night, was raw and distressing. I had no wish to repeat the experience.

Eventually the detective sergeant returned, still without handcuffs.

'You can have your car,' he said. 'And access to your house, but we will keep your phone and computer for the time being.'

It was a start – a move in the right direction.

'Okay,' I said. I held my hand out. 'I'll take the car and house keys now.'

'I can give you the keys for the house but not to your car. It's still at our forensic lab and needs to be returned here first to complete the paperwork.'

'So when will that happen?'

'Soon,' he said.

Soon could mean anything from just a few minutes to any length of time you chose. Something happening *soon* in geological terms meant in only a million years or so.

'Why can't I have my phone and computer?' I asked.

'Because the forensic team are still going through the data.'

'They won't find anything incriminating,' I said. 'Not implicating me, anyway. But you should take a look at the emails from Joe Bradbury over the past three years. They will show you the sort of man he really is. And there are more of those on Amelia's laptop. I presume you still have that?'

'Yes, we do. We've had it since the morning she was found.'

'Well, take a good look. You will see that there is no possible way that my wife would call Joe Bradbury and invite him over to our house, especially if I wasn't there. She hated him. Joe was lying about that in the Coroner's Court yesterday and you should ask him why. Check *his* phone records. There'll be no call.'

He looked at me in silence and I found it impossible to read what he was thinking.

'House keys?' I said, holding out my hand.

He handed over the padlock keys.

'Call me at home about the car and the other stuff,' I said.

And then I departed, inhaling the cold crisp air outside in great gulps. There was definitely something refreshing about freedom.

'Sounds like you had a good day,' Douglas said when I told him everything that evening.

'It could have been better. The damn police still won't release me from the investigation. They seem hung up on the life insurance thing.'

'You have to admit that it's a strong motive,' he said. 'Money being the root of all evil, and all that guff.'

'But that's not right,' I said. 'The correct quote is "*the love* of money is the root of all evil". Different thing altogether. It comes from the Bible. Saint Paul's first epistle to Timothy, chapter six, verse ten.'

Douglas looked at me and raised a questioning eyebrow.

I laughed. 'I calculate the church buildings insurance premium for the Diocese of London. The bishop quotes that verse at me every year when the premium goes up.'

And my love of money was like nothing compared to my love of Amelia. I'd give up every drop of monetary riches I owned just to have her back for an hour – or even a minute.

'How about you?' I asked, fighting back another wave of emotion. 'Did you have a good day?'

'Mixed,' he said. 'The damn jury convicted our man of manslaughter rather than murder. Complete cop-out, if you ask me. The judge was clearly furious with them. All but told them so, straight out.'

'So what happens now?' I asked.

'The CPS may decide to retry him for murder. Or they might take the view that this conviction is enough. We'll wait and see.'

'How long is the sentence for manslaughter?'

'The maximum possible is life imprisonment,' Douglas said. 'Same as for murder. But, in my experience, it's typically between two and ten years.'

'Couldn't the judge just sentence him to life anyway?'

'He could,' Douglas agreed, 'but it would likely be reduced in the Court of Appeal. Much better to get things right the first time round.'

Pity the Banbury police didn't take the same view.

*

Friday morning dawned bright and cold with the sun streaming through a crack in Philip's curtains.

'I think I'll go back home today,' I said to Douglas over breakfast.

'You know that you're welcome to stay here as long as you like,' he said between mouthfuls of toast.

'Thank you,' I said. 'But I can't run away for ever.'

'Are you sure you're ready?'

'No,' I said. 'I'm not at all sure, but I have to go back some-time, and today seems as good a day as any. At least the sun is shining.'

Douglas looked troubled.

'Would you like me to come with you? I've nothing scheduled for today now that my trial has finished. All I have to do is pre-pare my next brief.'

'My dear brother,' I said, 'I would love you to come but you've told me how busy you are in the coming weeks and I think this is something I have to do on my own.'

'At least you don't have to worry about the police any more.'

'Don't I?' I said. 'Try telling that to the investigating DS. He's still treating me as the only suspect.'

'Trust me,' Douglas said. 'I've been an advocate in criminal proceedings for more than twenty years now and I'm telling you that there is no chance the CPS would countenance charges against you with so little evidence, and with so many counter-indications. Your alibi is cast iron for a start. This DS might not want to admit it but, after what you proved to him yesterday, he will now be forced to look for someone else.'

'I hope you're right,' I said. 'I told him to check Joe Bradbury's phone records for the non-existent call he claims he received from Amelia.'

'That's a start,' Douglas agreed. 'But they will need more than that to charge him with her murder.'

'But, if nothing else, it will show him to be a liar and that might just stop them believing every word he says against me, and especially all that claptrap about me abusing his daughter.'

'I agree that is bizarre,' Douglas said. 'Why would he say such a thing without any evidence?'

'Because he's obsessed. He hates me so much that it clouds his judgement over everything. And I don't know why. He accuses me of bullying his mother but he's the real bully. Take all that nonsense over selling the family home a few years ago. He claimed that he was the world's expert on selling houses and then he made a complete cock-up of it. He berated Amelia for her choice of estate agent and then ended up appointing a cheap one who tried to mislead potential buyers with incomplete information. It would be a joke if it weren't so serious. The house was eventually sold for a hundred thousand pounds less than we believe it should have raised. All due to his incompetence. The man's an idiot.'

'I can tell that you don't like him much either,' Douglas said with a laugh.

'You're dead right there,' I agreed. 'But what he did to Amelia was even worse. I blame him completely for her mental illness and for putting her in hospital. He's done nothing except continually undermine her confidence for years and then he drove a wedge between her and their mother. And now he's killed her.' I choked back the emotion. 'I intend to nail him for that.'

But I felt better for having had a bit of a broadside against my brother-in-law and it was with a lighter heart that I packed up my stuff and caught the train from London to Banbury.

20

The first thing I did on arriving home was to paint over the 'killer' graffiti on the garage door.

I'd taken a taxi from Banbury station and had asked the driver to wait at a DIY superstore while I went in and bought some dark-green paint and a paintbrush.

I stood back and surveyed my handiwork.

The paint I had bought wasn't exactly the same shade of dark green as the rest of it but it would do. I would repaint the whole thing at another time.

Next I opened the padlock on the front door and went in.

As before, the house was cold and lifeless but, this time, I didn't dilly-dally in the hall but forced myself to go straight into the kitchen and then through into the utility room.

The central heating had been switched off by someone so I turned it back on again and the boiler sprang into action, bringing a sense of life back to the house as the pipework creaked as it heated.

I went round the house switching on all the lights and even set the music system in the sitting room so that Adele's 'Someone Like You' blared out of the speakers at full volume.

Adele had been Amelia's absolute favourite singer and we had been lucky enough to catch her final live concert at Wembley Stadium, buying horrendously inflated tickets off the internet with gay abandon. But it had been worth every penny to see my wife happy after so many desperate months of psychiatric treatments and mental institutions. Even Adele's mournful lyrics couldn't prevent me from now smiling at the memory.

For the next two and a half hours, I busied myself clearing up the mess left by the police forensic team, wiping away the mass of fine metallic fingerprint powder left on every surface, exercising the vacuum cleaner all around the house and tidying away stuff into the wardrobes and bathroom cabinet. I re-laid the fire in the hearth, plumped up all the cushions on the sofa, discarded a vase of flowers that were well past their best, and, finally, I swept up the broken wood by the back door and washed the kitchen floor, which I found very difficult.

I realised what I was doing.

I was keeping myself busy so as not to dwell on the fact that I was alone in this house and evermore would be.

It was the little things that I found the hardest to bear – Amelia's toothbrush still in a tumbler next to the bathroom sink; her shampoo in the shower; and particularly her multiple lip salves left at strategic points all over the house. Dry lips had always been a problem for her, however much I had tried to kiss them better.

Finally, when there was nothing left to clean and I was

pooped, I made myself a cup of instant black coffee and sat down in the sitting room, flicking on an afternoon TV programme about buying antiques to further distract my mind.

So far, so good.

But then there was a heavy knock on the front door.

Who could that be? I rather hoped it wasn't either the police or the press.

It was neither.

Standing on my doorstep was a smartly dressed slim woman with long blonde hair. She was holding a large plate on which sat a sponge cake, and she was fiddling nervously with a string of large pearls around her neck.

'Hello, Bill,' said Nancy Fadeley. 'I saw you earlier painting the garage door. I thought you might need something to eat. This is all I could think of. I've just baked it myself.'

She held out the plate and I took it.

'How lovely, Nancy,' I said. 'Thank you so much. Please come in.'

She hesitated, looking past me towards the kitchen, and fiddled some more with her pearls.

'It's okay,' I said. 'Amelia would have been so happy that you've come over.'

Just my mention of Amelia set her off crying, huge tears rolling down her face and dripping onto the doormat. I handed her my handkerchief.

'I can't believe she's gone,' she said between snuffles. 'I loved her so much.'

'So did I,' I said with a sigh.

'I know you did,' she said with more sniffs. 'You absolutely adored each other. That's why I can't believe what everyone in the village is saying. People can be so nasty.'

Tell me about it.

The two women had been best friends ever since we had first arrived in the village. I had also become friendly with her husband, Dave, a London-based jewellery dealer, and the four of us had regularly had boozy suppers in each other's homes, and had even once rented a villa together for a week in Greece.

'Won't you come in?' I said.

Nancy hesitated again and I wondered if she was worried about coming into a house alone with someone that everyone else in the village was calling a murderer. Hence I didn't push the point, remaining standing in the doorway.

'Amelia told me on the day before she died that she was going to have a drink with you at the pub.'

'Oh, yes, that's right,' Nancy said. 'She called me. But we only had a quick one. I had to get back to finish cooking supper for Dave. I asked her to join us, seeing that you were away, but she refused. She said she had some things to do and she wanted to have an early night.'

'What did you talk about?'

'Oh, you know, the usual.'

The 'usual' was the state of Amelia's health. Nancy and Dave had been there for us during the bad times as well as the good. Indeed, Nancy had been Amelia's rock and mainstay even in her darkest hours, and she was also well up to speed with all the problems between the Bradbury siblings.

'Was there any specific reason why she wanted to meet you that particular evening?'

'I don't think so.' She put her head on one side as if thinking back. 'We initially chatted about all sorts of mundane stuff but I now remember that there was one thing she told me as we were walking back that I thought was quite interesting.'

'Which was?' I asked.

'She said that her brother would soon be getting his come-uppance. She was convinced that he'd stolen some money from his mother during the sale of their family home. Something about him and the estate agent conspiring together to lower the reported sale price so that they could pocket the difference.'

Wow! Now, that really *was* interesting.

'I wonder why she didn't mention it to me.'

'She said was going to just as soon as she was sure of it. Seems she didn't want you going off half-cocked before she had the proof.'

'Did she tell you how she knew?' I asked.

'Not exactly,' Nancy said. 'It was something to do with a couple who were her parents' old neighbours in Surrey. Seems they came to visit her mum and it was something they said that made her wonder, but I don't know what it was.'

'Did you tell the police about this?' I asked.

'The police?'

'Yes. They told me that you were interviewed on the morning they found Amelia.'

'Oh, yes,' she said. 'So they did. A man in uniform knocked on our door to ask if we'd seen anyone unfamiliar in the village during the previous twenty-four hours. Or anyone at all near your house.'

'And had you?' I asked.

'No. We'd seen nothing. Not until an ambulance and the police turned up anyway. I remember asking him why he wanted to know but he wouldn't say. I only found out what had happened to Amelia much later, when all the TV people started arriving.'

I thought she was going to cry again.

'But you didn't say anything to the police about Amelia's suspicions that Joe Bradbury stole the money?'

'No,' she said. 'I didn't even tell Dave. It didn't seem important compared to . . .' She tailed off.

I personally thought it might be very important but I didn't say so to Nancy. She was distressed enough.

'Do you think that I should tell them?' she asked.

'No, not just yet,' I said. 'I'll do a bit of digging first and find out if there's anything to it.'

She seemed relieved. 'I don't want to make an unsubstantiated accusation to the police, now do I?'

'No,' I agreed. 'You don't.'

We'd had quite enough of those already.

But what if this one wasn't unsubstantiated?

What if it were true?

Nancy never did come in. Instead, she made her excuses and went back across the road to her own house, no doubt to prepare a sumptuous supper for Dave, for when he came home from work after another busy day buying and selling jewellery in Hatton Garden.

Her obsession with food preparation had been a source of secret amusement between Amelia and myself but there was no question that she was an excellent cook, and I greatly enjoyed some of her delicious sponge cake while I continued to watch afternoon TV.

But I found I couldn't concentrate on anything except what Nancy had told me.

What if the hundred thousand shortfall in the sale price of Mary Bradbury's home had not been down to Joe's incompetence, as I'd imagined, but was really due to him stealing the difference?

I wanted to believe it. Of course I did. But I couldn't see how it could have been done without the collusion of both the purchasers and the lawyers. Not that that would stop me investigating.

I had nothing else to do.

There was no sign of any paid employment coming my way. My email inbox, as accessed via my new phone, remained stubbornly empty, and the old phone, with the number that everyone knew, resided unanswered in some police forensic laboratory.

And on this day, I had originally been scheduled to be acting as a steward at Stratford-on-Avon Races, but I feared that that aspect of my life had now gone forever. Even if I could establish my innocence beyond any doubt, and find the true killer of Amelia, the horseracing authority was looking for a way to 'retire' most, if not all, its volunteer honorary stewards and to make the whole thing appear more businesslike, and I was likely to be a permanent casualty of that plan.

It was a move that many people in racing had been trying to resist, not least the honorary stewards themselves. It was felt that we brought a wealth of different experiences to the sport but, while there was no suggestion that our integrity was in question, the powers that be had decided that full-time 'professional' stewards were the best way forward.

I, personally, thought it would be a shame and a major loss. Many of the honoraries, myself included, had been former active participants in the sport rather than purely lifelong administrators, and I believed that a combination of the two should be the preferred solution, whether or not I was involved.

So here I was at a loose end, flapping wildly in the wind, and anything I could get my teeth into would be a distraction from the dreadful heartache in my chest.

I ate another slice of Nancy's cake but I was still hungry. I'd had no lunch, and breakfast seemed nothing more than a distant memory. I went back into the kitchen and opened the fridge, but I was out of luck. There was very little and what there was had a ring of green mould round the edges.

The freezer was not much better.

As I'd told the detective, Wednesday had always been Amelia's favourite day for food shopping. She would maintain that, by then, all the supermarket shelves had been restocked after the previous weekend's rush and it wasn't yet close to the following weekend to make the store too busy.

Hence, the fact that she had died early on a Wednesday

morning meant that the cupboards, while not being totally bare, were severely limited.

I took out a frozen loaf and put it on the worktop to defrost, but man shall not live by bread alone, nor even by cake, so I backed Amelia's much-loved cream Fiat 500 out of the garage and went into Banbury for some fish and chips.

21

Early on Saturday morning I went to see Mary Bradbury after yet another restless night.

I had, of course, often slept alone in our house, not least when Amelia had been in hospital, but this time it was totally different. There had been no one to call to say good night to, no loving moments on the telephone to make up for her absence, no warmth in my bed, or in my heart.

I had cried myself to sleep and then, to compound my suffering, I had dreamed about her murder, reliving the horrors that must have occurred in our kitchen on that awful morning.

I woke suddenly, in a cold sweat, and then I cried some more, so much so that I ended up with a thumping headache.

I got up and went to the medicine cabinet in the bathroom looking for some painkillers and, after much rummaging among tubes of foot cream, sticky plasters, eye makeup removal pads and numerous other bits and bobs, I found a bubble pack of paracetamol at the back with a couple of pills still left in it.

I swallowed them.

Having a supply of painkillers in the house had always been an area of contention between Amelia and myself, and I had finally tried to lay down the law by banning her from buying them.

I had not taken that step without good reason.

Twice she had tried to do herself harm by swallowing handfuls of pills and, thankfully, the only ones she could find at the time were her own anti-depressants and my statins, neither of which did her any permanent damage.

I thought about going back to bed but it was already getting light and I didn't want a repeat performance of the nightmare. So I had a shower, got dressed and went downstairs.

I then spent some time searching through the Queen Anne kneehole desk in the sitting room, which Amelia had used to store all her papers. I was looking for something specific and I found it at the back of the second drawer down on the left-hand side – information concerning the sale of her parents' Weybridge home.

There was a copy of a letter sent to Mary from the lawyer that Joe had engaged, together with the final statement of price and fees, both theirs and those of the estate agent.

The original listing had been at £3.2million but the final agreed purchase price, as I'd remembered, had been a hundred thousand less than that. The letter further stated that that amount had been paid to Mary Bradbury's bank account, minus the combined fees and disbursement charges of almost fifty thousand pounds.

I sat for a while memorising the figures and then, with my headache now fading away, I backed Amelia's Fiat out of the driveway and set off to Mary's cottage.

She had moved to a village near Chipping Norton, twenty-five minutes drive from us. 'Close but not too close,' she'd said at the time. 'Otherwise neither of us will get any privacy.'

It had been an excellent choice with good friends made among her new neighbours.

I parked on the driveway and rang the doorbell, hoping that she wasn't still in bed. She wasn't. The door slowly opened.

I hadn't seen her for some time, as I had decided that it was better to keep away rather than antagonise Joe, so I was shocked by her appearance. She had clearly aged considerably and her skin had a touch of yellow about it from jaundice, no doubt brought on by the cancer in her pancreas, or its treatment.

'Hello, Mary,' I said.

'What do you want?' she asked in an unfriendly tone. 'You should be in prison.'

'I didn't kill your daughter,' I said. 'I loved her.'

I could tell that she didn't believe me.

'Can I come in?'

'What for? To kill me as well?'

'Don't be silly,' I said. 'I loved Amelia with all my heart. I would never have hurt a single hair on her head and, if you think hard enough, you would realise that.'

'But Joe says . . .'

'Joe is lying to you,' I said.

'Why would he?'

It was a good question.

She was confused and I waited in silence. Eventually she stepped to one side to let me in.

'Do you want a coffee?' she asked.

'Yes, please. That would be lovely.'

We went through to her kitchen and she put the kettle on to boil.

'How are you?' I asked tentatively.

'Don't ask,' she said, throwing her hands up. 'The doctors have told me I should have three months but I feel so weak right now that I think it could be just three days.'

'I'm so sorry.'

'Comes to all of us in the end, I suppose. Always too soon.'

It certainly was for Amelia.

'I hear you had some friends from Weybridge come to see you,' I said, getting straight to the point of my visit. 'That was nice.'

'Jim and Gladys,' she agreed, nodding. 'They lived next door to Reg and me for nearly thirty years. They're a lovely couple. Our best friends.'

'Have I ever met them?' I asked.

'You may have. I'm sure they would have been invited to your wedding up in Wales. But maybe they didn't come. I can't really remember. Don't seem to remember much these days.'

'What's their surname?' I asked.

'Wilson,' she said, remembering that with ease. 'Jim and Gladys Wilson. He was a stockbroker, same as Reg. But he's been retired a long time now.'

Mary poured hot water into two cups containing instant coffee and handed one to me. 'Milk and sugar?'

'Just a little milk.'

She poured it from a plastic bottle and gave the mixture a stir. We both sat down at the kitchen table.

'What did you and the Wilsons talk about?' I asked.

'Our ailments mostly,' she said with a hollow laugh. 'We've all got so much wrong with us that it's a miracle we're still here.'

'Anything else?' I asked, pushing hard.

'Old neighbours and friends and how so many of them have recently dropped off the perch.'

'Do they get on well with the people who bought your house?' I asked.

'They seem to. Gladys said they are not as nice as neighbours as we were but I think she's just being kind. They're much younger than we were, of course. A new generation.'

Try as I might, I couldn't get Mary to speak any more about what the Wilsons had said about the sale of her house. Maybe she hadn't heard or perhaps she had forgotten. Probably the latter.

She sighed and looked at me. 'Don't get old, Bill. It's not much fun.'

Amelia would never get old. Just like James Dean and Marilyn Monroe. And neither of those two would have retained their fascination and glamour for such a long time if they were now in their dotage, confined to a nursing home, doubly incontinent and with senile dementia. Maybe there was some advantage in dying young, but not for those of us left behind.

I drank some more of my coffee and we sat in silence for a while.

'I miss her terribly, you know,' Mary said unhappily.

'So do I.'

Tears rolled down Mary's cheeks and dripped onto her scrubbed pine kitchen table. It was as much as I could do not to cry with her.

And straight into this tableau of misery walked Joe Bradbury.

'Hi, Mum, it's only me,' he called as he walked through the front door. 'What is Amelia's car doing outside?'

He came into the kitchen and saw me.

'What the fuck are you doing?' he shouted. 'Get out of here at once.'

'I'll leave only if your mother asks me to.'

He turned to her. 'Tell him to get out,' he demanded.

'Now, now, dear,' Mary said. 'Why can't you two be friends?'

'Friends?' he screamed. 'With him? Don't be stupid. He killed your daughter.'

'I did not,' I said. 'And you know it.'

'Get out,' he shouted at me again.

I remained exactly where I was. I was fed up with always taking the course of least resistance, of not antagonising him in order to have a quiet life. It was time to stand up to his bully-boy tactics and face him down. But what I hadn't expected was for him to grab a large carving knife from the block beside the cooker.

'Now, get out,' he said, brandishing the eight-inch blade in my direction. 'I won't ask you again.'

My heart was racing faster than a filly's in the Nunthorpe Stakes, but still I didn't stand up.

'What are you going to do?' I asked in as level a tone as I could manage. 'Kill me too?'

'Joe, put the knife down,' Mary said, but he took absolutely no notice of her and it suddenly dawned on me that he might use it. Perhaps it was time to heed the old adage that he who fights and runs away, lives to fight another day.

'Okay, okay,' I said, standing up. 'I'm going.'

I backed my way into the hall, never taking my eyes off the knife. Joe followed me.

'Bye, Mary,' I shouted past him.

'Bye, Bill dear,' she replied, seemingly totally unaware of the seriousness of the situation.

That seemed to make Joe even more angry.

'You leave my mother alone, do you hear,' he hissed. 'Come here again and I'll kill you.'

'Developed a taste for killing people, have you, Joe?'

'What do you mean by that?'

'I just wondered if you enjoyed strangling your own sister?'

'I didn't kill her,' he said, his lips drawn back in a frightening grimace of hate. 'You did that. You'd been killing her for years, cutting her off from her true family and driving her crazy. I loathe you. In fact, I'd be doing everyone a favour by killing you. Everyone knows you're a murderer. They'll say you got your just deserts.'

I now became genuinely worried. He was demented and, perhaps for the first time, I thought he was truly mad. And mad people act impulsively and to hell with the consequences.

The time for goading him was past. Now, I had to concentrate on getting out of this alive.

I continued to back across the hall until I could feel the front door behind me. He followed, getting ever closer, the knife held out in front, his manic staring eyes clearly visible behind his glasses.

'Come on, Joe,' I said in as consolatory a tone as I could muster under the circumstances. 'Don't do anything silly. Put the knife down.'

Try as I might, I couldn't keep the fear out of my voice, and Joe liked it.

He smiled at me. 'Frightened, are you?'

'Yes,' I said. 'I'm frightened how your mother will cope for her last few months on her own, without both her daughter and her son. Amelia is dead and you'll be in prison for murder.'

'I'll claim self-defence,' he said. 'Protecting myself from a murderer.'

'The police know that I didn't murder Amelia. I can prove I was in Birmingham all night.'

He took no notice, advancing to within a couple of feet. I pressed my back up against the door, and, to open it, I would have to move towards him.

I didn't.

'You're lying,' he barked. 'Everyone knows you're a killer. Read the papers. It even says so on your garage door.'

So had it been he who had painted that? I suppose I should be grateful he hadn't burned the whole place down while he was at it.

I felt around behind me with my hands, searching for some sort of weapon or at least something to shield me from the stabbing thrust that I knew was coming. But there was nothing.

He smiled again. He was enjoying himself.

His arm went back.

'Joseph!' snapped his mother from the kitchen door. 'Stop it! Stop it right now.'

He hesitated, just for an instant, glancing over his shoulder towards her.

I needed no second invitation. I lurched forward, pushed him away and was out through the front door quicker than a greyhound leaving the starting traps.

I ran to Amelia's car and jumped in, locking the doors from the inside.

Joe had parked his black Nissan immediately behind the Fiat so I couldn't reverse out. Instead I engaged forward gear, gunned the engine, and drove sharply left, bouncing over the front lawn and then out through the gate onto the road. Amelia would have been horrified at how I treated her beloved 500.

But I was shaking so much that I had to stop in order to avoid hitting something, all the while keeping my eyes firmly fixed on the rear-view mirror, just in case Joe had decided to follow. Thankfully, he hadn't, and the road behind remained clear.

Gradually, I recovered my composure and I drove to Banbury without mishap, pulling up in front of the police station.

I went in to report the incident.

DS Dowdeswell came out to the lobby to see me.

'Ah, Mr Gordon-Russell,' he said. 'I'm glad you've come in. I was about to come looking for you.'

'Why is that?' I asked with rising trepidation.

'We've just had an emergency call from Mr Joseph Bradbury. He's accused you of threatening him with a carving knife.'

22

I found myself back in the same interview room as before, this time questioned under caution on suspicion of engaging in threatening behaviour with a bladed weapon.

'It's not true,' I said. 'In fact, quite the reverse is the case. *He* threatened *me* with a carving knife and, what's more, he said he'd kill me if I ever went to see his mother again.'

'So you admit that you've been there this morning, then?' said the DS.

'Yes, of course. I went to visit Mary Bradbury.'

'Why was that?' he asked.

In the cold light of day, it seemed like a very good question. Why, indeed, had I gone there? I could have phoned her for the information about the Wilsons.

'Why shouldn't I go and see my mother-in-law?' I said. 'The poor woman has just been diagnosed with terminal cancer. Amelia and I were a huge part of her life for so many years, that was until Joe Bradbury convinced her that I'm the devil incarnate.'

I was getting quite worked up. To coin one of Joe Bradbury's favourite phrases: *How could he?* How could he accuse me when it had all been his doing?

I made a conscious effort to relax, as being angry wouldn't help my current predicament one bit.

'Have you spoken to Mary Bradbury?' I asked calmly. 'I am sure she will corroborate everything I've said. I'm in no doubt that it was only her intervention that enabled me to get out of her house alive.'

'Mr Bradbury claims you verbally abused his mother in a highly aggressive manner and he says that she is too upset by the incident to be interviewed at the present time.'

'And you believe him?' I asked incredulously. 'Have you learned nothing? The man is a pathological liar.'

'That's precisely what he says about you.'

'I will tell you exactly what happened.'

I went through everything, leaving out only the conversation I'd had with Mary about the Wilsons. I felt, right now, that it would simply confuse matters and I wanted to investigate what Nancy Fadeley had said a little more before I made any accusations to the authorities. It certainly wouldn't help my cause if the police investigated and it turned out to be all a pile of tosh.

'Get your forensic team over to Mary Bradbury's house,' I said. 'You won't find my fingerprints on any of her knives. I never touched them.'

He waved a dismissive hand, suggesting that his forensic team had far more important things to be dealing with.

'So,' I said. 'Are you going to charge me or not? I have other things I need to be getting on with, like fixing the lock on my back door.'

'Wait here,' he said, and he went out, no doubt to confer with his superiors.

I just couldn't believe what was happening.

How did Joe Bradbury have the nerve?

He must have worked out that I would go straight to the police and hence he'd decided to get his accusation in first. What I couldn't understand was why they believed him. It was a clear demonstration of how much they didn't trust me.

The detective sergeant returned.

'Okay,' he said. 'You're free to go for the time being. But we will continue to investigate this incident.'

'You just do that,' I said. 'It will prove what I'm saying is the truth.'

I started to walk out but I turned back.

'And when are you going to stop treating me as a suspect for my wife's murder? You must realise by now that I couldn't have done it.'

'Releasing you from the investigation would have to be a decision of DCI Priestly.'

'So where is he?'

'What? Now?'

'Yes. Right now,' I said. 'I want to speak to him.'

'But it's Saturday,' he said.

'So? You're working, aren't you?' Which I had to admit was a bit of a surprise. 'Get him on the phone.'

'I'm afraid that won't be possible,' said the detective. 'Yes, I am working, but he is not. He has the weekend off.'

I thought I could detect a slight touch of envy in his voice, as if weekends off during a murder investigation were the exclusive domain only of senior officers.

'Well, first thing on Monday morning, you tell him from me that I should no longer be under arrest or considered as a suspect. And I also demand a statement be made by the police to the press confirming that fact.'

He gave me a look, which implied that that was not going to happen.

'Otherwise,' I went on, 'I will lodge a lawsuit with the courts citing wrongful arrest and police harassment. You have no evidence against me, you never have had, and you know it. It is absolutely disgraceful the way I've been treated both by you and the media. I am one of the victims here. My darling wife has been murdered.'

'We did have reasonable grounds for arresting you,' the DS protested.

'What reasonable grounds? Accusations by Joe Bradbury and a life insurance policy? Don't make me laugh. That's not evidence. It's Joe Bradbury you should be arresting, both for killing his sister and for threatening to kill me.'

I didn't want to argue the point with him any further. I'd need to speak to a lawyer. So I marched out of the police station and climbed back into the Fiat.

Needless to say, I didn't go home and fix the lock on my back door.

I went to Weybridge instead.

I parked on Elgin Crescent, on St George's Hill, in front of the house that Reginald and Mary Bradbury had once lived in.

I had been to this address many times, both during the years I had courted their daughter and after we were married. Sunday lunches of roast beef plus all the trimmings had always been a favourite.

I got out of the car and stood looking at it through its wrought-iron gates.

Set back behind an evergreen yew hedge, the property had changed little in the three years since Mary had left, but I had forgotten how big it was. I suppose it would have had to be big to have been sold for more than three million quid. Such was the opulence of exclusive developments in London's leafy Surrey suburbs.

I walked up and down the road looking at the houses on either side, trying to see which of them was a likely candidate as a home for the Wilsons. The one on the right was undergoing some work with a concrete mixer and a stack of breeze blocks visible on the drive.

I decided to try the other side first, on the grounds that a mature couple might not bother with renovations after such a long time in the property. Also, it had no locked gates with an intercom button, as the others did. It was all too easy to tell someone standing at the gate to get lost via a disembodied speaker. Less so when they were face to face at the front door.

I pushed the bell and waited.

Nothing happened.

I pushed the bell again, longer this time, and I could faintly hear a ringing deep in the premises.

I was about to go when I heard a bolt being drawn back. Then the door opened about four inches, brought up short by a sturdy-looking security chain.

'I'm sorry,' said a male voice through the crack. 'We don't want to buy anything. Please go away.'

'That's all right then,' I replied jauntily. 'Because I'm not selling. Are you Mr Wilson?'

'Yes, that's right,' said the voice with a hint of surprise.

'Mr Jim Wilson,' I said. 'Married to Gladys?'

'Who are you?' asked the voice, the door still open just four inches against the chain.

'I'm Mary Bradbury's son-in-law.'

The door closed briefly and I could hear the chain being removed. When it reopened wide I could see a small grey-haired man I took to be in his late seventies standing there.

'Oh, dear,' he said. 'Have you come to tell us bad news? We saw Mary two weeks ago and she didn't look at all well then.'

'No,' I said. 'No bad news. I was with her earlier this morning.'

'Oh, good,' Jim Wilson said, now smiling. 'I'm so pleased. Gladys and I are very fond of Mary. But I do fear she won't be with us for much longer.'

'I'm afraid that you're right,' I said. 'She's had rather a bad diagnosis.'

'Yes,' he said gloomily. 'She told us.'

It was my turn to be surprised. If Mary had told the Wilsons two weeks ago that she had cancer, then why hadn't Amelia known about it?

Mr Wilson looked at me.

'So how can I help you?' he asked.

'It's a bit delicate to talk about out here,' I said. 'Could I come in?'

He hesitated, clearly debating with himself whether it was wise. He decided that it was, and he stepped to one side and waved me in.

'Come through to the kitchen,' he said. 'Gladys and I are just having a spot of breakfast.' He laughed. 'We tend not to get up very early these days so we never have breakfast before eleven, and then we have our lunch in the middle of the afternoon.'

'Very sensible,' I said. 'I hate getting up early. All those cold dark mornings are best avoided.'

He smiled at me and I wondered if he thought I was taking the mickey.

Because I was.

But I found I liked Jim Wilson, and Gladys turned out to be a treat as well.

They were having smoked salmon and cream cheese on toasted bagels. Quite a breakfast.

'Would you like one?' Gladys said. 'I have plenty more in the fridge.'

'That would be lovely,' I said, realising that I'd also had nothing to eat so far today.

Gladys fetched another bagel, cut it in two and put the halves in the toaster.

'Poor dear Mary,' Gladys said. 'First she hears about the cancer and then her sweet Amelia gets killed. We saw Amelia very recently, you know. She was with Mary when we went to visit. What a dreadful business. I just can't bear it that such a lovely girl was murdered. And in her own house, too. I hope that horrid husband of hers gets what's coming to him.'

'Now,' said Jim Wilson, cutting in. 'What was so delicate you couldn't . . .' He stopped and stared at me with his mouth hanging open. 'My God,' he said with a trembling voice. 'You're him.'

'Who?' Gladys asked, clearly confused.

'Amelia's husband.'

They both suddenly looked terrified, as if they had let a monster into their home.

'Please don't hurt us,' Gladys wailed pitifully.

'Get out of my house,' her husband demanded, standing up and pulling himself to his full height, which was still an inch or two shorter even than I.

I didn't move but sat there in silence and, at that moment, the bagel popped up in the toaster, making all of us jump.

'I didn't kill Amelia,' I said, for yet another time. 'I can prove that I was fifty miles away in Birmingham at the time she was killed. Otherwise the police wouldn't have let me go. It's only the damn press that are still accusing me of murder, and it isn't true.'

It wasn't quite the whole truth but . . . it seemed to do the trick. The Wilsons gradually relaxed and Gladys even took another bite of her bagel.

'I loved Amelia,' I went on. 'I loved her with all my heart. And I want to see the person responsible brought to justice more than anyone.'

Jim Wilson sat down again.

'So why *are* you here?' he asked.

'I know this sounds strange,' I said, 'but I believe that, during your recent visit to Mary, you said something about the price that her house next door was sold for, and I think that could be relevant in determining who killed Amelia.'

It was a tenuous connection but, if I could prove that Joe Bradbury was a liar and a fraudster, and one who would even steal from his own mother, then I might be some way to proving that he was a murderer too. If nothing else it would stop the police believing he was as honest as Mother Teresa.

'I don't know what that could be,' Jim said. 'We talked mostly about other long-standing friends of both ours and hers. I can't see how that could help find Amelia's killer.'

'How about the couple that bought Mary's house? Did you speak about them at all?'

'Alan and Margaret Newbould,' Gladys said. 'Nice couple.'

'Do you know them well?' I asked.

'Quite well,' she replied. 'They are friendly enough if we see them out somewhere or over the garden fence. But they're not like Mary and Reg.' She laughed. 'With them, we almost lived in each other's houses at times. Such a shock for us all when Reg died.'

She sighed.

Death was always a shock, all the more so when it was

216

unexpected, sudden and violent. Worse still when it was at the hand of another.

'Have you seen the Newboulds recently?' I asked. 'Perhaps that was what you told Mary about?'

They both thought in silence for a moment.

'I saw Margaret quite recently,' Gladys said. 'I was going for a walk and she was standing outside while some men were unloading a van. She waved at me and I stopped for a chat.'

'What was being unloaded?'

'Electrical goods, I think. A new washing machine and a dryer.'

'That's it,' Jim said excitedly. 'You were telling Mary that Alan wasn't very pleased that the ones she'd left in the house had broken down so soon, particularly after he'd spent so much to buy them from her in the first place. And they weren't still under an extended guarantee either, like he'd been promised.'

I inwardly groaned. If all that Joe had done was misrepresent the age of his mother's old washing machine, then it was hardly going to rate as grand theft auto.

But Amelia would surely have realised that too. So why had she said what she had to Nancy?

'A second-hand washing machine and tumble dryer can't have been that expensive,' I said.

'It wasn't just them,' Jim said. 'Alan Newbould told me he'd bought all sorts of other things too – carpets, curtains, light fittings, and so on. Even some nice pieces of furniture that Mary didn't have room for in her new place. He told me he'd done a deal with young Joseph to buy it all at a grossly inflated price so that he could effectively reduce the stamp duty a bit on the true cost of the house. Seems everyone does it.'

Indeed, they do. Amelia and I had done exactly the same when we'd bought the Old Forge. Stamp duty land tax was not levied on removable items such as white goods or wall and floor coverings, things that the taxman described as chattels, so why give the government more money than we had to?

But there had been no mention of any chattels payment in the letter sent by the lawyers to Mary.

'Do you know how he paid?' I asked.

'He wrote out a personal cheque to Joseph,' Jim said. 'Seems Joseph told him that it would be best if the lawyers on each side didn't know anything about it.'

'Do you happen to know how much the cheque was for?'

'A hundred thousand pounds.'

23

No crime would have been committed if Joe had given the cheque to his mother to deposit into her bank account. No crime, that was, other than defrauding the taxman of a few thousand pounds in stamp duty. And that would be nothing for me to get excited about, especially when paying the duty was the purchaser's responsibility, not the seller's.

But Nancy had told me that Amelia had been convinced that Joe had stolen the money from their mother.

Ever since we'd been helping Mary with her day-to-day expenses, Amelia had had access to her mother's online banking and she would have surely looked for the hundred thousand to have been paid in.

By mid-afternoon, I was back at Hanwell and on my knees in front of the Queen Anne desk.

When we were first married, Amelia had spent several weeks unsuccessfully trying to cancel an online film-streaming service for which she had forgotten the password and so, ever since then, she had kept a little blue-covered notebook, containing all her user names and passwords. With luck it would also contain her mother's bank login details.

All I had to do was find it.

I rifled through the drawers of the desk but it was nowhere to be seen.

In the end, I removed all the papers one by one, stacking them in piles on the sitting-room floor, but still there was no sign of the notebook.

But I did find one thing that made me gasp in shock, or in horror.

In the top right-hand drawer, hidden inside a cookery magazine, was a thin booklet entitled *Living or Dying with My Friend Suicide*.

The booklet was not only extremely well thumbed but Amelia had written copious notes in the margins alongside the text.

I couldn't tell whether they were recent or not. Probably not. There had been a time when almost all Amelia would talk about was taking her own life, but I thought that time had passed. But, nevertheless, finding the booklet brought it all back to me.

One of her notes caught my eye.

'THIS IS ME', she had written in large capital letters.

According to the title page, the booklet had been written by someone called Richard Schneider, MD, professor of psychiatry at New York University.

I sat on the floor with my back against the sofa and read it.

The professor started by stating that, in his considerable clinical experience, there were only six basic reasons why people kill themselves:

1. Psychosis – when schizophrenia or some other neurotic disorder generates 'voices' in the head telling sufferers to take their own lives, an instruction that is difficult or impossible for them to ignore.

2. Impulse – when someone takes their life on little more than a careless whim, mostly due to excessive use of alcohol or drugs. The 'watch me, I can fly' leap from a hotel balcony, or the 'I don't want to live any more' mournful cry of the maudlin drunk who then steps in front of a car or throws himself into a canal. These people wouldn't have dreamed of killing themselves if they'd been clean or sober.

3. Depression – when sufferers feel that they cannot bear for any longer the agony that it causes. Bizarrely, they often don't really want to die, they just want to stop living in pain, as if there was some halfway house from which they could return at some later stage when things were better. Depression can also blur a person's thinking, giving them the misplaced opinion that people would be better off without them and that they would be doing everyone a favour by ending it all.

4. A cry for help that goes wrong. Taking an overdose and then telling someone so that medical attention can be sought is a prime example. Such people don't really want to die, or expect to. They even frequently choose a method that they don't think will actually kill, only intending to alert or cause suffering to someone who has previously hurt *them*. But, if the overdose is sufficient or the medical help is too slow in coming, then death can occur, rendering the cry for help as misplaced as it is heart-wrenching.

5. Some people have a philosophical desire to die in a manner of their choosing. They often have a terminal illness, which may have future painful or debilitating consequences. They are not psychotic, impulsive, depressed or crying out for help, they simply wish to take control of where, when and how they pass on.

6. By mistake – a few people will always stab or shoot themselves by accident and, a generally more recent phenomenon, some men, seeking sexual arousal by deprivation of oxygen to the brain, either attempt self-strangulation by hanging or they place a plastic bag over their heads. Occasionally, such practices simply go too far, resulting in their unwanted deaths. The actor David Carradine, of *Kung Fu* and *Kill Bill* fame, died from auto-erotic asphyxiation caused by hanging from a rope in a hotel wardrobe in Bangkok. Although suspended at quite a low level, much lower than his own standing height, the

conclusion was that he had accidentally become unconscious, causing the majority of his bodyweight then to
hang on the rope, which had resulted in his death.

Well, one lived and learned.

Amelia had written 'THIS IS ME' in the margin alongside
number 3 – Depression. She had then underlined it twice with
such heavy strokes of the pen that they had almost torn right
through the paper.

I put the booklet down as tears again welled up in my eyes,
not so much from grief at her loss, even though that was raw too,
but at the frustration I felt that I hadn't been more useful to her
when she was alive. Why had she not shown me this? Why had
we not talked about it more?

But we had. Of course we had. All the time.

If I'd told her once, I'd told her a million times that I would
not be better off if she was dead, and here I was to prove it –
blubbing like a baby and totally lost without her.

Strangely, I clung to the fact that Amelia hadn't killed herself.
Autoerotic strangulation is almost exclusively a male activity
and, anyway, it is impossible to kill yourself with a ligature without actually hanging from something. As soon as you become
unconscious the pressure releases and you recover.

I sat on the floor and read through the rest of the booklet.

In its totality, it was far from being a manual of how to
commit suicide, more it was a recipe for how to stay alive
through difficult times, and I was glad of that. I hoped that
Amelia had found some strength from its pages.

The daylight was fading by the time I had finished reading so I stood up, turned on the electric replacement, and continued my search for Amelia's notebook.

I was sure it wasn't in the desk so I did a systematic search of the rest of the house, opening every cupboard and drawer in the kitchen, emptying the sideboard in the dining room and going through all Amelia's clothes in her wardrobes. I also searched her bedside cabinet and those in the bathroom, once again. I looked under all the beds and on top of all the bookcases. I even turned the pockets inside out in the coats hung near the back door.

Nothing. At least, no blue-covered notebook.

Amelia had always been extremely good at hiding things and I had never once come across my birthday or Christmas present by accident before the due day.

I tried all her multitude of handbags but they were mostly empty, and those that weren't contained such mundane items as tissues, hairclips and the ubiquitous lip salves. Hat boxes contained just hats, and there were no notebooks lurking in the depths of her boots, nor anything else for that matter.

I even opened the fridge and the freezer again to see if she had wrapped it in a plastic bag and popped it behind the butter or under a bag of frozen peas.

No joy.

I couldn't think of anywhere else to look.

Perhaps I'd try her car.

I was just collecting the keys when there was a knock on the front door.

Wary of what had happened that very morning in Mary Bradbury's cottage, and not wanting another confrontation with a knife-wielding Joe, I went into the sitting room and looked through the window to see who it was.

Dave and Nancy Fadeley stood expectantly on my doorstep, each of them bearing gifts.

'Hello, you two,' I said, opening the door.

'We thought you might need some company,' Dave said. He held up a bottle of red wine. 'And we can't have you getting blind drunk on your own, now can we?'

'And I thought you might need something more to eat,' Nancy added. 'So I've brought over a casserole for us all to share.'

'How wonderful, thank you. Come on in.'

I led them towards the kitchen but Nancy hung back.

'It's all right,' I said, but there were tears again in her eyes.

'Sorry,' she said, wiping them away with her sleeve.

'Don't be. I've been crying all over this house. It's very painful.'

'Would you prefer to go back over to our place?' Dave said. 'We nearly called you but we thought you might not answer.'

'No,' I said. 'It's fine. Somehow better to face the demons than to bury them. Let's have some of that wine.'

We went into the kitchen, Nancy included, and I fetched three glasses from a cupboard.

'None for me,' Nancy said. 'I have a slight infection – women's problem – and I'm on antibiotics. So I'm afraid it's no booze for me for another week.' She pulled a face.

'What would you like instead?' I asked. 'I don't have much that's non-alcoholic.'

'Tap water will do,' she said. 'Unless you have any coffee.'

'Instant?'

'Lovely.'

Dave poured two glasses of red while I switched on the kettle.

'I'm afraid I have no milk.'

'Black will be fine,' she said. 'But I'll have it with one sugar to take away the bitterness.'

Sugar, I thought. She'd be lucky. Neither Amelia nor I ever took sugar.

There were three white circular tins on the worktop behind the kettle with the words TEA, COFFEE and SUGAR painted on them.

I spooned some instant granules from the COFFEE tin into a mug and picked up the SUGAR one. It felt worryingly light. I pulled off the lid and was relieved to see just a little of the sweet stuff at the bottom.

And there, lying above it, was a small blue-covered notebook.

I laughed out loud, which Dave and Nancy found rather disconcerting.

'Sorry,' I said, lifting out the treasure and showing them. 'I've been searching for this notebook all afternoon. I've turned the whole house upside down. And I'd have never found it if you two hadn't come over. Thank the Lord for antibiotics.'

We sat on the bar stools at the kitchen counter and ate the casserole, which was excellent – would I expect anything else from Nancy? – and Dave and I drank all of his bottle of red wine and most of another of mine, with him consuming the lion's share. Not that I hadn't been a willing accomplice.

'So the police let you go,' Dave said when he had enough alcohol in his bloodstream to pluck up the courage.

'Yes,' I said. 'I can prove that I was in Birmingham the whole time.'

'So who the hell did kill her?' he said, slightly slurring his words.

Nancy gave him an exasperated look as if to express the view that he shouldn't be mentioning such things, not here, not now, and especially not in this kitchen.

But it was she who then answered the question.

'Her brother,' she said.

'Exactly,' I agreed, trying not to slide off my barstool. It had been some time since I had drunk so much claret.

'Amelia often told me she was frightened of him.'

'Did she really?'

'Yes, and she said it to me again last week, on the night before she died. Perhaps I should have done something about it like mention it to the police. Maybe I still should. I would have done but they seemed so sure that . . .'

'That it had been me who'd killed her,' I said, finishing her sentence for her.

'Yes,' she said sheepishly. She sighed. 'I wish so much that she had come to stay with us that night, with you being away and all. I asked her to. Then she would still be alive.'

Her tears returned and we all sat in silence for a moment, lost in our own thoughts. Dave took another large gulp of wine.

'Come on, Dave,' Nancy said finally. 'It's high time we went home.'

She collected her empty casserole dish and the plate that had held the cake, and then steered her unsteady husband across the hall and out through the front door. I smiled to myself. I reckoned he might be in for a bit of a roasting when they got back to the safety of their own home.

It was a difficult time for all of us who were left behind and we all dealt with our grief in different ways. Dave's method was clearly to hit the bottle, even though he didn't usually need any excuse to do that at the weekends. For Nancy and me, however, it was mostly dealing with the anger and the guilt – anger that it had happened at all, and guilt that we'd been unable to prevent it.

And the guilt was by far the worse of the two.

I had berated myself thousands of times for having gone to Birmingham without her, or having gone at all, and also for not coming home again that night. All to have had a few glasses of wine at the charity dinner.

For Nancy, it was the guilt of not insisting that Amelia stay over with her and Dave that night, and also for being just across the road from the disaster, almost in full view, but still helpless to stop it.

Nancy and Amelia had been very close, even though Nancy was a few years older. Closer even than sisters. They had shared a special bond insofar that neither of them was able to have children and they had each comforted the other in that respect. And now, just as for me, Nancy's best friend forever had suddenly gone, cruelly snatched away from life and laughter.

I loaded the dirty plates and glasses into the dishwasher. Then I noticed the little blue-covered notebook lying on the worktop.

I flicked through it and there, sure enough, all on one page near the back were all the login details for Mary Bradbury's bank accounts, written in Amelia's fair hand. Just seeing the neat flow of her handwriting caused me to choke back a wave of sorrow.

Thanks to the police, I had no computer to use, so I tried logging in with my replacement mobile phone.

Insert customer number – check.

1st, 3rd, 4th and 8th characters of the password – check.

Security questions: insert favourite place. I looked in the notebook. Venice – check.

Insert favourite book. *Rebecca* – check.

As if by some form of internet sorcery, Mary's bank account details suddenly appeared on my screen.

I felt slightly guilty looking at them.

Her balance was almost six thousand and I could see that monthly direct-debit payments would soon be due for such things as gas, electricity and telephone.

But it was the historical transactions that I was interested in.

Fortunately, all account activity for the past seven years could be recalled so I asked the system to look for credits only from three years previously.

One, for just over three million pounds, immediately caught my eye.

That would have been the proceeds of the house sale, wired to Mary's account by the lawyers, before being then invested in stocks and shares.

I searched for six months before that and for nine months after but there was no other credit remotely close to a hundred thousand, not even a tenth of it.

It didn't exactly prove that Joe had kept the money – he might have deposited it straight into his mother's investment plan – but it was enough for me to be suspicious. Plenty more than enough.

24

Sunday morning dawned with brilliant sunshine in a cloudless sky. Something I sorely needed to try and brighten the gloom and despair that had descended upon me once more.

It was the effect of excessive alcohol, I told myself, but that was only half the story.

For the past eleven days, I had been living in denial, dealing more with trying to prove my innocence of Amelia's murder rather than with the reality of being permanently left alone. I had been half-expecting her to walk in at any time, laughing that it had all been a great hoax, and I had often caught myself believing I'd heard her voice, maybe in another part of the house, or out in the garden.

But last evening, with the arrival at my door of Dave and Nancy, I had begun to realise the enormous actuality of what had really happened.

As if on automatic pilot, I got up, showered, shaved, brushed my teeth, combed my hair, put on my clothes and went downstairs.

Sunday mornings at the Old Forge had always been lazy affairs.

Amelia would wear her dressing gown, cooking ham and cheese omelettes for breakfast, while I went to collect the Sunday papers. And then we would nestle together on the sofa, eating and reading.

During the winter months, I would light a fire in the sitting-room grate and we would pass the day in happy contentment, often making love in the afternoon on the carpet in front of the fire, bathed in the warming glow from the hot embers.

But, on this particular Sunday, the only things lying on the sitting-room carpet were the stacks of papers I had removed from Amelia's desk.

I returned everything to the drawers from which it had come, even, for some reason, placing the *Living or Dying with My Friend Suicide* booklet back inside the cookery magazine as if accepting that, if Amelia had wanted it so hidden, I wasn't going to differ.

Next I went into the kitchen and made myself a cup of coffee.

Damn it. I should have asked Nancy if she had any spare milk. I also found black coffee rather bitter but I didn't fancy putting sugar in it.

Thinking about Nancy made me realise that there had been something else she'd mentioned on Friday that was relevant. She had said that Amelia had told her that Joe had conspired together with the estate agent. How had Amelia known? Had she simply assumed it was true, or had she been in contact with the agent directly?

With a jug in my hand as the pretext, even though it was true, I walked across the road and pushed the bell on the Fadeley front door.

From deep within, I heard a raised male voice ask, 'Who the bloody hell is that at this ungodly time on a Sunday morning?'

Oops.

'Dave, be quiet,' said a female voice from much closer. Nancy.

She opened the door, wearing a thin housecoat.

I glanced past her.

'Sorry about that,' she said. 'He can be a real pain when he's been drinking. Got a thumping hangover too, but it's no more than he deserves.'

'Tell whoever it is to get lost,' Dave shouted from somewhere out of sight upstairs.

'Shut up, Dave,' Nancy shouted back. 'It's Bill.'

A head with tousled brown hair appeared around a door frame, and bleary eyes finally focused on me.

'Bit bloody early for a Sunday.'

'Yes,' I said. 'I'm sorry, Dave. My fault entirely. Couldn't sleep.'

The head disappeared.

'What did you want?' Nancy asked sweetly.

I held up the jug. 'Do you have any spare milk?'

'Of course.'

I remained at the door as she went to the kitchen and returned with an unopened carton.

'Have this,' she said. 'We have plenty.'

'Thanks.' I took the carton from her.

'Just one other thing,' I said. 'You mentioned on Friday

that Amelia told you that her brother had conspired with the estate agent who sold her mother's house. Did she say how she knew that?'

'She phoned the agent and he told her. Something about it being common practice to reduce the tax or something. Apparently he was quite open and brazen about how he had talked the buyer into the scheme to save him some money.'

Perhaps the agent was unaware that the amount raised from the inflated sale of 'chattels' had been paid to Joe, and not to Mary.

'Did Amelia say anything else to you about it, anything at all?'

'She said that she really hoped the estate agent wouldn't tell Joe she'd called. She was worried that Joe would kill her if he knew.'

She left the last statement hanging in the air like a dense fog.

'Now that *is* something we should tell the police.'

Nancy and I called and made an appointment to go and see DS Dowdeswell first thing on Monday morning.

Then we spent a couple of hours in my dining room on Sunday afternoon going through everything again to make sure we had the chronology correct.

Dave came over as well, to listen.

Nancy made a written record of everything she could remember that Amelia had told her, and I also put down on paper all I had been able to glean from Jim and Gladys Wilson, from the lawyer's financial statement of the house sale in the desk drawer, and from Mary Bradbury's online banking system.

At one point, Dave stood up and went over to the French windows, looking out at the garden beyond, as if thinking.

'You know,' he said without turning round, 'it's not the stealing of the hundred grand that is the real story here. That's just peanuts.'

'What do you mean?' I asked.

'Who stands to inherit when Mary Bradbury dies?'

'I think her will states that everything was to be split equally between Amelia and Joe.'

He nodded. 'And, after them, to their issue, meaning their children. That's the usual way that wills are written. But Amelia doesn't have any issue.'

He stopped and turned back to stare at me.

'Good God,' I said, finally understanding what he was on about. 'So Joe will inherit everything.'

'He sure will,' Dave agreed. 'Unless there is a specific clause leaving Amelia's half to you, and I would severely doubt that.'

'Well, we won't have long to wait to find out,' I said. 'Mary Bradbury has been given only a few months to live, at most. She told me she thought she might have only a few days.'

'All the more reason for Joe to have killed Amelia quickly, before their mother died. If he'd done it after Mary was gone, even a minute later, Amelia's half of her mother's estate would have then come to you via her will.'

Nancy and I arrived at Banbury Police Station at nine o'clock as instructed and we were graced with the presence not only of Detective Sergeant Dowdeswell but also of Detective Chief Inspector Priestly.

I took that to be a good sign.

Shown back into the same interview room once again, I wondered if I should have arranged for Simon Bassett or Harriet Clark to be with us, especially as I was again cautioned before the interview started.

Douglas would have insisted on it.

But it was too late now. It would take hours for them to get here, even if one of them was free.

'How can we help?' asked the DCI politely, which I took to be another positive step. Seemingly gone was his belligerent style and his blinkered certainty that I was the killer.

'This is Mrs Nancy Fadeley,' I said, indicating my companion. 'She and her husband live across the road from me in Hanwell.'

He smiled and nodded in her direction.

'Nancy was my wife's best friend and we have some things to discuss with you.'

'Yes?' he said.

Nancy took out her piece of paper from her pocket and went through in detail every aspect of her conversation with Amelia on the night before she died. Nancy told them about Amelia having listened to her mother's former neighbours from Weybridge, how she had then spoken to the estate agent about the plan to lower the reported sale price, and how she was convinced that her brother had stolen the money, finishing with the bit about Amelia being worried that Joe would kill her if he knew that she was aware of it.

Then I had my turn, outlining to the detectives about the trip to see the Wilsons and what they had told me about the £100,000 cheque given to Joe Bradbury, and how I had accessed my mother-in-law's bank account to look for a deposit of that amount and had failed to do so.

The chief inspector raised his eyebrows at that.

'How did you access the accounts?'

'Online,' I said. 'Amelia has always had the login details in order to assist her mother with payments and such. Mary doesn't understand computers and couldn't cope with online banking.' In truth, she could no longer cope with much. 'I simply used the numbers and passwords that my wife had recorded in a notebook.'

'I'm not sure that's legal,' said the DCI.

'Arrest me then,' I said.

He smiled. 'I remind you, Mr Russell, that you have only been released under investigation. You are subject to re-arrest at any time.'

Mr Russell? Not Mr Gordon-Russell. Things were definitely on the way up.

'I know it doesn't prove that Joe Bradbury stole the money,' I said. 'He might have paid it back to his mother in another way or she might have even given it to him, but I would doubt that, as she would have then given the same to Amelia. But surely we've given you enough evidence to make it worth you investigating, or at least asking him.'

The DCI rubbed his chin in thought. 'One person describing what another person has said, even if it was said to them directly, is considered by the courts to be hearsay, and is only acceptable as evidence in certain very limited circumstances as laid down in part eleven, chapter two of the Criminal Justice Act 2003.'

Oh, for goodness' sake! How is it that all policemen are able to quote the law like that off the top of their heads? But, I suppose, I could quote almost all the 625 provisions of the Rules of Racing off mine, plus the 64 schedules and appendices.

But the DCI hadn't finished. 'However, even though a defence barrister wouldn't like it, I believe that this may be one of those circumstances, as the declarant is unavailable to be called in person as a witness. And it may not be necessary to introduce it as evidence anyway, not if other inquiries determine that what the declarant is purported to have said is indeed true.'

I hoped *he* knew what he was on about, because I didn't.

'And how about me?' I said. 'Isn't it also about time you officially stopped treating me as a suspect for my wife's murder?'

'We will consider our position on that as well, and we will let you know in due course.'

The DCI stood up as if to go.

Nancy nudged me. 'Aren't you going to tell him what Dave said?'

'Who is Dave?' asked the DCI.

'My husband,' Nancy said. 'And he said something very important.'

'Go on,' encouraged the detective.

'It's only a theory,' I said. 'And there's no actual evidence for it as there is for the other things we've just told you. But, it is a motive and I know from experience how keen you are on motives.'

The DCI sat down again. 'I'm listening.'

'Two weeks ago, just before Amelia was killed, Mary

Bradbury learned that she has pancreatic cancer and it had already spread to her liver. The doctors have given her a few months at most, but she told me she could go at any time. And Joe knew that too.'

'Yes?' said the DCI.

'Well, I believe that Mary's last will and testament states that her estate should be split equally between her two children, that's Amelia and Joe, and, if they predecease her, then their share goes to their further issue.'

The DCI nodded. It was normal.

'But Amelia and I don't have any children. There is no further issue on her side, so Joe Bradbury now stands to inherit the estate in its entirety. If Amelia had lived for just a few months longer, so that she had outlived her mother, then Joe would have been looking at only half.'

'And how big is the estate?' he asked.

'I don't know exactly but Mary Bradbury's house in Weybridge was sold for more than three million.'

25

In Wednesday morning's post I received a formal letter from Thames Valley Police, signed by the chief constable no less, stating that, unless new evidence against me were to come to light in the future, I would face no further action over my arrest on suspicion of the murder of Amelia Jane Gordon-Russell.

I didn't celebrate.

There was nothing to be joyous about. Indeed, I was angry.

I should never have been arrested in the first place.

The letter didn't exactly state that I was innocent of the crime but it was probably the best I could expect in the circumstances. My true innocence would only be confirmed when someone else, i.e. Joe Bradbury, was convicted.

It was too much to hope for that Thames Valley Police had sent copies of the letter to all the national daily newspapers and the broadcast media, so I wondered if I should send them copies myself. But the press are never particularly interested in innocence, only in guilt, and I didn't really want to remind them of the whole sorry saga again anyway. At last, after two long weeks, their interest in the gory details of Amelia's death had begun to wane as new sensational events took over the front pages and the news bulletins.

However, I did take a photo of the letter with my phone and then sent copies of that by email to all my contacts at the insurance companies, those firms for whom I had regularly done freelance work over the past two years, inviting them to again make use of my services.

I also sent a copy to the chairman of the British Horseracing Authority, and cc'd it to the chairman of the Honorary Stewards Appointment Board. Only time would tell if they responded favourably or not.

Probably *not*.

I thought fleetingly about sending a copy to Joe Bradbury but decided that it would be a bad idea, a very bad idea indeed. He'd go apeshit, and he was deranged enough already, especially as far as dealing with me was concerned. The letter would be like pouring petrol onto an already smouldering fuse – at best incendiary, at worst explosive.

He would find out soon enough when he was arrested. Not that there had been any word of that yet. It had been two days since Nancy and I had provided our signed statements to the police and I was becoming impatient.

I called DS Dowdeswell.

'Any news of an arrest?' I asked when he answered.

'All in good time, Mr Gordon-Russell. We like to get all our ducks in a row first.'

But the ducks had hardly been in a row before they'd arrested me, and I noticed we were back to Mr Gordon-Russell.

'So are you making any headway?' I asked ironically.

'Slow and steady,' he assured me, without giving me any specifics.

'I received a letter this morning from your chief constable.'

'Yes,' he said. 'I was aware that one had been drafted.'

I wanted to ask the DS if he now felt rather foolish for having gone all the way to North Wales to arrest me so dramatically when he'd had no evidence. But I resisted the temptation, just.

'How about your inquiries into the carving knife incident at Mary Bradbury's place?' I asked.

'They are ongoing,' he said in true police avoidance-of-detail speak, but I wasn't going to let him off that easily.

'In what way are they ongoing?' I asked. 'Have you interviewed Mrs Bradbury yet?'

'We may have done.'

'What sort of answer is that?' I said. 'Either you have or you haven't.'

'I am not at liberty to discuss the matter with you.'

'Don't be so stupid,' I said. 'If it wasn't for Nancy Fadeley and me, you'd have nothing to go on. You'd still be floundering in the dark trying your utmost to stick a murder charge on me when you've known all along that I couldn't have done it. I've given you Joe Bradbury on a plate – intent, opportunity and motive. What more do you want?'

'Intent?'

242

'Have you read the vile emails he's been sending my wife and me over the past three years? You still have our computers. Look at them. If those emails aren't a portent to murder, I don't know what is.'

There was a long silent pause from the other end of the line.

'Okay,' the DS said eventually. 'Yes, I have interviewed Mrs Mary Bradbury. I went to see her yesterday afternoon. And we have also removed from her premises an eight-inch carving knife for analysis.'

'And?' I said, encouraging him to go on.

'Mrs Bradbury was somewhat confused.'

Tell me about it.

'Initially she confirmed your version of events but, later, she said that her son was only kidding and he hadn't meant anything by it. Then, later still, she said that she couldn't in fact remember which of you had been holding the knife, and what did it matter anyway, as no one had been hurt.'

Silly old bat.

'I'm afraid,' the DS went on, 'that she would be a completely hopeless witness in any proceedings, so it is simply your word against his.'

'That doesn't mean it didn't happen,' I said.

'That's as maybe,' he said.

'How about the knife?' I asked. 'I assume you are testing that for fingerprints.'

'We are,' he said. 'But, according to Mrs Bradbury, it has since been through the dishwasher. Seems Mr Joseph Bradbury put it in there and set the thing off.'

243

I knew the police should have gone and got the knife straight away last Saturday, but even then they might have been too late.

'Did you ask her about the money from the house sale?'

'Not exactly,' he said.

'What is that supposed to mean?'

'I didn't mention the house sale specifically but I did ask her for written permission for us to access her bank account. I told her that there had been several local cases of elderly people, especially elderly widows, having had their accounts remotely hacked and emptied by criminals. I offered to ensure that it couldn't happened to her, and to put her bank on notice that we were on watch.'

Sneaky, I thought. 'And did she agree?'

'Readily.' I could detect some amusement in his voice. 'But it was important for us to get her permission as the access you had previously made was illegal and hence anything you found would have been inadmissible as evidence in court.'

'But won't someone argue that you gained access to her bank accounts by somewhat dubious means?'

'They might,' he said. 'But what I told her was completely true, there have been some local cases of fraud from people's bank accounts, and she did sign a wide-ranging permission. So the fact that we can look further than any potential hack is quite legal.'

'So have you looked?' I asked.

'We don't have online access to the account. We have had to make an application to her bank. We are still awaiting their response.'

'I hope Joe Bradbury doesn't find out in the meantime. Two years ago, he forced Mary to sign a power of attorney to give him sole responsibility over her finances. Cut Amelia out of the loop completely in spite of the fact that she had done everything for her mother for years. He convinced Mary that Amelia was crazy and not be trusted. That's a joke. But perhaps it's Joe that you need to get the permission from. I hope the bank don't ask you for it or, worse still, ask him directly.'

'So do I,' said the DS. 'He already knows I was there.'

'How?'

'He called his mother while I was talking to her.'

Bloody hell.

'Did she tell him *why* you were there?'

'She said that I was asking questions about the knife incident.'

'What did he say?' I asked.

'I couldn't hear him, only her, but it was after the call that she decided she couldn't remember which of you had been holding the knife.'

Unbelievable.

'He also told her to ask me why you weren't still in custody.'

'I hope you didn't tell her that I was no longer a suspect.'

There was a deafening silence from the other end of the line.

Oh, my God.

26

I walked round the house, checking that all the doors and windows were locked.

Was I frightened of Joe Bradbury and what he might do?

You bet I was.

The most certain way of getting away with murder was to ensure that someone else was convicted of the crime and now, for him, the chances of that happening had greatly diminished.

I went into the kitchen.

I still hadn't replaced the lock on the back door, nor the splintered wood surrounding it. Something about leaving it hanging there, twisted and broken, was important to me, perhaps as a reminder of what had occurred. Not that I really needed reminding – the appalling absence in my bed at night was more than enough for that.

But the broken lock also stood as a sign that matters remained unresolved and they would continue to be so until Joe was finally brought to book.

I had removed the police padlock and clasp from the outside of the door but had installed new bolts, top and bottom, on the inside. I now checked that they were fully slid over.

I also checked the French windows in the dining room and the door out into the garden from the conservatory. They still had the padlocks and clasps in place on the outside and both were secure, the snap-shut shackles clearly visible through the glass.

The front door was also locked but all of that hardly made the house totally impenetrable from the most determined would-be intruder. The ground-floor windows were comfortably accessible from outside and the glass in them could easily be smashed. For the first time ever, I wished I was living once more in a thirteenth-century castle with four-feet-thick fortified walls and high-up windows.

I wondered about going back to stay with my parents, but I felt I needed to be here, close to the action as it were, ready to assist the police as necessary.

I did another circuit of the ground floor to check everything was still in place and then propped the back of a chair under the handle on the inside of the front door, just in case someone tried to break the whole thing down.

'Pull yourself together,' I said out loud to myself. 'He's hardly likely to come here to try anything. It would simply prove his guilt.'

But I wasn't at all sure that Joe could think that rationally. In all his dealings with Amelia and with me in recent years, he had shown himself to be conspicuously short of logic and reason, and I had no grounds to imagine he would have suddenly changed now.

Not to mention the carving knife incident at his mother's house, which was still very fresh in my memory.

I would have felt so much safer if he was in one of the cells at Banbury Police Station, savouring the delights of a thin blue plastic-covered mattress, a musty blanket, lumpy pillow and one main meal a day.

Once I was happy that the Old Forge was as fortress-like as I could make it, I took a cup of coffee into my study, sat down at the desk, and took stock.

I had always felt huge sympathy for those people whose husband, wife or child had been murdered and that singular dreadful event had then defined their lives for ever more. For some, it was compounded by the killer never being identified or, worse still, the body never being found.

Suzy Lamplugh had been twenty-five years old when she disappeared in July 1986 from outside a house in Fulham. Numerous police searches spanning more than thirty years, including the dismantling of a whole building in October 2018, have failed to find a single trace of her.

Eight years after her disappearance, she was officially declared dead, probably murdered, but no evidence has ever been obtained to directly link any suspect to the crime.

Suzy's parents devoted the rest of their lives to keeping the search for her alive in the minds of both the police and the public but, nevertheless, they both went to their graves not knowing what had befallen their beautiful daughter, or where her remains now lie.

There have been others, too, for whom not knowing who killed their loved ones has resulted in a life of misery and despair. It has torn families apart, driven formerly quite perceptive and cogent individuals into gibbering wrecks, and laced them with an intensity of anger, with no target against which it could be vented.

In short, the murder had destroyed them as human beings as much as it had the victim.

Murder is a very special crime, uniquely evil.

Robbery, theft, fraud, and online hacking of old ladies' bank accounts are all despicable acts for which the perpetrator should be rightly punished and the funds recovered, but murder crosses a totally different line altogether.

By murder, you take away something that can never be given back.

I drank the rest of my coffee and resolved not to join the list of murder-family casualties. Not that I didn't miss Amelia terribly. I did. But she would not have wanted my life to stop with hers, whatever the circumstances. And I at least knew where her body lay, even if I hadn't actually seen it, and I also knew who was responsible. All I had to do now was help prove it.

By mid-afternoon, my security frenzy had subsided somewhat with me only doing a round of the house every half-hour rather than the every five minutes of this morning.

And I was hungry.

It was a Wednesday.

In order to keep life moving on in some semblance of

normality, I decided that a trip to Waitrose in Banbury was called for.

I went into the kitchen and made a list of essentials such as bread, coffee, milk, butter and eggs. I decided I would also buy a large supply of individual frozen ready meals to pop in the microwave whenever I needed one. It was so much easier for someone else to have done the cooking.

Not that I couldn't cook if required to, and I had been known to often, even when we'd had guests, but the kitchen had mostly been Amelia's domain, and I had no desire to cook for just myself anyway.

With my list complete, I now had the problem of leaving my fortress and venturing out into the big bad world, albeit only as far as Amelia's Fiat 500 parked on the driveway.

I again went round the house looking out of every window, searching for anyone lurking in the bushes. I even went upstairs and hung out of those windows to see if anyone was standing up close to the house waiting to lunge at me with a knife as I left.

There was no one.

However, my heart was still pumping rather faster than usual as I grabbed the keys, removed the chair from the front door, opened it, stepped out, slammed it shut again and ran to the car.

There was no shout, no call, and no one pounced from hiding to try and do me injury.

As I locked the car doors from the inside, I laughed at myself, but it was only the sort of laughter that comes from the sudden relaxation of stress.

I backed out onto the road and looked both ways, searching

for Joe's black Nissan, but there was nothing, just a courier's white van delivering to another house down the road. *Not to me*, I thought. I've ordered nothing.

Mind you, I still drove with my eyes almost as much on the rear-view mirror as they were on the road ahead and, when I arrived at Waitrose, I parked in one of the large parent-with-child spaces near the main door.

There were six such spaces and only one other was filled. I know that more room around the car makes it easier to get toddlers out and pushchairs in, but it also means it would be more difficult for someone to hide unnoticed when I came back.

No one gave me an accusing stare when I collected a trolley and walked into the shop without a small child in tow; indeed, no one took much notice of me at all, which was a huge improvement over my last excursion out in public.

I pushed the trolley up and down the aisles, collecting the items on my list from the shelves and much more besides, all the while being careful not to leave myself alone in the dark recesses of the beers, wines and spirits department, or in some quiet corner behind the shampoo and toothpaste section.

I had broken the cardinal rule of weekly food shopping, which was that one shouldn't do it while hungry. Hence, by the time I had finished, I had a huge load of food that included, in addition to the ready meals, many things I didn't really want or need, such as a large pack of freshly dressed Cornish crab, something that Amelia had absolutely loved but I was fairly indifferent towards. It was another example of me trying to make my life go on, if not quite as before, then in some sort of 'normal' fashion.

And it was not that I was unaccepting of the fact that Amelia had gone for good, it was more that I found some comfort in familiarity. To that end, I also bought some flowers to put in a vase on our hall table, as she had always done.

By the time I had put everything through the checkout and bagged it all up, it was getting dark outside. The clocks had now gone back and the long months of dark winter evenings had begun in earnest. How I wish I could have put the clocks back, not by just one single hour, but by two whole weeks, and thus prevented all this suffering.

I hung around in the well-lit entrance to the store until a group of other shoppers were also on the way out, and then I joined them as they walked back to their cars, keeping a keen lookout for any black Nissan lurking in dark corners of the car park.

Nothing happened and I managed to load everything onto the back seat of the Fiat without being attacked. But I was worried that getting it all out again safely at the other end might be a different matter. At home there would be no security in numbers.

I set off and thought about calling Nancy and asking her if she would come over and help me unload. Or would she think that I was a bit of a wuss, unable to carry a dozen or so shopping bags in on my own.

It would be completely insane for Joe to attack me, right?

Everyone would instantly know who was responsible, right?

It would be utter madness, right?

But I firmly believed that Joe was indeed mad.

So should I call Nancy?

Was it better to be a safe wuss or a brave corpse? Or was I just being over-dramatic?

All of these thoughts were going through my head as I drove out of Banbury.

Hanwell was to the right-hand side of the Warwick road, going north, and, whereas it had once sat isolated in the middle of the countryside, the village was now almost a part of Banbury itself.

Ever since Amelia and I had first arrived here just five or so years ago, the building of a thousand new homes on the northern edge of the town had gathered apace and now just a solitary green field stood between the new housing estates and the old village. It was only a matter of time, and a very short period of time at that, before the whole place was swallowed up by the tide of red brick sweeping up from the south. It was something we all, as village folk, were doing our best to resist, but with about as much chance of success as King Canute.

The closer I got to home, the more nervous I became, so I decided that I would call Nancy after all.

I reached down for my phone in the car's central console at the same time as I was slowing down to turn right into the village.

Only then did I notice a pair of headlights coming up very fast behind me. It was sadly not an uncommon occurrence at this particular junction due to the speed de-restriction signs just a short distance before.

Stupid man, I thought, *can't he see that I'm indicating to turn right?*

Only at the very last moment did it register in my crowded

thinking that it wasn't stupidity that was causing the lights not to slow down. It was a deliberate act and I should get out of the way.

But I was too slow. Much too slow.

Before I even had a chance to engage a gear, the vehicle behind ploughed into the back of Amelia's car, shunting it forward fast across the road. The Fiat then hit the raised grass verge and took off.

My very last thought before the car hit the tree was that my neck had been broken before and it was about to happen again, and I really didn't want to be paralysed from the shoulders down.

PART TWO

June the following year –
eight months later

'How are you getting on?' asked Detective Sergeant Dowdeswell.

'Slowly,' I said. 'Rehab is a very lengthy and painful process.'

'But I see you're now walking,' he said.

There was no wheelchair.

'After a fashion, but only with the help of these damn things.' I indicated towards the pair of crutches that were leaning up against the wall to my side.

'They might be a help,' he said with a forced smile. 'You may get more sympathy from the jury, and we could certainly do with all the help we can get.'

'Why?' I said with concern. 'Don't you think we have a strong case?'

'I've seen much stronger cases than this fail before now. Most of what we have is only circumstantial. There's not a lot of meat on the bones. It will all depend on how the jury react to it in its totality.'

I was sitting on a blue metal seat in the witness services suite of the Oxford Combined Court building. It was the third day of Joseph Bradbury's trial and I had been summonsed to appear for the prosecution.

I thought back to all the things that had happened to me since I'd hit that tree in October.

There had been plenty of them.

27

My first sensation was an itch on the side of my nose.

I tried to move to scratch it but I couldn't. Something seemed to be preventing my hands from working properly.

I began to panic.

Where was I?

In hospital, I thought. I could tell from the smell.

I'd been in hospitals before, too often, due to racing falls.

So where had I been riding this time? And on which horse?

I couldn't remember. It seemed that it was not only my hands that weren't working properly, my brain wasn't either.

And the itch wouldn't go away.

No matter. Amelia would be in to see me soon and she could scratch it, as she always did.

I opened my eyes.

Definitely a hospital. I could see privacy-curtain rails hanging from the ceiling and square lights. The curtains were pulled round my bed. Why did I need privacy?

I tried to turn my head to look at my right hand but it wouldn't move either, and I realised that I was wearing a very tight surgical collar that was squeezing into my chin. *That wasn't a particularly good sign*, I thought.

It must have been a heavy fall.

A face came into view looking down at me. Female, but not Amelia.

The face turned away briefly.

'He's awake.'

The face turned back to me.

'We've been worried about you,' she said. 'Glad you're back with us after so long.'

I tried to reply but the collar wouldn't let me open my mouth, so the muffled gurgling sound that did emerge was completely unintelligible, even to me.

Another face appeared in my field of view. A male one, this time.

'Don't try to speak,' he said, not that I could anyway. 'Blink your eyes twice if you can understand me.'

I blinked twice and both the faces smiled broadly.

'That's a relief,' the male said to the female.

I was confused. Of course I could understand them. What did they think I was, foreign?

'You were in a car accident,' the man said. 'A bad one. Ten days ago now.'

Car accident? Ten days ago!

Somewhere deep in my head an alarm bell started ringing.

Accident? Car accident?

I knew there was something I should be remembering but, try as I might, I couldn't recall what.

I felt tired.

I closed my eyes again and went back to sleep.

When I woke the next time it was not just an itch on my nose that I was worried about; everything else now hurt.

'Ah, he's back with us,' said a voice from somewhere over my right shoulder. 'I thought he might be soon, now we've shut off his pain relief.'

Oh, thanks, I thought. *Turn the damn thing back on again.*

But I also realised that pain was a good thing. My arms hurt, and my legs too, so I wasn't paralysed. That was a huge relief.

But why did I think that I might be?

Another face appeared and I focused on it.

'Hello,' it said. 'I'm Mr Constance, one of the orthopaedic consultants. You're a lucky man – a very lucky man. We thought we'd lost you several times.'

I tried to ask where I was but again without any success.

'You just rest,' he said. 'I'll give you some more pain relief now that you're awake. Your whole system had quite a nasty shock from the accident. And we can't take the collar off just yet, or let you move, because your neck is totally unstable. You need another urgent operation on it.'

Another?

Did he mean after the one I'd had several years ago?

I suddenly realised I could remember that, and then all sorts of other things came flooding back in a rush, not least the awful realisation that Amelia wouldn't be coming in to scratch my nose.

Car accident?

But she hadn't died in a car accident.

I was still confused.

I did as the doctor had said – I rested, drifting in and out of sleep or unconsciousness – I wasn't sure which.

When I woke for the third time, I was in a different place. The lights in the ceiling above me were round, not square, and the sounds were different too, with beeping and bells going off regularly in the background.

And there was also a large tube fixed into my mouth. I could feel it with my tongue.

I looked up at the round lights and wondered what else had changed. I still couldn't move anything, but the collar round my neck was seemingly less tight.

My body might not be much improved but my mind definitely felt clearer.

'Hello,' said a voice.

I swung my eyes round to my right and they settled on the face of a nurse wearing blue scrubs. I tried to reply but without any success whatsoever, not even the internal gurgling of last time.

'I won't ask how you're feeling,' she said, 'because you can't answer. That's an endotracheal tube in your throat. You were intubated to put you on a ventilator during the operation, to assist your breathing. But it can probably come out now, since you're awake.'

That was encouraging.

So I'd had an operation. This must be the recovery ward.

After a while the nurse returned with another woman, this time in mauve scrubs, and, between them, they removed the tape around my mouth and then slid the tube out. As it passed my eyes, I was amazed how long it was. It seemed to go on forever and must have stretched all the way down into my lungs. No wonder I hadn't been able to talk.

Boy, that felt better.

'Take it easy at first,' said mauve scrubs. 'You might be a bit hoarse.'

Did she say that I was a bit of a horse? I almost laughed. Which bit?

Then I realised what she had really said and the amusement subsided. My brain obviously wasn't completely back to normal.

'Where am I?' I croaked.

'Oxford,' she said, smiling down at me. 'The JR.'

I looked quizzically at her.

'The John Radcliffe Hospital. You're in the intensive care unit.'

The John Radcliffe Hospital.

What was it I knew about the John Radcliffe Hospital in Oxford?

Then I remembered. But I wish I hadn't.

The John Radcliffe Hospital was where the Home Office pathologist had done the post-mortem on Amelia. Perhaps she was still here, lying in the mortuary. Maybe she was just down the corridor.

A wave of panic rose in my chest.

Oh, Amelia.

I could feel tears running down the sides of my head and into my ears.

'Are you in pain?' asked mauve scrubs with a concerned look on her face. 'Do you need something for it?'

Yes, I was in pain, but it was not the sort of pain that drugs could alleviate.

A new face came into view, one that I recognised.

'Hello again,' said Mr Constance, the orthopaedic surgeon. 'How are you doing? I have managed to stabilise your neck using two small metal plates. They should hold everything in place. Your spinal cord is intact but I don't know how much it's been affected by the bruising. You gave it quite a clout. It's now just a matter of time to see how you get on.' He smiled down at me. 'Just don't be having any more road accidents.'

'It wasn't an accident,' I croaked up at him. 'It was done on purpose. Someone tried to kill me.'

His smile disappeared and then, after a moment or two, so did the rest of him.

When he came back he had someone else with him, as if needing a witness.

'Now,' Mr Constance said seriously. 'Please say again what you said to me just now.'

'I said that it wasn't in an accident. Someone tried to kill me.'

And we all knew who that was, didn't we?

28

It's now just a matter of time to see how you get on, was what the orthopaedic man had said, and how I was getting on during the next couple of weeks was variable.

Some things had improved hugely while others remained frustratingly the same. At least physically.

I was moved out of intensive care and into a side room of a regular ward and, thanks to the electrically controlled hospital bed, I was able to sit up, which was a huge advance. It meant I could see more than just the ceiling. The cervical collar around my neck was also removed, which made talking much easier.

Doctors came and went, each of them seemingly testing something different. Neurologists came and poked and prodded me with needles and declared that, as I could feel them pricking me all down my legs and arms, there should be no reason why I couldn't also move them.

But I couldn't. All I could move was my eyes and my mouth, although I could also breathe on my own and swallow, but the nursing staff had to spoon-feed me, and also to deal with my other bodily functions, which was desperately humiliating.

Every moment of every day, I tried to move my arms and legs, God help me I tried, but nothing happened. It was as if I had been robbed, not of sensation, but of action.

And it made me hugely frustrated, and very angry.

More doctors came, and then some medical students too, as if I'd become something of a celebrity, or maybe it was just because I was a clinical oddity.

It was during one of these visits, when a member of the clinical teaching staff was talking about me in the third person to his students, as if I wasn't actually there in the room with him listening, that I noticed something extraordinary.

Movement. Down by my feet.

It must be a mouse, I thought, *caught under the sheet.*

There, it moved again.

'Excuse me,' I said loudly, interrupting the medical class. 'Can you please pull back the bedclothes?'

The teacher smiled broadly. 'Indeed I can. I was just about to do that anyway.'

He removed the sheet with a bit of a flourish as if he were revealing some great treasure.

There was no mouse.

The movement was caused by the big toe on my right foot waving back and forth like some demented digit with a life of its own. Except that I was making it happen and I could stop and start it at will.

If anything, the poor man looked rather disappointed, as if

his prized freak exhibit was now not so much of an anomaly after all.

I, meanwhile, had more tears streaming down my face.

Tears, on this occasion, of joy rather than of sorrow.

It was around this time that I had a visitor in the form of Detective Sergeant Dowdeswell.

'Hello,' he said, standing at the foot of my bed. 'How's it going?'

'Badly,' I replied.

He pulled up the chair and sat down next to me on my right-hand side.

'You'll have to sit at the end,' I said. 'I can't move my head to see you.'

'What, not at all?'

'Not at all. In fact the only thing I can move is one big toe.'

He shook his head. 'I knew you were bad but not that bad.'

He moved the chair until he was in my eyeline.

'You took your time,' I said.

'Not from lack of trying, I assure you,' he said. 'The medics wouldn't let us in. Seems you almost died. They placed you into an induced coma at the scene and it took them ten whole days to wake you up again. They were worried you had brain damage. I'm only allowed in here now because I've promised to be quick and not to upset you.'

'You not being here before now has upset me a lot more,' I said. 'You know that it wasn't an accident.'

'One of the doctors told me you'd said that.'

'But surely you knew that already.'

He looked rather sheepish.

'Traffic attended the scene and the assumption by them was that you had tried to take the corner too fast, skidded on some loose gravel, gone through the hedge and hit the tree beyond. Seems the car was a complete write-off, and that was even before the fire brigade had to cut it to pieces to get you out.'

'What about the other car?'

'There was no other car.'

'Yes there was. It struck me violently from behind and sent me flying towards the tree. I didn't go through the hedge, I went over it.'

He looked horrified.

'There was no other car there when you were found. But God knows how long it was before someone spotted the wreck.'

'When was that?'

'About eight o'clock on Thursday morning. Someone walking their dog saw the car over the hedge and then they noticed that there was a body still inside.'

'Thursday morning?' I said with incredulity. 'That means I'd been there all night.'

I received more horrified looks.

Overall, I was quite grateful that I couldn't remember anything after flying towards the tree.

As the doctor had said, I was a very lucky man.

'It also wasn't very helpful that Traffic didn't initially identify you.'

'Why not?'

'It seems that both the car's number plates, front and rear, had been shattered in the crash and were unreadable, so the officers on site used your mobile phone number to run a check. But those records indicated that the phone was registered to a man called Henry Jones from Coventry, so they had to contact West Midlands Police. Only when they tried to go there, did they find that the address didn't exist.'

It was my turn to be embarrassed. 'I'm afraid that was my fault. I gave a false name to the shop when I bought it.'

The sergeant looked at me in a highly disapproving manner. 'Only drug dealers do that.'

'I was fed up with you lot tracking my movements.'

He snorted.

'But, never mind all that,' I said, even though I did mind. 'Tell me about Joe Bradbury. Have you arrested him yet?'

At that point the senior ward nurse burst into the room.

'That's enough,' she said aggressively. 'Time for you to go now, officer. We can't have our patient getting over-tired.'

'No!' I shouted loudly back, with equal aggression. 'The sergeant stays right where he is. We're not finished.'

She stared at me and pursed her lips.

To totally bastardise the speech by the first Queen Elizabeth, I may have had the body of a weak and feeble invalid, but I had the heart and stomach of an Olympic athlete and there was no way I was going to let her send the detective away right now, just in case I became a little tired. And she could see it.

'Okay,' she said finally. 'You can have five more minutes.'

'Ten,' I said, but she ignored me and stormed out. The

old battleaxe clearly didn't much enjoy having her authority challenged.

'Go on,' I said to the DS. 'Have you arrested Joe?'

'Indeed we have.'

I sighed in huge relief.

'He was arrested two weeks ago on suspicion of theft from his mother and for conspiracy to defraud Her Majesty's Revenue and Customs.'

'Not for murder?'

'In their infinite wisdom, the CPS consider that we have insufficient evidence for a charge of murder.' He said it in a manner that made it obvious he thought the Crown Prosecution Service to be a bunch of idiots.

And I agreed with him.

'But at least his arrest has allowed us to have access to his phone and computer. We are processing the information they hold, so all is not lost.'

'Where's he being held?' I asked.

'He's not. He's out on bail.'

My heart skipped a beat.

'Bail?'

'Yes, he was charged and appeared before magistrates in Guildford. Sadly, they gave him bail, but that was to be expected for those charges.'

'Why Guildford?'

'It's close to where the offences were said to have occurred.'

'So it wasn't you who arrested him?'

'No. Surrey Police did that. But we have requested all his

phone and computer data from them. After all, it was us at Thames Valley that gave Surrey the lead in the first place.'

And Nancy and I had given it to them before that.

'You know he'll go straight to his mother and convince her that she agreed all along that he could have the money. You'll have no case.'

'Having no contact with his mother is part of the bail conditions. If he goes near her he'll end up in prison.'

'That will be very hard on her when she's dying of cancer.'

'She doesn't want to see him anyway.'

'Why ever not?' I asked.

'I've spent quite a long time with Mrs Mary Bradbury over the past three weeks. Nice old lady. I showed her some of the emails our man sent to your wife. To say she was horrified was an understatement. She couldn't believe how she'd been taken in by him for so long.'

'But are you sure it will stick?' I said. 'She probably won't remember anything about it by next week.'

'Don't be so certain. I found her much more lucid than I'd been expecting, especially after the last time I spoke to her over the carving knife incident. She even told me that she hasn't lost all her marbles, like everyone thinks she has. Seems this confusion thing is all a bit of an act she puts on to make her life easier. No one expects her to be able to make any important decisions, so she doesn't have to. Saves arguing with her son all the time, apparently. But she thinks he's gone too far this time.'

Well I never did. The devious old witch.

'She was particularly angry with him for stealing money

from her. She said she would happily have given him some cash if he'd asked her, so why did he have to go and take it without telling her?'

'Right, that really is enough now.' The battleaxe was back. 'Time for you to go.'

I could tell that defiance was not going to work this time.

'Come back and see me again,' I said to the detective. 'And make it soon.'

He stood up and turned to go.

'How about a police guard?' I asked to his back.

He turned round once more to face me. 'Why do you need one?'

'Because, with Joe Bradbury on the loose, I don't feel safe. That's why. He's now tried to kill me twice and I fear he'll try to do it again, and I can hardly fight back when I'm like this. At the moment, a five-year-old could bump me off in a heartbeat.'

'But what would he gain by it?'

The battleaxe started to tap her foot with impatience.

'Don't you ever learn anything?' I said. 'Joe Bradbury doesn't need a reason to try and do me harm. He simply thinks of me as his enemy, someone that needs to be destroyed.'

It was how I was beginning to think of him too.

The DS stared at me. 'I'll have a word with the DCI.'

'You do that,' I said. 'And also find that other car. Start with Joe's Nissan. Then you can add attempted murder to his charge sheet.'

29

The day after my visit from the detective sergeant, the big toe on my left foot started moving, and gradually, during the following week, most of my fingers began to obey my mental commands too, and then my ankles would flex when I asked them to.

My whole body started to feel human again, rather than just a disconnected brain, uselessly attached to an inert lump of meat.

And the improvement seemed to please the neurologists and also Mr Constance, the surgeon.

'Now that your neck is orthopaedically stable, and the operation site has healed well, I think it's time we moved you on,' he announced. 'You need to go to a specialist rehabilitation centre rather than staying here in hospital. The physiotherapy there is more intensive and they will try and get you back walking again. I'll arrange it.'

I suppose it was the obvious next step but part of me wanted to stay right here at the John Radcliffe. Stupid as it sounded, I found some comfort in being in the same building, or at least on the same site, as Amelia.

Even though it had now been more than a month since her death, there had still been no mention by anyone of a funeral. I was in no fit state to organise anything, so I just went with the flow and kept quiet. But it was a bridge that would have to be crossed at some stage, although bridge was hardly the right word – minefield, more like.

Mr Constance returned to say that it was all sorted and I would be transferred by ambulance the following Monday.

'Where to?' I asked.

'The National Spinal Injuries Centre,' he said. 'At Stoke Mandeville Hospital in Aylesbury.'

'But isn't that for disabled people?'

He laughed, even though I thought it particularly insensitive under the circumstances.

'So what do you think you are?' he said, still chuckling.

He could see that I wasn't joining in with his mirth.

'Look,' he said more seriously. 'The problems you are currently experiencing are due to the trauma your spinal cord received in the accident.'

'It wasn't an accident,' I said, interrupting him.

'Okay,' he said. 'In the incident, then. The nerves in your neck were heavily bruised and we know from experience that bruised nerves often stop working. In your case, it was specifically the motor nerves that shut down. Thankfully, they are slowly beginning to work again, but there are no guarantees that they will ever return to normal function.'

He didn't pull his punches. He gave it to me straight.

'Some patients in your situation regain full use and sensation, but there are others who are confined to a wheelchair for the rest of their lives.'

'Oh.'

'The spinal injuries centre will give you the best chance. Yes, they have specialist therapies to treat people whose cords have been totally snapped, but they also deal with people like you. If anyone can get you back on your feet, they can.'

'Right, then,' I said more positively. 'The sooner I get there the better.'

Over my last weekend at the JR, I had three visitors.

The first two, on the Saturday afternoon, were Nancy and Dave Fadeley.

'How are you doing?' Nancy asked, again nervously fiddling with her ever-present pearl necklace. 'We would have come before but the hospital . . .'

'It's okay,' I said. 'I'm only just well enough to have visitors, and it's so lovely to see you both.'

I smiled, and she relaxed a bit and smiled back.

By now I could move my head a little from side to side, which was just as well as Dave and Nancy sat down on chairs placed on either side of the bed.

'How are things in Hanwell?' I asked.

'Much the same,' Dave replied. 'We've been over to your place a couple of times. We used the key you gave us.'

They had been keyholders for the alarm company since we first arrived.

'I threw away some stuff from the fridge,' Nancy said. 'It had gone off.'

'Thank you. Was everything else okay?'

'I turned off the hot water and put the heating right down,' Dave said. 'But everything seemed fine.'

No sign of Joe Bradbury, I assumed.

'It was Mark Thornton who found you. It's been the talk of the pub.'

Mark Thornton, the local publican. After the way he'd spoken to me when I'd collected my car from his car park, I suppose I should be grateful that he'd called the emergency services at all. Perhaps he hadn't realised it was me, or maybe he'd thought I was already dead.

We chatted on for a while about a number of mundane things, such as the weather, until I sensed a slight unease in them.

'Have you heard from the police at all?' I asked, thinking that must be reason.

'Not a dicky,' Dave said.

So it was not that.

I then wondered if their unease was just that of the hospital visitor who wants to leave but doesn't know quite how to say so to the patient.

'I'm sorry.' I forced a yawn. 'I'm getting quite tired.'

'Yes,' said Nancy, her unease disappearing in an instant. 'Sorry. We've just been prattling on without thinking. Come on, Dave. It's time to go.'

They both stood up just a tad too eagerly.

'We'll come again.'

'I'm moving on Monday,' I said. 'To Stoke Mandeville.'

'Oh, right. Then we'll come and see you there.'

'I'll call you,' I said, and we left it at that.

Everybody happy.

My third visitor came on Sunday morning.

The return of movement to my feet had been accompanied by a feeling of intense pins and needles in my soles, something that was quite painful. And it had been particularly bad during Saturday night and hence I had slept rather badly.

So, on Sunday morning, I was snoozing quite a lot.

I woke from one such doze to find Mary Bradbury sitting at the side of my bed. She looked concerned, with deep furrows across her brow.

'Bad, is it?' she asked.

'Only when I think about it.' Which was all the time.

'I needed to come and see you,' Mary said. 'Before I can't.'

She did look much more frail than when I'd seen her only a few weeks before, and her skin was noticeably more yellow. Her cheeks had also sunken in somewhat and her face had a pronounced skull-like appearance. There was not much doubt that the cancer within was taking its dreadful toll on her body.

'I need to talk,' she said, and tears welled up in her deep-set eyes.

'It's okay, Mary,' I said. 'Don't worry.'

'It's not okay,' she said, the tears now openly flowing. 'And I do worry. I accused you of killing her. I now know that wasn't true. And I am so very, very sorry.'

'Mary, my dear, forget it. Everyone else was accusing me as well. I promise, you have nothing to be sorry about.'

'Yes, I do,' she said. 'And it wasn't just that.'

She paused as if plucking up the courage to go on.

'I had no idea that Joseph was being so horrid to you and to my dear Amelia. That nice policeman showed me his dreadful emails.' She cried some more. 'Why didn't Amelia tell me?'

She had tried, often, but Mary hadn't wanted to know – and she certainly hadn't wanted to believe. Not least because, all the time, Joe had been whispering in her ear that Amelia was mad and untrustworthy.

But I didn't say that.

'Maybe she hadn't wanted to distress you.'

But she was distressed now, and seemingly the more so because it was now too late to tell Amelia how sorry she was.

'I so wish she was still here so I could speak to her,' Mary said, the tears still flowing.

So did I. It would have done so much good for her mental health.

'That is all Joe's doing,' I said, twisting the knife in Mary's heart. 'He is the reason Amelia isn't here.'

She nodded, as if aware of the fact.

'Will the police be able to prove that?'

'I hope so,' I said.

She nodded again. 'I won't see it, though,' she said miserably. 'I've not got long now.' She suddenly smiled. 'But I'll be able to put things right with Amelia on the other side.'

'Maybe,' I agreed, even though I didn't really believe in all that. But if the thought gave Mary some comfort, then I would not be the one to mock it.

As DS Dowdeswell had told me, the old dear seemed more alert and more mentally perceptive than in the past, and I so wished that Amelia had known that too.

'I must go now,' she said. 'Fred and Jill, my neighbours, they brought me here. They're waiting outside.'

'Thank you so much for coming.' It had obviously been quite an effort.

She managed another smile. 'You take care, my dear.'

I watched her go in the sure knowledge that it would be the last time I would see her, and my eyes filled with tears too.

But I was wrong.

No sooner had she disappeared from my sight through the door, than she was suddenly back again.

'One more thing,' she said. 'I've changed my will. You will now receive Amelia's half of my estate, and Joseph's half goes directly to his children.'

Did I detect a slight degree of amusement in her voice?

'It'll serve him right.'

30

Three weeks after my arrival at the National Spinal Injuries Centre, I took my first steps, albeit between parallel bars for support and with lots of help from the team of physiotherapists.

My housemaster at school had been very fond of using the expression *There's no such word as can't*, whenever one of his charges had moaned, 'I can't do it, sir.'

Here in the rehabilitation gym at Stoke Mandeville, that expression should have been inscribed on the walls in huge flashing letters.

And what the patients could do was remarkable.

Wheelchairs, rather than being simply the inanimate objects that most of us see, take on a personality of their own in the hands of men and women so badly damaged that half their bodies have no use whatsoever, other than to be an encumbrance.

But that didn't mean that these remarkable people would not participate to the full in love, in life and, especially, in sport.

The precursor to the Paralympic Games was first held at Stoke Mandeville way back in 1948, on the very day that the Olympic Games were declared open in London by King George VI.

In those first Stoke Mandeville Games, there was just one event in one sport, archery, and a mere sixteen competitors took part, all of them from the United Kingdom.

By 2016 the games had grown somewhat such that, in Rio de Janeiro, nearly four and a half thousand athletes from a hundred and sixty countries competed in twenty-two Paralympic sports, still including archery, winning 528 gold medals and setting 220 world records.

And most of the patients at Stoke Mandeville had seemingly set their sights on being on the next Paralympic flight to Tokyo, or the one after that to Paris, or after that to Los Angeles.

The level of determination to make the best of life's bad deal was inspirational, to put it mildly, and it was as much the encouragement from the other patients as that from the staff that made things happen.

'Come on, Bill,' shouted Robin, a fellow patient who couldn't even sit upright without being strapped to a high-backed wheel-chair, and who was unable to breathe without the aid of a ventilator that rhythmically pushed and pulled his chest in and out. 'You can do it.'

It had taken all his strength to shout like that, and all his breath, and I wasn't about to let him down, now was I?

Walking was simple, right?

Even tiny kids could do it, right?

Just put one foot in front of the other, and then repeat.

I took five of the smallest steps ever, and I was totally exhausted.

I sat back down heavily into the wheelchair that one of the staff had been pushing behind me.

'Good job,' shouted Robin, and then, when the contraption he was wearing gave him another breath, 'Way to go, Bill.'

And so my life progressed, one tiny step at a time, each one feeling like a gold-medal winning achievement.

By the end of the fourth week, I could walk along the total length of the bars, albeit in a manner that made Hopalong Cassidy look more like a marching guardsman.

And it was after another particularly lengthy stint in the gym that DS Dowdeswell came to see me again.

'We got him,' he said, echoing the words that Barack Obama had used when he was informed that a US Special Forces soldier had shot and killed Osama bin Laden.

'Who?' I asked, my mind clearly not working properly after such a strenuous session.

'Who do you think? Joe Bradbury.'

'How?' I asked.

'Cell-site evidence.'

'What's that?'

'Evidence from his mobile phone,' the detective said with a laugh. 'It's always their mobile phones that give them away. They can't resist taking the damn things with them wherever they go as if they're a part of their own bodies. Criminals are so stupid. It's almost as if they want to get caught.'

And the clever ones never are, I thought.

'Anyway, like you said to, we examined Bradbury's black Nissan, but there was no damage on it, not even a scratch.'

'It could have been fixed. It's been long enough.'

He shook his head. 'We can always tell. There are minor changes to the paintwork of the repaired bit compared to the rest. He would have had to have the whole vehicle resprayed and, even then, there would still be telltale signs in the door recesses and also in the boot and the engine compartments. No, we were certain the Nissan was not the car that hit yours.'

I sat silently in the wheelchair and waited for him to go on.

'But,' he said, 'we did a check on his phone and, sure enough, it showed that he'd been in Banbury around four o'clock on the day of your accident.'

'It was not an accident.'

'Yeah, that's right – your non-accident. We get so used to describing every road-traffic collision as an accident. Difficult to forget sometimes.' He paused. 'Anyway, the cell-site records show that his phone was switched off for most of the afternoon but he did turn it on for a while when he was in Banbury to make a call to his office. Maybe he forgot, but the phone wasn't switched off again until later, and it was still on when automatically passed from a mast in Banbury to one close to Hanwell village at twenty-six minutes past five.'

'The exact time I was on my way home from Waitrose.'

'Exactly. So if he wasn't driving his Nissan, what was he driving?'

'Could have been a tank if the force of the impact was anything to go by.'

'Anyway,' the DS said, ignoring my flippancy. 'Next we checked if his wife had a car, but she doesn't. So what other vehicles did he have access to? And, sure enough, the first thing we tried came up trumps.'

'Which was?' I asked eagerly.

'I remembered him saying in the Coroner's Court in Oxford that he was an officer of the High Court. And, if I recall correctly, he was rather pompous about it.'

No kidding. Ever since I'd first met him, Joe had used that phrase to anyone who'd listen, always using the same patronising, self-righteous air, as if it somehow gave him greater importance.

'So I contacted the High Court,' said the DS. 'And they told me that, yes indeed, they did have someone called Joseph Bradbury registered on their books as an enforcement officer, although his registration was currently suspended because he's been arrested for fraud.'

'So it's definitely him, then.'

'No doubt about it. But he hadn't been either arrested or suspended on the day of your acc— . . . incident. He's attached to one of the west London firms that deals mostly in private rent arrears. We've checked the firm's records and, guess what, he signed out one of their vans on that particular Wednesday. Not that that in itself is incriminating. He signed out a van on most days in order to do his job, which was to enforce High Court writs. Enforcement officers have the power to seize goods from debtors up to the value of the outstanding debts, so he would need a van to transport them.'

He paused and I nodded for him to go on.

'Well,' he said. 'It transpires that the van that Joe had that day was involved in an altercation at one of his jobs. At least, that's what he claimed. He told his office that someone drove straight into the front of it while he was waiting outside some premises for the occupier to return. Apparently, it's not that unusual for their vehicles to be attacked. Seems some of the debtors can turn really nasty.'

I wasn't surprised.

When you have absolutely nothing with which to pay your rent, it must be devastating when some heartless court official arrives in a van to take away the few possessions that you actually do own. It explained why Joe Bradbury's demeanour was so hard. Over the years, he must have developed a skin as thick as a rhinoceros against the pleading of those in desperate need.

Maybe smashing up the debt-collector's vehicle made them feel a little better, even if it got them into deeper water, and greater debt, in the long run.

'The van in question has now been fully repaired and is back in service. It went straight to the body shop so there's no chance of any forensics. But . . .' He smiled. 'There were ANPR records showing that, rather than being in Ealing as Joe Bradbury had claimed, the van made a journey down the M40, leaving the motorway at junction eleven.'

'For Banbury,' I said.

'Indeed. And, what's more, forensic examination of what was left of your vehicle has shown that there are traces of white paint on the back end with a chemical composition consistent with that used on Ford Transit vans of the identical type.'

285

'My goodness,' I said to the detective. 'You have been a busy bee.'

He smiled again. 'And, after they'd seen what we had, it took the geniuses at the CPS less than five minutes to agree that he should be charged with attempted murder.'

I thought for a moment.

'Did you say there were traces of *white* paint on the Fiat?' I asked.

'Yes, the van was white.'

I remembered back to when I'd driven away from the Old Forge on that Wednesday afternoon. I'd been looking only for Joe's black Nissan but I could recall seeing what I had assumed at the time was one of the many white courier vans that regularly delivered to houses in the village.

I now realised that it must have been Joe, watching and waiting for his chance.

'But it seems incredible to me that he was able to drive that van at all after hitting the Fiat. You'd think it would have been too badly damaged.'

'Robust things, Transit vans. Especially the long-wheelbase versions as in this case. Much stronger and much heavier than a tiny Fiat 500 runabout. But we did have difficulty in tracking it back to London. I wonder if the front number plate was too badly damaged to be read by the automatic camera system, or maybe it was missing altogether. He should have thought of ANPR beforehand and taken the plates off, or replaced them with ones nicked off another vehicle.' He smiled at me once more. 'I'd make a much better villain than most of them.'

'So where is Joe Bradbury now?'

'He's still out on bail.'

I looked at him incredulously. 'But—'

The DS held up his hand to stop me.

'Bradbury doesn't know anything about all of this yet. He's due to return to court in Guildford tomorrow morning to answer his bail on the theft and fraud charges. He'll be expecting to have his bail renewed and a trial date set. But little does he realise that I'll be there waiting there for him, ready to arrest him again, this time for attempted murder.'

'How about also arresting him for murdering Amelia?' I said.

'I'm still working on that.'

31

Mary Bradbury died exactly three months to the day after her daughter. So the doctors had been spot on with their prediction.

It happened four days before I was discharged from the spinal-injury centre, but I didn't find out until after I arrived home and opened a letter from Mary's local Chipping Norton solicitor. It informed me of her death and that, not only was I one of the beneficiaries of Mary's estate, she had also named me in her will as her sole executor.

Joe won't like this, I thought, and I was dead right.

Further on in the same letter, the solicitor advised me that he was aware that Mrs Bradbury's son had already lodged a challenge to his mother's will, claiming she had been bullied into signing it, but, subject to the outcome of the challenge, my appointment as executor would continue for the time being, and what would I like to do about organising her funeral? He hoped that I wouldn't object that he had taken it upon himself to arrange for her body to be removed from her home by a firm of undertakers, as he wasn't sure of my whereabouts.

He finished by offering himself as the solicitor I should appoint to obtain a grant of probate, together with a breakdown of the fees he would charge for such a service.

I sat in my wheelchair in the hall of the Old Forge reading and rereading the letter, and all I could feel was deep sorrow.

Poor Mary.

Her last few months on this earth had been pretty dreadful. Not only had she had to deal with a cancer that had eaten away her body from the inside, but her only daughter had been murdered and her only son was now on remand in prison accused of having done it.

Detective Sergeant Dowdeswell had been back to see me at Stoke Mandeville with the news that the CPS had finally agreed to charge Joe Bradbury with Amelia's murder.

'What's the reason for their change of heart?' I'd asked.

'New evidence.'

'Do tell.'

'We could find no trace in either his or your wife's phone records of any call made by her to him on the Tuesday evening. We checked all his numbers – work, home and mobile – against all of hers. Nothing.'

'I told you there was no way Amelia would have called him.'

'And the location devices on both mobiles showed they didn't move the whole evening. Joe Bradbury is still maintaining that he received a call from his sister and that was the sole reason he went to your house on Wednesday morning.'

'He's lying.'

'There's something else as well. The ANPR records for the M40, plus some CCTV footage we have obtained from a petrol station near the motorway junction, indicate beyond any doubt whatsoever that Joseph Bradbury and his black Nissan were in Banbury by eight-twenty on the morning of the murder. Yet he didn't call the police emergency line to report his sister's death until ten-seventeen. Almost two whole hours later. Now why was that?'

Why, indeed.

'Have you asked him?'

'Yes, I have. I went to arrest him at Bullingdon Prison where he was already being held on remand for your attempted murder. And, with a new arrest, we had another opportunity to question him.'

'And?'

'He said that he had agreed to meet your wife at nine o'clock but she didn't turn up. The traffic had been lighter than he'd expected, so he was early, but he claims that he waited for her at the chosen rendezvous point for an hour before deciding to drive to your house.'

'And where was this mysterious rendezvous point supposed to have been?'

'At a disused pub car park in Wroxton.'

'The Hare and Hounds?'

'That's the one. The pub's all boarded up now.'

'But why there?'

'I've no idea,' the DS had said. 'But that's what he told us.'

Amelia and I had enjoyed going to the Hare and Hounds in Wroxton, when it was open. The food had been very good and, in happier times, it had been where we had occasionally met Joe and his family for lunch on a Saturday. It had a nice garden with swings for their young girls to play on. But that had been back in the days when we had all been talking, rather than how things were now.

I'd sighed. Nothing ever stays the same.

'Can Joe prove that he waited there for an hour? And, if Amelia was meant to turn up and didn't, why didn't he phone her?'

'There's no CCTV footage to prove either way if he was there or not and, because it's in a dip, there's no phone signal at that particular spot.'

That had been one of the reasons Amelia and I had loved the place so much. We couldn't be interrupted by the continuous ringing of phones, both ours and other peoples.

'He could have always driven up the hill to make a call. There's plenty of signal there.'

'He claims that he didn't want to leave the car park, even for a few minutes, in case he missed Amelia.'

'It all sounds a bit convenient to me,' I'd said. 'Joe knew the place, and also that it didn't have any phone signal, so I think he's just made it up about waiting there for an hour while he was, in fact, at my house killing my wife.'

'As do the big brains at the CPS. That's why they've sanctioned a charge of murder against him.'

I read the letter from Mary Bradbury's solicitor one more time.

What did I want to do about her funeral?

It didn't seem quite right, somehow, that it was my decision, but Joe wasn't exactly in a position to do much about it, and his wife was as far away in family terms as I was – an in-law – and it had been Amelia and I who had done most for Mary when she'd been alive, so why shouldn't I perform the necessary final duties after she was gone?

I rang the solicitor, a Mr James Fairbrother, MA (Oxon), TEP, according to the letterhead.

'Oh, yes, um,' he said hesitantly. 'Mr Gordon-Russell. Thank you for calling.'

'Please call me Mr Russell,' I said. 'Or even, just Bill.'

'Oh, yes, right. Okay then . . . Bill.'

'Shall I call you James?' I asked.

'Oh, yes.' There was a very small nervous chuckle. 'James. Or Jim. I answer to both.'

'Okay then, James,' I said. 'I have received your letter concerning Mrs Mary Bradbury, my mother-in-law.'

'Oh, yes, well, thank you. Yes. Such a dear old lady. So sad, so sad.'

I feared that this telephone conversation was going to be a bit sad too.

'In your letter, you state that she has made me her sole executor.'

'Oh, yes, well, that's true. But . . .' He stopped.

This was getting painful.

'I understand that Mr Joseph Bradbury is challenging the will,' I said, prompting what I thought he was about to say.

'Oh, yes, well, I understand he's trying to. But he won't succeed.'

'Are you sure?'

'Oh, yes,' he said. 'Quite sure. Mrs Bradbury's last will and testament was properly made and executed. I was present myself at the signing and there were several independent witnesses.'

'I ought to warn you that Joseph Bradbury can be quite determined.'

'Oh, yes, well, I know. Mrs Bradbury told me. But so was she. That's why she insisted on having everything explained to her not just by one solicitor – that was me.' He laughed nervously again. 'But also by the head of my firm. Very adamant, she was.'

'Who were the witnesses?' I asked.

'Oh, yes, well. The witnesses.' I could hear papers being shuffled. 'A Mr Frederick Marchant and a Mrs Jillian Marchant. I believe they were her neighbours.'

Yes, I thought. *The ones who had taken her to Oxford on the day she'd come to see me at the John Radcliffe.*

'They are the ones who signed the document as the two legally required witnesses. But there were others present too. I was there, as was Mr Kaplan, he's the head of our firm. Plus there was also Mrs Bradbury's doctor.'

'Her doctor? What was he there for?'

'Oh, yes, well. After we'd arrived at her house, when we were all having tea in her sitting room, Mary asked her doctor to perform some cognitive assessment tests on her.'

'Cognitive assessment tests?'

'Oh, yes, well, to satisfy the golden rule.'

293

'The golden rule?' I asked.

'Oh, yes, well, one always has to satisfy the golden rule. It states that "the making of a will by an aged or seriously ill testator ought to be witnessed or approved by a medical practitioner who has satisfied himself of the capacity and understanding of the testator, and records and preserves his examination or findings". So the cognitive tests proved that Mary had full testamentary capacity at the time of the signing, in accordance with sections one to four of the Mental Capacity Act 2005. She also insisted on telling us all, several times, that she knew what she was doing, that her decision to sign was being taken freely of her own volition, that she was not being coerced, nor signing against her own free will. She then made us all write witness notes to that effect, which I have kept on file. Finally the executed will was lodged at the Probate Department Registry of the Family Division at the Royal Courts of Justice.'

The canny old bird. She had known that Joe would challenge her will so she had done her best to prevent him succeeding – and it was the full belt-and-braces job by the sound of it.

'She seems to have covered everything,' I said.

'Oh, yes, well, I hope so. But Mr Bradbury could always still apply to the courts and make a claim against the estate under the Inheritance (Provision for Family and Dependants) Act 1975 on the grounds that he is in need of funds to provide for his wellbeing but, from what I know of his previous conduct, I think such a claim is also unlikely to succeed.'

'His previous conduct?'

'Oh, yes, well, the Inheritance Act 1975 does allow for the

court to consider any conduct of the claimant which the court may consider relevant. In 2014, during the case of *Wright v. Waters*, the High Court of England and Wales had ruled that the treatment by a daughter of her late mother had been so deplorable that it outweighed all the other compelling factors in her favour, including the fact that the daughter was in poor health, confined to a wheelchair, and in financial difficulties.' James paused and took breath. 'I believe that, in this case, the High Court would similarly decide that Joseph Bradbury's despicable conduct, having allegedly stolen a hundred thousand pounds from his mother during the sale of her house, outweighs all other factors.'

How delicious, I thought. Joe was set to be undone by a ruling from his own beloved High Court.

'Hence,' James laughed nervously once more, 'I am quite certain Mr Bradbury's challenge will fail on every count.'

'How on earth did Mary think all that up?' I asked. 'You know, the second solicitor, the doctor tests, the golden rule, the Mental Capacity Act, the Royal Courts of Justice thing and all that other legal stuff.'

He laughed again. This time without the nervousness. It was as if he was quite enjoying himself.

'Oh, yes, well,' he said. 'That may all have been at my suggestion after she explained what she was going to do. We agreed that we should apply the three tests from the judgement in the case of *Banks v. Goodfellow* way back in 1870. The tests may be a hundred and fifty years old but the High Court ruled only last year that they are still relevant. First, the testator must understand the nature of the will and its effect. Second, the testator must have an understanding of the extent and value of her property, and third, the testator must be aware of the persons for whom she would usually be expected to provide, even if she chose not to, and must be free from any delusion of the mind that would cause her reason not to benefit those people.'

Now I laughed. So it was *he* who was the canny old bird.

'So what does the TEP stand for?' I asked.

'Eh?'

'TEP. The letters after your name on your letterhead.'

'Oh, yes, well,' he said. 'It means that I'm qualified as a Trust and Estate Practitioner, so I specialise in wills and probate.'

Oh, yes, well, more like a Totally Extraordinary Person, if you asked me.

I agreed that, yes indeed, I very much did want to appoint him to assist me in obtaining probate of Mary's estate, and I also said that I'd get back to him about her funeral.

'Oh, yes, well, the undertakers are rather waiting on your instructions.'

He gave me their details.

'I'll call them.'

'Oh, yes, well, good idea.'

32

I bowed my head as a simple oak coffin was carried past me. Then I repeated the process as a second identical coffin followed it.

I had applied to the Oxford Coroner for permission to have Amelia's body returned to me and, having consulted both the CPS and Joe Bradbury's defence team, he had agreed.

So here I was, living a nightmare, sitting in a wheelchair inside Hanwell village church for the double funeral of both my wife and my mother-in-law.

Mother and daughter together, and with no Joe here to come between them this time.

I had asked DS Dowdeswell if it were possible to prevent Joe from attending from prison and he had readily agreed to ensure it, citing the likelihood of a public disturbance as the official reason. And it was quite possibly a true one too.

I could clearly remember back to the day I had collected my car from the local pub car park, when Mark Thornton had told me that Amelia had been very popular in the village and that feelings were running high. At the time, their anger had been directed squarely at me as the prime suspect but now, with Joe Bradbury awaiting trial for her murder, the ire of the locals was thankfully aimed at him.

Not that many of the village folk had been round to apologise for jumping so quickly to the wrong conclusion. In fact, only Nancy and Dave of my neighbours had been to see me during the twelve long lonely days since I'd arrived home from Stoke Mandeville, and I was not sure how I would have coped without them.

I had found that living in hospital for an extended period, with its strict daily regime, was a perfect way of shutting out the real world, and the agonies that came with it.

Wake, wash, dress, eat breakfast, go to the gym for physiotherapy, have lunch, return to the gym for walking practice, have tea, watch TV, hot milk drink, undress, go to bed, sleep – every day the same. It numbed the mind. Even Christmas had come and gone without any noticeable change other than the physiotherapy stopped because the staff were off work enjoying themselves.

But I'd gone to the gym anyway, on my own.

Routine was, well . . . routine. And comforting.

Douglas had been down from London a few times to see me, and my parents had even made the long journey across the international border from Wrexham to Aylesbury but, overall, my mental life had stood still for the seven weeks I was there.

Fortunately, my physical side improved gradually such that,

by the time I was discharged, I could walk a short distance with only the aid of crutches, and even climb a step or two before my legs began to shake uncontrollably and I had to sit down again. But it was enough, and I had finally convinced the doctors I was well enough to go home.

Coming back to my empty house in the dead of winter, however, had been much harder than I had imagined, both physically and mentally.

It was the human-to-human interaction, both with the staff and with the other patients, that I missed the most. For weeks, I had done my utmost to get myself out of hospital and now all I wanted to do was to go back in.

I also found that I had to do for myself all the things that had previously been done for me. Simple tasks like turning on lights or drawing the curtains required a huge effort, not to mention the much more complicated pursuits of washing my clothes and preparing my own food.

The supply of microwaveable frozen ready meals, which I'd so carefully selected at Waitrose on my big food-shopping trip, had disappeared on the back of the recovery truck along with Amelia's broken and dismembered Fiat 500.

Hence the cupboards were still almost bare.

And, of course, to top it all, there was always the problem of the stairs.

I had lied to the doctors, telling them I lived in a bungalow, just to ensure they would let me go. But now the reality of the undertaking faced me. Not just a single tread or two as I had been practising on, but a whole flight of them, twelve in all.

They might as have well been the north face of the Eiger.

On my first two nights back in the house, I had addressed all of these difficulties by simply sitting hungrily in the dark, and then sleeping fully dressed on the sofa in the sitting room with the curtains wide open.

Thank goodness for remote-controlled television sets. As far as I was concerned, the inventor should have been awarded a Nobel Prize.

But then, on the third morning back, Dave and Nancy had come to my rescue.

Nancy had fed me while Dave had carried one of the twin beds down from the guest room and set it up in my study.

'Only a temporary measure, mind,' he'd said. 'We want you up those stairs in no time.'

I had smiled at him and almost cried at their kindness.

But, all the while, and in spite of Dave and Nancy's best efforts, the greatest agony was the loneliness and the unspeakable hole that remained in my heart.

Even after more than three months, I found myself bursting into tears for the smallest of reasons, maybe catching a glimpse of the photo of Amelia pinned to the noticeboard in the kitchen, or coming across a lip salve, hidden between the seat cushions on the sofa.

Both were more than enough to turn on the taps and leave me sobbing.

The church was packed, with even the standing room at the back overflowing out through the doors into the graveyard.

My parents, together with my brother Edward and his wife Stella, had made the journey from Wales, and Douglas had come down from London.

DS Dowdeswell and DCI Priestly were both present, representing Thames Valley Police in their dress blue uniforms, as were Fred and Jill Marchant, Mary's current neighbours, and Gladys and Jim Wilson, her former ones from Weybridge.

Jack Westcott, our GP and the doctor from Warwick Racecourse, was also there with his wife. As was Simon Bassett from Underwood, Duffin and Wimbourne of Chancery Lane.

And, in death as they had done so in life, the village people of Hanwell did Amelia proud, gathering together in great numbers to bid her farewell.

Even, oh, yes, well, solicitor James Fairbrother, MA (Oxon), TEP, had turned up to pay his respects to his 'dear old lady'.

For me, however, it felt like I existed in my own little bubble of solitude and isolation, an unreality that I found difficult to comprehend.

But it was all too real.

Three days earlier I had finally been taken by a police family-liaison officer to the John Radcliffe Hospital mortuary to say goodbye to my wife. It was a dreadful experience and, once again, I should have taken Douglas's advice to stay away.

'Remember her as she was,' he had told me. 'Not as she is now.'

But it was something I had needed to do, if only to prove to myself that it really was her and that she was gone for good.

More than three months in a deep freeze had done its worst but the body presented to me under a white sheet on a trolley in the mortuary chapel was undeniably that of Amelia Jane Gordon-Russell.

But, somehow, it wasn't her – it was just a shell of her.

My vibrant, funny and beautiful wife, full of life and love, had departed long ago, and it was as close as I'd ever come to believing that the souls of the dead go elsewhere.

I had taken her favourite dress with me to the hospital so that she could be buried in it and that was all I could now think of as I sat staring at the right-hand of the two coffins positioned side by side below the altar.

I only half-heard the service although everyone told me afterwards that it was very moving.

Douglas read a eulogy on my behalf.

I had written it the previous afternoon but I had bottled out of delivering it as I wouldn't have been able to do so without breaking down, and that would have displayed my raw emotions for everyone to see.

'No one will mind a few tears,' Douglas had said, but even he could see that it would be too much for me to bear.

As it was, even he cried through the whole thing and maybe I was the only person in the church at that moment with dry eyes. I had done all my weeping as I'd written it, huge splashes of tears on the paper making the words so unclear that Douglas had had to copy the whole thing out again so he could read it.

After forty minutes the sad little procession was reversed, with Mary carried out first and Amelia following, both coffins placed in the waiting hearses ready for the short trip to their final resting place.

Long gone were the days when most village churchyards had the space available for modern burials.

And, anyway, the two women had lived in different parishes. The solution had been to arrange for them to lie side by side in a single grave in the cemetery at Hardwick Hill on the edge of Banbury.

Douglas pushed my wheelchair outside and I sat by the church door as all the mourners filed past in front of me, each one shaking my hand and expressing their condolences.

It was another ordeal I could have done without, but it was also another that had to be done.

How was it, I wondered, that convention and tradition forced a bereaved and broken-hearted husband to suffer the mental trauma of a public funeral of his recently departed lover, at the very moment when he was least able to cope with it?

Mark Thornton came up and stood in front of me. He tentatively held out his hand towards me. I reached out and shook it. He nodded at me twice, before turning away. No words were necessary. We had both understood the significance of that moment.

Mark had arranged that, while the immediate family went away to the cemetery for the burials, everyone else would go along the road to his pub for refreshments, all at his own expense.

Maybe that was the price of a guilty conscience.

At least Joseph Bradbury hadn't been in the line but, at the very end, when I had thought that the church must be empty, his wife Rachael appeared. It was as if she had been hiding at the back and plucking up the courage to show herself.

'Hello, Rachael,' I said.

'I wish you were dead too,' she said acidly by way of a greeting.

'If all you were going to do was to be unpleasant,' I replied, 'why did you bother to come?'

'To tell you that Joe didn't kill Amelia.'

'How do you know?' I said. 'Were you there?'

'No, of course not,' she said. 'But I still know he didn't kill her. He wouldn't have.'

The ever-loyal wife, I thought. Still believing in her husband's innocence in the face of overwhelming evidence. Like Primrose, wife of Harold Shipman, the UK's most prolific serial killer, who persistently refused to believe that her husband had done anything wrong, and even offered chocolates to the families of his victims during breaks in his trial at Preston Crown Court.

'And do you also deny that Joe tried to kill me?' I asked Rachael.

'Of course,' she said. 'You just had a car accident.'

'And stealing a hundred thousand pounds from his own mother? Was that an accident as well?'

'She didn't need it while we did. Stupid old bag was loaded.'

I stared at Rachael and wondered if it had been she who had actually thought up that particular venture.

'Go home,' I said to her. 'Before someone finds out that you are married to Joe. Your husband is not very popular hereabouts and I'd hate it to be taken out on you.'

If she thought I was threatening her, she'd be right.

And, as if to reinforce my threat, the two Thames Valley policemen came walking over towards me. Seeing them coming,

Rachael scuttled away past the waiting hearses and out of sight along the road. I couldn't imagine why she had come in the first place.

'How's it going?' asked the chief inspector, shaking my hand.

'You mean apart from being at the funeral of my wife and her mother?'

If he'd expected me to make things easy for him, he was much mistaken.

'I'm so sorry,' he said, looking appropriately contrite.

If anything, his sidekick appeared slightly amused by the exchange, and I found that, somewhat surprisingly, I was becoming quite fond of Detective Sergeant Dowdeswell.

'I want my car back,' I said to the DCI.

'But can you drive like that?' he asked insensitively.

'That's not the point,' I replied angrily. 'I want my car back now, whether I can drive it or not. And my computer, and my mobile phone. I also want my wife's things that you lot took away.'

The DCI looked somewhat stunned that I was being so aggressive, but they'd been hanging on to my stuff now for three months and I felt that, if it didn't come back very soon, it never would.

'I'll sort it,' said the detective sergeant, getting his boss out of a hole. 'I'll get someone to drive the car over and leave it in your driveway. I'll put the other things in the boot, that's unless the CPS need to keep something for the trial. I'll speak to them about it.'

'Thank you,' I said, and I smiled at him.

Douglas came over and stood behind the wheelchair, ready for action.

It was time to go.

'Will you excuse me now?' I said to the policemen. 'I have to go and bury my wife.'

33

So here I was in June sitting in the witness services area of Oxford Crown Court.

'How do you think it's going so far?' I asked the detective sergeant.

'Much too early to say, and I shouldn't be saying anyway, not to you as a witness.' He paused for a moment, looking around him, but he then continued. 'But I can tell you that most of the Monday was taken up with swearing in the jury, plus legal arguments and the other formal stuff. The defence were again doing their best to have the indictments separated so that Joe would face three trials instead of one.'

'Why on earth would they want that?' I said. 'I would have thought three trials would be much more of an ordeal for their client.'

'Yeah, but they think that the evidence for the theft and the attempted murder are much stronger than that for the murder. They are worried that if found guilty for the other two, it will taint the jury in making their decision on the murder. And they're probably right, although attempted murder is notoriously difficult to prove. Did he really try to kill you or was he just wanting to cause you some pain and suffering? Difficult question to answer.'

'Trust me,' I said. 'He was trying to kill me.'

'Anyway, the Oxford resident judge had ruled back in March that all three counts should be tried together, but the Justice Department have parachuted in a High Court judge from London for this case because of its high media profile. So the defence tried again.'

He smiled. 'Thankfully, after hearing the arguments, the new judge agreed with the old one and made the same ruling. And he's right. The indictments are all interconnected. The motive for the murder is related to the theft, and the motive for the attempted is related to the murder. The defence weren't happy but we were delighted because we think it gives us a better chance of getting convictions on all three.'

'How about the conspiracy to defraud the HMRC?'

'That's been dropped by the CPS. At least as far as Joseph Bradbury is concerned. They felt that it clouded the issue on the other charges.'

I could understand that.

'So, after all that was settled on Monday, there was the opening by the prosecution yesterday, laying out the case to the jury and giving an indication of the evidence that's to come. That took several hours.'

'So am I the first witness?' I asked.

'No, no. The Home Office pathologist was first up, yesterday afternoon. He would have given his findings from the post-mortem. The CPS thought it was a good idea to get that in early, to make the jury fully understand that this is a very nasty murder case.'

I was very relieved that I hadn't been in court for that. What I'd heard in the Coroner's Court had been quite sufficient, thank you very much. It had been enough to give me nightmares for weeks, at least it would have if I hadn't been in a coma for some of the time.

'And then I'm on before you,' said the DS. 'And I'm afraid you might be waiting here for some time. In fact, I'm quite surprised they called you at all for today. I'm quite expecting to be in the witness box all day, and maybe for most of tomorrow as well. I've got lots to go over.'

'That's fine,' I said. 'I'm happy to wait.'

I had lots to go over as well – in my mind.

'Detective Sergeant Dowdeswell,' shouted a voice. 'You've been called.'

'That's me,' replied the DS, standing up.

'Good luck,' I said.

'Thanks,' he said, and departed, presumably to go to the court.

I spent the next two complete days sitting in the witness suite waiting, thinking, and twiddling my thumbs.

One of the idiosyncrasies of the British legal system is that witnesses who are yet to be called cannot listen to the evidence that others are giving before their turn, in case their accounts of events become tainted by, or are argumentative with, what someone else has said earlier.

Only after having given their evidence are witnesses allowed to sit in the body of the court to observe further proceedings.

Hence, I felt somewhat detached from the trial and that made me hugely frustrated, especially as everyone was in there talking about my wife and me.

It was all too easy to speculate on what was being said in the courtroom and how the jury were reacting to it, so I tried to take my mind off things by thinking back to what had happened to me over the months since the funeral.

I'd heard it often said that a funeral can bring some sort of closure to one's grief, and I was certainly glad to have put the ordeal behind me, but in my case it did little to ease the pain of loss.

I had spent weeks moping around the Old Forge feeling sorry for myself, eating little and sleeping less, but all the while my motor nerves had improved their communication skills and my mobility improved, such that I could finally manage the full flight of stairs and venture outside into the garden. I had even contemplated having a go at driving my car, which had been returned by the police along with all my other stuff.

So my life went on, lonely, rudderless and miserable.

But I had to earn a living.

I had discovered that, while it could take many years, decades even, to establish a persuasive reputation within the insurance family as a highly accomplished actuary, it could all be undone almost overnight by a single false accusation and malicious gossip.

Insurance, after all, was based on the assessment and control of risk, and hence underwriting companies and practitioners were largely of the opinion that any potential risk to their business had to be mitigated. So it was easier not to employ someone against whom there existed any sort of black mark, real or imagined.

And that was me.

No matter that I had been released from any sort of investigation into Amelia's murder, and that someone else had been charged with the crime; hiring me, it seemed, even on a freelance single-task basis, was a gamble not worth taking.

'I'm so sorry,' said one of my regular account managers. 'If it were up to me . . .'

He had left the sentence up in the air because . . . it had been up to him.

'Try again after the trial,' he'd said. 'Provided her brother gets convicted.'

At least my enforced unemployment had given me time to sort out Mary Bradbury's estate.

I had placed her cottage with a local office of one of the national estate-agent chains and had almost instantly received an offer of the full asking price, on condition that it was immediately taken off the market.

'No way,' I'd said to the prospective buyer. 'If you want it taken off the market, sign the contract and pay the deposit.'

In the end, this had resulted in a bidding war between three interested parties and I had eventually agreed to accept the highest of three binding, sealed bids, which had resulted in the property raising more than twenty-five thousand pounds above the asking price.

It had taken quite a lot of toing and froing from the agent, but it had all been worth it, not least because half of the sum raised would be coming in my direction. That was, after deduction of the fees, legal charges and inheritance taxes.

As the completion date of the sale had approached, I'd sent an email to Rachael inviting her to come to the property and choose some of the contents for her daughters to have in memory of their grandmother, but she had sent me a rude message back telling me to get lost, and to do whatever I wanted with Mary's 'dreadful' belongings. She also wrote in her missive that she'd never liked any of Mary's stuff and, as far as she was concerned, 'it could all go on a bloody big bonfire'.

Charming, I thought.

Needless to say, it hadn't gone on a bonfire, bloody big or otherwise.

I had kept some of the more personal items for myself, such as some photos and mementoes of holidays that Mary had spent with Amelia and me. Plus I'd retained a few pieces of her best antique furniture, but the remainder had been taken away by a house-clearance company and sold for peanuts at a local Sunday-morning auction.

I, meanwhile, made sure that I maintained a meticulous record of every transaction as I was certain that, at some time in the future, Joe Bradbury would accuse me of stealing.

And, oh, yes, well, Mr James Fairbrother, MA (Oxon), TEP, had lived up to his billing as a trust and estate practitioner. He had proved to be a great help, first seeing off Joe Bradbury's fatuous challenge to his mother's will, and then applying on my behalf for a grant of probate from the Chancery Division of the High Court, in order that I could distribute the estate funds to the beneficiaries of the will, plus, of course, a sizable share to the taxman.

As a result, I wasn't too concerned yet at my lack of paid employment, not with a seven-figure bank balance suddenly to my name. And, at the very least, that had silenced the bank's threats to foreclose on my property.

At four-thirty on Thursday afternoon, the court rose after the fourth day of the trial, and I still hadn't been called.

No one apologised that I had spent two whole days sitting on a hard seat facing a blank wall. But at least the Crown Prosecution Service would pay expenses towards my unnecessary taxi journeys both ways from the far side of Banbury. Shame I couldn't also claim for loss of earnings.

'Be back tomorrow,' the witness service instructed. 'Court reconvenes at ten o'clock sharp.'

My trusty taxi picked me up from outside the court building and we worked our way through the Oxford rush-hour traffic congestion and on towards Banbury.

I had finally been cleared by the medics as fit enough to drive, but only for short distances and Oxford was too far, plus the problem of parking near to the court made a taxi the only sensible option.

'How's it going?' the driver asked cheerfully.

'No idea,' I said. 'All I've done so far is wait in a room. But I should be called tomorrow. I'll need to be there by ten.'

'I'll pick you up at half past eight,' he said. 'Same as today. Just to be on the safe side.'

'Fine.'

He drove on in silence. He knew I didn't really want to talk.

In spite of my loneliness, no amount of conversation with anyone other than Amelia seemed to make me feel any better. After eight months, I was trying to get my life back onto some sort of track, where I could look forward to a future rather than always backwards at the past.

But it wasn't easy.

Everyone else had done their grieving. They spoke to me about Amelia as if she had somehow once been a character in a film, and one that had now been relegated to DVD, or some old-movie channel on satellite TV. But, for me, her role had been worthy of an Oscar and deserved to be forever in lights above the title for everyone to see.

The taxi dropped me outside the house and I hobbled up the path to the front door.

The trial had put everything in my life on hold and I had been advised by the police that it would go on for several weeks at least, and maybe for a month or more. Long gone were the days when even high-profile murder trials lasted less than a week.

In October 1910, the infamous dentist Dr Crippen was tried, convicted and sentenced to death within the space of just five days, with the jury taking as little as twenty-seven minutes of deliberation to unanimously find him guilty. Within a month he was dead, hanged at nine in the morning at Pentonville Prison in London.

Even forty-three years later in 1953, the trial of John Christie, of 10 Rillington Place fame, was over quicker still, in only four days, and a mere three weeks was to pass between the start of his trial and his execution on the same gallows as Crippen.

And John Haigh, the 'acid bath murderer', was amazingly convicted of six murders in just two days, the 18th and 19th of July 1949, with the jury taking no more than seventeen minutes to find him guilty. He was hanged on 10th August.

'Evidence tends to be far more complicated these days,' DS Dowdeswell had told me. 'What with forensics, DNA profiles, phone records and such. And modern juries are also much more sceptical than in the past. They need greater convincing. No one believes the police without question any more.'

He had made it sound like a major failing on the part of the public, but there had been too many examples where police evidence at a trial was later found to have been fabricated in the misplaced desire to guarantee a conviction.

I let myself in through the front door and wished for the millionth time that Amelia were here to greet me. The trial might provide me with some sense of justice, provided Joe was convicted, but it could never bring back what I'd lost.

I popped one of my replenished supply of ready meals into the microwave.

Four minutes at full power.

While I waited for the timer to count down to zero, I again looked at the broken back-door lock and decided that I'd fix it after the trial was over, whatever the outcome.

Life had to go on.

34

'William Gordon-Russell.'

'Here,' I said, struggling to stand up while not dropping the crutches.

The court usher held open the doors for me as I made my way into the courtroom.

It was eerily quiet as I went slowly past the massed rows of court reporters to the witness box, the only sound being the *clink-clink* of the crutches on the hard blue-carpeted floor.

'Do you need a chair?' asked the usher.

'No,' I said. 'Not to start with.'

I was determined to stand, if only to demonstrate to Joe Bradbury that I was not the invalid he had tried to make me. I leaned the crutches up against the front of the wooden witness box.

'Take the testament in your right hand and read from the card,' said the usher.

I did as he asked. 'I swear by Almighty God that the evidence

I shall give shall be the truth, the whole truth and nothing but the truth.'

The usher took back the card and Bible, and I looked around the court.

Slightly to my right and in front was the imposing red-robed and bewigged judge sitting alone behind his raised bench. On the rear wall, above the judge's head, was a painted moulding of the Royal Coat of Arms of the United Kingdom – a reminder that all criminal cases are tried in British Crown Courts in the name of the reigning monarch.

Beyond the judge, on the far side of the court, was the jury and I was facing them directly as they were me. Five men and seven women in two rows of six.

I turned to my left and there he was – the defendant, Joseph Reginald Bradbury, sitting behind vertically slatted glass panels in the dock at the back of the court, opposite the judge, flanked by two uniformed security officers.

The very sight of Joe staring at me with his cold eyes sent a shiver down my damaged spine.

There was a slight pause and then the prosecuting barrister stood up from his place and turned to me.

'Please state your full name,' he said.

'William Herbert Millgate Gordon-Russell.'

'And are you the widower of Amelia Jane Gordon-Russell, the victim of the murder in this case.'

'I am.'

So it was now official, I was a widower.

And there was no point in asking to be referred to as just plain

Bill Russell. Even I could see that. The whole court atmosphere was extremely formal, from the judge in his red robes and horse-hair wig, the barristers in their black gowns, also with wigs, and then the court officials in dark suits, some also with black gowns over. I was in my Sunday best, as was Joe Bradbury in the dock, both, no doubt, trying to make a good impression as honest and respectable citizens.

Only the jury appeared to have been dragged in off the street in their leisure attire, which of course they effectively had. And they had clearly not received any memo concerning an expected dress code. Most of them appeared to be completely out of place in slogan-printed T-shirts and skimpy blouses. But perhaps their choice of apparel was more in keeping with the hot June weather than the heavy garb of the lawyers. One of the young men in the back row, I noticed later, was even sporting Bermuda shorts and flip-flops.

But, I suppose, the jury could wear what they liked. They didn't have to impress anyone.

The judge might think that he was in charge, and he was in terms of the law, but the jury were the final arbitrators of the facts and it was they who ultimately pronounced on the guilt or otherwise of the man in the dock. They were the kings of the court and everybody knew it, the judge included, bowing down at their every behest, flip-flops or not.

'Thank you for coming to court today, Mr Gordon-Russell,' continued the prosecution barrister. 'I hope the journey wasn't too onerous for you, especially in your, shall we say, delicate condition.'

He made it sound as if I were eight and a half months pregnant.

'No,' I replied. 'The journey was fine, thank you.'

'Are you sure you wouldn't prefer to sit down? The usher will bring you a chair.'

'I may need to later,' I said. 'But I will stand for the time being.'

If anything the poor man looked rather disappointed and I realised too late that, as DS Dowdeswell had suggested, the prosecution were attempting to use my physical incapacity as a lever to extract greater sympathy from the jury.

'Now, Mr Gordon-Russell,' he went on. 'I intend taking you through the events of last October. We will try and keep everything in chronological order and I would appreciate it if you could tell the jury everything and anything that you consider might be relevant to them in making up their minds as to the circumstances of the case. I should warn you, however, against making any form of speculation or opinion. It is for the jury to make their own assessment of the evidence. Just confine yourself to the facts as you remember them. Do you understand?'

I nodded at him. 'Yes.'

'Good. So could you please tell the jury where and when you last saw your wife, and where you were, and how you discovered that she had been murdered.'

I knew this would be where he would start. He had told me so beforehand. And I had tried to prepare myself but, even so, I found the next hour or so, while describing the events of that Tuesday evening and Wednesday morning, far more difficult than I had expected.

I told the jury how I had left home, leaving Amelia in the garden and how she had waved at me as I drove away. I explained how I had called home when I'd arrived at the hotel and then gone to a charity dinner. I told them how I had been unable to contact Amelia on the Wednesday morning but hadn't been overly concerned. Not, that was, until I had been informed by the police at Warwick Racecourse that my wife had been murdered.

'Take your time,' the barrister said to me as I took some deep breaths to prevent myself from bursting into tears – and I was determined not to do that.

'How would you describe your relationship with your brother-in-law, the defendant?'

'Hostile,' I said. 'Especially on his side towards me.'

'Has it always been like that?'

'Not at all. For many years we got on well. We visited each other's homes. Joe was an usher at my wedding, and our families were close. Amelia especially loved her young nieces.'

'So when did it all go wrong?'

'About four years ago. When Amelia and Joe's mother moved from Weybridge to near Chipping Norton. Joe seemed to become insanely jealous of the closeness between Amelia and her mother and he clearly set out to destroy it.'

'Did that affect the bond between the siblings?'

'Absolutely,' I said. 'They had been close as children, with Amelia often telling me that she used to look out for her little brother at school but, over the last three years of her life, Amelia grew to hate him over what he was doing to her. She couldn't even stand talking about him and wanted nothing to do with him ever again.'

'So she wouldn't have invited him into her home on the day she died?'

'No way,' I said, glancing over towards the dock. 'She wouldn't have invited him anywhere, ever.'

Joe was staring at me intensely through the glass and he moved as if to stand up, but one of the security officers put a hand on his arm and he slowly relaxed back into the chair.

I turned back to the prosecutor.

'And how would you describe your own relationship with your wife?'

'Very loving,' I replied. 'Amelia was not only my wife, she was also my best friend. She was my constant companion, my confidante and my lover.'

My voice almost broke and I fought back the tears once again. It was talking about her in the past tense that I found so distressing.

'I think we will break for lunch now,' announced the judge, looking up from his copious note-taking. 'Mr Gordon-Russell, you may take the time to compose yourself. We will restart at two o'clock.'

'All rise,' shouted the usher, and everyone did. The prosecution and defence barristers bowed towards the judge and he returned the gesture, before departing through his own special door. Then the jury filed out through theirs. Joe was taken out of the dock by the security officers through yet another door, and finally I shuffled unsteadily across the court, out to the lobby, and back down to the witness services suite.

At least, with all these separate entrances and exits, I wouldn't run into my brother-in-law by accident, as had happened outside the Coroner's Court.

'Well done,' said DS Dowdeswell, who was waiting for me. 'Bit of an ordeal, isn't it? Do you fancy a coffee or a bite to eat?'

'Something to eat would be great.'

He went to the canteen and returned with ham and cheese sandwiches, plus two cups of coffee.

'Overly generous,' I commented, somewhat flippantly.

'Court expenses,' he said, making sure he put the till receipt carefully in his wallet.

We sat down.

'It seems to be going pretty well so far,' I said. 'Have I said the right things?'

The DS shook his head. 'I can't discuss your evidence with you, but it always does seem to go well when the prosecution are asking you the questions. But it will be a different matter when you get cross-examined. And you need to be very careful with this particular defence barrister. He's a right slimy eel. He'll do his best to tie you in knots and get you contradicting yourself. He'll also try to convince the jury that you're lying, so watch out. Never hesitate or he'll jump at you.'

It sounded like a barrel of laughs.

'And if he asks you something you don't know, say so. Don't let him lead you off on a tangent, and then agree with him that he might be right – because he won't be.'

'I thought they weren't allowed to ask leading questions.'

He gave me a look that I took to mean 'Don't be so naive.'

*

'I remind you, Mr Gordon-Russell, that you are still under oath.'

'Yes, my lord,' I replied to the judge.

We were all back in court after the lunch break, everyone in their allotted places.

The prosecuting barrister briefly went back over the events that we had covered during the morning, as if to emphasise the horror of discovering one's wife had been murdered, and to remind the jury of its significance.

'Now, Mr Gordon-Russell,' he said finally. 'Let us move on to the events of the last Wednesday in October, exactly two weeks after the murder of your wife, the day on which the defendant also attempted to kill *you*.'

The judge raised his eyes from his note-taking and gave the barrister a stare as if to admonish him slightly for his forwardness. But he said nothing.

'Please could you describe to the jury what happened to you on that afternoon, specifically concerning your visit to the Waitrose supermarket in Banbury.'

I wanted to tell him, and the jury, that it wasn't the first time Joe Bradbury had tried to kill me. I wanted to tell them that on the Saturday prior to the last Wednesday in October, Joe had tried to stab me with a carving knife and I had only escaped thanks to the timely intervention of his mother.

But the CPS didn't want that episode to 'cloud the issue', as they considered that there was insufficient evidence to charge him over it. I, however, felt that it was another prime example of Joe's obsession with doing away with me.

I also wanted to tell them that, prior to that Wednesday, I had been down to Weybridge to speak to Jim and Gladys Wilson, and I had found evidence that proved Joe had stolen a hundred thousand pounds from his mother. And I wanted to tell them that, on the Tuesday afternoon, Joe had just learned that I was no longer considered a suspect in the death of his sister and he mistakenly believed that killing me was a way of getting himself off the hook.

But the CPS didn't want me to bring any of those things up either.

'Just answer the questions that you are asked,' the prosecuting barrister had said to me in earnest during our pre-trial meeting. 'And nothing else.'

He was strongly implying that I shouldn't try and answer those that I wasn't asked.

He told me they had good reasons for keeping quiet at this stage, and that these matters would be introduced later. Not that they were coaching me or anything. That would have been illegal.

In addition, the CPS had made it perfectly clear that they would prefer it if I also didn't mention anything about me having been arrested on suspicion of murdering Amelia.

'But surely the defence will bring that up,' I'd said.

'They might or they might not. Depends on how desperate they are. If they do, then they will show themselves as trying to blacken the character of a bereaved widower. Juries tend not to like that. And we would have the last word in re-examination to confirm absolutely that you have an unbreakable alibi and that the police no longer have any interest in you as a suspect.'

So I simply explained to the jury how I had driven my wife's cream Fiat 500 from my home to Waitrose supermarket in Banbury on that Wednesday afternoon.

'Did you notice anything during the journey?' the prosecutor asked.

'As I backed out of my drive, I spotted a large white van parked further down the road. I assumed at the time it was one of the many similar courier vans that deliver online-shopping packages. I remembered thinking that he wouldn't be delivering to me as I hadn't ordered anything. Other than that, I noticed nothing unusual and I arrived at the Waitrose car park about half past four.'

I went on to describe how, after doing my shopping and loading everything into the car, I had set off to drive home a little before five-thirty, and by that time on a dull dank late October afternoon, it was already completely dark.

I had driven out of Banbury and, after indicating to turn right off the main road into Hanwell village, I had realised far too late that the headlights behind were not slowing down.

I told them how someone had driven straight into the back of Amelia's Fiat 500, shunting it forward with such force that hitting the opposite grass verge had sent the car airborne. It had passed over the hedge, crashing into the tree in the field beyond.

'And what happened after that?' asked the barrister.

'The next thing I remember was waking up in the John Radcliffe Hospital some ten days later.'

'And what were your injuries?'

I catalogued everything, starting with the break to my neck

and the bruising of my spinal cord, which had resulted in my motor-nerve paralysis.

'And are you fully recovered now?' asked the prosecutor.

'No,' I replied. 'Over the past eight months, with constant physiotherapy, much of my mobility has returned. But I still have problems, with my legs in particular, and I am informed that I may never recover full movement and control.'

'So would you describe your injuries as being life-changing?'

'Yes,' I said. 'Very much so.'

But not as life-changing as losing my wife.

'Thank you, Mr Gordon-Russell. No more questions.'

The prosecuting barrister sat down, leaving me still standing there in the witness box with a look of total surprise on my face.

No more questions?

But I had more to say.

How about asking me about Joe's vile emails? And his threats? What about his attempts to brainwash his mother? And the theft of the money? And his false accusation that I had assaulted his daughter?

I had *so* much more to say.

35

'Am I right in thinking that you refer to yourself as Bill Russell rather than using your full name?'

The 'right slimy eel' defence barrister was on his feet and asking the questions in cross-examination.

'Yes,' I said. 'I do.'

'Why is that? Is it some kind of reverse snobbery?'

He made it sound like a major failing.

'No,' I said. 'It's just simpler.'

Specifically, it had been simpler when I'd been riding as an amateur jockey, as 'Mr W. Gordon-Russell' had been too long to fit on the racecourse number boards, not that many of them had those any longer.

But maybe the eel was right too, in a way. Being the son of an earl, and with a double-barrelled surname to boot, didn't make getting spare rides any easier.

Historically, in British horse racing, the jockey was always considered to be the owner's servant, and the earliest race records show only the names of the horse and its owner, and not that of its rider. Even in modern times, for some of the old school, offering a ride to someone who they considered had a higher social standing than them was a no-no.

'Mr Russell,' said the eel, 'I put it to you that much of what you have told the court today has been a pack of lies.'

'No,' I said. 'It has been the truth.'

'An intricate tissue of lies to cover up your own carelessness and wrongdoing?'

'Not at all. I have told you the truth.'

'You have told the jury that your relationship with your wife was a loving one, but I suggest this is far from the reality?'

'No. I loved my wife deeply. We had a blissful marriage.'

'But was it not your mental cruelty towards your wife that resulted in her being admitted to a psychiatric institution on several occasions?'

I was doing my best to keep my cool. This was clearly a line that Joe had spun to his defence team. It was what he had accused me of many times in his ranting emails, when it had been his doing all along.

'No,' I said.

'But your wife had been admitted to such institutions?'

'Yes,' I agreed. 'But not due to any cruelty on my behalf. I suggest you look at your client's behaviour to find the true reason.'

He ignored me. 'Your wife suffered from depression. Is that correct?'

'Yes.'

'Would you say that a happily married person would be depressed? Does not the very word *depression* imply unhappiness?'

'That is far too simplistic a view, and one that is totally wrong,' I said. 'Depression is a complicated issue and doesn't necessarily relate to someone's happiness or unhappiness.'

'Was your wife suicidal?'

'She had been, in the past.'

'Yes,' he said. 'And had your wife not been rushed to accident and emergency several times as a result of trying to take her own life?'

'Yes.'

'Hardly the behaviour of someone in a blissful marriage, wouldn't you say?'

'You are misrepresenting the situation,' I said.

'No, Mr Russell. It is *you* that is misrepresenting the situation. Was your wife not desperately unhappy in your marriage, to the point of trying to end her own life on multiple occasions? Is that not the true situation?'

'No,' I said. 'That was absolutely not the case.'

He ignored my answer yet again.

'And was your wife's inability to have children a source of further friction between you?'

'I wouldn't call it friction,' I said. 'It was a source of great sadness for us both.'

'So it put your marriage under strain?'

'Yes, it did,' I said. 'It was a difficult time for us both.'

I could see DS Dowdeswell sitting behind the prosecution

team staring purposefully at me. Then I remembered his warning over lunch.

'But,' I went on, 'it didn't ever affect the deep love we had for each other. It put us under strain in other ways and, if anything, those difficulties brought us closer together as a couple.'

The detective sergeant nodded at me in approval.

The eel didn't.

'Did you stand to benefit financially from the death of your wife?' he asked.

'In what way do you mean?' I asked back, sure that he was on about the life insurance policy. But I wanted him to mention it first.

'Was your wife's life insured?' he asked.

'Yes, of course,' I said. 'I have been employed in the insurance business all my working life. It would be remiss of me not to have insured my wife, as indeed it would have been if I had not also insured myself.'

'But is it not the case that you took out a new policy just a few months before her death? A policy that pays out a million pounds to you as the sole beneficiary?'

'Yes,' I said. 'That is the case. But I can assure you that no amount of money can compensate for the loss of my wife.'

DS Dowdeswell was nodding furiously.

But the eel pressed his point again. 'However, you did stand to benefit financially from her death?'

'No,' I said. 'I did not.'

The eel was slightly taken aback. 'But you have just told the court that you are the sole beneficiary to a life insurance policy worth a million pounds. How is that not a financial benefit?'

'Because, according to her mother's will at the time, Amelia stood to inherit half of her mother's substantial estate, something that would have happened very soon as her mother had been diagnosed with inoperative stage-four pancreatic cancer. However, as my wife was murdered and hence predeceased her mother, and we have no children, the whole estate would have gone to her brother.' I turned and faced the dock, pointing my left forefinger in Joe's direction just in case the jury hadn't understood what I was saying. 'My wife's death would have resulted in a huge financial benefit to him, not to me.'

The detective sergeant looked so happy that I thought he was about to burst into applause, and the eel looked like he'd swallowed a wasp.

I could see what the defence were attempting to do. They were trying to sow a seed of doubt in the minds of the jury that it had been the wicked cruel husband whodunit but, in trying to establish a financial motive for me to have killed her, they had only provided me with the opportunity to do exactly the same for their client sitting in the dock.

But the eel wasn't giving up the thread that easily.

He played what he obviously thought was his trump card.

'Mr Russell,' he said, 'was it not the case that you were arrested by the police on suspicion of murdering your wife?'

'Yes,' I said unhesitatingly. 'But I was wrongly arrested. As I have explained earlier, I was away in Birmingham at the time of my wife's death – and CCTV has proved it beyond any doubt. The police have accepted that. I have a letter signed by the chief constable of Thames Valley Police.'

I decided not to mention that the letter didn't exactly state that I was innocent, just that the police would not be pursuing charges against me unless any new evidence emerged. But, even so, I could tell from the eel's body language that he was suddenly regretting having brought up my arrest in the first place.

But I wasn't. It had given me the chance to show that I had a watertight alibi.

For the first time, I was even quite enjoying myself and eager to see the eel's next tactic.

I was pretty sure that he couldn't refer to the police caution I had accepted as an undergraduate for having had sex with Tracy Higgins when she was only fifteen. That had been twenty-one years ago and was hardly relevant to the matter in hand, but I wouldn't put anything past him.

'Mr Russell,' he said. 'Would you consider yourself a risk taker?'

'My work as an actuary involves the evaluation of risk,' I replied. 'Every activity we perform carries some level of risk – crossing the road, flying away on holiday, scuba diving, everything. My job is to calculate that level, however small. So, in some respects, everyone is a risk taker.'

'But would you say that you personally take *unnecessary* risks?'

'No.'

I wondered where he was going with this.

'But did you not ride in steeplechase races, including over the Grand National fences? Would you not consider that an unnecessary risk?'

'Possibly,' I said. 'But it was a calculated risk.' I smiled at him. 'If you are on a good horse then the level of risk is acceptable.'

'But did you not have to give up riding in races due to injury?'

'Yes.'

'And what was that injury?'

'I damaged my neck.'

'You damaged your neck?' he sounded incredulous, spreading his hands wide towards the jury. 'But is it not the case that you broke vertebrae in your neck, the same vertebrae that have caused the current problem with your walking?'

'Yes.'

'So your present difficulties may, in some large part, be due to the injury you received several years ago while riding.'

'I can't answer that as I'm not a doctor,' I said. 'All I know is that I could walk perfectly well before the recent crash, and I can't afterwards.'

'Do you like speed, Mr Russell?'

I wasn't quite sure what he meant by speed. Did he mean amphetamines?

He clarified. 'Does going fast give you a thrill? An adrenalin rush?'

'I think everyone gets a thrill from riding a fast roller coaster.'

'But not everyone rides racehorses at thirty miles per hour over Becher's Brook. Did that give you a thrill, Mr Russell?'

'Yes,' I said.

'Do you miss that thrill, now that you have stopped riding?'

'Yes.'

'So you drive a fast, powerful sports car instead?'

'I wouldn't call it fast,' I said.

'No? A four-point-two-litre V8 supercharged Jaguar XKR-S sports car? With a top speed of one hundred and seventy-four miles per hour? I think I'd call that fast.'

'It is now more than ten years old,' I said.

I had bought it during the bountiful years, before the financial crisis, when all City bonuses had been overly extravagant.

'As maybe,' said the eel. 'But I bet it still shifts along pretty nicely, doesn't it? Enjoy driving it, do you, Mr Russell?'

'Yes.'

There was no point in denying it. I loved driving my Jag.

'Do you like going fast? Taking a few risks?'

'No,' I said.

'How many penalty points do you have on your driving licence, Mr Russell?

'Nine.'

'Are they all for speeding convictions?'

'Yes.'

He paused to allow that fact to settle into the brains of the members of the jury.

'Going fast on the night of the crash, were you, Mr Russell?'

'No,' I said, smiling. 'And I wasn't driving that car.'

'Exactly,' he said triumphantly. 'A Jaguar sports car is built to corner well. You are very familiar with it. But on that day you were driving a Fiat 500. Is it not the case, Mr Russell, that you simply took the corner too fast in a car you were not used to driving, and one that is not designed for the high-speed manoeuvres that you regularly perform, and far from being hit from behind by another vehicle, you simply lost control and crashed due to your own excessive speed and negligence?'

As the detective sergeant had said, he was, indeed, a right slimy eel.

'No,' I replied strongly and loudly. 'That is not what happened at all. The Fiat was almost stationary when it was struck from behind by another vehicle.'

The eel snorted his disbelief.

'No further questions.'

He sat down and the prosecuting counsel made no move to stand up again.

'Thank you, Mr Gordon-Russell,' said the judge. 'You may step down.'

In truth, I was somewhat disappointed. I'd been on a roll, and I'd been in the witness box for less than one day when I had quite expected to be there for much longer.

Clearly, so did the court, as the next prosecution witness had not been called to appear.

'We will adjourn until ten o'clock on Monday morning,' announced the judge.

'All rise!'

36

'Sounds to me like you did pretty well,' Douglas said.

I had taken the train from Oxford to spend the weekend with my brother and we were talking through the events of the day over a glass of Rioja.

'The defence barrister was a bit of a bastard.'

He laughed. 'All barristers can be bastards when we need to be. It's the defence's job to throw doubt on the testimony of the prosecution witnesses.'

'But he didn't need to be so unkind about Amelia and her problems.'

'From what you've said, I think he was quite mild. When I'm defending I can be far worse than that.'

'Oh, thanks,' I said. 'Then I'm glad you weren't there.'

He laughed again and we drank some more wine.

Whereas it would have been illegal for the prosecution to coach me as one of their witnesses in the case, there were no such qualms for my brother, the QC, provided we did not discuss the actual evidence.

Over the past few weeks, Douglas and I had spent quite a lot of time on the telephone together. He had taught me what to expect in the court, how to handle difficult moments, and to keep my composure at all times. His wide experience with juries had given me an insight into what they were looking for and how to present them with it.

Without his guidance, mine would have been a far more nervous performance.

'How are things in general?' Douglas asked. 'Other than the trial?'

'Much the same,' I said. 'I still can't walk properly and no one will employ me.'

'But they can't still believe that you were responsible?'

'No. I don't think so. But it's all to do with risk – all insurance is. They see it as a risk to employ me at the present time with all the publicity still going on. Who was it who claimed there was no such thing as bad publicity?'

'Phineas T. Barnum,' Douglas replied. 'The American circus owner. It was either him or Oscar Wilde.'

I shook my head. 'Oscar Wilde said that the only thing worse than being talked about is *not* being talked about.'

'Same thing, surely. Or maybe it was Brendan Behan?'

'Who?' I asked.

'Brendan Behan. You know, the Irish poet and playwright. Used to describe himself as a drinker with a writing problem. Claimed he drank only on only two occasions – when he was thirsty and when he wasn't. And his favourite tipple was a mixture of champagne and sherry. Totally lethal.'

We laughed, and then took large sips of our own alcoholic beverages.

'But, come to think of it, I'm pretty sure that Behan said that there was no such thing as bad publicity, except your own obituary.'

We both laughed again. It felt good.

Laughter had been in short supply in my life during the past eight months.

'Anyway,' I said. 'Whoever said it was an idiot. All the fund managers are telling me to wait until the trial is over. Maybe things will settle down then, they say. Thank the Lord for Mary Bradbury, that's what I say. Without her legacy I'd probably be losing my house by now.'

'How about Amelia's life insurance money?'

I rolled my eyes. 'You know what insurance companies are like. They won't pay out until the death certificate is registered by the coroner. And that won't be until the inquest concludes, and that won't happen until after the criminal proceedings are finished. They'll drag it out as long as they can.'

'So how did you have Amelia's funeral without a death certificate?'

'I applied to the coroner for a temporary one. That allowed the funeral to take place on condition she was buried and not cremated.'

He gave me a sideways look, which implied I was giving him too much information.

'How about you?' I said, changing the subject. 'Have you seen your boys recently?'

He smiled broadly.

'They were here last week for half-term. Charlotte came with them for some of the time.'

'That's great news.'

'Don't get excited. We're not getting back together. In fact, she left a day earlier than originally planned because we found we couldn't stand being together. Kept arguing over the smallest of things.' He laughed nervously. 'I've obviously got used to living on my own.'

I wished I could.

One of the main reasons why I had come to stay this weekend with Douglas in London was because I now found the Old Forge to be such a lonely place and I had thought that, after giving my evidence, I would have hated being alone there even more.

And I was right.

The experience had clearly affected me.

I had been building up to this day for so long, believing that it would be the decisive day in the trial, but, somehow, I felt it had been a bit of an anticlimax.

After going up to bed, now back in Douglas's guest bedroom after the repairs from the water leak, I lay in the dark for a long time, worrying about it.

Should I have done more?

Could I have done more?

By the time I finally went to sleep, I had convinced myself that, in spite of Douglas's help, I hadn't done enough, and that Joe Bradbury would get off.

The very thought gave me nightmares.

*

On Saturday afternoon I went to the races at Sandown Park.

It wasn't a spur-of-the-moment decision. I had been invited by the chairman of the Honorary Stewards Appointment Board to discuss my future, a move I had taken as being hugely positive, so I had accepted at once.

My legs were still not up to a journey to the Esher course by train as there was a good half-mile between the railway station and the racecourse entrance. So I booked a car with a driver, one who would wait and bring me back when I became tired.

I asked Douglas if he would like to come with me and, much to my surprise and delight, he agreed.

'I've only been to a horse race once before in my life,' he announced in the car on the way. 'And that was to see you ride at Lingfield. Long time ago, now, mind. I was a junior in a trial at Southwark and it was postponed for a day due to a bout of sickness in the jury. So, in a moment of weakness, I caught a train from Victoria.'

I turned in my seat to stare at him. 'You've never told me that before. Did I win?'

'No,' he said. 'You were miles in front and I thought you were going to, but you fell off at the last fence.'

I remembered it well. Failures like that seem to stick in the memory longer than the successes.

'I think you'll find that the horse itself fell,' I said. 'Rather than I fell off it.'

'Same thing, surely.'

No, it wasn't, I thought. *Totally different thing altogether.* But, I suppose, the result was the same. And, in truth, it had been my fault. It had been early in my riding career. I could recall being so elated that I was about to win my first race that I hadn't concentrated enough in getting my mount balanced for the last. And we had both paid the price, hitting the turf hard.

The incident had bruised my ego even more than it had bruised my body.

'You didn't say anything to me at the time about being there.'

'I would have if you'd won. But I thought, under the circumstances, it was best simply to drift away.'

He was right.

My clever lawyer brother was always right.

He had worked out that I would have been doubly embarrassed and distraught if I had known that he had witnessed the debacle. But, almost two decades on since the event, I was pleased that he had taken the effort to go and see me ride, albeit with such a disaster. Even now, my heart ached with the desire to have done better for him on that day. Maybe it wouldn't have been his only previous trip to the races if I'd won. Indeed, I was sure of it.

'At least no one will fall at the last fence here today,' I said as the car pulled up in front of the Sandown main entrance. 'It's flat racing.'

I had never returned my official BHA steward's pass and I used it to gain access. I even managed to acquire a complimentary entrance badge for Douglas and a racecard.

It felt so good to be back on a racecourse.

I hadn't been to the races since that appalling day at Ascot just three days after Amelia had died and, even now, I went hot and cold wondering what on earth I'd been thinking of in going.

I clearly hadn't been myself.

I wasn't sure I was myself even now.

It was as if the death of my wife had also killed off a large part of me. Sure, I went on breathing and eating, sleeping and thinking, but it was in a parallel universe to how I had been before, seemingly not living in reality.

Part of me even expected to wake up from this torment and find everything was fine again.

I knew it wasn't really going to happen but, somehow, I received some degree of solace from believing that it might, and I could understand absolutely how Mary had been comforted by her certainty that she would soon meet Amelia again on the 'other side'.

'Fancy some lunch?' I asked Douglas.

'What time's your meeting?'

'After the first race. That's at five past two. We have plenty of time.'

We went to the champagne and seafood bar and found a table in the window that someone else was just vacating.

'I'll get the food,' Douglas said. 'You keep the table.'

Walking with crutches was not conducive to carrying anything so I sat and waited while Douglas fetched a bottle of Moët in an ice bucket, two glasses, and a couple of plates of prawn salad with lashings of Marie Rose sauce.

'Cheers,' he said, raising a glass of bubbles. 'Here's to a fun afternoon.'

'A fun afternoon,' I echoed, somewhat forlornly, also raising mine.

I knew that I hadn't been any fun to be around for months. Maybe it was time I started looking on the brighter side of life. Perhaps I'd be able to soon, once the trial was over, provided we got the right result.

Douglas and I ate our lunch and we finished the bottle of champagne, which was perhaps not the best preparation for an important appointment with the stewarding boss.

'Where's your meeting?' Douglas asked.

'In the Stewards' Room,' I said. 'It's in the weighing-room complex. After the first race, unless there's an enquiry, in which case it will be after the second.'

We went outside into the sunshine to watch the horses circling in the paddock for the first race, a five-furlong sprint for two-year-olds.

'Which one do you fancy?' Douglas asked, looking at the racecard. 'Where should I stake my shirt?'

'Your guess is as good as mine.'

'But I thought you knew about racing,' he said with a laugh.

'I know the rules,' I said. 'Not which horse will win.'

Somewhat surprisingly, honorary stewards *were* allowed to bet provided they were not acting for the particular race in question. However, I usually didn't bet at all while at the races, as I didn't consider it was the best advertisement for the sport for a known steward to be seen gambling, even if he was 'off duty'.

And, far more importantly, I didn't like losing my money, which I invariably did.

'They look awfully small,' Douglas said as the runners paraded past us.

'These are just babies,' I said. 'For many it's their first time on a racecourse. Jump horses are generally much bigger because they're older.'

'So will these go jumping when they grow up?'

I laughed. 'Some might but I doubt it. These days, horses are mostly bred to be either flat or jumps specialists. But that wasn't always the case. Red Rum, he of three-wins-plus-two-seconds-in-the-Grand-National fame, ran eight times on the flat as a two-year-old. In fact, his first ever race was a dead-heat win in a five-furlong selling plate at Aintree the day before Foinavon famously won the National, after that massive pile-up at the twenty-third fence. But that was back when Aintree used to stage flat races as well as jumps.'

'Don't they any more?'

'No. Aintree is now jumping only.'

'So how many racecourses are there in total?' Douglas asked.

'Sixty in Great Britain. About a third are flat only, a little over a third jumps only, and the rest have both, but not usually on the same day. Mixed meetings used to be quite common but now there are only a very few in the whole year. I know there's one at Haydock in May. In fact, that might be the only one left.'

'Why not more?'

'Different clientele, I suppose. Different trainers. And different jockeys.'

'But the same stewards?'

'Absolutely,' I said, smiling. 'Rules is rules, either code.'

Douglas decided to keep his shirt on his back and to invest just ten pounds to win on a horse whose jockey's silks were in his college colours.

'Bookmakers will love you,' I said, laughing.

We watched the race from the main grandstand.

The babies broke evenly and ran as fast as they could down the five-furlong straight course, the whole thing over in less than a minute – blink and you missed it.

Douglas enthusiastically shouted his support for his selection at maximum decibels, urging it to go faster, but to no avail. It finished sixth out of the nine runners.

'Mug's game,' he said, tearing up his betting slip into confetti.

We went to the unsaddling enclosure to watch the winner come in; as there were no controversial incidents that required any action, I left Douglas there, leaning on the rail, as I went through to the Stewards' Room.

The chairman of the Honorary Stewards Appointment Board was already waiting for me.

'Ah, there you are, Bill,' he said, stretching out a hand for me to shake, which I ignored.

'Sorry,' I said. 'I currently need both my hands to walk with.'

Especially after half a bottle of champers.

Why did I do that?

'Yes, of course,' said the chairman. 'Silly me.'

He pulled over a couple of the chairs and we sat down.

'How are things?' he asked.

'Physically or mentally?'

'Both.'

'Physically, I am getting better very slowly. I can now walk pretty well with the crutches and I haven't brought a wheelchair with me here today, which I would have had to do until about a week or two ago. The doctors tell me they have little or no idea if I will ever be back to normal, but I'm working on it.'

The chairman smiled.

'As for the mental side,' I said, 'I hope things will be better after the trial is over. I am finding that quite stressful at present.'

'Yes, of course,' the chairman said again. 'But other than that?'

'Well, I won't say that life has been a bunch of laughs these last eight months. It hasn't. But I'm still here. And I'm ready and eager to resume my duties as a race-day steward.'

'Yes, well, that's why I asked you to come here today.'

Suddenly, I feared that he was going to tell me I wasn't wanted, and to demand back my official pass card, but he could have surely done that by email or post. And my fears were unfounded.

'I am pleased to tell you,' he said, 'that I will be recommending to the full BHA board that your name be reinstated on the official List of Stewards.'

I smiled broadly.

'That is very good news,' I said. 'But George Longcross won't be pleased. He told me in no uncertain terms that I'd brought racing into disrepute.'

It was a comment that still irritated me.

'Yes, well, George can be a bit of a dinosaur at times. But you have always impressed me by the solid reasoning of your arguments and the clarity of your decisions. Welcome back to the team.'

He held out his hand again and, this time, I shook it, warmly.

'Let's hope the main board agree with you.'

'They will,' he said. 'I have the Authority chairman's blessing to hold this meeting. You will hear officially very soon.' He stood up to indicate that our meeting was over. He smiled. 'I must now get back to my job of stewarding here today. My colleagues have been holding the fort for me outside.'

I also stood up and gathered my walking aids together.

'Thank you,' I said, meaning it.

There was almost a spring in my faltering steps as I went back outside to Douglas and I didn't need to tell him the outcome – he could tell by the huge grin that I couldn't wipe off my face.

It *was* going to be a fun afternoon, after all.

'I'll order some more bubbly,' he said.

'Only if you want me to fall over.'

We settled on a coffee from a concession stand, which we drank while perusing the runners in the next race.

Douglas chose to place another wager, again ten pounds, this time on a horse with a legal-sounding name, but his renewed high hopes ended once again with more confetti in the wind.

It was a good job my brother was a better lawyer than he was a punter.

37

Week two of the trial was taken up by the prosecution as they slowly tried to build a solid wall of evidence with which to surround the defendant, a wall that we all hoped the defence would be unable to knock down.

After I'd finished giving my own testimony on the first Friday, I sat in the public area of the court for every moment of the trial, and I watched as a steady stream of witnesses made their way in and out again.

First up was Nancy Fadeley. She stood bolt upright in the witness box dressed in a smart floral-printed summer dress, and wearing her signature pearl necklace, this time with matching drop-pearl earrings. The prosecutor began by asking her to tell the jury of her trip to the pub with Amelia on the evening before she died, and to recount the conversation that had taken place between the two of them.

As DCI Priestly had predicted, the defence barrister didn't like it one bit and, in spite of his complaints having been dismissed once at a previous hearing, he now again protested vociferously to the judge that what Amelia had said to a third party was mere hearsay and should be inadmissible as evidence.

The jury were sent out of the court while the matter was discussed at length between the lawyers. Eventually, the judge ruled that, as Amelia wasn't able to attend court herself to be questioned due to having been the victim of the murder and hence she was dead, evidence of what she had said to a third party was relevant and admissible.

The jury were brought back in and Nancy continued, explaining how Amelia had told her that she was certain that Joe had stolen money from their mother, and how he would have killed her if he'd known she was aware of it.

The next witness was someone I didn't recognise, who turned out to be Alan Newbould, the man who had bought the house in Weybridge from Mary Bradbury.

Yes, he agreed, he had given Joe Bradbury a personal cheque for one hundred thousand pounds as payment for fixtures and fittings, plus some of the carpets and pieces of furniture and, yes, Joe had indicated to him that it was best if the lawyers used by each side for the transaction knew nothing about it.

The eel gave him a bit of a hard time in cross-examination, claiming that it had been he who had committed a crime by avoiding a proportion of the stamp duty land tax, but Mr Newbould never wavered from his story that, as far as he was concerned, the payment had been a legitimate settlement for goods received, and he had been unaware of any intention by Joe Bradbury to keep the money for himself.

An executive of one of the High Street banks then arrived to testify that no sum of any amount, let alone one of a hundred thousand pounds, had been deposited at any time into Mary Bradbury's account by Mr Joseph Bradbury. And, because her son had banked with the same company as his mother, the same executive was also able to provide bank statements to the jury that showed Mr Newbould's funds being cleared into Mr Bradbury's personal account just three days after he'd received the cheque.

Next to appear was the solicitor Mr James Fairbrother, MA (Oxon), TEP, who confirmed that, oh, yes, well, prior to her death, Mrs Mary Bradbury had expressed to him her belief that her son had indeed stolen a hundred thousand pounds from her. As a result, she had cut him out of her will, passing his share of her estate directly to his children.

The eel had made another attempt to prevent hearsay testimony being admitted but with the same result – abject failure – and for the same reason: the relevant person was unable to attend the court in person to give it herself as she was dead.

There were brief appearances by Fred Marchant, Mary's neighbour, followed by his wife Jill, both of whom stated that they had been witnesses to Mary's signing of her new will, the one excluding Joe, and that, as far as they were concerned, she had been quite aware of what she was doing, and why, at the time of the signing.

The eel had been quick to ask them what qualifications they had for making such a claim and, reluctantly, they both had to admit they had none.

351

However, this played straight into the hands of the prosecution as they then called Mary's doctor, the one who had
performed the cognitive assessment tests on her, and he
did have the necessary qualifications to assert that Mary
Bradbury had been of sound mind and did have the required
testamentary capacity under sections 1 to 4 of the Mental
Capacity Act 2005.

There was a smug self-satisfied air to the prosecution counsel
as he dismissed the doctor and then moved on from the theft to
the attempted murder.

First up in this section was a Thames Valley Police traffic
officer, who testified that he had attended a road-traffic incident
at the Hanwell village interchange after a call from a member of
the public to the 999 emergency line.

'And what did you find?' asked the prosecuting barrister.

'A cream-coloured Fiat 500 in the field beyond the hedge. It
was in a heavily damaged condition and there was evidence that
it had been in collision with a nearby large oak tree. The ambulance service were already in attendance and they, together with
the fire brigade, removed the occupant who had been placed in
an induced coma. He was subsequently transported to the John
Radcliffe Hospital by air ambulance.'

How disappointing, I thought. I'd always wanted to go in a
helicopter and now I had, but I'd been unconscious throughout
the whole trip.

'And what then happened to the vehicle?'

'What was left of it, after the fire brigade had cut the roof
off, was collected by a mobile crane onto a low-loader and

removed to a vehicle breakers yard near Bicester. I supervised the removal myself.'

The next witness was a police forensic specialist who testified that he had examined the remains of the Fiat at the breakers yard and had obtained samples of white paint found on the rear of the vehicle. He had further found, by chemical analysis, that the paint was identical to that used on long-wheelbase Ford Transit vans.

An office employee of Joe Bradbury's High Court enforcement company then told the jury that Joe had signed out one of their vehicles on the day in question, a long-wheelbase white Transit van, and the vehicle had then been sent by Mr Bradbury direct to their regularly used body shop for repair after he had informed the company that it had been driven into by a disgruntled loan defaulter.

Next, another police specialist, this time in IT, gave evidence to show that ANPR cameras had recorded the passage of the van along the M40 motorway from London to Banbury, and mobile phone records had shown Joe Bradbury's phone connecting to a mast near Hanwell village just before the supposed time of the collision.

Finally in this sequence, my friend Mr Constance, the orthopaedic surgeon, appeared to describe the injuries that he had encountered on my arrival at the John Radcliffe Hospital.

'He's a very lucky man,' said the surgeon, turning towards where I sat at the back of the courtroom. 'And particularly as he had been in that car all night before being found. Any sudden movement, even involuntary, during that time would have likely severed his spinal cord rendering him, at best, paralysed.'

'So do you consider,' said the prosecutor, 'that, in your expert opinion, the injuries sustained by Mr Gordon-Russell were life-threatening?'

'Absolutely,' said Mr Constance. 'There is no doubt in my mind that more than ninety per cent of people would have died in those circumstances. Mr Gordon-Russell must have the constitution of a horse.'

Oh, no, he's wrong there, I thought. Horses, for all their great bulk, are very delicate creatures; but we all knew what he meant.

The eel had been mostly conspicuous by his absence during this string of testimonies, only briefly rising to ask the police forensic specialist to speculate on how many vehicles on British roads had that same white paint as a Ford Transit van, but now he stood up again.

'Mr Constance,' he said. 'Are you saying that the injuries sustained by Mr Gordon-Russell are consistent only with there having been an attempt on his life? Could the same injuries not have been caused by an accidental collision with the tree caused only by his own excessive speed?'

'Yes, of course.'

'Thank you, Mr Constance. No further questions.'

The eel sat down and the surgeon was dismissed by the judge.

The final strand of the prosecution's case concerned the murder of Amelia.

One of the other detectives on the case gave evidence, playing on the court televisions the CCTV footage from a petrol station near the Banbury motorway junction, in which Joe Bradbury was clearly shown filling his black Nissan with fuel. The time and date on the footage indicated that he was there at 8.20 a.m. on the morning Amelia died.

The same detective then told the jury that the emergency call from Joe to report his sister's death was taken at 10.17 on that same morning. He further stated that the distance between the petrol station and the Old Forge in Hanwell had been measured by him at precisely 4.2 miles.

The prosecutor didn't need to ask him why he thought it had taken Joe almost two hours to cover such a small distance by car. I could tell from the faces of the jury that they had worked that one out for themselves.

Next up was a forensic scene-of-crime officer who testified that he had attended the house in Hanwell on the morning of the murder.

He explained how he had examined the broken lock on the back door, damage he considered consistent with a violent forced entry into the premises from outside. He also described how he had obtained DNA swab samples from the body of the victim and from various surfaces in the kitchen.

'And what did those samples reveal?' asked the prosecutor.

'DNA from three different individuals was found on the kitchen surfaces. Comparison with known profiles has allowed me to identify those individuals as the victim, her husband and the defendant.'

'From just three individuals, you say?' asked the prosecutor. 'Was there any other person's DNA present?'

'No, sir.'

'And how about on the body?'

'Swabs taken from the victim's skin provided just two profiles. That of the victim and another of the defendant.'

'From whereabouts on the body were the swabs taken?'

'From the exposed skin,' said the forensic officer. 'From the hands, face and especially round the neck.'

'And where exactly on the victim's skin was the defendant's DNA found?' asked the prosecutor with a rather smug look on his face. It is said that no barrister should ever ask a question in court to which he doesn't already know the answer, and the prosecuting barrister in this case clearly did.

'On the neck.'

'And did you also take swabs from the ligature used as the murder weapon?'

'Yes, sir, I did.'

The prosecutor waiting expectantly and waved a hand to the witness in encouragement to go on.

'DNA from both the victim and the defendant were present on the leather dog lead.'

'Thank you, officer,' said the prosecutor. 'No further questions.'

The eel was quickly to his feet.

'But would it not be the case,' he said, 'that you would expect the defendant's DNA to be present on the victim's neck and on the ligature if he had been attempting to remove the dog lead from around his sister's throat?'

'I couldn't say,' said the forensic officer. 'My job is only to determine if DNA is present, not to speculate on how it got there.'

*

'They'll surely find him guilty after all that,' I said to DS Dowdeswell over another coffee.

'I very much hope so,' he replied somewhat hesitantly. 'But it's all rather circumstantial.'

'There's surely nothing circumstantial about Joe's DNA being all over Amelia's neck,' I said.

'That's true but, according to his defence statement, he found your wife dead with the dog lead already in place. He claims that he broke in through the back door to try and remove it, and that is how his DNA would have been transferred to both her neck and the lead.'

'What do you mean by his defence statement?' I asked.

'Before the trial starts, the prosecution have to disclose to the accused all the evidence they have, along with the list of any prosecution witnesses. They also have to disclose anything that might help the accused or undermine their own case, even if they don't intend to raise it at the trial. Basically, the prosecution have to disclose everything they know.' The sergeant didn't sound like he much approved of the practice. 'Then the accused has to deliver a document back to the prosecution outlining his intended line of defence, including any defence witnesses he will be calling. That document is what's known as the defence statement.'

'So what else does Joe's defence statement say?'

'On the theft, he says that his mother knew about the payment and it was a gift from her to him for all his help in selling the house.'

'But that's nonsense,' I said.

357

'You know it and I know it, but that's what he will be telling the jury. And, on the attempted murder, he claims that no collision ever took place and you simply must have crashed into the tree by going too fast round the corner.'

'How about the white paint found on the back of the Fiat, and the fact that his mobile phone was in the Hanwell area at the same time?'

'He maintains that those are merely coincidences.'

'Surely the jury won't believe that.'

'In my experience, juries can believe all sorts of strange things. And remember, he doesn't need to convince all twelve of them. Just three would be enough to ensure he's not convicted.'

Now he really had me worried.

38

Joseph Bradbury took the stand at the start of the third week of the trial, as the defence opened their case.

I watched as one of the security guards used his key to unlock the door from the dock to the courtroom proper, and as he then escorted Joe across the floor of the court to the witness box, sitting down right beside him. Meanwhile, the second security officer also took up station, standing four-square in front of the exit double doors out to the concourse.

They were clearly taking no chances that their prisoner might escape.

For the second time I listened as Joseph Bradbury swore to tell the truth, the whole truth and nothing but the truth and, for the second time, I didn't believe a word of it.

The defence barrister was quickly on his feet and there was no building up to the murder indictment for him, he went straight into it from the off.

'Why did you go to see your sister on that fateful Wednesday morning?' he asked Joe.

'Because she called me on the previous evening and asked me to go and see her. Our mother had just been diagnosed with cancer and she wanted to discuss her treatment.'

I knew better than to repeat my shout of 'liar', as I had done in the Coroner's Court. So I just sat on my hands and ground my teeth in frustration.

'But why could you not discuss it with her over the telephone?' asked the eel.

'Amelia was quite emotional when she called me and she said she didn't want to discuss matters over the phone. Hence, she specifically asked me to go over and see her the following morning.'

'But not at her house?'

'No,' Joe said. 'She wanted me to go to her house but recent relations between Amelia's husband and me have not been as good as I would have liked, so I suggested we meet elsewhere so that her husband wouldn't be around to be rude to me, as he always is.'

He turned and looked towards me with his usual pretentious sneer.

It was as much as I could do not to jump to my feet and shout out that it was he who was always rude to me, rather than vice versa. In actual fact, I did my utmost to have no communication with him whatsoever, in order to not inflame the situation. I refused to answer his calls and I certainly did not reply to his ranting, vile emails. Not that that had stopped him sending them. Only him being on remand in Bullingdon Prison had done that.

I pressed my lips together tightly, and gripped the sides of my seat hard to keep myself from standing up.

'So where *did* you arrange to meet your sister?' asked the eel.

'She said that if I wouldn't come to her house then we should meet in a pub car park in Wroxton. The Hare and Hounds pub. It's closed now but we both knew where it was because we had met there before. It's only three miles from where she lived'

'Why not meet at your mother's house?'

'I suggested that but Amelia was insistent that we couldn't speak about mum's future when she was there listening, so we finally agreed on the pub.'

'And at what time was this meeting due to take place?'

'Nine o'clock in the morning. I was there a few minutes early so I waited but Amelia didn't come. In all, I waited there for about an hour. I tried calling her in case she had forgotten but there was no mobile phone signal at that point in Wroxton, so, in the end, I did drive to her house. I rang the front-door bell but there was no answer and it was locked, so I went round the back. It was then that I saw Amelia through the kitchen window. She was lying face down on the kitchen floor.'

His voice trembled. He always had been a good actor.

'The back door was also locked so I broke in by kicking the lock off. I went straight to Amelia and tried to remove the dog lead wrapped around her neck. Her skin was so cold and her lips were blue. I was quite certain she was dead. I've never felt so helpless.'

This time he made out that he was actually crying, covering his face with his hands and blowing his nose loudly into a tissue.

God, it made me so angry.

I knew what real tears were like. I'd wept buckets of them.

'Then what did you do?' asked the eel.

'I immediately called the police and waited for them to arrive.'

The eel shuffled his papers.

'Now let us move on to the supposed theft,' he said. 'Do you admit that you received a personal cheque for one hundred thousand pounds from Mr Newbould in payment for fixtures and fittings, and for some pieces of furniture left at your late mother's property in Weybridge, which Mr Newbould was purchasing at the time?'

'Yes,' said Joe. 'That's right.'

'Was your mother aware of this payment to you?'

'Of course she was. It was her property that I was selling. She was fully aware of the fact and she agreed that I should keep the money in recognition of the work I had done in selling the house for her.'

'But we have heard from the detective in this case, and also from your late mother's solicitor, that she told them both shortly before her untimely death from cancer that she was convinced that you had stolen the money from her. How do you explain that?'

'Convinced is the right word,' Joe said. 'My mother was a frail old lady who was often confused and forgetful, whatever her doctor might say. Just prior to her death, she was convinced by my brother-in-law, William Gordon-Russell, that, among other things, I had stolen this money from her when the reality could not have been more different. She had given it to me as a gift. I remember her clearly saying so to me at the time of her house sale. The fact that, all these years later, she couldn't remember doesn't mean it didn't happen. If it was stolen, would I have been so stupid as to pay the cheque straight into my own bank account for all to see? There simply was no theft. No theft, that is, other than that of half my mother's estate by him.'

He pointed straight at me and I could see the members of the jury looking across the courtroom to where I was sitting.

He sounded so damn convincing and believable, when I was so sure that what he was saying was completely untrue. But neither Mary nor Amelia were here to refute his lies.

Could the jury not see through this travesty?

I found it impossible to read their thoughts.

Only time would tell.

'And finally,' said the eel. 'Let us move on to the attempted murder charge. Please tell the court what you were doing on that particular Wednesday.'

'I was at work in the morning, in Ealing, west London. I was carrying out my duties as a High Court enforcement officer, executing a writ of repossession on a property where the tenants were in arrears with their rent.'

'And did you have a company vehicle for this purpose?'

'Yes, I did,' Joe said. 'A long-wheelbase white-painted Ford Transit van.'

'And how about in the afternoon?'

'The repossession took a lot less time than I had expected.

The tenants had already packed up their stuff before I arrived, and it was simply a matter of seeing them out of the property and then changing the locks. An hour's work at most. So I found myself with time on my hands. I regret it now, but I decided to go to Banbury. I had been bereft over the loss of my sister and I somehow felt that being close to where she had died would give me some sort of comfort.'

'And did it?' asked the eel.

'It did at the time but it has caused me all sorts of trouble since.'

'The prosecution have claimed that you were there in order, on purpose, to crash into a car driven by your brother-in-law. Is that right?'

'No, of course not. I've never crashed into anything on purpose and certainly not near Banbury. That would have been really stupid. If, as they say, the crash was so severe, how come the van wasn't so badly damaged that it was impossible to drive? How would I have then got back to London?'

'So where did you have the crash?'

'It's a bit embarrassing, really. I wasn't concentrating and I ran into a concrete post near the company vehicle depot in Harrow. I know I told the staff in the office that someone else had driven into the van, but that was so I wouldn't get the blame. Things like that happen all the time. That's also why I took the van straight to the body shop.'

He looked shamefaced at the jury and some of them even nodded back at him in understanding.

How could they believe such a load of claptrap?

'So let me just confirm what you're saying to us, Mr Bradbury,' said the eel. 'You say there was no theft because the money was a gift from your mother to you; you say that you did not crash into any other cars; and you say that your sister was already dead when you arrived at her home. Is that correct?'

'Yes,' Joe said, smiling. 'Totally correct on all three counts.'

He confidently removed his spectacles and polished the lenses with a handkerchief.

'No more questions,' said the eel, and he sat down.

The prosecution barrister stood up eagerly, but the judge quickly intervened.

'I think we'll take a short break there,' he said. 'Before the cross-examination. To allow the jury to stretch their legs.' He looked at the clock situated on the wall above the exit doors. 'We will reconvene in twenty minutes.'

'All rise!'

'He's going to get off, isn't he?' I said to DS Dowdeswell over a cup of coffee. 'I could see the jury believing every damn lie he uttered.'

'It always looks bad just after the defence have asked their questions of the defendant. Let's wait until after our man has had a go at him. I'm sure he has some tricks up his sleeve to catch Bradbury out.'

'I hope you're right,' I said. 'At the moment I'd put all my money on an acquittal.'

39

'How would you describe your relationship with Amelia Jane Gordon-Russell?'

The prosecuting counsel was opening his cross-examination.

'We loved each other,' Joe said. 'As a brother and a sister.'

'I suggest to you that you did no such thing. When did you last talk to your sister prior to the supposed telephone call the night before she died?'

'The call was real, I tell you,' Joe said. 'She called me.'

'But when did you speak to her prior to that night?'

'I can't recall for sure.'

'Would you say that you were in regular communication?'

'Quite regular, yes. I sent her emails.'

'Yes,' said the prosecutor dryly. 'Your emails. We will come to those.'

Joe suddenly looked rather worried. As well he might.

'But when did you last actually speak to your sister prior to the call you say she made to you on that Tuesday evening?'

'I've already told you. I can't remember the exact date.'

'Is that not because your sister hadn't spoken to you for nearly two years prior to her death? Indeed, did she not refuse to speak to you after you had been so nasty to her and her husband?'

Joe said nothing.

'Do you recall receiving an email from your sister in the January, twenty-one months before she died?'

'No, I don't,' replied Joe.

'Then I'll read it out to you, to remind you,' said the prosecutor. He lifted a piece of paper. '*Joseph, I hate you, I hate you. You are causing so much hurt and pain. I never want to see you again, ever. I have blocked your calls and I do not want to receive any more of your horrid emails. Leave us alone.*' He waited in silence for a few moments before looking up at the witness. 'Would you say that was the sort of email you might expect to be sent between two people who love each other as a brother and a sister?'

'All siblings have their minor problems occasionally.'

'But this is not a minor problem, is it, Mr Bradbury? Let me read your reply to that email, a reply sent by you in spite of being asked not to.' He picked up another piece of paper. 'This was found in Amelia Gordon-Russell's inbox on her computer. It arrived the day after your sister sent the previous one to you. *Amelia, it is not me that is causing so much hurt and pain, it is you and your vile husband. He is like a cancer in our family and the sooner you get rid of him, the better. He has destroyed his own family and he is now trying to destroy ours too. He is a hateful, hateful man who is trying to ruin my relationship with*

367

my mother. I wish he were dead. The whole family hate him and I have the evidence to prove it. He is a fraud and a liar and I am building a dossier against him.'

He laid the piece of paper back down on the table.

'Not much brotherly love shown there, wouldn't you say, Mr Bradbury?'

Joe said nothing and the prosecutor waited patiently, looking at him.

'The witness will answer the question,' interjected the judge.

'No,' Joe said in a whisper.

'Speak up,' commanded the judge. 'The recording equipment won't catch what is said if you whisper.'

'No,' Joe said again, louder.

'And that is not the only email you have sent to your sister since that time, is it, Mr Bradbury?'

'No,' Joe said again.

'No, indeed,' replied the prosecutor. 'In fact, since then you have sent no fewer than twenty-six equally unpleasant emails to either your sister or your brother-in-law, in spite of receiving not a single reply back from either of them. Would you call that harassment, Mr Bradbury?'

Joe said nothing and, this time, the judge let it go.

But the prosecutor wasn't finished with the emails just yet. 'The jury will be given printed copies of all these emails as an evidence bundle.' He held up a wad of papers. 'It is not contested by the defence that these emails were sent by you to your sister and brother-in-law from your personal computer. Isn't that right, Mr Bradbury?'

'Yes,' he said quietly.

'Let me remind you of just one more of them. You sent the following to your sister just five days before she died.' He picked up one of the pieces of paper from the wad and read from it. '*I hear from Mum that you have been bullying her again, telling her that I am wicked and evil. Her words not mine. I am hugely disappointed that you should choose to target a frail old lady with such abusive comments about her own son, shouting at her and threatening her. You are a stupid, stupid woman. Are you aware how much of a relief it is to everyone else that you can't have children, so that you can't pass on your crazy genes to the next generation? I will not tolerate behaviour like this towards our mother and will take severe action against you if it continues.*' The prosecutor paused. 'What sort of severe action would that be, Mr Bradbury?'

'It was just a turn of phrase,' he mumbled.

The prosecutor left it hanging, and the jury looked suitably horrified by what they'd just heard. After a fitting pause, the prosecutor went on.

'Let us now turn to why you drove a Ford Transit van belonging to your High Court enforcement firm all the way from Ealing in west London to Banbury and back, a distance of some seventy miles each way. You have told the jury that you undertook the journey solely because you believed that being close to where your sister died might give you some comfort in your grief. Is that right?'

'Yes,' Joe said.

'But when you were first questioned by the police, did you

not deny ever having been in Banbury on that day, and then, when confronted with the automatic number plate recognition evidence that showed the van on the M40, did you not then deny being the driver? Were you lying to the police then, Mr Bradbury, or are you lying to us now?'

'I was lying to the police then,' Joe said at little more than a mumble.

'And why would that be?' the prosecutor asked.

'I don't know. Maybe I panicked.'

'Now let us turn to this concrete post that you claim to have hit. Where is this post exactly? Does it also have white paint on it from the Transit van?'

'I don't know of its exact location. I can't remember.'

'I suggest, Mr Bradbury, that you can't remember because the post doesn't exist. I further suggest that the white paint found on the back of Mr Gordon-Russell's car was from the white van you drove to Banbury. And you went there with the express intention of murdering Mr Gordon-Russell and that is exactly what you attempted to do by crashing the van into his car.'

'No,' Joe said. 'I can't think why you would say that.'

'Maybe because it's true.'

The prosecutor picked up yet more papers.

'Finally, let us turn to this supposed telephone call of the Tuesday evening. I have here the phone records of both Mrs Gordon-Russell and yourself, for your landlines and mobile phones. In them, there is no indication of any call from her to you on that evening, from any of her numbers to any of yours. How do you account for that, Mr Bradbury?'

'I don't know,' said Joe. 'She definitely made the call. Perhaps she used a public call box.'

'If so, then that too would be shown on the documentation. But it isn't. The records show that only one call was received by you on that evening, at five past eight, from your mother.'

'Then the records must be wrong. I'm telling you, Amelia called me.'

'I suggest,' said the prosecutor, 'that no such call was ever made. That you made it up to justify your actions in going to your sister's house on that Wednesday morning, and there you strangled her as the *severe action* that you had previously threatened her with.'

'No,' Joe shouted at him in desperation. 'That's not true. I didn't kill her.'

I looked at the jury and wondered how many of them were believing him now.

And then, if things weren't bad enough already for Joe, they were about to get a great deal worse.

The second witness for the defence was Rachael Bradbury, Joe's wife.

In the United Kingdom, as in the United States, other than in very limited circumstances of domestic or child abuse, a wife cannot be compelled to give evidence in court against her husband, nor a husband against his wife.

This is known as spousal privilege and stems from the English common law position that a husband and wife are considered, by 'legal fiction', to be one person.

Every individual has the right in law not to incriminate them-selves through their testimony, a right originally established by common law in England, and by the fifth amendment to the constitution in the United States, which states that 'no person . . . shall be compelled in any criminal case to be a witness against himself'. Hence the term 'taking the fifth' as the excuse for a witness not to answer a question in a US court.

It is also the basis for the 'right to remain silent' on arrest and in police questioning.

As 'one person', therefore, a wife also has the right to remain silent and cannot be forced to testify against her husband.

But she could do so voluntarily.

Or by mistake.

Rachael had been called by the defence to further the claim by Joe that he had received a telephone call from Amelia on the night before she died.

Having given her testimony in answer to questions by the eel, she was then open to cross-examination.

'Hello, Mrs Bradbury,' said the prosecutor, smiling at her. 'It must be very difficult for you to come to this court and give evidence when your husband is sitting in the dock.'

'Yes, it is,' she replied, glancing across at Joe. 'Very diffi-cult indeed.'

'Now, tell me,' went on the prosecutor, 'did you personally speak with Mrs Gordon-Russell on the telephone during the evening in question?'

'She spoke to my husband.'

'But not to you?'

'No,' she said. 'But I could hear their conversation.'

'All of the conversation?' asked the prosecutor. 'Or just your husband's side?'

'Well, just his side, I suppose, but I could hear a voice from the other end of the phone even if I couldn't hear the exact words.'

'Then I suggest that your evidence is of no value to the court. For all you know, your husband could have been talking to the speaking clock. Isn't that right, Mrs Bradbury?'

'The speaking clock doesn't call us,' she said. 'I know he was talking to his sister.' There was a touch of desperation in her voice, as if she was trying to convince herself as much as the jury, and they all heard it.

And the prosecuting barrister wasn't finished with her, not by a long way.

'Now, Mrs Bradbury,' he said. 'Were you aware at the time that your husband received a hundred thousand pounds from the sale of some of your mother-in-law's belongings?'

'Yes, of course,' replied Rachael. 'It was a gift from his mother. I was there when she gave it to Joe.'

'And what did you do with the money?'

She seemed somewhat surprised by the question, but I had briefed the barrister and we both thought it was a question worth asking.

'Some of it went to paying off debts, and some on a new car.'

'A black Nissan?'

'Yes.'

'So were you heavily in debt before he received the hundred thousand?'

'Quite heavily,' she said. Then she smiled. 'You know what it's like with three small kids. They can be a considerable draw on the family finances.'

Perhaps she said it as a way of trying to garner a little sympathy from the jury. But she didn't get it.

The prosecutor pounced. 'Did your mother-in-law not help you out with some of your children's expenses, as their grandmother?'

'You've got to be joking. She was tighter than a duck's arse when it came to money.' She emitted a hollow laugh.

There was a long pause in which her laughter died away. And no one else joined in.

'And yet,' said the prosecutor gleefully, 'you would have us believe that she simply gave your husband a hundred thousand pounds. I suggest to you that the hundred thousand was stolen by your husband because of the financial difficulties in which you found yourself as a couple. It was just too good an opportunity not to take what you felt was rightly yours, don't you agree, Mrs Bradbury?'

Just as at the funeral, Rachael stupidly couldn't resist having a dig at her late mother-in-law.

'She wouldn't miss it,' she said. 'She had millions.'

There was a groan from the dock that the whole court could hear, in spite of the glass panels. Rachael looked over to her husband with shock and surprise on her face, but the damage had been done, and everyone knew it – everyone, that was, except her. But she soon worked it out.

'No further questions,' said the prosecutor, and he sat down.

Rachael, now in floods of tears, was dismissed.

How the fortunes in a criminal trial could ebb and flow like the tide.

Such was the power of cross-examination.

Just a few hours ago, I'd have staked my house on an acquittal, but now, and especially after Rachael's debacle, I was more confident of a conviction.

40

The last two days of the trial proper were taken up with closing arguments by the barristers, legal submissions and the summing-up by the judge.

First up was the prosecutor, still on a roll after his cross-examination of the defendant and his wife.

'Ladies and gentlemen of the jury,' he said, facing them. 'I have laid before you a compelling banquet of evidence in this case, evidence that must lead you to the inevitable conclusion that the defendant, Mr Joseph Bradbury, is guilty of all three of the indictments he faces: theft, attempted murder and murder itself – the murder, no less, of his own sister, his own flesh and blood.'

He was like an actor on stage, giving everything to his performance.

He outlined the prosecution evidence, reminding the jury of what his witnesses had said about the hundred thousand pounds, the ANPR results of the Ford Transit van on the road to Banbury, the white paint found on the back of the Fiat 500, the CCTV footage of the black Nissan at the petrol station early on the morning of the murder, the defendant's DNA on the neck of the victim and on the murder weapon, and the lack of any record of a supposed telephone call made by the victim to the defendant on the night before.

He also reminded them of the monetary gain that Joe had stood to receive as a result of Amelia predeceasing her mother, and of his financial plight that Rachael had so clearly signalled in her testimony.

Finally, he turned to Joe's emails, reading out some of his most offensive comments, many of which contained veiled, and not so veiled, threats against both Amelia and me.

'I am sure that you are all fair-minded individuals and you may say that much of the evidence in this case is circumstantial, and you would be right. But circumstantial evidence is like a jigsaw puzzle. Each piece on its own may seem fairly meaning-less but, when all of them are fitted together, they build up a picture of guilt that should be clear for you all to see.'

And we had to hope that the defence couldn't knock enough pieces out of the jigsaw puzzle such that the picture became impossible to discern.

'My learned friend, the counsel for the defence, will try and tell you that there is uncertainty in this case, that there is no "smoking gun" that would prove, beyond any shadow of doubt whatsoever, that the defendant is guilty. But I say to you, that there is ample evidence to demonstrate the defendant's guilt beyond any reasonable doubt. This is not a fantasy movie where special effects can defy the laws of nature and the most improbable and unlikely exploits can seem commonplace. This is the real world and the heinous crime of murder has been committed, depriving Amelia Gordon-Russell of the most precious commodity that each of us possess, life itself. We have shown that Mr Bradbury had both the opportunity and the motive, as well as the mental attitude to kill and to attempt to kill, and his DNA was found all over the murder scene. It is now your duty, as the jury in this case, to ensure that the perpetrator of these appalling offences, that is the defendant in the dock, is justly condemned and punished for his actions by finding him guilty.'

He sat down. Those would be the prosecution's last words in the case. He had done all he could.

The eel stood up and straightened his gown and wig.

'Members of the jury,' he said. 'There has been much argument and counter-argument in this case but one fact stands out above all others: there is no direct evidence to prove that Mr Joseph Bradbury has committed any of these offences, and you must, therefore, return verdicts of not guilty.'

He took a drink of water from his glass to give time for that sentence to be absorbed by the jury.

'Mr Bradbury does not need to prove his innocence, that is presumed by the law until shown otherwise. Instead, it is for the prosecution to prove to you that he is guilty, something that I contend they have singularly failed to do.'

Another sip of water.

'The term *beyond reasonable doubt* is one that my learned friend has raised with you. "What is beyond reasonable doubt?"

I hear you ask. So I will tell you. It is the burden and standard of proof that you must apply in this case. In order to convict you have to be sure, not just almost sure, that the defendant has performed the actions of which he is accused. If you only think that he *might* have done them, or even that he *probably* did them, then that is not good enough and you must acquit. In order to convict, you must be sure he did them.'

The eel is good, I thought.

No reasonable doubt about that.

'And I put it to you, members of the jury, that you cannot be sure of what happened in that kitchen on that fateful morning, you cannot be sure that Mrs Gordon-Russell wasn't already dead by the time the defendant arrived at her house, you cannot be sure that the van driven by the defendant did collide with a car driven by Mr Gordon-Russell, and you cannot be sure that Mrs Mary Bradbury didn't give a hundred thousand pounds to her only son. And, because you cannot be sure of any of these things, it is your solemn duty to return three verdicts of not guilty.'

He sat down. His time was up too.

I was totally confused. And if I was, then how were the jury faring? They were the ones that now had to make the decisions and I had absolutely no idea of what was going on in their minds.

I was thinking that an acquittal was back to being odds-on favourite.

Next it was the judge's turn.

'Ladies and gentlemen of the jury,' he said, turning towards them. 'You and I have separate functions in this trial. My job is twofold. Firstly, to rule on all aspects of the law to ensure a fair hearing for the defendant, and secondly, to sum up the evidence and give you direction in the law to assist you in reaching your verdict. Your function, however, is to determine the facts in the case. The facts are your domain, and solely yours.'

He paused and looked at each of them in turn.

'You have heard the closing speeches of the prosecution and the defence counsels but those were just that, speeches. They are not evidence in this case. The evidence is what you have heard from the witness box, or read in the uncontested evidence bundle provided to you by the prosecution. You have the responsibility of deciding upon the evidence that has been brought before you, and only upon that evidence, whether the defendant is guilty or not guilty of the offences of which he has been accused.'

He paused again.

'Now that all the evidence has been heard, and the prosecution and defence counsels have addressed their arguments to you as to the conflicting conclusions they would each ask you to draw from that evidence, I will give you directions upon the law, which you are required to apply.

'The prosecution have the burden of proving the guilt of the defendant. That burden never shifts. The defence at no stage in this case have to prove anything whatsoever to you. Before you can convict the defendant on any of the counts, the prosecution have to satisfy you so that you are sure that he is guilty of that count. If you are sure, you convict him. If you are not, you acquit him. That is all there is to it.

'Let me deal with the three indictments in turn. First, on the matter of the theft, there is no dispute that the defendant did receive a payment of one hundred thousand pounds from Mr Newbould. The only matter in contention is whether that payment was known to Mrs Mary Bradbury and, furthermore, if she had then sanctioned it as a gift to her son. If you think that the defendant and his wife may be telling the truth when they say that the hundred thousand was a gift, then you must find him not guilty. If, on the other hand, you believe the evidence given concerning Mrs Mary Bradbury's belief that it was stolen, and also that you are sure the defendant knowingly kept the payment for himself even though he was fully aware that he was not entitled to it, then you must find him guilty of theft.'

The judge took a drink of water.

'Secondly, let me turn to the attempted murder charge. There is agreement between the prosecution and defence concerning the fact that the defendant drove a white Ford Transit van from London to Banbury. Even though he initially denied the fact to the police, and you may apply whatever weight to that denial as you may decide, he now admits that he was the driver of the van and he was in the vicinity of the crash in which Mr Gordon-Russell was seriously injured. You don't have to worry about whether that bit is true. It is. What is in dispute is whether he was the cause of the crash. If you think that the defendant's account may be true and that he did not crash into the car, and that he damaged the van later by striking a concrete post in Harrow, then you should find him not guilty.'

There was a hefty degree of scepticism in his tone.

'However, if you believe the prosecution's claim that he

was responsible for the crash and that the white paint found on the rear of Mr Gordon-Russell's car was from the van that the defendant was driving, and you are sure, not only that the defendant did purposely crash into the car, but also that he did so in an attempt, not just to injure Mr Gordon-Russell but to kill him, then you should find him guilty of attempted murder.

'Now let us turn to the murder itself. The prosecution have told you that the defendant had both the opportunity and the motive to have carried out this murder. It has been established by a forensic expert that the defendant's DNA was present on the victim's neck and on the dog lead used to strangle her. This is not contested by the defence. What is in contention is whether Mrs Gordon-Russell was alive or dead when the defendant arrived at her house. If you think that the defendant may be telling the truth that she was already dead when he arrived and that someone else was responsible, then you should find him not guilty. If, however, you believe that the defendant is lying and you are sure that he did, in fact, break in and strangle Mrs Gordon-Russell, then you should find him guilty of murder.

'Now, members of the jury,' went on the judge, 'you will retire to consider your verdicts. You should elect a foreman from your number who will act as a conduit for your discussion and your spokesperson, but be aware that each of you has an equal voice and your deliberations should be as a complete jury of twelve. Do not split up into smaller groups, or discuss matters when some of you are not present. By a process of discussion of the evidence, the group of twelve of you must decide, after applying the law as I have directed you, whether your verdict should be guilty or not guilty on each count, and it should be the verdict of you all. You may have heard of something called a majority verdict, but that does not apply in this case. If, at some time in the future, it does become relevant, then I will give you the necessary direction in the law. Until that time, I require a unanimous decision.'

The usher then led the jury out of the court.

I watched them go, trying but failing to read what was going on in their minds. One or two of them glanced across at Joe sitting in the dock behind the glass but, even then, I found it impossible to discern if they were pro or anti.

Now it was up to them.

What had Douglas said? *In my experience, juries are always a bit of a lottery.*

My own profession was all about measuring chance and calculating probability, but still I had little or no idea what would happen.

Would the jury believe Joe or not? He had certainly been resolute and unwavering about finding Amelia already dead. And I had to admit he'd been fairly convincing on that point, even if his hitting-the-concrete-post-with-the-van story had been far more suspect.

All we could do was wait for the jury to decide.

Now where was my money?

41

And wait we did. For hours. No 'seventeen or twenty-seven minutes of deliberation' in *this* murder trial.

'Is it a good sign or a bad one?' I asked DS Dowdeswell.

'You never can tell,' he replied unhelpfully. 'Juries are a law unto themselves. But if they're spending the time reading through all those nasty emails, it might be a good one.'

We waited.

And then we waited some more.

'I wonder what they're saying in there,' I said absentmindedly.

'We will never know,' said the detective. 'Unlike in the United States where jurors are interviewed on television after high-profile cases, and some of them even write books about their jury deliberations, here they are not allowed to speak about it – not then, not ever.'

We went on waiting.

At the end of the day the judge had the jury brought back into court.

'Members of the jury,' he said. 'I am going to send you home now for the night. You will reconvene here tomorrow morning at ten o'clock to continue your deliberations. Please take note, you must not discuss the case with anyone else, not anyone else at all, and that includes your family. Nor are you at liberty to discuss it between yourselves unless all twelve of you are together in the jury room. And, as I have told you before, you must not seek to discover any details of this case in the newspapers, on the television or radio, or via the internet or social media. To do any of those things would be to hold this court in contempt and may make you subject to imprisonment.'

And, with that dire warning still ringing in their ears, the twelve trooped out of the court.

As on most nights during the trial, I went home by taxi to the Old Forge.

This waiting and not knowing was interminable torture but, if it was bad for me, it must be so much worse for Joe. I almost felt sorry for him, but only almost. He had brought all of this on himself. I just hoped that the jury could see through his lies and protestations.

I kicked my heels around the house all evening and wondered if I would still be living here a year from now. My love for the place had evaporated on that October morning, and it had never returned.

Maybe I'd move back to London.

A new home? A new job? A new life?

Same old heartache.

I tried to watch some television but I was too nervous to concentrate. I went to bed but I couldn't sleep. By the early hours,
when I finally dozed off, I had convinced myself that the jury
would find him innocent.

What would I do then?

By lunchtime of the second day of jury deliberation, I was almost
climbing the walls with tension, fear and frustration, at least I
would have been if my legs had been working correctly. As it
was, I couldn't even pace up and down properly to rid myself of
the nervous energy.

Why was the jury taking so long? What were they doing in there?

Midway through the afternoon, the judge called them back
into court to ask how things were going and whether it was likely
that they would be able to reach a decision on which they were
all agreed.

The foreman stood up. He was the man who had been in shorts
and flip-flops for much of the trial but now was wearing a sober
shirt and trousers, maybe in deference to his position. 'Yes,' he
said. 'I think we may be able to reach verdicts if given a little
more time.'

So the judge sent them back to the jury room.

And his intervention must have galvanised their thinking
because, less than an hour later, word came through that the jury
were ready with their verdicts.

I wasn't.

My heart was beating nineteen to the dozen and, as I took my
seat in the court, I could hardly breathe.

Everyone took their allotted places and, when all were ready, the jury were brought in.

Douglas had told me that he reckoned he could always tell if the jury were going to give a 'not guilty' verdict. 'They will look at the defendant,' he'd said. 'If it's guilty they tend to keep their eyes down.'

But I couldn't tell however hard I tried by watching them walk in. Most of them just looked at the judge.

When they were all seated, the clerk of the court stood up and turned to them. 'Would the foreman of the jury please stand.'

He did so.

'Ladies and gentlemen of the jury,' said the clerk. 'Have you reached verdicts on the indictments upon which you are all agreed?

'Yes,' replied the foreman.

'To my next questions,' said the clerk, 'only answer guilty or not guilty: on count one, theft, do you find the defendant guilty or not guilty?'

'Not guilty.'

NOT GUILTY!

I couldn't believe my ears. Were the jury stupid or something? Hadn't they been listening? How could they not find him guilty based on the evidence?

I glanced briefly at Joe in the dock and he was smiling.

I felt sick.

I could hear the blood rushing in my head and my hands were shaking. Was this all going to be for nothing?

But the court clerk moved swiftly on regardless.

'On count two, attempted murder, do you find the defendant guilty or not guilty?'

'Guilty.'

I hardly heard it, such was my panic. I looked again at Joe. He wasn't smiling now. And we weren't finished yet.

'On count three, murder, do you find the defendant guilty or not guilty?'

I held my breath and my heart pounded even more. I really had no idea which way it would go.

The foreman stood bolt upright facing the judge.

'Guilty.'

It felt to me that he had said it in slow motion, the word seemingly stretched over several seconds.

I started breathing again, letting out a small sigh of satisfaction.

But the reaction from the dock was far more dramatic.

Joe stood up and banged on the glass with his hands while shouting at the jury. 'No. No. You're wrong. You're wrong. I never killed her. It was him.' He pointed at me. 'He killed her. It wasn't me. He did it.'

The two security guards in the dock moved quickly to either side of Joe and they manhandled him back into his seat, where he sat in a heap.

He started crying.

The judge just watched and waited for calm to be restored. Contrary to popular belief, judges in British courts don't have gavels to bang as they do in the United States.

'Ladies and gentlemen of the jury,' he said finally, facing

them. 'Thank you for your diligence in this trial and for doing your duty as citizens. You are hereby discharged.'

Then he turned to the body of the court.

'This case is now adjourned until tomorrow morning at eleven o'clock, when sentence will be passed.'

After all that waiting, the verdicts had been over so quickly.

It felt surreal.

'All rise,' shouted the usher and we all did, except for Joe, who remained seated with his head down. He was then led away by the security guards, out through the door at the back of the dock.

I watched him being taken away with a mixed bag of emotions: disbelief that he had been found not guilty of the theft; pleasure that he'd at least been convicted of murder and attempted murder; anger at what he'd done to Amelia; plus a huge amount of sorrow.

And the sorrow won.

How had we come to this?

Joe and I had once been good friends, so much so that I had nearly asked him to be my best man at my wedding. And Amelia and I had both been so pleased when his and Rachael's girls had been born, revelling in being an uncle and aunt, even if we couldn't be parents ourselves.

And, now, all of that was gone for ever.

Amelia was dead and Joe was facing a life term in prison.

After the apparent disaster of her testimony, Rachael hadn't returned to the court and she hadn't been present for the verdict. But her life, too, had been destroyed. As had her children's.

They would now have no father around during their formative years, with only infrequent visits to see him in prison to look forward to.

The whole situation was a complete tragedy for all of us.

There was nothing to celebrate.

Not that that stopped DS Dowdeswell from doing so.

'What a great result,' he said to me, all smiles, slapping me on the back outside the court.

'I can't believe he was acquitted of the theft.'

'The jury may have thought the money was a gift,' said the DS, shaking his head in disbelief. 'But don't worry about that. Bradbury was convicted of the other two, and they were the big ones. You must be so pleased.'

How could I tell him that I wasn't?

'I suppose I'm happy it's finally over,' I said.

But was I?

The build-up and then the trial itself had given me a purpose in life. Now, with the delivery of the jury's verdicts, it had suddenly finished, and in spite of mostly getting the result I wanted, I was already feeling a sense of loss.

'I expect you'll be reading your Victim Personal Statement to the court in the morning prior to sentencing,' said the detective.

I shook my head. 'I haven't written one.'

'Why on earth not?'

'What good would it do?'

'You could explain to the judge how much the attempted murder has caused you such physical pain and hardship, and also how your wife's murder has affected your life and made it so much worse.'

It had certainly done that.

'He'll get a life sentence anyway,' I said. 'All murderers do.'

'But the judge also has to decide the minimum term. Your statement might make a difference to the length of that.'

Did I really want that responsibility?

'There's still time,' said the DS enthusiastically. 'You can do it tonight.'

'I suppose I could,' I replied, but without his eagerness.

'Great. I'll make sure the CPS know it's coming.'

My cheerful taxi driver dropped me outside the Old Forge.

'Same time tomorrow?' he said.

'Yes, please,' I replied. 'But it will be the last day.'

I wasn't sure whether he was pleased or not. For him, the trial had been a nice little earner, with guaranteed journeys to and from Oxford.

I paid his fare and went into the house. As always, it was cold and quiet, in spite of the warmth of the day.

Perhaps I should have been elated. At long last, Joe was going to get his just deserts. But it did nothing for me. The torment of loneliness continued.

When alone, I had taken to talking to Amelia.

I knew it was irrational but, nevertheless, I did it, imagining what she might have said in reply. It helped.

'The jury found Joe guilty of your murder,' I said out loud in the kitchen. 'He's going to prison for a very long time.'

I think she would have been pleased, certainly more pleased than I.

Over the past three or four years, Amelia had grown to hate her brother with a passion.

Any inter-sibling love that had once existed had been totally overridden by the pain and mental suffering he had caused to her. She had been one for whom forgiveness was something other people did, especially with respect to her brother.

'One day I'm going to explode,' she would often say. 'You watch, I'll wipe the floor with the bastard.'

I had tried my best to keep her calm, not least because anger was a serious precursor to her becoming depressed.

It had been I who had insisted that she have nothing to do with Joe, and I would plead with her not to read his emails. But I know she did, and they stoked her fury. I encouraged her to let it all wash right over her. But she couldn't, and every one of his insults was like a dagger in her heart.

But now the court had wiped its hard blue-carpeted floor with him and, whatever the judge might say in the morning, a long stretch in the slammer awaited.

However, no length of sentence could ever bring Amelia back.

How long did I want as sufficient punishment?

Or was it revenge that I needed?

I went and sat at my desk in the study, trying to write a Victim Personal Statement.

According to the Ministry of Justice website, my statement should explain the impact the crime had had on me.

It had totally destroyed my life, but how could I put that into words?

What I wasn't allowed to include was any comment concerning the length of the sentence that I was hoping for. *Lock him into a dank fetid dungeon and throw the key into the River Thames* was not appropriate, even if I'd wanted it.

I tried four times, explaining not only the physical injuries I had suffered but also the emotional and psychological ones. I wrote about how the loss of my wife had immeasurably damaged the quality of my life on a day-to-day basis, and how any hopes for my future had been extinguished by her death.

But every time I read through what I'd typed on the computer screen, it all seemed inadequate and somehow rather trite.

For the fourth time, I deleted the words and then closed my laptop.

I had made my feelings perfectly clear during my testimony, so I decided I would now leave it up to the judge.

42

'The prisoner will stand,' said the clerk of the court.

Joe stood up and faced the judge.

If anyone had been hoping for a quick 'I sentence you to life imprisonment – take him down', after which the rest of us could go for an early lunch, they were to be disappointed.

Sentencing took the best part of an hour and a half, and Joe stood in the dock throughout.

The judge didn't once mention the theft. Instead he merely summarised the actual convictions and applied the Sentencing Council guidelines to each, taking into account any aggravating or mitigating circumstances.

For the attempted murder, the judge took into account Joe's forward planning and his premeditation in driving all the way from London, as well as the seriousness of my injuries and the long-term effects on my health. He did give Joe credit for his previous exemplary record and his previous good character but, nevertheless, he sentenced him to fifteen years imprisonment.

I glanced at Joe in the dock. He wobbled a bit but remained standing.

In England and Wales, there is a mandatory life sentence for murder. All the judge had to decide on was the tariff, the minimum term to be served before he was eligible for parole.

In mitigation, the judge ruled that, as Joe had not taken the murder weapon with him but had used something already to hand in the kitchen of the Old Forge, it suggested that the degree of pre-planning had been small, but that was more than offset by his breaking into the premises and killing within the victim's own home, a place where she should have felt safe.

The guidelines stated that the minimum term of imprisonment for a person over the age of eighteen sentenced to life for murder started at fifteen years but, with the aggravating circumstances, plus the degree of violence used on a blood relative for financial gain, and bearing in mind the sentence already passed for the attempted murder, the judge set the tariff at twenty-five years.

Joe did more than wobble this time. He stepped backwards and sat down heavily.

And there was a gasp from some of the others in the court, me included.

Even without a Victim Personal Statement from me, the judge had thrown the book at him.

However, DS Dowdeswell, understandably, was delighted.

When I'd met him earlier he'd been disappointed, and not a little angry, that I had declined the opportunity to read out a victim statement prior to the sentencing, but all that had now gone. He was in jovial spirits.

I suppose, for the detectives in a murder case, the length of the sentence handed down to a guilty offender must be a measure of their success in the investigation. For some, and that obviously included DS Dowdeswell, life should mean life, but a tariff of more than twenty years was the next best thing.

But for me, the deep sorrow of yesterday returned. It was such a waste of so many lives, and especially of Amelia's.

I declined an invitation from the police team to join them for a celebratory lunchtime drink in a local pub, and managed to avoid the media scrum outside the court by slipping away during the statement read by DCI Priestly to the waiting TV cameras.

I'd phoned my taxi driver, and he picked me up around the corner in Speedwell Street and took me home.

'Good result?' he asked as I settled into the back seat.

'I suppose so,' I said.

And, indeed, it was, in spite of my lack of enthusiasm. And I'd have been much more devastated if Joe had been acquitted of all the charges and had walked free.

But there were no winners here, just losers.

The driver took me to Hanwell in silence, for which I was grateful.

Life now had to get back to normal, at least as normal as I could make it.

Perhaps I'd give those insurance account managers a call and ask them to put me back on their *persona grata* lists, and maybe I'd invite a few estate agents round to value the Old Forge with a view to selling. Would a high-profile murder in the kitchen increase or decrease the price?

'Don't s'pose you need me any more,' said the driver as he dropped me.

'Not immediately,' I said, giving him a generous tip. 'But I'm sure I'll use you again sometime.'

'Always available,' he said with a smile. 'Give me a call.'

I stood and watched him drive away. Even though he didn't know it, his friendly face every morning and evening had done much to keep me sane during the stress of the past weeks. And I'd miss him.

I went in to my quiet, lonely house.

Now what did I do?

I wandered aimlessly from room to room, unable to settle to anything, and ended up, as always, in the kitchen.

I looked at the broken lock.

'I think it's finally time I fixed you,' I said out loud to it, and I dug out my toolbox from beneath the sink.

I had hoped it was just a matter of securing everything back into place, but the lock wasn't just hanging off the wooden door, its metal casing was also twisted and useless, so I used a screwdriver and a pair of pliers to remove it completely.

I tried to straighten out the casing but without success and, if anything, I made it worse. I decided that I'd need a replacement lock, which was a bit of a shame as the broken one was old and in keeping with the age of the house.

Maybe I'd be able to match it with a modern reproduction. *No time like the present*, I thought, and I knew exactly where to go to find one.

There have been markets in Banbury since Anglo-Saxon

times and one was still held in the centre of the town every Thursday and Saturday.

One of the regular stalls was run by a man with whom Amelia and I had become quite friendly over the years, since we'd moved into the Old Forge. He dealt in specialist hardware, especially little bits and bobs that you couldn't get anywhere else. And much of his stuff was aimed at people like us, owners of listed buildings, for whom English Heritage laid down strict regulations concerning what we could and couldn't use in repairs on our houses.

If anyone had a replacement lock of the right sort, it would be him.

Today was a Thursday and, if I asked him now, he might be able to delve into his huge stock at home to get the right part by Saturday. Otherwise I'd have to wait a whole week.

I drove my 174 m.p.h. supercharged Jaguar sports car into Banbury at a very sedate pace, and not just because I was worried about picking up another three points on my licence, something which would have triggered a ban. The collision with the tree and my resulting injuries had undeniably made me far more wary.

I parked as close as I could and shuffled down to the market square.

'Hi, Bill,' said my friend, warmly shaking my hand. 'Haven't seen you for a very long while.'

'No,' I replied. 'I've been rather busy.'

'I'm so sorry to hear about your lovely wife,' he said. 'Dreadful thing. I was so shocked, as I'd been talking to her

only a few days before she died. She dropped by for a chat and
to buy something.'

He spent several minutes talking about Amelia's last visit to
his stall, not that it made me feel any better. Would I ever get
used to her not being around? Eventually, I showed him the
broken lock.

'I can't match it exactly,' he said. 'But I think I can get pretty
close. Come again on Saturday and I'll see what I can find in
the meantime.'

'Thanks,' I said.

As I drove home, I mulled over what the market stallholder
had told me and, instead of immediately going in through my
own front door, I went across the road to the Fadeleys' place
and rang their bell.

Nancy answered.

'Hello, Bill,' she said. 'Dave and I have been thinking of you
a lot these last few days. You must be pleased with the outcome
of the trial. I heard it on the news.'

'I suppose so,' I said. 'At least no one will still think that I'm
responsible for Amelia's death.'

'Would you like to come in for a cuppa?'

We sat in her kitchen, alongside her vast array of cookbooks,
and, while we were drinking the tea, I asked her a question.

After about fifteen minutes or so, I got up to go.

'Dave will be home from London around seven,' Nancy said.
'Would you like to come over and join us for supper? I'm making
seared scallops in a champagne cream sauce.'

It sounded delicious and a huge improvement on my usual

individual ready meals, but I didn't want company – not tonight.

And I had far more important things on my mind than eating.

I sat on the cold hard stone kitchen floor of the Old Forge and sobbed.

I had come straight home from Nancy's house and searched for something and, to my absolute horror, I had found it almost immediately.

Not that I was pleased that I'd found it. Far from it.

It would have been infinitely better if I hadn't.

For all her mental health problems, and whatever her brother might have claimed, Amelia hadn't been stupid. Quite the reverse. She had been a very smart lady, very smart indeed. But she hadn't been able to hide everything – not forever – and not from me.

I couldn't drag my eyes away from what I'd found. It was only small and I might have never noticed it, that was if I hadn't been expressly looking for it.

But I had been, and there it was.

Again, I felt sick.

Just like the jury, I deliberated with myself and came to the only logical conclusion from the evidence, a verdict beyond a reasonable doubt.

Amelia hadn't been murdered at all.

She had committed suicide.

The police were very accustomed to investigating unex-plained violent deaths to determine if they were really murders made to look like suicides. But now they needed to have a closer look at Amelia's death, as I had done, and then they would likely come to the same conclusion as I had, that this had been a suicide made to look like murder.

Was she really that scheming?

Yes, she was. Especially when it came to her brother.

Furthermore, Joe hadn't been lying after all.

Amelia had indeed called her brother on that Tuesday evening to arrange their strange rendezvous at the disused pub car park in Wroxton for the following morning, knowing that, when she failed to appear, he would eventually drive to our house and find her cold dead body. And she had done that partly to prevent me from having the trauma of finding her, but mostly in the hope and expectation that Joe would be accused of her murder.

She had killed herself at a time when she knew I had the cast-iron alibi of being at a charity dinner in Birmingham, and made it look like murder so I could still collect her life insurance money. Perhaps she hadn't realised that, by pre-deceasing her mother, Joe would have inherited all of the estate.

But maybe she had.

Had she appreciated how important motive was to the police? Was that, indeed, part of her scheme to frame her brother from beyond the grave?

I thought she had been much better in the few months before her death, and her talk of 'ending it all' had seemingly faded. But it had always been there in the background and her mother's cancer diagnosis, together with Joe's final hate-filled email, had caused it to rear its ugly head again, only more so.

Amelia had known all about her mother's cancer – Jim and Gladys Wilson from Weybridge had made that perfectly clear. Had she just not told me in order to prevent me from working out her plan?

I wanted so much *not* to believe that she had killed herself after all that expensive therapy, and after I had worked so hard to prevent it, but . . .

Let us consider the evidence.

Amelia was dead.

Of that there was absolutely no doubt. I'd seen her lifeless body with my own two eyes. And she had died of strangulation with our old leather dog lead round her neck – I didn't doubt the pathologist on that one.

But the man from the market stall in Banbury had told me that Amelia had bought something from him that totally changed everything else.

'She was after one of those self-locking buckles,' he'd said. 'You know the type, like those on a compression strap that you put round a sleeping bag or such when you're trying to get it really small to fit into your rucksack. She said she wanted it for a belt.'

A belt?

What had DCI Priestly said to me in my first interview with him at Banbury Police Station?

This dog lead was the murder weapon. Mrs Gordon-Russell was found with it still tight round her neck.

Tight.

That had been the important word, but I hadn't realised it at the time.

Then I'd been across to talk to Nancy, to ask her a single question about that Tuesday evening.

'Yes,' she'd agreed. 'I did see Amelia go out in her little car shortly after we'd walked back from the pub. But she was only gone for an hour. I saw her coming back again later. She put the car away in the garage.'

Nancy was ever the inquisitive neighbour, watching all the village comings and goings.

Only gone for an hour.

Amelia might have nipped out to the shops for milk, or for bread, or for any number of other things, but I knew she hadn't. An hour was just long enough to have driven over to her mother's house and used the landline there to call her brother, a call the prosecutor had claimed in court was made by Mary.

And Amelia had made sure that she'd left her mobile phone at home.

Normally, she didn't go anywhere without her phone, certainly not to the shops, not even to the loo. It had been like an extension of her own arm. The fact that records showed her phone hadn't moved that night had made me believe that she hadn't either.

I'd been wrong.

And the final piece in this particular circumstantial jigsaw puzzle was the thing I'd just found.

I sat on the kitchen floor and stared at it, willing it not to be there.

But it was.

A small, almost insignificant blemish in the woodwork between the frame and the door from the kitchen to the hall. A bruise in the paint about five feet from the floor, just below the top hinge. A mark the width of the dog lead.

Amelia had pinched the leather between the door and the frame to hold it tight and had then used that anchor point to jerk the ligature very tight around her own neck, and the self-locking buckle had done the rest.

As the pathologist had so rightly said, it had then taken a minute or two for Amelia to lose consciousness. Plenty of time to open the door and remove the dog lead from its fixing point before falling to the floor.

Had she dug her fingernails into her own neck in a true attempt to remove the lead because she had suddenly changed her mind, or had that been a calculated move to further the lie that she'd been murdered?

No one would ever know, and I wasn't sure which of those thoughts gave me the most comfort.

Neither of them.

'Oh, my darling Amelia,' I cried out loud in pain. 'Why didn't you talk to me?'

I sobbed some more, a lot more.

I sat on my kitchen floor deep into the night, not knowing what to do next, and I spent the time thinking.

The simple answer, of course, was to call DS Dowdeswell and tell him what I'd found. Maybe that was also the right and proper thing to do.

But was it really that simple?

As far as DS Dowdeswell and his colleagues were concerned

the case was over – arrest, charge, conviction and sentence. Job done and dusted. Now off to the pub to celebrate.

How had they or the pathologist not seen what was under their noses? Why had they not recognised the relevance of a self-locking buckle? Had they been so blinkered by their determination to find a culprit for their 'murder', first me and then Joe, that it had overridden simple common sense?

The law courts take their time over correcting any perceived mistakes. The decision of a jury to convict is not one that is overturned lightly, or quickly, by the Court of Appeal. Not that time was really an issue here. It was only the murder conviction that was in doubt, not that for attempted murder.

And would the police or the courts take any notice of me anyway? They certainly wouldn't thank me.

And Joe *was* guilty of Amelia's murder.

There was no uncertainty in my mind about that.

He may not have physically strangled her, as the jury in Oxford had believed and decided, but he'd killed her nevertheless. He'd been the one who had driven her to suicide with his merciless attacks on her state of mind over a period of three years. That final vicious email, sent just five days before she died, had simply been the last straw.

Yes, I thought, *Joe deserves to be convicted of her murder.*

So what should I do?

If Amelia's soul was indeed somewhere else, lost in the ether, and she could somehow read my mind, what would she be saying now? She would be screaming in frustration that I had discovered the truth, and urging me to do nothing about it.

So would I be betraying her if I went to the police?

However, there was also the financial position to consider.

All my life I had been an insurance man, and an honest one too. Other than the occasional speeding conviction, I'd done nothing for which I felt any sense of guilt. I'd never fiddled my taxes, nor even exaggerated my expense claims.

So was I about to accept a million-pound payout for my wife's life insurance when I knew it to be a fraud?

But no one else knew, or even suspected. The market stall-holder hadn't appreciated the significance of what he'd told me. He'd been simply making conversation. Similarly, Nancy didn't realise why Amelia having gone out on that Tuesday evening was important.

And I hadn't lied under oath in court. I had told the truth, the whole truth and nothing but the truth – as I'd then believed it to be.

All I had to do now was to keep quiet.

But *I* would always know, and one cannot unlearn something. If the human race could unlearn how to make nuclear bombs, the world would be a safer place.

However, that was not an option, and nor was this.

Around four in the morning it started to get light and I was still sitting on the kitchen floor. And still considering my options.

I was certain that Joe would appeal his conviction and sentence – anyone would in these circumstances.

Did that not mean that it was his defence team's responsibility to produce any new evidence to indicate that his conviction was unsafe?

Was I under any obligation to assist them?

Would Joe have done the same for me if the roles had been reversed?

Not a snowball's chance in hell.

Then I thought about Rachael and her girls. Twenty-five years is a very long time. Without the life-sentence tariff, Joe would be out on parole in under a third of that, having served half his sentence for attempted murder.

But did that really make me feel any safer?

He had tried to kill me twice, that's if you counted the knife attack at his mother's house, which I certainly did. Wouldn't the long years in prison simply make him more determined to be *third time lucky* just as soon as he was released?

Very likely.

So wasn't it better for me to keep him in prison for as long as possible?

Undeniably.

So what should I do?

I decided to sleep on it and went to bed.

Have you read the previous novel from
bestselling crime author Felix Francis ...

FELIX FRANCIS

A DICK FRANCIS NOVEL

Crisis

Harry Foster, a lawyer by training, is a crisis manager
for a London firm. When a fire in the Newmarket
stables of Oliver Chadwick slaughters seven
very valuable horses – including the short-priced
favourite for the Derby – Harry is thrust into the
unpredictable world of Thoroughbred horse racing.

As Harry delves deeper into the unanswered
questions around the tragedy, he unearths disturbing
information about the Chadwick family, a
dysfunctional racing dynasty where resentment runs
deep. And when human remains are also discovered
at the crime scene, only two questions remain:

Who is the mystery victim?
And who might be next?

AVAILABLE NOW IN PAPERBACK AND EBOOK

SIMON &
SCHUSTER